Praise for Claire Delacroix

"Beautifully written, intensely passionate, and gripping, *Fallen* grabbed me from the first sentence and didn't let go. Its eerie future world and frightening mores provide an unforgettable backdrop to the story of Lilia Desjardins, the shade-hunter, and fallen-angel-turned-cop Adam Montgomery. It's *The Matrix, Blade Runner,* and *The Terminator* rolled into a riveting love story and made better. Perfect. A must-read by an author who keeps you on the edge of your seat."

—Linnea Sinclair,
RITA Award–winning author of
The Down Home Zombie Blues and
Shades of Dark

Fallen

CLAIRE DELACROIX

TOR®
paranormal romance

A TOM DOHERTY ASSOCIATES BOOK
NEW YORK

This is a work of fiction. All the characters and events portrayed in this novel are either fictitious or are used fictitiously.

FALLEN

Copyright © 2008 by Claire Delacroix, Inc.

All rights reserved.

A Tor Book
Published by Tom Doherty Associates, LLC
175 Fifth Avenue
New York, NY 10010

www.tor-forge.com

Tor® is a registered trademark of Tom Doherty Associates, LLC.

ISBN-13: 978-0-7653-5949-0
ISBN-10: 0-7653-5949-9

First Edition: October 2008

Printed in the United States of America

0 9 8 7 6 5 4 3 2 1

Authors's Note

In my research for this series, an indispensable reference has been *Hiroshima and Nagasaki: The Physical, Medical, and Social Effects of the Bombings*, translated by Eisei Ishikawa and David L. Swain, published by Basic Books, Inc., in New York, in 1981.

This book was a departure for me, and I owe a debt to all of those friends and associates who read Lilia's story in one (or several) of its incarnations. Thanks to Pam Trader, Ingrid Caris, Cindy Hwang, Anna Genoese, Lisa Stone Hardt, Dominick Abel, and Jennifer Taylor. Thanks also to my husband, Kon, who not only endured many soliloquies on structure and plot but always knew when it was time for a walk or a glass of wine. Many thanks to all of you—this book would not have come to fruition without your generosity.

I hope you enjoy the result.

Fallen

Prologue

THE SURGERY hurt far more than he'd expected.

But then, how could he have prepared for an experience so new? He'd known nothing of pain.

Until the first cut.

A line of fire ripped across his back and he screamed. It was the first audible sound he'd ever made.

Feathers were falling, surrounding him with a curtain of drifting white. It took him a moment to realize that they were his own feathers. They had lost their familiar luminescence and looked alien.

He was becoming alien himself. The idea horrified him, until the surgeon sealed the wound. Heat seared across his back, following the line of the incision. Wetness spilled onto his cheeks and he tasted the salt of his tears.

Another first.

His bellow made the floor vibrate. The smell of burned flesh was new as well, and sickening.

He reminded himself that he had volunteered.

The second cut hurt less, maybe because he knew what to expect. Maybe it was the way of earthly matter, so susceptible to sensation, to learn to ignore stimuli once they had been experienced.

Munkar didn't know. He crouched on the floor, shaking, his flesh pulsing and wet. He waited for the surgeon's fingertip to sear the second wound. He caught his breath at the burn on his skin, then heard the steady pound of his heart. He spread his hands and looked at the flesh he had become.

He felt heavy and slow, bound by gravity in a way he'd never known before. The physical constraints of his body were inescapable, unforgettable, impossible to ignore.

He felt weak.

No, he felt diminished.

There were other cuts—one in the back of his neck, one in the palm of his left hand—but they seemed almost incidental in comparison to losing his wings.

Munkar couldn't even look at the furious blaze that was his attendants. Had he been so radiant himself, just moments ago? It seemed impossible, but he knew it was so.

The taller one bent and kissed his cheeks in turn, a flush of heat on each side of his face that left his skin burning.

"You will forget." The words filled his thoughts, and he knew there was an elusive familiarity about the way he felt rather than heard them.

But he couldn't grasp the memory.

He certainly couldn't reply in kind.

Already, much of what he had known was slipping away. He had doubts. He felt fear. He'd never been vulnerable before and he didn't like it.

The brilliant light faded and when he opened his eyes, he was alone in an empty building.

No, not alone. A woman stepped out of the shadows and smiled.

"Raziel," he whispered in amazement, forcing his first word over his tongue and past his lips. It was slow and lacked elegance. He didn't like the sound of his voice.

"They call me Rachel here," she said with the confident ease he had always associated with her.

She offered him a pile of dark cloth and he took it, because she expected as much. His fingers stroked the surfaces—leather, fur, velvet—sensation overwhelming his thoughts.

"Come on, Adam Montgomery, I'll show you around."

"Adam Montgomery?" He repeated the unfamiliar name, pleased to hear his words becoming more fluid. Was the earth completely without grace?

"That's you, at least in this place. It's all set up. I'll tell you more as we walk."

"Adam Montgomery," he repeated.

"It was as close as I could get, what with the list of authorized names and all."

"As close to what?"

She smiled, a bit of that old radiance in her eyes. "You're forgetting already. That's okay, it's easier."

He dressed with Rachel's assistance. Her presence made it easier to adjust to so many changes in short order. As he finished, she tapped her toe and checked her left hand, her impatience obvious.

"We're running out of time," she said and he understood her urgency. "I'm glad you volunteered, especially now. You were always the best at reading the secrets of men, and I'm not sure who's telling me the truth anymore." Montgomery's confusion must have been obvious, because she laughed. "Don't worry, you'll learn fast. It's just the shock that slows you down at first."

She took his hand and they left the building, each step increasing his familiarity with his body and how it worked. He found pleasure in the flex of his muscles, in the soft fur brushing his chin, in the weight of Rachel's hand in his own.

Dawn tinged the eastern horizon. The sky was deep indigo overhead, and Montgomery marveled at its color.

A shooting star suddenly etched a blazing line across the sky, heading for the rosy eastern horizon.

"That one must be for you," Rachel said.

Montgomery didn't reply. He watched the star, feeling his memory slip away. He knew it had to be so, but regretted the loss all the same.

By the time the star was lost in the light of the rising sun, he remembered only his mission.

He was to aid Rachel in saving the earth.

It was the only thing he needed to know.

From *THE REPUBLICAN RECORD*, August 13, 2099.

FITZGERALD, GIDEON—Esteemed fellow of the Society of Nuclear Darwinists, himself a Nuclear Darwinist of the Seventh Degree. Suddenly, in New Gotham, on August 2, 2099. Sadly missed by his wife, Lilia Desjardins, and his mother-in-law, Lillian Desjardins. Services to be held at the Practical Chapel at 2 p.m. on August 15 in Nouveau Mont Royal. Donations, at the request of the family, will be welcomed by any local chapter of the S.H.A.D.E. Beneficiary Society in Gideon's honor.

I

Wednesday, October 28, 2099

LILIA'S PLAN was simple:

1. She would attend the Nuclear Darwinists' conference in New Gotham to present the award to be given in honor of Gid. Renaming the existing award had been her idea, after all, and was the perfect cover for what she really wanted to do.
2. She would discover the truth about Gid's death.
3. She would quit the Society after the award was presented, preferably with some panache.
4. She would stay out of trouble.

The last item was the only one Lilia expected to be an issue: she had only added it to her list to keep her mother happy.

Her mother didn't need to know how quickly that item had been ditched.

Lilia had only been in New Gotham for an hour and she was wearing Gid's second best pseudoskin, idling a rented Kawasaki and considering the best way to enter the old city of Gotham unobserved. Revving the bike and wasting precious canola were the least of the multiple offenses either committed or pending.

She didn't idle the bike because she was worried about breaking the law. Lilia did that all the time. Old cities were off-limits, by senatorial decree, which meant those who ventured into them had to fend for themselves. Usually Lilia welcomed that edict—it meant less interference.

What troubled her was that the guys in the bike rental place had been joking about the wolves in Central Park.

Wolves. Was it true? It was one detail she hadn't planned for. Lilia hadn't given their chatter much credence, not until there was just the muck of the Hudson between herself and Gotham.

The sight of the old city was what gave her pause.

Gotham was big, dark, and legendary—she'd known that before. In this moment, though, it crouched on the other side of the river, a blackened wreck of what had been a glittering metropolis. It was hard to imagine that once it had shone with so many lights that its illumination had obscured the stars above.

Now the stars had no competition. The steady rain and the darkness didn't do the old city any favors—it looked like hell.

Maybe it was.

Lilia was sure that Gotham wolves would be bigger, more numerous, and more nasty than most.

But rumor wasn't going to stop her. This was a one-time shot. She kicked the bike into gear and turned into the darkness of the Lincoln Tunnel. Her geiger was already ticking faster than she might have liked, which meant she was soaking up radiation faster than would have been ideal.

As she drove down the curving ramp, Lilia held her breath, hoping that the tunnel wasn't blocked. She turned onto the straightaway and the bike's high beam showed that the snaking length of the tunnel was unobstructed. There was just a couple of inches of water on the roadway and the vehicles—there must have been some—were gone.

Pilfered, most likely, and raided for parts.

Her geiger settled to a slow tick.

Lilia grinned. Her legendary good luck was holding.

She accelerated and the roar of the bike's engine reverberated in the tunnel. It felt good to ride, as good as being cut loose from a corset, as good as kicking five pounds of underskirts aside. Even better, the Kawasaki had guts.

As the darkness closed behind her, she felt a prickle of fear. Lilia didn't like darkness, never had. Logic, though, had dictated that the tunnel was the best option for entering the city. The tunnel shielded her from the radiation on approach, giving her more range once in Gotham, and it muffled the noise of the motorcycle from curious ears.

Had Gid, the king of logic, come this way?

The tunnel was long, or seemed longer than it should have been. It said something about Lilia's fear of darkness that she was relieved to emerge into the hot zone of Gotham itself.

She burst from the tunnel like a bat out of hell and her geiger went wild. She had a heartbeat to note the wet road, gleaming like obsidian, before the bike tried to skid from beneath her.

Lilia swore as she corrected the skid.

The wolves chose that moment to howl.

The rumor *was* true.

Even better, there were a lot of them; their howls echoed one after the other.

Wolf telegraph. Lilia knew enough about wolves to know that they were summoning each other as a little welcome committee.

It made sense to move fast when she looked like lunch. Her heart was pounding as she turned to race into the valleys of the old city.

Lilia wasn't unprepared for this adventure: she carried her nifty new laze, the one Joachim had bought her as a bonus for snagging the angel-shades. She'd brought Gid's old suit because even his second-string pseudoskin was a better quality than any of her own. They'd been almost the same height and if it was a little snug around Lilia's curves, well, there wouldn't be a fashion show in the old city. And her dark cape would keep the eyes of Sumptuary & Decency averted when she was in public areas.

Like the bike rental shop.

Since there were multiple hungry carnivores in her vicinity, Lilia fretted about the extra-heavy-weight-gauge mesh in the polymer of Gid's pseudoskin. How much would it slow her down? Her calculations had suffered from a small omission—would it be a fatal one?

Better not to dwell on that.

She'd memorized the map of Gotham from the archives, using a public reader to access it rather than her own palm. She'd told no one where she was going. It was a bit late for Lilia to see the parallels with Gid's last fatal trip.

She'd avoided radiation for the past two weeks to allow herself maximum time in Gotham. Even so, the required monitoring patch on her sternum was already emanating a slight glow. There was no question of turning back. The shade who had contacted her out of the blue had implied that he knew something about Gid. Lilia didn't know how to find the shade again.

It was now or never.

She drove faster. Skeletal hulks of old buildings stretched like fingers into the night sky, their height cast in impenetrable shadows. The thrum of the bike's engine echoed and was magnified, as if a herd of motorcycles had invaded the ruin. Audacious young trees pushed their way through the cracks in the pavement, as opportunistic as the wolves.

There were no lights anywhere in Gotham, but the moon was nearly full and the night was surprisingly clear. Silver light slipped into more than one apartment, creating snapshots Lilia didn't want to see. The streets were slick with water that reflected the moon and stars.

The gray dust was thick and dark over everything beyond the road, and it was probably mixed with ashes. Lilia didn't have to speculate on what those ashes might have been: she knew. They had studied the hit on Gotham at the Institute for Radiation Studies—it was, quite literally, textbook stuff. Ten million people had made their homes in the city and roughly a quarter of a million had managed to evacuate before the firestorm started.

Lilia had never thought she'd see the damage live.

Few did.

Maybe more people should see it, she thought. Maybe the Republic should offer tours. The old city of Gotham was a poster for disarmament.

Maybe that was the real reason why old cities were off-limits.

Not that Lilia was cynical about the objectives of central authority. Nuh-uh.

The odd thing about Gotham was that it seemed to be awake. Everything she could see was destroyed, broken, trashed, and abandoned, yet there was a strange watchfulness. She wasn't at all convinced that she was alone, much less unobserved.

Gotham felt sentient. Most old cities didn't have that kind of aura. Lilia had visited enough of them to know.

She shivered, although she wasn't cold.

Maybe it was the wolves. Lilia was sure she saw the yellow eyes of wolves in every shadow. She was sure she heard the pad of their footfalls as they tracked her course.

But it would have been weird for wolves to have so much presence, even if they were starving.

Was someone else watching?

Or was the city haunted?

Lilia didn't want to know.

It shouldn't have been far from the end of the tunnel to her destination, but the city didn't quite look as it had when the archived map had been made. The debris piled into the streets wasn't that easily distinguishable in the dark from actual buildings in decay. Lilia took a turn, realized she'd made a mistake, turned back, and tried again.

Precious time was slipping away. She accelerated the bike even more, choosing one risk over another. Broadway and Seventh had become one cavernous pit, so Lilia made a quick U-turn. She had to retrace her course and go up Eighth, across Fiftieth, wasting precious moments.

Two blocks left, then one. She was breathing hard, perspiring beneath her pseudoskin.

It was 20:59. Was she too late?

Would she get out of Gotham alive?

Or would she die here, just like Gid?

Lilia turned the last corner to her destination, sprayed an arc of water as she skidded the bike to a halt, and stared. Unlike the rest of the city, Rockefeller Plaza was eerily similar to the way it looked in the archival photos.

But dark.

Extinguished.

Creepy. Lilia hesitated, revving the bike. The plaza appeared to be closed box, a sculpture at the far end being its focal point. There was a black hole in front of the statue, a pit of darkness that seemed to devour what little light there was.

"There's a place in Old Gotham where the shadows are darker . . ."

She remembered the shade's reedy voice all too well and her mouth went dry. His signal had been bootleg, on an unauthorized frequency, and the audio had broken up. Most people couldn't have received the signal, but Lilia had her palm tuned to pirate frequencies. Even so, his voice had sounded as if he was pinging her from another world.

But then, Gotham could have been another world.

Lilia considered the plaza and didn't like the lack of exit options. She turned up the audio on her helm and heard only the pattering of rain on stone. She tried very hard to be prudent, but being prudent wasn't one of Lilia's best tricks.

Her palm chimed the hour.

It was time for the rendezvous.

She roared into the plaza.

As she drew closer, she saw that the statue at the far end still had enough of its gilding to glint in the moonlight. It depicted Prometheus, bringing fire to mortals and risking the wrath of the gods by so doing. Considering what the human race had done with that bit of technology, to Lilia's thinking the gods had good reason to be pissed off with him.

Two dark sentinels loomed on either side of the steps that descended into the darkness before Prometheus, but she didn't spare those sculptures more than a glance. Lilia parked between them at the top of the stairs.

No one was waiting there.

There was, however, something below.

That something was human in form. There had once been a pool beneath Prometheus, at the base of the stairs, and that something was on the pool's lip. He was lying one one side, but not moving.

Maybe not even breathing.

The moonlight touched the small figure, the spaces on either side of the stairs left in impenetrable shadows.

Lilia had a very bad feeling, but there was only one way to be sure. She'd come this far, and she wasn't coming back. She glanced over her shoulder and saw a line of yellow eyes closing into the shadows behind her.

So much for her luck.

She left the bike running and leapt down the stairs. Under the weight of Gid's pseudoskin, she felt as if it took half of forever to get to the bottom. The wolves, she knew, were moving faster.

Lilia was sweating furiously when she turned on the external speaker in her helm. "Y654892?"

Big surprise—he didn't answer. Lilia glanced back and found eyes glinting at the top of the steps. The wolves were drawing closer to the idling bike than she'd expected.

Hunger made them brave.

"Y654892?" Lilia shook his shoulder, because there was an off-chance that he'd settled for a doze while waiting for her.

At her touch, he rolled to his back. Even though she'd not expected anything good, Lilia screamed at what she saw.

The visor on his helm was open, as if to deliberately display the "third eye" right in the middle of his forehead. His normal eyes were staring back at Lilia, their blue irises glassy and lifeless. His skin was already puffing from the radiation exposure, his face mottled and red.

Lilia didn't scream because he was dead.

She screamed because he had been eviscerated.

Y654892 HAD been cut open from gullet to groin, then sliced crosswise from shoulder to shoulder and hip to hip. His skin was pulled open, like the doors to a secret chamber, the four corners pinned fastidiously to his patched and ancient pseudoskin. What Lilia had thought was shadow and rainwater beneath his body was actually guts and blood.

She retched when the first whiff made it through her filters. He hadn't been dead long. Lilia fought her gag reflex, having learned that hurling in one's helm is never the best choice.

She managed to control herself, then looked again. In case she'd had any doubt as to his identity, his pseudoskin had also been cut away to display the tattoo on the inside of his left forearm.

Y654892.

Point taken. He was never going to tell Lilia, or anyone else, anything about Gideon Fitzgerald.

Somehow Lilia snagged images of Y654892's mutilated body. Some routine kicked in, a learned response to document and catalog. She could thank the Institute for Radiation Studies for that much.

The wolves howled behind her, probably salivating in anticipation of the special du jour, but she tried to ignore them. She had a few moments, no more, to look for clues.

Where had the shade come from? There was no sign of his transport, which could have told Lilia a lot. She didn't have time to search for it, not with her radiation patch glowing so hot.

Y654892's bootleg palm was the best source of information. It would have been easiest to datashare with him, but Lilia couldn't bring herself to do it.

Not with a corpse.

She rationalized that she'd have to expose her own skin to release her probe and that sounded persuasive. Either way, it was infinitely preferable to use the camera in her helm to grab images of the last dozen things he'd pulled up himself, in the hope one of them was what he'd planned to share with her.

She still had to touch him to operate his palm, and that was bad enough. Standing in his blood and guts, even in the rain, just about finished her.

Lilia didn't really see the images she captured—she was too busy fighting the urge to vomit. His palm faded to nothing after she snagged the sixth image.

That was that. The last spark of electricity in his nervous system had died. The only option was to datashare, letting his palm borrow the power of hers.

Fat chance.

Time to go.

Lilia pivoted to find the first wolf descending the steps.

The big shaggy leader eyed her, and his manner couldn't have been called friendly. She held his gaze, meeting canine challenge with one of her own. He snarled. Lilia walked toward the stairs with deliberate steps, removing her cloak as she walked. She also pulled her laze.

As she climbed the stairs, he growled. The others hung back, waiting to share the spoils, or letting him do their dirty work.

Maybe wolves weren't so different from humans.

He was a mangy-looking beast, a few open sores on his back, his fur matted. He was so emaciated that Lilia could see his ribs. All he had left was determination and she felt a certain respect for that. She could have fried him, but it didn't seem fair.

They'd negotiate this the old way.

Lilia climbed another step and he descended another

one. He was completely on the steps, front paws two steps lower than his hinds. It was likely to be the only advantage Lilia got.

She moved very slowly, as if hesitant, and he crouched to leap, assuming he had time on his side. Wrong. As soon as he was bent, Lilia flung her cloak over his head. She fired the laze into the pack surrounding the bike. They scattered.

Lilia ran to the bike.

The big male was faster than Lilia had expected— older and wiser, or maybe someone had played this trick on him before. He tore through her cloak in record time. He lunged and snapped at her leg, only missing because Lilia was a bit faster.

Or a bit luckier.

"So, it's true that no good deed goes unpunished." Lilia kicked him square in the chops. He stumbled, growled, and came up to fight, blood running from his chin. He leapt toward her, fangs bared.

To hell with respect. Lilia fired right into his chest.

He fell, whimpered, and shuddered one last time. There was a smell of cooked meat and another little puddle of blood on the stone, both of which she could have done without.

The other wolves retreated to the shadows ringing the plaza, growling with dissatisfaction. Lilia lunged for the bike, her heart pounding that it took so long to get there. She didn't dare waste an instant of the pack's uncertainty.

When she rode out of the plaza, she looked back. The rest of the wolves had gotten over the shock of losing their leader: they were slipping down the stairs to partake of the feast. There wouldn't be much left of Y654892 soon.

Would they eat their leader too?

Better not to think about that.

She had one beat to feel relief and turn the bike toward the tunnel before she heard deep laughter, right in between her own ears. It came from everywhere and nowhere; it echoed inside her own thoughts.

Lilia tried to tell herself that she had picked up a stray signal, and that the frequency had somehow resonated with the speakers embedded in her helmet, producing an apparent echo in her own thoughts, but even she knew that was crap.

It was as impossible to bullshit a bullshitter as she'd always believed. What had just happened was impossible.

Alone in the old city—or maybe not quite as alone as she'd thought—Lilia panicked. She rode carelessly, pushing the bike to its max speed, intent only on getting her butt out of Gotham ASAP.

Then she went straight to the police station in New Gotham to report Y654892's murder. She was in the door of the precinct before she realized her mistake.

By then it was too late.

REPUBLIC OF THE UNITED STATES OF THE AMERICAS

LAW CODE 201/8-349

SECTION IV: DETERMINANTS FOR POSITIVE DESIGNATION OF SUB-HUMAN ATOMIC DEVIANT EVALUATION (S.H.A.D.E.)

Any individual within the geographic boundaries of the Republic, or any individual coming under the geographic boundaries of the Republic by dint of Republican expansion, will be evaluated to be a Sub-Human Atomic Deviant if any of the following criteria manifest in his or her physical person, and that individual can be documented to have been exposed to radiation:

i) Microcephaly—being a head circumference of less than two standard deviations below the age- and sex-specific mean;

ii) Keloids—being the presence of irregularly-shaped three-dimensional scar tissue, most characteristically in the shape of a crab and copper-red in color;

iii) Ocular lesions;

iv) Other visible birth defects—being inclusive but not limited to: Brachycephaly; Oxycephaly; Scaphocephaly; Megacephaly; Strabismus; Narrow Palpabral Fissure; Radiation-Induced Cataract; Corneal Opacity; Abnormality of Iris; Epicanthus; Mongoloidism; Saddle Nose; Curved Concha; Gothic Palate; Odontoloxia; Harelip; Cleft Palate; Uvula Bifida; Micrognathia; Megaloglossia; Vascular Engorgement; Digitus Varus of the Fifth Finger; Brachydactylia; Arachnodactylia; Polydactylia; Syndactylia; Adactylia; Simian Crease; Axial Triradius; Cubitus Valgus; Cubitus Vaurs; Heart Murmurs; Pigeon Breast; Funnel Chest; Umbilical Hernia; Accessory Mamma; Pterygoid Neck; Leukoplakia; Hypertrichosis; Hemangioma; Skin Sinus; Cryptorchidism; Hypospodias; Vaginal Fistula; Aproctia; Hermaphroditism.

In addition, possessing two or more of the following chronic conditions—which may or may not result in outward physical manifestation—when caused by radiation exposure, will designate a positive evaluation:

i) Thyroid cancer;

ii) Leukemia and other radiation-specific blood disorders including, Multiple Myeloma, Malignant Lymphoma, Polycythemia Vera, Myelofibrosis, and Aplastic Anemia;

iii) Mental Retardation in any child that was in utero, particularly during the third and fourth month of gestation, when the biological mother was exposed.

First passed in New D.C., May 2025, with major amendments in 2034, 2056, and 2078.

II

MONTGOMERY WAS in a foul mood.

Again.

He'd argued with Rachel.

Again.

Her refusal to share information was a persistent sore point. He felt as if he had no role and no objective. She was adamant that he should watch for abnormalities from his post at New Gotham Police Department. Her belief in the divine plan was getting to him.

Probably because he couldn't see any plan at work at all. The mortal world was a mess and getting worse. He hadn't volunteered just to have it disintegrate while he watched.

Montgomery took foot patrol duty as often as possible, in the hope that he might see something. He scanned records and reviewed cold cases, under the guise of learning the workings of his new precinct. He haunted the pleasure fringe of New Gotham, certain that it would be the first place he would hear gossip from the underworld. No luck. It felt futile and ineffective.

Rachel insisted that good would inevitably triumph over evil.

It looked to Montgomery as if evil had good on the run.

Maybe he'd made a mistake in volunteering.

Maybe it was too late for second thoughts. The only way back to the world he knew was through this one—he had to complete his mission to regain his wings.

He didn't have to like it.

Montgomery took the broad stone steps to the precinct three at a time, knowing he was late. He fabricated an excuse about walking patrol, knowing that it was only a matter of time before his disguise was destroyed.

He automatically removed his helm and bent his head as he crossed the threshold, granting an unobscured view of his identification bead to the reader installed overhead. He wasn't surprised to see Thompson on desk duty again—the rookie was about as incompetent as was humanly possible, but the computers managed most of the functions of reception. It was comparatively risk-free to leave Thompson loose on the reception desk.

Montgomery *was* surprised to find a woman waiting there.

She wearing a tight pseudoskin that left little to the imagination and defied every line item on the Sumptuary & Decency Code. She was tall and slender, as athletically built as he'd expect given that she was wearing such a heavy-gauge pseudoskin. She was wearing black biker boots, much like his own, and had black gauntlets hooked into her belt. Her helm was tucked under her arm and her dark braid fell down her back almost to her knees.

She was dressed for active duty in a hot zone, but women were never dispatched to hot zones. She was waiting on Thompson, her impatience evident in her tapping toe, and as yet unaware of Montgomery's presence.

He noticed the datachip that she moved between her fingers. She was agitated, not just impatient, and he wondered why.

The answer, he would bet, was on that chip.

She took a step away from the desk, her gaze on Thompson. Montgomery realized that she'd reconsidered. She was going to leave, without sharing the reason she had come in the first place.

He decided that was sufficiently strange to merit his attention.

Thompson frowned at his display, bending over the desktop, and the woman made her move. She spun and bolted for the door. It was a small foyer and she moved so quickly that she nearly collided with Montgomery.

She would have, if he hadn't caught her shoulders in his hands.

She looked up in surprise and he was shocked by her beauty. Her face was heart-shaped, her eyes blue and thickly lashed. There was intelligence in her gaze and defiance in the set of her lips.

Something quickened within him, something that had never yet been awakened by the whores in the pleasure fringe. He recognized her, though he couldn't have said why, and that surprise kept him from hiding his attraction.

The spark was reciprocal: she looked him up and down with appreciation. Montgomery felt a very natural response to this bold show of female interest, then suspicion clouded her eyes again.

"Excuse me," she said, frost in her tone. "I was just leaving."

When she shrugged off his hands and made to step around him, Montgomery blocked her passage. He saw the flash of anger in her eyes.

The lady liked to have her way. He'd have to remember that.

Thompson glanced up and cleared his throat. "Detective, I was just looking for you. Weren't you supposed to be in your cube?"

"No. Patrol." Montgomery didn't imagine the way the lady's eyes narrowed when Thompson used his title.

"But the database says . . ."

Montgomery spoke dismissively. "Then it must be wrong."

Only Thompson would believe that and he did.

The woman hesitated, pausing to consider Montgomery through her lashes. Interesting. So few people questioned the databanks of the Republic that it was refreshing to find one who thought it possible.

Meanwhile Thompson leaned over the desk. "I was looking for you because this, um, *lady* says she's witnessed a murder."

Montgomery ignored the younger cop's implication and met the lady's gaze. "Is that correct?"

Her lips tightened as she tried to step past him again. If nothing else, he could be a formidable obstacle. He moved to block her again and almost smiled at her visible irritation. "No, it's not. I made a mistake."

"A mistake?" He kept his tone mild. "About a murder?"

"Things happen," she said darkly, looking daggers at both him and Thompson. She and Montgomery stepped sideways in unison again. "You're starting to annoy me," she muttered and Montgomery couldn't stifle his smile. She stared at him for a heartbeat, then a touch of color stained her cheeks as she averted her gaze.

Montgomery felt hot.

"It was probably in the pleasure fringe," Thompson said with a snicker. "Some kinky game. You know how it is down there."

"Do I?"

"That's what the boys say, that Montgomery knows his way around the pleasure fringes better than most."

Montgomery ignored that bit of innuendo too.

The lady, though, studied Montgomery with new interest.

"Maybe we should ask the witness what she observed instead of speculating on what she saw and where she saw it." Montgomery spoke with smooth authority. Thompson had the grace to flush.

She frowned. "I'm not a witness because I didn't see anything."

"Then why are you here?" Montgomery asked.

She glared at him for this reasonable question. "Because I made a mistake. Let's forget I even said anything." She tried to step around him one more time.

"No. Let's not." Montgomery blocked her path again. "What did you see where?"

"It doesn't matter," she said, steel in her tone.

"This says it does." Montgomery tapped a single finger

on the radiation patch on her sternum, which was glowing from recent exposure, and she jumped slightly. "Where?"

She grimaced then, betrayed as she was by her own equipment. Still, she didn't back down and he admired that. "You shouldn't be standing so close, not if you know I'm hot."

Thompson snickered. "Montgomery prefers the glow girls."

Montgomery held her gaze. "I'll take my chances."

"What did he say your name was?"

"Detective Sergeant Adam Montgomery, New Gotham Homicide." He offered his hand to her. "And you are?"

"Leaving," she said flatly, her manner hostile. This time she put a hand on his arm to push him aside.

Montgomery glanced toward Thompson, who peered at his display. "Lilia Desjardins," he supplied and Montgomery felt his eyes widen.

That was why she looked familiar. She was Fitzgerald's widow.

What was she doing here, so far from her home on the Frontier?

Witnessing a murder that she didn't want to talk about.

Montgomery had been part of the team that had brought her bad news, so he couldn't blame her for being angry. She probably recognized his name. He hadn't been happy with the resolution of Fitzgerald's case himself. It had smelled like a cover-up to him and Rachel had been very interested in the details.

He dared to hope that Lilia knew something Fitzgerald had known.

Lilia's gaze slid over his shoulder and her lips tightened. "Damn government databanks," she muttered.

"The eyes of the Republic are everywhere," he said, when he really wanted to agree with her. He offered his hand. "Pleased to meet you."

She looked down at his outstretched hand as if surprised that he offered to shake hands with her. Because she was a

woman? Or because she was hot? She put her hand in his
with some reluctance. "I can't say it's reciprocal."

Her fingers felt slender within his grip, and he was surprised by the strength of his protective urge. Worse, the
brush of her skin against his own distracted him in a very
earthy way.

"Then the pleasure is all mine," he said, and she flushed
again. She pulled her hand from his abruptly.

He reminded himself that she must be a grieving widow.
She still wore a heavy silver ring on her left hand, after all.
"And what did you see tonight, Mrs. Fitzgerald?"

Her expression turned stony. "Ms. Desjardins. Please."

There was an issue there of some kind, one that he
wanted to explore. He arched a brow instead of repeating
the question.

She sighed. "You aren't going to do anything about what
I saw so it might as well have not happened. It wasn't a
murder because the victim was a shade."

"Technically, you're right," Montgomery allowed.
"The killing of a shade is not murder under Republic law.
It is, however, of considerable interest to me."

She met his gaze again, skepticism shining in her own.
"Why?"

"Professional interest."

"Strange hobby."

"No. A disregard for other life can escalate. There are
patterns of violent behavior that are first revealed in a
perp doing injury to small animals, then shades, then fre-
quently citizens."

It looked as if Lilia was persuaded, then changed her
mind. Against him. "All happy PR talk aside, we both
know that you're not going to do anything about a shade's
death. I need to go."

Montgomery was keenly aware of the watchful eyes of
the Republic—and the leer of Thompson—and knew there
was only one way to keep the lady in the building.

He'd have to trick her.

Now.

It would infuriate her, but it would keep her from leaving.

"Not so fast." Montgomery surveyed her curves leisurely, then lowered his voice to a murmur. He held her gaze, seeing a flicker of heat in her own. "I'd like to see what you've got first."

Her eyes widened in shock. Thompson gave a low whistle. Lilia took a step back, but not before Montgomery snagged the datachip from her fingers.

He'd distracted her, just as he'd intended, and he saw the moment she realized as much.

He also saw her fury.

At least, he had her attention.

He stepped past her and headed to his cubicle, knowing that she'd follow him. He smiled when he heard her swear.

Then she marched in pursuit, so angry that her heels pounded on the floor.

Point to Montgomery.

IF IT wasn't for bad luck, Lilia clearly wouldn't have any luck in New Gotham at all. She'd made a mistake in coming to the precinct, courtesy of being freaked out by Y654892's corpse, and met none other than one of the team who had been dense enough to declare Gid's death an accident.

Plus Montgomery was so yummy that she wanted to jump his bones. Even if Lilia hadn't almost collided with him, the eye candy he offered would have stopped her in her tracks. It had been a long time since she'd seen such a prime male specimen.

There was a complication her life didn't need.

If she'd had any taste for cops, Montgomery would have made a tasty morsel. But Lilia had an allergy to cops, especially NGPD Homicide detectives.

She'd seen him on the CC list of the official correspondence over Gid's death. Montgomery was on the NGPD team, and that meant he wasn't on Lilia's team.

The only upside of following him and her disappearing datachip into the warren of the precinct was the view. Lilia had always been convinced that there was nothing more spectacular than a man in a heavy mesh pseudoskin, especially when he had the muscle tone to wear it as if it weighed nothing at all.

Montgomery did.

The view of him striding away was worth the price of admission. Raw biological response reminded Lilia that she'd become a widow too young. Gid was dead, but she was entering her sexual prime, and doing it solo. The way she tingled in the proximity of a buff example of the male of the species was proof positive of that.

It was the last proof she needed, in the last place she wanted it, from the last man she wanted it from.

Montgomery reached his cube and held the door. Lilia had to step past him, almost brushing his chest with her shoulder as she did so. Female bits of her began to sing. He shut the door behind them, the size of him making the space seem smaller and more intimate than Lilia had anticipated.

Or maybe it was the way he watched her so carefully.

In the close proximity of his cube, her awareness of him was impossible to ignore. Montgomery's pseudoskin seemed barely able to contain his broad chest and highlighted the musculature of his legs. This boy was no desk jockey: he was out there, every day in his pseudoskin, doing the dirty work.

Lilia respected that, even if she didn't want to.

Montgomery's uniform was all black, as was customary, and his laser weapon was standard issue. She felt pity for him on that account. The spherical stud implanted in his left earlobe gleamed like a polished jet bead, a reminder Lilia didn't need that nothing seen by a cop went unwitnessed by the Republic.

His hair was shaved to almost nothing, and Lilia was

jealous. The Sumptuary & Decency laws forbade a woman from cutting her hair, but Lilia had always thought it would be easier.

She stood in Montgomery's cube, felt the weight of his gaze, and knew she had to get out of the copshop immediately, if not sooner.

She wasn't going without her property, however.

Montgomery was perceptive, so there was no point in playing games. Lilia put out her hand. "Give me the chip, please."

"You'll have it back momentarily."

"You have no right. It's personal property and illegal for you to have seized without a warrant." It was outrageous that Lilia, of all people, was quoting Republic law to an NGPD detective, but there it was.

Montgomery spoke with infuriating calm as he passed a hand over his desktop to awaken it. Lilia saw it do a security scan of his iris before the display appeared. "You came here to report a crime. You brought the datachip to support your charge. You had it in your hand, prepared to surrender it as evidence." He gave her a steady look. "Correct me when I go wrong."

"This is a waste of your time."

"I'll decide what's a waste of my time and what's not." Montgomery spoke more dispassionately than anyone Lilia had ever known, which said something, given her years among the cold-blooded scientists at the Institute. She wondered what he was thinking, then wondered what it would take to rattle his composure.

She shouldn't have wanted to do so, not so badly.

He was a Republic team player, so he'd probably give her a lecture first. She put down her helm and folded her arms across her chest, ready to endure a few minutes of official admonitions.

On the upside, that gave her ample chance to look.

Lilia decided to be blunt. "Let it go, Montgomery. NGPD probably won't even retrieve the body."

"Where is it?" His gaze danced to her radiation badge and she knew there was no point in lying.

"In the old city."

He straightened. "Gotham is within NGPD's jurisdiction . . ."

"I'm not sure it's there to be retrieved . . ."

He frowned. "Did you move it?"

Lilia shook her head. "You must know about the wolves."

"The patrols say they migrated down from Maine and mixed with the feral dogs in the city."

"Of course. Old cities are full of predators." She smiled, wanting to shock him. "Not all of them have four legs."

Montgomery studied her and she felt like squirming under his bright gaze. He was so still, so intent, that she halfway thought he could read her thoughts.

They would surprise him, she was sure. Maybe she just had a soft spot for yummy cops who visited the pleasure fringe.

Cops who walked the beat.

Cops who argued that the Republic's databases were fallible.

Cops who filled their pseudoskins so very well.

"You know a lot about old cities," he said.

Lilia put out her hand. "Give me my chip and let's just forget I ever said anything."

Montgomery rolled the chip between his fingers. "Why did you come here if you were so sure there was no point in doing so?"

"I was frightened." Lilia tried to look demure and was sure that she failed. "I've never seen anyone dead before." That wasn't quite true, but he couldn't know as much.

"I thought it was only a shade."

Lilia straightened, angered by his insinuation. Before she spoke, she saw the glint in his eyes and knew she'd been provoked.

On purpose.

Montgomery smiled ever so slightly, and Lilia's heart skipped a beat at the way his features softened. He looked younger, even with a half-smile, and even more tasty.

She really needed to get to the pleasure fringe herself and buy some orgasmic relief.

Montgomery pushed the datachip into the port on his desk and Lilia caught her breath as her images spilled across his digital blotter. She had to look away. They were gruesome.

Montgomery gave a low whistle, revealing that he was a bit shocked himself. "You know this shade?"

"No."

He looked up, inviting more.

To her shame, Lilia gave him a little bit of information. She blamed too much blood and guts for throwing her game. "I was supposed to meet him there."

Montgomery glared at her. "Whose stupid idea was that?"

Lilia said nothing, the better to not further condemn herself. There was no doubt that she had Montgomery's undivided attention.

Or that his eyes were a delicious shade of green. He had dark lashes that would have been the envy of any woman, and which made the hue of his eyes seem more intense.

"Why Gotham?" he demanded when she didn't reply.

"That's not really your concern."

"I think it is." He looked away to compose himself and she was surprised that he could be so angry with her over something that shouldn't have bothered him at all. Then he spoke and revealed the real reason for his annoyance. "It is illegal to enter old cities without prior authorization, Mrs. Desjardins . . ."

"*Ms.* Desjardins," she corrected automatically.

His gaze lingered on the platinum ring on her left hand. "And unless you can prove to me that you had such authorization, I can arrest you." His expression was determined. "Or you can answer my question, *Ms.* Desjardins. Your choice."

Being a Nuclear Darwinist had its advantages: one was that Lilia could go pretty much anywhere and claim it to be "research." Nobody ever said it had to be research sanctioned by the Society or by the Republic, mostly because there was no way to prove what either were researching at any given point in time. Old cities were a natural haunt for such activities.

"I'm a shade hunter, a Nuclear Darwinist," she said, oozing confidence. "This shade had a third eye, so I wanted to talk to him for my current research project."

Montgomery looked her up and down. Lilia was the best liar on the Frontier, but she had a feeling that he didn't believe her.

Why not? Her excuse had always worked in the past.

Montgomery's perusal made her feel very aware of the close fit of Gid's pseudoskin, and gave her a rare attack of modesty. His glance lingered on her boots, then on her breasts (which were both splendid and original equipment), then on her laze, before his gaze locked with hers again.

Lilia couldn't deny that she liked how Montgomery looked and how he looked at her. It was just biology, nothing more than that. It wasn't illegal for a woman to be heterosexual.

At least not in this state of the union.

If she'd expected a compliment after that perusal, she was due to be disappointed.

"You work for the Society?" he asked.

"No," Lilia said, hiding her feelings with attitude, as usual. "I work for the circus."

As expected, the tone of their interview changed for the worst with that confession. Lilia knew shouldn't have been disappointed that Montgomery was so predictable.

Republic Announces New Decency Code

New D.C.—This morning, in response to the recent spate of violent crimes against women, the President announced a new decency code, to be put into practice throughout the Republic.

"It's clear that women's apparel in public spaces is a major factor in the increase of personal crime against women," he told a press conference. "Provocative clothing is at the root of this recent problem, and it's past time to make changes to stop the trend. It's our responsibility to make the streets of the Republic safe for all citizens of both genders. The elimination of unseemly attire in public spaces will protect women everywhere."

The Sumptuary & Decency Code (<u>hotlink for the full text of the Code</u>) calls for all women to cover themselves in public in the name of modesty. No skin other than that of the face may be exposed to casual view—although the Code recommends the wearing of veils, they remain optional at this point in time—and traditional attire, including long skirts, gloves, and hats, is proscribed. The Code applies to all women citizens, which it defines as those females being more than twelve years of age. Similarly, women are not to be seen in public while visibly pregnant, an obvious nod to the felon known as "The Third Trimester Rapist" who has terrorized Gotham's expectant mothers in the past year.

The S&D Code, as it has already been termed, explicitly refers to attire worn in public, including offices, and does not apply to what is worn at private residences: behind closed doors, women are free to wear what they like.

The President also announced a budget for a new police corps, to be created purely to enforce the new Code, which is to become effective May 1 throughout the Republic.

The President's conclusions, although shared by Congress and the Senate, both of which rapidly approved the bill, were not greeted with enthusiasm by others. Sharon Woodsworth, of the National Force for Women (NFW) criticized the legislation as "a giant step backward. The President is blaming women everywhere for the fact that men can't control themselves or their desires. It's not a new strategy, but history has already proven this kind of misogynism, time and again, to be ineffective thinking. What we really need is more aggressive sentencing for sex offenders." NFW plans to picket the White House and Congress in protest against the bill, as well as to undertake a fund-raising campaign to mount legal opposition to the bill.

The Republican Civil Liberties Union (RCLU) compared the legislation to restrictions upon women proposed by religious fundamentalists throughout the world. The RCLU, however, had no plans at press time for legally contesting the bill.

The United Republic Workers (URW), which has recently negotiated a new contract on behalf of sex workers in the Republic, also condemned the legislation, stating in a press release that the bill will make the lives of sex workers more dangerous. The URW's rationale is that provocative clothing is "necessary self-promotion for sex workers in a competitive marketplace," but that this bill will ensure that sex workers "showing entrepreneurial initiative" will draw the attention of those with violent tendencies toward women. The President dismissed this criticism, insisting that all sex workers have the opportunity, if not the obligation, to "repent of their sins and find alternative, respectable, employment."

III

IN HINDSIGHT, bringing Lilia to his cube had been a mistake. She filled the space with her vitality and defiance. She moved and spoke like no woman he had ever known and he was fascinated by her. She distracted him in a very earthy way.

All Montgomery had wanted to do was assess her motives away from Thompson's eye, to determine whether she knew whatever Fitzgerald had known.

But in such close proximity, his thoughts became inappropriate. He could smell the scent of her skin and was intrigued by the curve of her lips. Away from the public space, he could only think of doing private things.

It didn't help his professional composure that Lilia was temptation personified in her snug pseudoskin. Montgomery was definitely feeling the constraints of his reevlar codpiece.

Lilia watched him after her confession, one hand on her hip and challenge bright in her eyes. She expected him to disapprove of her place of employment, and he could work with that. A little dissent between them would be anticipated by the Republic.

"Not interested in furthering the cause of research?" he asked.

She shrugged. "The good guys don't pay so well. I like having the best toys when I go in, and the Society's troops are underfunded." She paused for a heartbeat. "Kind of like the Republic's troops."

Montgomery looked pointedly at her laze, a new design of breathtaking accuracy, power, and compact size. His own laze was perhaps twenty-year-old technology.

"It's not what you're packing that makes the difference, Lil," he said quietly. "It's how fast you move."

She bristled at his use of her first name and her eyes widened ever so slightly. Montgomery felt a tentative accord—even if it was just mutual desire—then she lifted her chin.

"Go ahead and believe what you need to, Montgomery. More is better in my scheme of the world. And it's Ms. Desjardins."

Montgomery changed the subject. He touched one of the images displayed on his blotter, his fingertip indicating the bump on the shade's forehead. "Is this what you're calling a third eye?"

"You know that it is."

"Actually, I don't."

She sighed and threw herself into the chair opposite his desk, crossing her legs. The musculature in her calves was just enough to be sexy. Her breasts seemed more round, and from this angle, she looked lusciously feminine.

More than her physical assets, he liked the spark of her intellect. She seemed more alive than most mortals he'd met, as if she was lit by an inner fire. She wasn't marking time on earth, but was savoring every minute of it.

He could respect that.

She shrugged. "It's not that rare of a mutation, but it's not very common either."

"What does that mean?"

"That most norms wouldn't have ever seen one, that most Nuclear Darwinists would have seen at least one, and that I've seen several dozen."

He magnified the image with a touch. "It looks like a wart."

"It's a skin nodule. There are mystical associations with it."

"Like?"

"It's often credited with vision of things beyond the physical."

Montgomery glanced up. She seemed so pragmatic that he was surprised by her explanation. "Do you believe that?"

Lilia smiled with confident ease. "Who cares?"

Montgomery couldn't tell her that he did.

Well aware that everything he said and did was observed, Montgomery let his tone fill with disapproval. "So, you were planning to offer this shade employment as a circus freak?"

Lilia was clearly insulted—the flash of her eyes gave her away—but she replied calmly. "No. We just were meeting to talk."

"In the old city? That's a big risk for a vague promise."

Lilia's expression made it clear that it hadn't been a vague promise. "I check out all the angles," was all she said.

What had the shade promised her?

"What brings you to New Gotham?" he asked. He touched his blotter and a list came up. He felt Lilia try to read the display. There was a notation that she had arrived on the train from the Frontier earlier this same day and her name was hotlinked to Gideon Fitzgerald's obituary.

"I'm in town for the Nuclear Darwinists' annual conference."

That all seemed reasonable, except that her file showed she hadn't left the Frontier since graduating from the Institute for Radiation Studies nine years before.

Montgomery would have bet his last cred that Lilia's journey was related to Fitzgerald's death.

She knew *something*.

"You live on the Frontier," he said.

Lilia's expression hardened. "Born and raised."

That explained her rebellious attitude.

Montgomery stalled. He flipped through the images of the dead shade from her datachip, bringing each to the fore in turn, shuffling them like so many cards. It would take a ruthless killer to do this to another human.

But then, a Nuclear Darwinist wouldn't consider a shade to be human, would she? Nuclear Darwinists, after all, were the scientists who used shades for research and shade hunters, like Lilia, captured shades in the field.

"What are these?" Montgomery asked as half a dozen images scattered themselves across the blotter. They were the last ones loaded onto the datachip.

The images were blurry but they seemed to be of packing crates in industrial settings. Warehouses and loading docks and trucks. They were images taken of a palm: he could see the outline of someone's hand around the perimeter of each shot.

Lilia leaned closer to look. "Orv the Orange," she murmured and shook her head.

"Excuse me?"

"That's the name of the cartoon mascot for *Sunshine Heals.*" Lilia touched the logo on one of the crates and Montgomery saw that it was on a number of them. "I guess everyone needs a hobby."

"Yours or the shade's?"

Lilia looked as if she would have liked to lie. It was clear where she'd snagged these, from the time and date posted on the images, and maybe that prompted her honesty. "His, obviously."

He decided to provoke her. "You just took images of his palm? Couldn't you bring yourself to datashare with a shade?"

"With a corpse, more like." She couldn't suppress her shudder.

Montgomery watched her, intrigued by her squeamishness. Was it an act? "Do you often take images of the palms of corpses?"

She glared at him. "No. That's not one of my hobbies either."

He returned to the images of the dead shade and noted how she had to turn away. She was pale, as if she'd be physically ill.

She wasn't as tough as she wanted him to believe.

Could she have killed the shade? He thought not. "So, why did you take the images at all?"

"I thought it might be helpful in identifying his killer," Lilia said, her tone challenging. "After all, he's probably wolf-chow by now. Anyone who cared how or why this shade died would need all the help he could get. Of course, that was assuming that someone *would* care."

Maybe frightening her was the best way to persuade Lilia to be quiet. "Do you know how long a palm stays live after its host dies?"

She blinked. "Five or ten minutes?" Hers was obviously a guess.

Montgomery gave her a sharp look. "Two minutes. Max."

Lilia was visibly startled.

Montgomery ran a hand over the display and continued his officious lecture. "Yet you were confident that it would stay live long enough for you to take these images. How many do we have? Five? Six? How long would it take to snag them? A minute? Two? Anyone who cared how or why this shade died would be very interested in that timing."

"No!" Lilia pushed to her feet, furious. "That's not how it was . . ."

Montgomery let his voice harden. "Your appearance on the scene was virtually simultaneous with the shade's death. There were no other witnesses and no one else was apparently present. The location where you met would have facilitated that, and you have yet to say who chose it."

"He did," she admitted with quiet force. "He pinged me."

"That's your story."

"It is."

"When did he ping you? Why?"

She clamped her lips shut and glared at him.

Montgomery could see that she was thinking furiously, and thought it was about time. He leaned closer and tapped his fingertip on his desk. "If this has anything to do with an amateur investigation of the death of Gideon Fitzgerald, you should be aware that his death was officially declared an accident."

"I know," she said with hostility. "I got the memo."

"Lucky for you the death of a shade *isn't* considered a homicide under Republic law." Montgomery saw her alarm, but went one better. "Although there remains the issue of damaging federal property."

"I wouldn't. I didn't. That's why I work at the circus . . ." she began then fell into mutinous silence.

"I don't understand."

She gritted her teeth. "Individuals in the employ of the circus can't be harvested by the Society or the Republic, under Section 3002/45 of Republic law. They can't be declared shades." She took a shaking breath and spoke so softly that Montgomery almost missed the words. "They're safe there, so long as they're on the payroll and paying their taxes." Her features softened slightly. "And they get to have names instead of numbers."

It wasn't every day that a Nuclear Darwinist defended the rights of shades, which were, by legal definition, not human. Montgomery was both surprised and intrigued by her passion about the matter. It didn't jive with her choice of career.

"Why did you meet the shade in the old city?" he asked. "Another safe zone?

"I told you that he picked the place. I don't know what he wanted to tell me." She flicked a quick glance at the images on the desktop. "But someone made sure he couldn't say anything."

Montgomery realized that the shade's killer must have been close at hand when Lilia arrived, close enough that she could have been killed in the old city herself.

Like Fitzgerald.

"You might plan your alibi with more care in future, Ms. Desjardins." Montgomery touched his desktop, consigning her images to a database with apparent impatience. "I could charge you with trespassing, given your own admission that you entered the old city without authorization."

That made her lift her chin again. "Why bother? You'd never make it stick. Nuclear Darwinists head into old cities all the time. The most radically mutated shades are there, after all."

There it was again, her protective tone when she spoke of shades. "I thought those shades were in the pleasure fringes," he said mildly, hoping to draw her out.

"Not the bad mutations. They're hidden." She inhaled with disapproval. "Only those with genital mutations can make a living in the pleasure fringe, selling themselves to the norms who find such sights thrilling."

"Do you?"

She met his gaze, her own hard. "That's a pretty personal question. Maybe I should ask about your hobbies since you apparently spend so much time in the pleasure fringe."

Their gazes locked and held for an electric moment.

Montgomery frowned down at his desktop. "People have lots of reasons for becoming Nuclear Darwinists. What was yours?"

To his surprise, Lilia smiled. "Filthy lucre."

It was a lie and he knew it, although he couldn't fathom a guess as to the truth. "That's it?"

"That's it." Lilia pointedly glanced around his cube, which was small and cheaply furnished, then met his gaze steadily. "Isn't that good enough?"

"So, you would have sold this shade to the circus, if he'd been alive?"

Again he glimpsed her annoyance before she managed to contain it. There was a moral principle guiding her actions, he would have bet upon it, but he didn't expect her to confide in him. "My motivation isn't that important, not now."

Montgomery leaned his hips on the lip of his desk. "I think it is. Were you going to return the Republic's property? He had a Republic tattoo and was obviously a fugitive."

"There's no comp in that, is there?"

"Is everything about compensation to you?"

"Pretty much, yes." Lilia pretended to consider this and nodded again. "I like a little luxury, after all."

"So you hunt shades for bounty." He almost sneered, knowing that this wasn't her true motivation. She was an idealist, he knew it in his gut, and he wanted very much to know which cause had won her allegiance.

Lilia swung to her feet and retrieved her chip from the port, her gesture quick enough that Montgomery didn't try to stop her. "Maybe it is about how quick you are," she mused.

Montgomery let her have it. There was no reason for him to keep the chip, as the images had already been captured by his desktop. She spun to leave and he waited to speak until she had her hand on the door. "Funny, but I've never met anyone who did something distasteful purely for the comp."

When she glanced over her shoulder, her expression was mischievous. "Maybe you need to get out more, Montgomery."

"You must have had another reason to become a Nuclear Darwinist. Few of them defend the rights of shades."

"And maybe they should." She pivoted then, her eyes flashing. "I'm the best shade-hunter that there is, and I do my best to snag shades first." There was pride in her tone.

"First?"

"Before they get dispatched to the mines and the slave-dens and the research labs." Her disgust was apparent, then she continued with pride. "The first two angel-shades ever discovered and captured were mine. Maybe you saw that on the vid."

A chill slipped down Montgomery's spine. "I did read about that. It was earlier this year."

"A major coup." Lilia jabbed her thumb into her chest. "*My* coup and I got a bonus for it." She patted her fancy laze with pride. "The Society would have just cut a regular pay amount, without even a thank-you-very-much. There's nothing wrong with being compensated accordingly for your skills. It's the Republican way."

"Is it?"

"They forget to tell you boys about the joys of capitalism when you get drafted."

"I volunteered."

"Well, then, you have my sympathies."

That made Montgomery smile, a sight that disconcerted her for a heartbeat. "Thanks for sharing your status with me," he said softly. "Knowing who to call is a good thing for a cop to know."

Lilia looked him up and down. "You can't afford me."

Montgomery couldn't resist. "There are other forms of comp, besides credits."

To his surprise, she blushed scarlet.

Maybe Lilia wasn't such a grieving widow, after all. Their gazes locked and the air in his office seemed to sizzle.

"But creds buy them all," she concluded. She pivoted to leave, but Montgomery stopped her on the threshold with four low words.

"Watch your ass, Lil."

She glanced back, maybe expecting to catch him in the act of checking it out himself.

Montgomery met her defiant gaze instead. "Either your acquaintance was left for you to find, or you're the most likely person to have killed him."

She was visibly insulted. "I'd never savage another being."

"Not even for the right price?"

Lilia looked away.

"I could confiscate all your weapons right here and right now, as well as charge you with trespassing, but for the moment, I'll just keep copies of your images. A little advice, Lil—"

"My name is Ms. Desjardins and I think you've dispensed plenty of advice already . . ."

"A little advice, Lil," Montgomery repeated, his voice hard. "Follow the rules while you're in town. We do things a bit differently here than on the Frontier."

She put her hands on her hips. "Or?"

"Or you could find yourself on the wrong side of the Republic. Take it from me, that's not a good place to be."

"Really? And what would you know about it?" Lilia crossed the office and leaned her fists on his desk, rising to his warning in a way most women never would. Montgomery was fascinated. "Or is that your speciality? Making life miserable for those who don't play the Republic way? Are you *threatening* a citizen, Montgomery?"

How could she be so reckless? How could she be so unaware—or uncaring—that the eyes of the Republic were everywhere? He wanted to protect her from herself more than he'd ever wanted to protect anyone.

He knew his expression was cold. "Of course not. Just doing my part to serve and protect."

She glared at him for a long moment, and the tension between them changed—again—from anger to another flavor of passion. She pivoted and marched back to reception, refusing his escort with a dismissive wave.

Montgomery didn't believe Lilia was as foolish as she wanted others to believe and he didn't believe her presence in New Gotham was a coincidence. If nothing else, as a Nuclear Darwinist, she knew the risks of going into the old city.

What had the shade offered to make a trip into Gotham's hot zones seem worthwhile?

Montgomery wanted to know.

He was going to find out.

THE LAST thing Lilia needed was a reminder that she wasn't on her usual turf, but she got it anyway.

The courtesy shuttle from the bike rental shop dropped her off—discourteously—on the opposite street corner from her hotel. Lilia had a few choice things to say about service fees for lack of service, but that made no difference.

The prudent choice would have been to descend into the netherzones, the underground service network that ran beneath the streets of every city in the Republic, but Lilia couldn't face more darkness.

It was no more than a fifty-yard dash to the hotel's entrance and the street was quiet. She'd be in bed in a quarter of the time it would take to navigate an alternative route through the unfamiliar netherzones. There was a silvery fog in the street, one that Lilia didn't much like. The fog and the events of the evening combined to make her go for the easy choice. It was a bold move, but the kind of thing Lilia did all the time.

On the Frontier.

That was the critical difference. Lilia hadn't taken more than half a dozen steps before they were on her.

Six burly soldiers leapt out of nowhere. They were wearing dark uniforms and balaclavas. Lilia didn't recognize their insignia—not that she had a lot of time to peruse their badges. They took her down hard, probably because they enjoyed it that way.

She assumed they were serving with Sumptuary & Decency, because it wasn't just a joke that S&D liked going undercover. It took a certain kind of man to savor a job enforcing the Decency Code. The unspoken assumption was that all women who violated the code were harlots or slaves or both.

Lilia's pseudoskin didn't fit well with this view of the world. She'd forgotten how rigorously the rules could be enforced: everyone was lax about the S&D laws on the Frontier.

The men slammed Lilia into the wall, one twisting her arm behind her back. She couldn't defend herself well because of the unfamiliar weight of Gid's suit. Another grabbed her braid and pulled it back, exposing the I.D. bead embedded in the back of her neck. Her helmet fell and rolled. A third snagged Lilia's laze and fired it once across the street, then whistled through his teeth.

"Nice piece," he said.

Lilia might have complained about the wasted firepower but the first rammed his armored hips into hers. He squeezed her between the wall and his pelvis, then ground himself against her.

It had to be military-grade recvlar on that codpiece—there was nothing mortal that could be so hard. Lilia wasn't going to tell him how much it hurt, though. Attitude would only get her into more trouble.

Even if it was difficult to define at this point exactly what *more* trouble might be.

"Bet that's what you want, isn't it?" he muttered in Lilia's ear. The perverts with him laughed, but she kept her mouth shut.

She was outnumbered and on the wrong side of the law.

Hadn't she just been warned of the price of that? Montgomery must have ordered her up a 3-D version of his verbal warning.

"What're you doing out in the world without an escort, slut?" asked the commander. He ran his reader over her neck with more force than was necessary. Lilia knew she'd have a bruise.

She also knew they'd love to give her a few more.

"Just going home," she said meekly.

"Lilia Desjardins," he read. "What kind of name is that?"

"The one my mother gave me."

"But not the one your father gave you." They snickered together, reassured that they'd called her occupation correctly. "Maybe she didn't know who your father was, slut."

"I don't know." Lilia tried for the demure tone she found so elusive.

"What're you doing out alone? It's past curfew."

"I was working." Admitting—again—that she'd been in the old city wasn't going to improve anything. She didn't imagine they'd believe that her cloak had been eaten by a wolf either.

"Looking to find a sperm donor of your own?" asked the one pressed against her. He rolled his hips and her pelvis ground against the brick building. " 'Cause, baby, I'll volunteer."

They found this so funny that it didn't seem any of them would be able to catch a breath anytime soon.

"I'm a shade hunter," Lilia said when their laughter finally slowed.

"You won't have to look far to find a shade willing to get a piece of that," the one holding her hair said, then pinched her butt cheek hard. Lilia winced but didn't complain.

"Hey, you're a Nuclear Darwinist." The leader looked at her with narrowed eyes. "Or did you steal someone's I.D.?"

Lilia refrained from telling him how difficult it would be to not only steal someone's identification bead, but to have it embedded in one's own neck. They faked I.D. all the time at the circus, after all, but it was a refined art requiring special, illegal equipment.

"It's all mine," she said. "Check the description."

He read from the display of his reader, then nodded.

"Check the sign," Lilia suggested, pointing upward, ever the helpful citizen. The hotel had a big sign welcoming Nuclear Darwinists to their annual convention.

"Huh, that's you then." He snapped his fingers and the two thugs released her. "Catch anything?"

"Not tonight."

"You're looking pretty hot." He gestured to her radiation reading badge while his fellows snickered.

"Oh, it's the end of the month and I've been working overtime," Lilia said, dismissing the high reading. The tenor of their exchange had altered, presumably because she was a tourist contributing to the local economy.

She guessed that she was about to contribute more.

"Thirty creds," he pronounced, giving Lilia a hard look. He wanted her to challenge him, she could see, because the fine should have been twenty creds, max.

But he would have loved to have made it forty.

As much as Lilia would have liked to have argued the matter, she ceded. That was the smart choice.

Maybe it was even prudent.

When she shrugged acquiescence, he logged the charge onto the I.D. bead in the back of her neck. Lilia knew that the creds were being removed from her bank account and deposited somewhere, presumably the account of the police department or of the metropolis of New Gotham itself.

She wouldn't have bet on that, though.

He scowled at her. "Now, don't let us catch you again."

Lilia practiced her demure smile. "I wouldn't dream of it."

"Chester will," one of the guys teased the one who had slammed her into the wall. He eyed Lilia, the way a stray dog eyes lunch.

She put out her hand for her laze and there was a pause in the festivities. She knew that if they didn't give it back to her, she wouldn't be able to hide her anger.

"It's in her I.D.," their leader said finally. "She's licensed and it's registered in her name."

"She could lodge a complaint," noted the one who had been silent so far.

The ape with Lilia's laze gave it a slight caress and handed it back. At home, she would have gone down the street and pretended to be staying elsewhere, but Lilia had learned her lesson: less time on New Gotham's streets was better, as long as she was wearing her pseudoskin. They already knew where she was staying, anyway.

Lilia strode straight to the hotel, aware of their hungry gazes the whole way. She was starting to see a pattern: ever since she'd gotten to New Gotham, she'd been feeling like prey.

She didn't have to like it.

And she didn't have to like Montgomery's role in this little tutorial.

Maybe she would hunt him down again, just to tell him off.

"Angels" Among Us?

NOUVEAU MONT ROYAL—Circus proprietor Joachim Delorenzo presented his two newest shade performers as "angels" yesterday for the first time, in defiance of widespread suspicion. The capture of the two shades, somewhere in the wilderness by Nuclear Darwinist Lilia Desjardins, has been controversial since the news was first leaked.

Delorenzo insisted yesterday that the shades are the result of spontaneous mutation and not surgical alteration. The pair, which both have large luminous wings, appeared in the nude. Delorenzo exhibited X-rays and certifications from several medical authorities to support his claim of authenticity. When pressed, he admitted the extremely low probability of two such mutations occurring simultaneously.

"Truth is stranger than fiction," was Delorenzo's conclusion.

The Society of Nuclear Darwinists has refrained from acknowledging the shades or confirming their safety within the Frontier Circus, and has called instead for their immediate surrender to the Society's labs for further study. In a prepared statement, Ernestine Sinclair, president of the Society, declared the angel-shades to be "a remarkably complex mutation, well beyond the evidence currently gathered with respect to radiation effects. We owe it to the citizens of the Republic—present and future—to not only to verify that these are genuine mutations, but to isolate any conditions responsible for such radical deformity."

In an interview, Ernestine expressed her own doubts of

the pair's authenticity. "It's so unlikely as to be impossible," she said with a smile. She quoted the probabilities of such a mutation occurring twice simultaneously to be "lower than one in 76 million, according to our foremost statistician, Gideon Fitzgerald."

In an uncommon expression of defiance from a Society fellow, shade hunter Lilia Desjardins declared that the angel-shades, known in the Frontier Circus as Armaros and Baraqiel, "would be surrendered to the Society's labs over my dead body."

The Republic, when asked, confirmed that the shades cannot be harvested by the Republic or the Society, under Republic law, as long as they remain within the bounds of the circus and upon its payroll. Delorenzo and his legal counsel were quick to provide evidence of pay statements to the Republic Inspectors who attended yesterday's show.

If others had doubts, the five hundred citizens who flocked to see the first public appearance of the angel-shades were unanimous in accepting the celestial nature of the shades. Angel enthusiasts thronged the streets of Nouveau Mont Royal and images of the two angel-shades were available for download from virtually every kiosk in town. The main tent of the circus was filled to capacity and a line had already formed for today's exhibition.

Armaros and Baraqiel themselves had nothing to say during their appearance, but their smiles and their presence were seemingly sufficient for the adoring crowd. Many attendees fell to their knees before the pair. Others spoke in whispers or prayed quietly. Delorenzo acknowledged that the exhibit lasted three times as long as he had intended, but declared himself reluctant to force people to move quickly. "They've come far: they deserve a good look for their creds," he said. "This is a wonderful event."

Yesterday's admissions at the Frontier Circus for the angel-shades alone surpassed ten thousand creds.

"It's a miracle," declared Georgina MacKay, who had traveled from New Houston to see the angel-shades. She declared herself satisfied with their authenticity. "They're not human: there's something otherworldly about them. They've come from God."

Popular vid-evangelist Reverend Billie Jo Estevez evidently agreed. She was unsuccessful in arranging a live vid service with the pair, later citing Delorenzo's insistence that the circus was a secular forum (per Republic law). Undaunted, the Reverend conducted a prayer service outside the bounds of the circus. The live broadcast was cut with vid captured during Estevez's private encounter with the pair, and instantly became the Republic's most-forwarded and most-downloaded broadcast of the decade.

The Society for Nuclear Darwinists, simultaneous to the first public display of the angel-shades, filed a motion for the shades' immediate surrender in the Chicago District Court.

IV

AFTER HIS shift, Montgomery strode into the darkness, his faux leather cloak swinging. He moved like a wraith though the quiet streets of New Gotham, a shadow blending into the shadows.

He ducked into the netherzones, moving with purpose through the primary level. Despite the curfew on the street, there was still some foot traffic. Attractive shades assigned as personal assistants to the rich and powerful took breaks at all hours, their owners inclined to be indulgent. Other shade domestics walked colicky babies and ran late errands.

Montgomery slipped the stud from his ear with practiced ease and stashed it inside his glove. He bought a daily download on a chip, declining the privilege of datasharing with the vendor, and headed to a beverage bar close to the pleasure fringe.

He settled in front of a public reader with a steaming cup of dark brew at his elbow, spared a wink for the curvy blonde smiling at him from the bar, and palmed a scrambler hidden in the top of his boot. The scrambler was a thin biodegradable film, encoded to disrupt the tracking abilities of the Republic's central databases. It began to disintegrate upon exposure to air.

Montgomery spread the scrambler quickly on the datachip, noting that he only had two left, and pushed the datachip into the port.

The daily download was displayed, along with an additional window with a prompt. Montgomery accessed Lilia's file, following the link to her capture of what she called angel-shades. He was struck by the fact that it had been Fitzgerald who had provided stats to the Society to discredit her find.

The firewall on the coroner's reports was easily breached, especially as Montgomery had done it before, and in a heartbeat he was reviewing the autopsy report of Gideon Fitzgerald.

The decedent had initially been a John Doe, discovered in the old city by a routine security patrol. The death had been assumed to be accidental from the outset—there were no images, much less a description, of the scene of death. There was a physical description: a Caucasian male, mid- to late thirties, unidentifiable due to the extensive radiation burns to his face and hands. The victim had died of a concussion, having been struck on the head, presumably by a piece of stone cornice found in his proximity, but not before removing his helm and gloves.

Bad choice, Montgomery thought. Part of the danger of old cities was the lack of maintenance upon damaged structures; falling chunks of buildings were a constant hazard.

Anyone with a speck of sense should have known that. Had Fitzgerald been one of those clever types who couldn't deal with practical realities? Montgomery couldn't see Lilia marrying such a man.

Or maybe he didn't want to.

Face and fingertips had been burned beyond recognition. The identification bead that should have been in the decedent's neck had been removed before his death. The coroner suggested that the angle of the wound indicated that it had been self-inflicted. The rationale had been that the decedent, knowing he intended to do something illegal, had tried to disguise his identity.

But Fitzgerald couldn't have planned on the radiation burns.

Not unless his death had been a suicide. The surprising possibility made Montgomery blink before he continued reading.

He pulled up the image and wasn't so sure that the

wound had been self-inflicted. There was a black market in reprogrammed I.D. beads, one sufficiently lucrative that someone might have taken his chances in the old city for a retrieval. Old cities were so poorly secured that it was comparatively easy for people to enter them.

Of course, the health hazard provided a certain deterrent.

The decedent's palm had been wiped, except for the address of a shipping and expediting company in New Gotham. It was Breisach and Turner. The receptionist, Rachel Gottlieb, had confirmed that no one of that name or description had ever worked there.

It wasn't quite a lie. Fitzgerald had been there to talk to her, twice, but she hadn't told NGPD that.

She *had* told Montgomery.

The investigating officer had concluded that the decedent had had a software worm installed on his palm, one programmed to wipe his palm clean upon his death. According to this logic, the subroutine had missed one random piece of data.

Montgomery didn't believe in random.

The decedent's pseudoskin had provided the clue to a positive identification. It was a good suit, custom made, and had been traced by its maker's mark to a customer named Gideon Fitzgerald.

Who hadn't been reported missing, even though a corpse wearing his pseudoskin had been lying in Gotham for a good week before the patrols found the body. The pseudoskin might have been sold or borrowed—except that no one knew Fitzgerald's location, once they were asked.

Fitzgerald's wife, Lilia Desjardins, had said that he was on assignment, and although she hadn't heard from him in months, that wasn't uncommon. Montgomery had smelled a lie even then in Lilia's tone, but maybe she had been sworn to secrecy.

What kind of marriage had they had?

The Society had nothing to say to the police about one of their members and refused to confirm Fitzgerald's whereabouts. The dental records had been declared insufficient for identification. Fortunately, the cadaver had been ornamented with a number of distinctive tattoos.

Some in quite personal locations.

Montgomery squinted at the images, still amazed by them. The occult practices of Nuclear Darwinists didn't officially occur according to the Society, but Fitzgerald's body proved otherwise.

Did Lilia have tattoos?

Montgomery frowned in concentration as he reread Lilia's list of the eight tattoos that her husband possessed. The first tattoo was a Pictish knot on the top of Fitzgerald's head. That and the Eye of Horus she'd claimed was on Fitzgerald's forehead had been impossible to verify due to the radiation burns.

But then the investigating officer hit paydirt. The bee Lilia had said was on the front of Fitzgerald's throat matched the tattoo on the body in the morgue.

The first hundred digits of pi were tattooed around her husband's chest, according to Lilia, the spiral of numbers beginning over his heart and ending less than two turns later under his right arm. The corpse had the same tattoo. Montgomery was struck again by the distinctiveness of the tattoos and Lilia's very precise descriptions.

Did the tattoos have specific meanings?

There had been a universal man around Gideon's navel, a man with outstretched arms and legs standing in a pentacle, and the decedent had also possessed that tattoo.

On the base of the decedent's spine was a smiling sun that matched Lilia's description and also looked vaguely familiar to Montgomery. He tracked back to the images Lilia had snagged earlier that evening and recognized Orv the Orange. He made a mental note to find out more about Orv.

On the top of Fitzgerald's right foot was a symbol that Lilia had said was the symbol for Mercury. It looked like a circle on a stem, with a crescent lying atop it. The decedent had it too.

The most shocking tattoo to Montgomery was the one

at the decedent's groin. In her list, Lilia had called it a
melusine. To Montgomery, it looked like a mermaid with
a split tail, one that had been tattooed on the decedent's
pubis. The melusine smiled coyly, her breasts bare and
her dark hair flowing loose. She held one end of her tail
in each hand and the split in her tail was right at the root
of the decedent's penis.

Montgomery was incredulous that anyone would have
endured the pain of a detailed tattoo in such a tender location. His heart stopped cold when he realized why he'd
recognized Lilia earlier.

The mermaid had Lilia's coy smile and heart-shaped
face.

Montgomery would have bet everything he had that
Fitzgerald had loved his wife. Yet he had denounced her
and what she called her angel-shades.

Publicly.

Had she loved Fitzgerald?

Did she still?

Montgomery couldn't believe that the Lilia he had met
would have let that pass without comment.

Would she have killed Fitzgerald for trying to discredit
her? He couldn't believe it.

Or did he just not want to believe it? She was clearly a
passionate woman, one unafraid to act on her convictions.

Had she hired the shade to kill Fitzgerald and gone into
the old city to silence the shade forever? No. Montgomery
couldn't reconcile that kind of cold-blooded strategizing
with the woman who had lost her temper so readily in his
office. She seemed to wear her heart on her sleeve.

Or was that an act?

His old question still remained: what had Fitzgerald been
doing in the old city? Montgomery was starting to think
that Lilia knew exactly why he had been there, and that she
had gone there to finish what Fitzgerald had started.

Whatever that had been.

"What the hell are you doing?" a woman demanded.
Montgomery turned in surprise to find a furious

Rachel at his elbow. She was early, just his luck. "I'm following a lead," he began, but Rachel wasn't listening.

"You've wasted a scrambler," she snapped, glancing at the reader's display. "The Republic doesn't care if you look at porn vid. Do you think these tools come out of the air?"

"That's not what I'm doing," Montgomery argued. "It's about Fitzgerald." He backtracked through the record to prove it to her. He had a feeling it was a losing battle.

He was right.

"GOOD EVENING," the shade on the front desk said to Lilia, sounding as welcoming as a badly programmed robot. It was the same shade who had checked Lilia in earlier, and she had been struck then by the woman's detachment.

Maybe it was the particular sedative cocktail she was being given.

Lilia didn't ask and didn't answer; she just went to her unit. She felt the shade following her progress across the lobby and was surprised. She'd seemed too zoned out to be watchful.

Maybe it was a trick. Maybe she sold dirt. The Republic employed many tattles, after all, some of whom were in the most unlikely of places. Lilia was too tired to care whom the shade told about her pseudoskin now.

What else could go wrong?

She knew she shouldn't have wondered. She took the stairs to the third floor, unwilling to take the elevator even in her exhaustion. She plodded down the hall to her unit, entertaining a fantasy of a long undisturbed sleep.

Maybe Montgomery could make a cameo appearance in her dreams. The Republic, at least so far, hadn't figured out a way to record that little indulgence and use it against citizens.

Lilia silently gave them another decade to conquer the technical obstacles.

She locked the unit door behind herself, leaned back against it, and closed her eyes. No matter how she consid-

ered it, this hadn't been one of her better evenings.
Clearly, someone didn't want Lilia to know whatever it
had been that Y654892 had known.

This was both good and bad. On the upside, it meant
that there was a greater probability that she was right about
Gid's death not having been an accident. The shade's death
could have been a random act of violence. Unlikely, given
the location, but not impossible.

On the downside, it meant that someone with a tendency to violence didn't want Lilia being nosy.

Danger had never stopped her before, and neither had
a fear of repercussions. Gid deserved justice and Lilia
was going to get it for him.

She hadn't, after all, given him much else.

Lilia glanced down and saw a white plastic envelope on
the dark carpet. It must have been slipped under her door
while she was out. *Lilia Desjardins* was written across the
front of it, but that wasn't what made her heart stop.

Her name was written in Gid's handwriting.

But Gid had been dead for two months and was unlikely to be keeping up with his correspondence.

"SO WHAT?" Rachel said. "People come around asking
questions all the time. I've got a few of my own."

Montgomery spared her a glance. "This is the guy you
wanted me to assess, remember. Maybe his widow knows
whatever he knew."

Rachel shrugged. "It's not important anymore. We have
to go to Chicago tomorrow. There's new evidence . . ."

"Chicago?" Montgomery's gaze fell to the tattoo on
her forearm that Rachel always kept hidden. "Are you
sure?"

"This isn't about me," she said with impatience.

"It could be. You should be careful." Montgomery
pulled up the images of the savagely murdered shade.
"This happened tonight."

Rachel caught her breath. "A dissection cut," she

murmured. "Made on a shade. Sounds like Nuclear Darwinists to me."

"Their convention is in town this week."

"Great," she said wryly. "Thousands of them underfoot. All the more reason to go to Chicago."

"Even though the Institute for Radiation Studies is there."

Rachel shuddered. "And the labs. Don't forget the research labs."

"Is that why you're going there?"

"No. I heard something. We need to check out this lead, and besides, we've done everything possible in New Gotham." She spoke brusquely. "I've made the arrangements and you'll leave tomorrow on the express train."

Montgomery didn't want to go. "Fitzgerald's widow is the one who captured Armaros and Baraqiel last spring."

"Oh, that explains everything." Rachel laughed under her breath. "Maybe you *are* looking at vid porn." Before he could ask, she leaned over him and tapped back to Lilia's record, pulling up the image of Lilia.

Even in the official image, she looked mutinous, clever, and gorgeous. Montgomery's mouth went dry.

Rachel lowered her voice. "She's beautiful, isn't she? A renegade and a rebel, a liar and a fellow barely tolerated by the Society. Anything she tells you is completely suspect."

"She found the dead shade in Gotham."

"Maybe she killed the shade in Gotham. There's no way to know."

"No. I trust her motives. I think she's an idealist . . ."

"We have better things to do, Montgomery." She gave him a hard look. "I chose you for my team because you were always such a good judge of human character. I'd really hoped that you wouldn't suffer the usual affliction of male volunteers."

"This isn't about lust," Montgomery began to argue.

"Isn't it?" Rachel demanded. "You're all the same. You

get earthbound and you can't control yourselves. It's as if mortal women are fatal to your ability to reason . . ."

"That's not true. She knows something."

Rachel snorted. "What I know is that you have the hots for her and it's not convenient. I don't have time to fight, Montgomery, and I don't have time to help you get lucky. Our mission is important, more important than sex. Don't you want to go back?"

"Of course I do . . ."

"Then you don't be seduced by earthly pleasure. You can enjoy it, but don't surrender to it. Don't let it drive your choices. That puts you on the other side—it gives power to the dark one and can keep you from going back."

Montgomery blinked. It was the most information Rachel had given him in months.

She pivoted and would have walked away, but he caught at her arm. "You haven't told me why you're going to Chicago."

"I'll tell you on the way."

Montgomery shook his head. "I'm not going, not tomorrow. I need to find out what Lilia knows." At her skeptical expression, he shook his head. "It's not lust. She knows something. This is the clue we've been waiting for."

Rachel's lips tightened. "Do me a favor, Montgomery, and get Lilia Desjardins out of your system quickly. You know where to find me when you're ready." With that, Rachel left him there, her displeasure hanging between them.

As he watched her stride away, Montgomery noticed a strange silvery fog sliding across the floors of the netherzones. He heard a faint echo of laughter, and knew it had to be carrying from another beverage bar.

Even if it sounded as if it was inside his own head.

He turned back to the reader. Rachel was wrong about Lilia. Lilia wasn't completely playing on the Nuclear Darwinist team, and he was going to find out why.

Montgomery took one last survey of Lilia's file, not expecting to see anything new.

Maybe that was why he was so shocked when he did.

Mother of E562008

He blinked and read the line item again.

Lilia had borne a mutant child.

Montgomery stared at the words but they didn't disappear. This had to be a malicious lie planted on her file to discredit her. He clicked through the hotlink on the child's assigned number, which brought up a much shorter record.

E562008
daughter of Lilia Desjardins
father unknown
harvested at birth
2081–2090

That was it. A short life, and one apparently unworthy of documentation.

As Montgomery stared, the scrambler fizzled. The window disappeared and only the daily news remained on the screen.

Everything Lilia said indicated that she held shades in higher regard than the law did, so why would she have joined the ranks of those who harvested shades when they had taken her own? He couldn't imagine that she could have been so indifferent to the fate of her child. The fact that there was no father listed made Montgomery doubt its truth even more.

It had to be a lie.

Giving birth to a shade was scandalous, especially for a Nuclear Darwinist. Citizens paid good cred to see these kinds of damning details buried deeper in the databanks, where fewer eyes could see them. Lilia wouldn't have ethical issues with doing that, or fail to find the cred necessary to see it done.

It was a malicious information plant to discredit Lilia, left where a great many people could see it, a great many people who could use it against her.

Lilia should know about the false data, and if he told her, Montgomery might gain some goodwill.

She might exchange one truth for another. It wasn't much of a card, but it was the only one he had and Montgomery would play it.

Fortunately, he knew just where to find the lady.

LILIA PEELED off Gid's pseudoskin and hung it up in the bathroom of her unit. She wasn't that tired anymore, not since she'd seen the envelope. She propped it up against the bathroom mirror, and stole glances at it from the shower stall as she soaped down. It never hurt to have another chemical shower and she'd brought the appropriate soap with her.

Either it was Gid's writing, which was against the odds, or someone had copied his writing brilliantly.

What were the chances that Gid had left her a last message? Lilia would have said slim to none, but she looked at that envelope and wasn't so sure.

She considered the price of opening the envelope. The room would be infested with monitors, but then the Republic was already aware of the envelope.

It might look more suspicious to *not* open it.

There was no good answer, not without knowing the contents of the envelope itself. Lilia wondered whether the shade on the front desk had been tipped to deliver it—that would explain her interest in Lilia's return.

Maybe it was a love poem from an ardent admirer. Lilia thought immediately of Montgomery and wondered if he was the type to compose love poems. The idea made her smile.

He'd be more likely to have ordered S&D to take her down for violating the law code of the Republic. Montgomery was not a fun date, even though he was a delicious beast.

A woman couldn't have everything, apparently.

Not that Lilia wanted *anything* Montgomery had.

Well, maybe that wasn't quite true.

Lilia plucked the envelope off the vanity with an impatient gesture. The plastic envelope crackled as she opened it.

Inside it was a temporary tattoo.

The tattoo was the cheap kind included with breakfast cereal granules. To pacify moms everywhere, it would wash off in any time frame from a couple of hours to a couple of days—which moved the battleground from permanent disfigurement to personal hygiene.

Lilia's mom, of course, didn't possess any maternal prejudice against tattoos, a good thing since Lilia had a variety of them.

Like Gid. Lilia's stomach rolled at the unwelcome reminder of her last exchange with NGPD, and she considered this gift instead.

This image wasn't ancient or symbolic of anything beyond the power of centralized authority. It was the logo used by the Republic as a reminder and a warning: a pair of eyes drawn in black. It was apparent that they were feminine eyes, even in the simple line drawing, because they were tilted exotically upward at the outer corners as if they had been outlined in kohl. Women were the heart and soul of trouble, as every citizen knew.

These were the eyes displayed throughout the Republic on billboards, on official notices from the Republic to its citizens. There were lots of them at the circus, fluttering on little colored banners that were strung between the tents, not that anyone ever heeded that warning.

The eyes of the Republic are everywhere.

As messages from beyond the grave went, this one had to count as a disappointment. On a whim, Lilia applied it to her upper left arm. Who knew? Maybe it would open a secret door somewhere. Lilia checked it out in the mirror, then made the connection.

The tattoo was a warning.

The envelope was from someone who knew that Gid's death hadn't been an accident—Lilia was being warned, probably by someone very much alive, that what she did would not go unwitnessed.

The hair stood up on the back of her neck.

There was someone other than Y654892 who knew more about Gid's death, probably the same someone who had been responsible for the shade's untimely demise.

This person or persons unknown knew exactly where Lilia was.

Lilia shivered. This wasn't the most reassuring note on which to end her day. It seemed pointless to go anywhere else, to try to hide from someone who could apparently find her so readily.

It wasn't like Lilia to be afraid, but her heart was pumping. She went to bed anyway. Unlike a real tattoo, the temporary one pulled against her skin. It couldn't have been just the persistent tug that kept her awake long into the night.

It wasn't a guilty conscience either.

It was Montgomery's terse words: "Two minutes. Max."

In two minutes, the shade's killer couldn't have gotten far from the dead shade, whether or not there was another exit to the plaza. He couldn't have started another bike without Lilia having heard it.

Which meant the killer had lingered, maybe even watched her discover the shade's body, then left after Lilia was gone. It would have been easy for him to kill Lilia, but the choice had been made to let her live.

Why? Lilia couldn't get warm once she made that realization. She tossed and turned, exhausted but unable to fall asleep.

The Republic's eyes weren't the only ones watching her.

75TH ANNUAL CONVENTION
OF THE SOCIETY OF NUCLEAR DARWINISTS

OCTOBER 28–31, 2099, IN NEW GOTHAM

• HIGHLIGHTED SCHEDULE OF EVENTS •

THURSDAY

- 7-11–Mix and Mingle in the Lobby Bar

FRIDAY

- 9–NOON–Special Session–Wilhelmina Olsendatter on her recent work (*Angels and Demons: Past and Present Perceptions of Good and Evil,* Institute of Radiation Studies Press, Chicago, 2098)
- NOON-3–Opening Keynote Luncheon: Mike MacPherson: Annual Review of the Society's New and Pending Drug Patents
- 2-3–*Sunshine Heals*: Vid Feed of Official Launch into Frontier
- 7-9–Cocktail Reception for new 7th Degree Fellows.

SATURDAY

- 9-11–Incumbent President Ernestine Sinclair and Declared Candidate Blake Patterson present their election platforms for 2100 Presidency
- NOON-3–Closing keynote: "A Mathematical Model of the Society's Future" : Abraham Malachy
- 3-6–Special Session–"Harvesting in the Field"–Rhys Ibn Ali shares his shade-hunting techniques and strategies
- 6-10–Annual Gala and Dinner: a Tribute to the first 75 years of the Society and the Memory of Ernest Sinclair, Society Founder. Presentation of Gideon Fitzgerald Award for Academic Excellence at the Institute for Radiation Studies (presented by Lilia Desjardins)

V

Thursday, October 29, 2099

LILIA DIDN'T imagine that there could be much worse than being roughed up by S&D, but she was soon proven wrong.

Being snagged before breakfast by a videvangelist on a mission was much worse.

"Lilia Desjardins!" boomed a familiar voice. "Here she is, ladies and gentlemen, the mortal designated by God to welcome angels into our midst!"

The Reverend Billie Jo Estevez had finally found her. The exchange Lilia had been ducking for months finally caught up with her, in the hotel lobby. On the upside, Lilia had dressed to the full measure of the decency code, if only because she had been so spooked the night before — at least, she'd look good on the vid.

Maybe if Lilia cooperated, the reverend would go away.

It was worth a shot.

Lilia pivoted and tried not to wince at the brightness of the lights. The reverend was closing fast, her arms outspread, as if they were old friends who had finally met.

Not as if Lilia had spent the last six months deleting the reverend's pings with no reply.

"Lilia, Lilia! *Lilia!*"

The reverend was much more imposing in person than on her daily vid upload. Her hair was silvery white and she wore flowing garments in bright colors. She was a woman whose only punctuation was an exclamation mark.

She always reminded Lilia of the cross-dressers in the Frontier's pleasure fringe. In person, that effect was amplified a hundred times. The reverend was too large, too vivid, too loud—visually and aurally—to be real.

But the bear hug she gave Lilia wasn't imaginary. "Lilia, I am so delighted to have found you!" She caught Lilia close, stunning her victim with a cloud of perfume.

"How are you?" she demanded. Her gaze was steely, for all her apparent down-home friendliness.

"I think I've cracked a rib," Lilia murmured.

The reverend laughed, then gathered her upload team with a flick of the wrist. Lilia was positioned with the reverend's arm around her shoulders—holding her captive.

"For those of you as yet unaware," the reverend boomed in the direction of one feed, "angels are among us, and here, with me, is their divinely appointed trustee."

"Well, actually, those two angel-shades have signed a contract to work with Joachim Delorenzo's circus . . ."

"Nonsense!" The reverend boomed, burying Lilia's words beneath her own. "We cannot know the mind of God, but we can see his workings upon the face of the earth and in our midst." The reverend's fingers dug into Lilia's flesh as a warning. "You, Lilia, were chosen as the trustee of God's appointed messengers. You, Lilia, hold the secret to their arrival among us. You, Lilia, have almost seen the face of God!"

If she hadn't made such a stretch for the superlative, Lilia could have played along. "Actually, Reverend, I just found them in a little clearing in the woods . . ."

"Remember the parable of the Good Samaritan!" the reverend interrupted. "The apostle Luke tells us of a lawyer who asked Jesus *'And who is my neighbor whom I should love as well as my own self?'*"

The reverend paused. "Who is my neighbor, Lord?" She drew herself up to her full height. "Who is my neighbor? Luke records the reply Jesus gave to the lawyer, the story we know as that of the Good Samaritan." She began to recount scripture and Lilia's thoughts wandered to escape and breakfast, in that order.

She wondered how the reverend remembered so many

verses so well. It was impressive, at least until Lilia saw the tiny feed in the reverend's left ear.

The Reverend finished her lesson and raised a mighty finger. "And so it was that Lilia offered aid to a neighbor, much as did the Good Samaritan, and so perhaps, in God's great mercy, might Lilia have gained the kingdom of eternal life."

Lilia cleared her throat. "It wasn't exactly like that."

"Humility and modesty! Paul tells us in I Timothy, 2:10–15, that what becomes a woman best is modesty and good works. '*Let a woman learn in silence with all submission.*'" The reverend gave a rapturous sigh. "And so it is, Lilia, that we see the reason for the divine choice, in your modesty and willingness to serve."

"Demure, that's me," Lilia said and someone made a choking sound behind her. She couldn't see who because of the lights, but the choke was definitely feminine.

Therefore not Montgomery, unfortunately.

The reverend leaned closer, so close that Lilia could see the pores on her nose beneath her rosy-hued mask of makeup. "So, tell us, Lilia, what message did the angels bring to humankind?"

Lilia blinked. "Message?"

"God dispatched angels throughout the Old Testament to deliver his messages to his faithful," the reverend explained. "An angel came unto Joseph in a dream and counseled him to not put Mary aside, that she carried a child in truth but one conceived by the Holy Spirit. The angel Gabriel appeared to Zacharias to tell him that his wife, Elisabeth, should conceive a son, John, and that this son should smooth the way for Jesus and his teachings."

She turned to the vid feed and her voice rose to majestic proportions. "And the angel of the annunciation came unto Mary herself, our Virgin Mother, and said '*Do not be afraid, Mary, for you have found favor with God. And now you will conceive in your womb and bear a son and you will name him Jesus. He will be great, and will be called the Son of the Most High, and the Lord God will*

*give to him the throne of his ancestor David. He will
reign over the house of Jacob forever, and of his kingdom
there will be no end.'* And so it is writ in the gospel of
Saint Luke and so it has been."

The reverend gave Lilia a stern glance. "There are angels, Lilia, of this we have no doubt, and further, they are
the emissaries of God. What message did the angels
bring to us from our Lord the Most High?"

Everyone in the lobby seemed to be listening, waiting
for the divine wisdom to spill from Lilia's lips to their
ears.

It seemed a bad time to admit that there had been no
message.

Or that Lilia hadn't thought to ask for one.

All the same, the reverend expected an answer.

Lilia debated the merit of *"Eat more fiber"* or even
"Peace be unto you." "Love your neighbor" had some potential given the Good Samaritan reference, but seemed a
bit thin, especially seeing as *two* angel-shades had been en-
trusted with its delivery.

That alone seemed to require a certain weight, message-
wise.

"Um." Lilia stalled for time, quite badly. "I'm not sure
I should just say it."

"Of course not!" someone interjected in an imperious
tone.

Was salvation at hand?

Someone pried the reverend's fingers from Lilia's
shoulder. The interrupter tut-tutted, which gave a hint of
her identity.

Lilia remembered that tut.

"A message of this import is for the ears of the highest
officials, first and foremost, and must be considered carefully before it is disseminated amongst the masses." Dr.
Wilhelmina Olsendatter seized Lilia's shoulder with her
own iron grip and tut-tutted again. "Really, Reverend, you
must show an increment of social responsibility."

Before the reverend could recover from the fact that she

had been chided on vid—by a stranger—Dr. Olsendatter swept Lilia away.

"Demure," she snorted. "I thought about abandoning you when you said *that*. You couldn't be demure to save your life. It's part of what I like about you, dear."

"Sorry. And thanks." Lilia felt as if she'd jumped from the fat into the fire. Dr. Olsendatter was heading to the hotel café, dragging Lilia into a restaurant thick with hungry Nuclear Darwinists.

Lilia upgraded her assessment: being snagged by the oldest living professor on the face of the earth was worse than being beaten up by S&D *or* cornered by a vid-evangelist on a mission.

The day could only get better.

"FOOL WOMAN," Dr. Wilhelmina Olsendatter grumbled. She hailed a wait-shade, demanded two orders of the largest breakfast platters on the menu, then picked up her rant where she'd left off. "How utterly predictable that she would edit the verses she recounts."

"Excuse me?"

"That bit from Timothy about women being submissive has a verse in the middle of it, declaring that women shall not teach: '*Let the woman learn in silence with full submission. I permit no woman to teach or to have authority over man; she is to keep silent. For Adam was formed first . . .*' etc., etc. But then, that would be problematic for a female evangelist, wouldn't it?"

Doc Mina, as her students had been instructed to call her, lowered her voice somewhat. Everything was relative: Doc Mina had one of those high voices that carried well over long distances. "That is, as you must know, one of the verses most often cited against the notion of ordaining women as priests."

Lilia didn't know that, so she pretended otherwise. "Of course."

"It's nonsense, naturally," Doc Mina fumed. "We've

known for more than a hundred years that Paul didn't compose either of the gospels called Timothy. They're simply not coherent in terms of style or references to the letters that he did write, but that doesn't stop people from making references to them as if they were, well, gospel." Doc Mina smiled at her own joke.

The reverend's voice carried from the lobby. She was expounding upon the wisdom of God in sending the light of his word into the deepest darkness. Lilia supposed that was a reference to the low incidence of religious devotion among Nuclear Darwinists.

The fire was definitely a better choice than the fat, so Lilia settled in. She'd always liked Doc Mina. Because so few Nuclear Darwinists took an interest in "the dovetailing of religious belief with historiography in the wake of nuclear destruction," Doc Mina had always been thrilled to find anyone in her lectures.

To be present and conscious merited an instant A.

Lilia had received a flurry of messages from Doc Mina after the angel-shades had been revealed but she had been ducking her old prof. After the argument with Gid over Armaros and Baraqiel, Lilia hadn't been ready to go toe to toe with any other experts.

Doc Mina, however, could trigger guilt like a forgotten maiden aunt and served some up right on cue. "Now, Lilia, I've had the very devil of a time getting hold of you. Did you receive my messages?"

"Well, yes—" Lilia thought she improvised brilliantly "—but I didn't want to be offhand about something so important."

"Ah! Well, you might have acknowledged receipt. I had always believed you to be a woman with an increment of good manners."

"I've misplaced them, in the field."

She gave Lilia a stern look. "Well, you certainly must realize the importance of this discovery to my own research. Why, it's remarkable and yet so utterly predictable."

"Excuse me?" Lilia was sure she'd heard incorrectly.

"In terms of human mythology, of course. Even the Reverend Billie Jo knows that angels are the traditional bearers of messages from the divine source itself, or Himself, depending upon your choice of terminology. Myself, I've always thought of the divine as sexless—I mean, really, wouldn't you expect a cosmic force to have evolved beyond mere biology?—but to each, his or her own."

Doc Mina spread her napkin across her lap as the meals came. It looked like three eggs over easy with sausages, fruit salad, and toast, but Lilia knew better. The eggs were too gelatinous to be real and she was deeply suspicious of the sausages.

They could have been biologic foam.

"Faux flesh and extruded fruit." Doc Mina sighed, then frowned at the black liquid optimistically labeled "tea." "You'd think they'd just go with supplements. I so dislike compromise. Go one way or the other, is what I say, don't dither about in between."

"Real tea, if less of it." Lilia had gotten spoiled by the contraband readily available at the circus—this stuff tasted so foul that she wanted to spit it out.

Doc Mina nodded. "Exactly. Like the opening keynote lecture. They should have booked something different when Paul fell ill, as I'm sure I wasn't the only one looking forward to his anecdotes. But no. This person from the labs is stepping in and won't be nearly as entertaining as Paul."

"Paul?" Lilia had forgotten about Doc Mina's tendency to meander from topic to topic.

"Paul Cosmopoulos," Doc Mina chided. "You remember him, of course. Director of the Institute's Research Labs? Paul would have sparkled, making the most painfully dry material fascinating. Doubtless the substitute will drone on about research results and drug patents, which is so boring even though it is important, of course, to both the Society and society at large." She shook her head and chewed on her "toast." "The revenue from such things funds my own research, of course, although it's vulgar to say so."

Maybe it was better that there was a little social vacuum around them. Lilia knew from experience that Nuclear Darwinists didn't take kindly to suggestions that their research was dull.

"They should have fetched Paul and compelled him to come, or canceled the talk. Enough compromise!" Doc Mina boomed this last bit, which created more space around them as more Nuclear Darwinists moved farther away.

"It's not like you to be so critical," Lilia said carefully, distrusting this new sense that she had an ally in the Society.

"I'm tired of pretending," Doc Mina said with a snort. "And there's not much more they can do to me now. They've given me a smaller office and cut my salary."

Lilia was surprised. "What's going on?"

"Oh, it's all the old nonsense about my courses not being relevant to the curriculum." Doc Mina chomped through her "sausage" with gusto. "It seems that I've been classed as a 'frill.' Ernest Sinclair, you know, insisted that Nuclear Darwinists embrace a broad range of studies, not just science and research, in order to make them more balanced individuals and thus better scientists, but no one seems to remember *that*."

"Are they going to fire you?"

She shrugged, her brave posture not fully hiding her disappointment. "Anything is possible, of course, once the Council gets involved. I'm sure they'd rather I just quit. Can you believe that students hate my course and find it irrelevant?" She looked at Lilia, obviously needing verification that this was madness.

Unfortunately, Lilia knew it was true.

So she changed the subject. "The Council? Do you mean the Council of Three? I thought they didn't exist."

Doc Mina snorted. "Of course they exist, they'd just prefer that you weren't sure." She jabbed her butter knife in Lilia's direction. "You worry about whether they exist and speculate upon who they are, instead of concerning yourself with what the hell they're doing. That's how this kind of travesty gets as far as it does. Who do you think makes all of the decisions? The Board of Governors?" Doc Mina laughed uproariously at her own joke. "They can't even find the restrooms on their own."

"I didn't know."

"You didn't pay attention."

"Well, who is the Council of Three?"

"There you go, worrying about who they are instead of what they're doing." Doc Mina wagged a slice of toast at Lilia, changing the subject herself. "Which reminds me, Lilia, you must tell me *all* that you can about the angels, especially since you've been ignoring my messages."

Lilia felt a smidgen of guilt. "What do you want to know?"

"Begin at the beginning, my dear. How did you find them?"

"You know, it almost seemed that they found me."

"Of course. Angels are said to be, if not omniscient, then far closer to that divine perfection of knowledge than mere mortals. What was the first thing they said?"

Lilia didn't even have to think about that. " *'Do not be afraid.'* They stole my line, if you must know."

"Classic," Doc Mina muttered. "Were you afraid?"

"Startled." Lilia took a bite of her cultivated fruit. "And they were . . . bemused."

Doc Mina laughed. "Oh, that is simply too perfect."

Lilia felt the need to set her former prof straight. "Doc Mina, you do understand that they aren't actually angels, not really messengers from the divine. Theirs is a rare mutation, but they're shades, not angels."

Doc Mina was unpersuaded. "How do you know?"

"Because there's no such thing as an angel."

"Is that so?"

"Armaros and Baraqiel exhibit an extremely rare mutation . . ." Lilia tried to argue, but didn't get far.

Doc Mina, after all, was giving her a weapons-grade glare. "What did you call them?"

"Armaros and Baraqiel."

Doc Mina was so intent upon Lilia that she put down her toast and her fork. "Who gave them those names?"

"They already had them. They told me their names."

"Interesting." Doc Mina gnawed through the rest of her breakfast, then glanced down at her empty plate with surprise. Lilia pushed her own toast plate closer to the professor.

"You must have researched those names," she said slowly.

Lilia knew she'd made a mistake. "No. I never thought of it."

"Lilia, Lilia." Doc Mina tut-tutted. "Word was that you'd never made a good Nuclear Darwinist but I had hopes that you would make a decent scholar. Armaros and Baraqiel are the names of two of the fallen angels, two of the angels accounted by the Essenes to have been Watchers or *Grigori*."

"Fallen angels? Don't you mean demons?"

"No, no, no. Keep your sources straight, my dear. The Essenes were a Jewish religious sect, most active around the time of Jesus himself. Demonology really didn't come into its own until the middle ages, after angelology had been exhausted by theologians."

"Oh."

She pounced on Lilia's toast, margarined each slice with gusto, and launched into lecture mode, spewing bread crumbs as she did so. Evidently no one had ever told Doc Mina that it was inappropriate to eat and lecture simultaneously.

Lilia wasn't going to be first.

"To fully understand, we must return to the story of Adam and Eve in the Garden of Eden, put there by God to tend the garden, instructed as they were to not touch the fruit of the central tree, the Tree of Knowledge. The Latin Christian tradition insists that Eve, tempted by the serpent, ate of the fruit then shared it with Adam. In so doing, the pair became aware of their nakedness, and when God learned of their disobedience, they were expelled from the garden, forced to work the land to feed themselves. Eve, for her transgression, was cursed with pain in childbirth, a legacy to all women. And so, because of this defiance of God's will, the garden is lost to mankind for all time."

"I've heard that story before."

"Of course you have. We all have. It's almost as old as time, and has its parallels in many other cultural traditions. What is important here is that the story had other variations, before this official version was decided upon." She chewed the last of the toast, looking around for more fuel. Lilia surrendered the rest of her faux fruit and Doc Mina began to devour it.

"Did those variations include the Watchers?"

"Funny you should ask. I was just thinking about them this morning, for some reason."

"Armaros and Baraqiel."

"Very good, Lilia. We'll make a scholar of you yet. Those were the names of two of the Watchers, as recorded in the *First Book of Enoch*. These angels descended to the earth to teach important skills to mankind, skills which God would have preferred to deny to man, just as He denied us the fruit of the Tree of Knowledge."

She looked at the ceiling of the hall. "Let's see now. Armaros was said to have taught men to free themselves from enchantment, which one wouldn't have thought was a problem until someone knew how to cast enchantments. Maybe that was the job of another Watcher. I forget. Baraqiel taught men the secrets of astrology. There are others, of course, a dozen or so all together, but you get the idea. The Watchers were given credit for teaching mankind what passed for science several thousand years ago." Doc Mina licked her fork. "Few divinities are fond of those who challenge their edicts, so these angels came to be described as 'fallen' and equated with evil."

"But did they really mean to be good, or just to be

defiant?" Lilia asked, fully able to identify with the urge to challenge expectations for a just cause.

Doc Mina smiled. "It is written that they felt lust for the daughters of men, and that was why they descended to earth. After they had had their pleasure, *then* they shared some of what they knew."

"Not everything?"

"We'd know a lot more than we do, if they'd done that."

Lilia was intrigued by all of this. "You don't really think that Armaros and Baraqiel are these same Watchers, do you? I mean, that would make them several thousand years old."

And angels, immortal beings made of light.

Impossible.

"Angels are immortal, my dear, or close to it. At the very least, they mean to put us in mind of those old stories."

"But why?"

Doc Mina sighed. "It's interpreted as a sign of the end times, of course. The angels gathering, the Antichrist making one last bid for the souls of men, blah blah blah. You'd think that over the millennia, we could have come up with some new stories, but we keep fiddling around with the same old themes and elements. I'm surprised, actually, that you don't have more people like the Reverend Billie Jo following you around."

"You sound skeptical."

"Well, the world has been scheduled to end so many times and failed to do so that I've lost count. It seems to be much more resilient than one might have expected. Just look at what we've done to it in the last century, never mind what we've done to each other." She winked. "I'll wait until the Devil himself shows up for his last cameo appearance before I get worried."

Lilia picked at the rest of her breakfast, thinking.

Doc Mina cleared her throat. "I do have to wonder, Lilia, why these angels appeared to you. I mean no offense, but why you? If they'd appeared to the reverend, she would have asked after their message to mankind. And if they'd appeared to me, well, they'd have saved my academic career." She fixed Lilia with an accusatory glance. "You could have at least given me a first interview."

Lilia thought that if angels had any foresight, then they would have seen her as their best bet for survival. There had to be some advantage in not being sliced and diced for research purposes when on a mission from God. Lilia tried to think of a way to express that politely, given present company, but failed.

Doc Mina gestured toward Lilia's plate with her fork, indicating the two faux-flesh sausages left on it. "Are you going to eat the rest of that, dear?"

LILIA STEPPED out of the hotel with relief. That sense evaporated when she saw someone who resembled the most annoying cop in the Republic, apparently waiting for her.

But looking—if it were possible—even more delicious than Montgomery had looked the night before. This man had the same build, the same handsome features, but he was dressed like a norm.

Well, a norm with pizzazz.

He wore a black faux leather greatcoat that was halfway to being a cape, one that was faced with velvet and trimmed with faux fur and would swing with flair when he strode. And he would stride. Mere walking wouldn't be sufficiently debonair for this vision of masculinity.

His tall black boots were remarkably similar to the ones the cop-Montgomery had worn the night before, and his tapered black trousers showed his muscled legs to as much advantage as the pseudoskin had. There was a froth of lace at his throat, one that made him look all the more of a male animal for the contrast, and he wore dark gloves.

He leaned in the shadows opposite, his arms folded across his chest and his legs crossed at the ankles. His collar was turned up, his eyes smoking, dark and mysterious. He looked long and lean and observant, a predator pretending to be relaxed. Lilia wasn't fooled—and for the first time since arriving in New Gotham, she wouldn't have minded being on the menu.

He smiled at her and Lilia decided her day *was* looking up.

Montgomery's secretive smile hinted at knowledge of places beyond the view of the Republic's many eyes, and what activities would be best practiced there.

Lilia had a few ideas of her own.

The obvious conclusion was that by-the-book Montgomery had an evil twin. If so—or even, if not—he was Lilia's first choice to solve her chastity problem.

The one that hadn't been bothering her until the night before.

The streets were busy, filled with people walking to work, the crowd interspersed with bicycles and rickshaws. Those on bicycles wove in and out of the bustle. It was chaotic and noisy, but mercifully everyone seemed to be headed in much the same direction.

Downtown New Gotham.

A vendor was shouting into the crowd, waving a newspaper feed. "Get your morning edition of *The Republican Record*! Thirtieth-anniversary commemorative ceremonies planned for Gotham! Mount St. Helens erupts and ten thousand believed dead! The president set to head home from successful treaty discussions in China! Get the details in today's download!"

Montgomery's twin straightened and headed toward Lilia. En route, his smile broadened slightly. Dangerously. Attractively. He looked roguish, unpredictable and irresistible. That must have been what made her palms go damp and an icy trickle of sweat meander down her spine.

It couldn't really be Montgomery; Lilia was certain that the impassive cop was incapable of showing so much emotion.

She wouldn't have put the sex appeal past Montgomery, though. And the gleam in his eye revealed that they *had* met. He moved toward her with purpose. He wasn't even going to pretend that he had run into her accidentally.

It had to be Montgomery. He might be off-duty and out of uniform, but he was a straight arrow through and through.

There was something to be said for honesty.

All the same, Montgomery had a lot of nerve to show up after what he had done, or had ordered to be done, the night before.

Lilia held her ground and waited for him, telling herself that it was simply for the pleasure of telling him off.

"Good morning." That voice could easily lead Lilia into temptation, as well as give her ideas of what to do once she arrived. He bowed before her and offered his elbow, as if they had agreed to meet.

The man was smooth, she'd give him that. And just being in the presence of so much testosterone made Lilia weak in the knees.

She needed to get herself a date.

Or loosen her corset.

A twinkle appeared in his eyes, as if he guessed her thoughts. Lilia took a deep breath, knowing from the pounding of her heart that she was in big trouble. She put her hand into the crook of his elbow and felt the muscles of his arm flex under her fingers. Even the man's arm gave her shivers.

What she really needed to get was some sex.

Lots of sex.

Soon.

She'd find out where New Gotham's pleasure fringe was before the end of the day and buy herself a treat. She pulled her hand from his elbow, missing the contact immediately, and simply walked beside him.

That made her hot enough.

"Sleep well, Lil?" His use of her name was every bit as alluring as it had been the night before.

Unfortunately, his words reminded her of her suspicions.

"Should I have?" she asked, not caring that her tone was sharp.

Montgomery fell into step beside her, but Lilia hadn't really expected otherwise. This was the kind of man who would always get what he came for. He'd come to talk to her apparently, so barring nuclear disaster—which was never out of the question in the late twenty-first-century Republic—he'd talk to her before he left.

Lilia admired that determination, though she'd die before confessing as much to him or anyone else.

"Not taking the conveyor?"

"It's better exercise to walk."

"Depends how far you're going."

Lilia said nothing. She'd let him work for it.

He cleared his throat. "How far *are* you walking?"

Lilia smiled sweetly. "I don't know. It's such a lovely day and I'm sightseeing."

His skepticism was evident. "I thought you'd come to New Gotham for other reasons."

"The conference, of course."

"That's not all, Lil. If you're going to Breisach and Turner this morning, it's about eight blocks, off to the right. Maybe the conveyor would be a good choice."

VI

LILIA'S HEART stopped at both Montgomery's accurate guess and his conviction, then galloped ahead without her. He had guessed the real reason for her trip.

It shouldn't have been a surprise. Gid's name had probably flashed along with her name on his desktop. Montgomery was smart enough to have made the connections, even if his desktop hadn't helpfully hotlinked them for him.

"I don't know what you're talking about," she lied. "I'm just out for a walk."

"Good choice," he said under his breath. "No one will be able to overhear us this way."

There was a surprising comment, given its source. Lilia wondered what Montgomery might have to discuss that he didn't want recorded by the Republic's many cameras and recorders, gossips and spies. She glanced up and saw that he wore no ear stud.

Why had he come looking for her? What didn't he want anyone to witness? Her heart began to beat a bit faster. "Where's your monitor?"

"I must have forgotten to put it in this morning."

"I thought they were surgically embedded."

He shrugged. "Sometimes they're loose."

Lilia halted. "I thought it was against the law code of the Republic for a police officer to willingly remove his ear monitor. For your own protection, of course."

That half-smile touched his lips again, launching a chain reaction under Lilia's skin. "The Republic doesn't need to know everything about me."

Lilia was surprised. Montgomery hadn't impressed her as a rule breaker, but here he was, breaking a rule.

A big one.

"I'm thinking that's a sentiment that could get you fired."

He gave her no more than a steady look in response.

Lilia suddenly had a bad feeling. She realized there were some things the authorities might prefer to *not* have recorded and archived. Montgomery was the type who would remove his monitor on command, not as a rebel.

Lilia had enough experience with being in deep trouble to recognize the view when she ended up there.

She spun away from Montgomery and walked a bit faster, not liking that whatever he intended to say—or do—to her wouldn't be observed. He, of course, easily matched his steps to hers, taking a long stride for every three of her mincing steps.

Lilia tried to walk faster, despite her heels. "I suppose you've come to confirm that I've been persuaded to your view?"

"Of what?"

"That being on the wrong side of the Republic is an undesirable situation."

He was visibly surprised.

A more gullible woman than Lilia might have believed him innocent of any involvement in her little welcome wagon. Lilia, though, suspected that he was faking his surprise. "Don't pretend you don't know about my exchange with S&D last night."

"What exchange?"

So much for honesty. "I was roughed up by S&D and don't pretend you don't know it. It was a warning to play by the rules in New Gotham, just a little emphasis of the verbal warning you gave me, and it wasn't appreciated."

Lilia marched onward. Montgomery strode beside her, making her whirlwind pace look effortless. She was hot and angry and afraid, and he was impassive. It made her want to kick him.

"Were you hurt?"

She gave him a lethal glance. "Don't pretend to be sympathetic when you ordered it."

"It wasn't my fault."

"No? Then who else?"

He frowned. "Sumptuary & Decency report to no one. And you have to admit that you took a risk in being seen in your pseudoskin. I expected you to be more sensible—"

Lilia was not going to endure a lecture on that incident being her own fault, or any intimation that she had gotten what she deserved. Her mother had taught her everything she knew.

"Oh, bull." Lilia interrupted Montgomery with a force that clearly surprised him. "Look around you! This is a tourist area, filled with people from afar, happily filling the city's coffers, as well as middle-class taxpayers trotting off to work, which also fills the city's coffers. This isn't the usual stomping ground of S&D. It's bad publicity to beat up tourists and taxpayers."

Lilia saw the barest flicker of doubt in his eyes. Then right before her eyes, he morphed into Montgomery, police detective.

Which was too bad, because she much preferred his evil twin.

"S&D docs their rounds everywhere, without warning . . ."

Lilia hadn't slept well enough to be particularly patient. "Time for some plain talk, Montgomery. They were waiting for me, which means that someone tipped them off, which had to have been someone who knew not only when I was coming back to the hotel but what I was wearing." Lilia spread her hands. "Sorry, but there aren't a lot of eligible candidates for Tipster of the Day here. You win. Thanks for nothing."

His eyes narrowed. "I didn't do it, Lil."

It made Lilia even more angry that she was tempted to believe him. "I suppose you came around to see my bruises, but I'm not inclined to play show-and-tell, even if that sort of thing does make you strain your pseudoskin." He flushed ever so slightly. "Have a great day, Montgomery."

Lilia spun, flicking her skirts, and carried on. She would have left him there, but Montgomery wasn't having any of that.

Big surprise.

She heard his steps, then he caught her elbow in his hand and pulled her to a slower pace. She would have liked to have fought him, but she knew that she would lose. Lilia was tall, but he was taller. She was buff, but he was more buff.

He was irritating in oh-so-many ways.

Worse, Montgomery wouldn't have let her win, as Gid so often had done. There was, after all, not going to be an erotic bonus awarded for chivalrous behavior.

That soured Lilia's mood even further.

"Damned heels," she muttered and he made a sound that might have been a chuckle. A ghost of a smile touched his lips before it was dismissed from active duty. She allowed herself a small rant against the Decency Code. "You would never have caught me otherwise."

"I wouldn't be so sure of that."

"They slow me down, which is the point, of course." Lilia knew she sounded like her mother and she didn't care. "No one wants women to be able to run. None of you might ever get lucky again."

"And here I was going to compliment you on your appearance."

This time Lilia was skeptical. "You don't fool me. You liked the pseudoskin better."

Montgomery chuckled. It was indisputable. Lilia looked up in disbelief, only to find him grinning.

"Guilty as charged," he said and winked.

The evil twin was back.

Lilia could tell by the leap of her pulse. She wasn't

nearly as immune to his so-called charm as would have
been prudent.

Never mind demure.

It was startling how much younger Montgomery seemed
when he smiled, but maybe not very surprising how much
more sexy he looked. The prospect of flirting with him—of
doing more than flirting with him—was much *much* easier
to entertain when his evil twin was in town.

Montgomery leaned closer and his voice dropped low,
down to a timber that launched little earthquakes in
Lilia's belly.

Or maybe the earthquakes were a bit farther south.

"I didn't send them, Lil." He lifted her veil to the brim
of her hat, as if he seduced women in broad daylight all the
time, and Lilia only wanted him to hurry. She couldn't
even tear her gaze away from his.

"I swear it to you." He touched his chest over his heart
with his gloved fingertips, his eyes gleaming with sincer-
ity, and brushed those fingertips across his lips.

Then touched his fingertips to her lips.

Right there in the street.

Lilia's heart stopped cold. He held his fingertips against
her lips, his gaze knowing. All of the air left her lungs.
She went sweaty then shivery in rapid succession. Worst
of all, she couldn't even blame the unfamiliarity of her
corset.

It was Montgomery doing this to her, on purpose, and
she couldn't stop him. She felt the smooth faux leather of
his gloves eased across her lips, smelled his skin, saw the
way his dark lashes spiked around the unbelievable green
of his eyes.

She was sure he would kiss her.

She wanted him to kiss her.

Montgomery would have to say her name like that.
Lil. It threw her game completely. It ought to be illegal
for a man to roll a woman's name across his tongue, like
a caress, or a purr.

Like they were lounging in bed together, sheets knotted around their naked bodies, after a night of physical exertion of the best kind.

She had to get away from him, so that she could think.

She reached up slowly and took his gloved hand in hers, lifting his fingers away from her lips. Her move didn't work as well as would have been ideal, because Montgomery kept the connection. He turned his hand and caught her fingers in his, as if they were lovers. His hand closed around hers and his eyes darkened, giving him the intent look of a man on an erotic mission.

Was he?

Lilia felt herself blush, watched him smile, and knew she was sinking fast. He gave her hand a little tug and she fell against his chest, looking every inch the fainting heroine she wasn't. Before she could step away, he bent and brushed his lips across hers.

It was a light kiss, a teasing kiss, a kiss intended to leave her hungry for more.

Lilia wished it hadn't worked quite so well.

But Montgomery, she was sure, had played this particular game before.

Then again, so had she.

"Okay," she said, trying to sound indifferent, collected and unaffected by either his kiss or his proximity. "Let's pretend for the moment that you didn't send them. Just for the sake of argument. Why weren't you surprised when I mentioned it, then?"

His lashes swept low, dark, and thick and hiding the emerald of his eyes. He looked sleepy yet intent, and Lilia was fascinated when his voice dropped lower. "The line-item charge showed up on your file late last night."

She was so busy looking that it took her a moment to understand what he had said. Before she could reply, Montgomery leaned closer and kissed her again.

This time, it wasn't quick or teasing. He tasted her, savored her, left her gasping. Lilia closed her eyes when he lifted his lips from hers, swallowed, and fought to think straight.

Of course he'd seen the charge on her file. As a cop, he had access to the central databanks, where the government stored all its tasty titbits about all of its loyal citizens. Even the titbits about disloyal citizens like Lilia were there.

"I thought you had just been fined, Lil, not that you had been assaulted." He took her hand to his chest, so her fingertips were over his heart. Her hand was flat, pressed against his chest, trapped under his much larger hand.

He was pretending they were a courting couple, maybe to distract attention, but Lilia melted when she felt the pounding of his heart under her fingertips. It was beating as quickly as her own. She wondered how far he would take his amorous assault, and was ready to find out.

Not just because it would be cheaper than going to the pleasure fringe either.

Lilia tried to focus on the business at hand. "And why were you looking at my file last night?"

He leaned even closer and whispered. "To decide what the chances were that you were lying."

His breath brushed her cheek, stirred her hair, jangled her equilibrium. "How?"

Montgomery studied her, his gaze warm. "By examining your history, and whatever deeds of yours have been recorded. By looking for behavior patterns."

It made sense, and Lilia was already beginning to understand that Montgomery was a creature of logic. Well, she'd been married to one of those and had survived to tell about it.

"And? How'd I do?"

He averted his gaze, thoughtful. His thumb slid across the back of her hand, launching an army of shivers even with the faux leather barriers between them. "I think you believe what you told me about the shade. And I think that you were frightened." He paused and Lilia glanced upward, sensing there was more. "I also think that you're not telling all of the truth about the reason for your visit to New Gotham, Lil."

"Me?" Lilia feigned surprise, probably pretty well. Practice should have made perfect. "What makes you think such a thing?"

"Because I've read your file."

"What's there?"

His tone turned officious and he stepped away from her. Lilia immediately felt the absence of his body heat. "It is not the right of any citizen of the Republic to have full access to the data maintained by the Republic for its own protection upon that citizen or any other citizen . . ."

"If you had any idea how infuriating that is, you'd know better than to spout law code to me," Lilia growled. This time, she was the one matching her pace to his. "It's bad for your health, Montgomery."

"You're usually the one spouting law code to me."

"I'm getting over it."

He arched a brow, his expression wicked. "How do you intend to affect my health? Are you carrying your laze this morning?"

"What do you think? Did you leave yours at home?"

He looked Lilia up and down, and she had the sense he'd been waiting for an excuse to do that. "I can't see it."

"Surprise. What does the S&D Code say about women visibly packing heat?"

He shut up, but he smiled. That alone told Lilia that he wasn't going to confiscate her weapon. He kept walking beside her, as if giving her time to remember what he had said and to consider it.

What *could* be in Lilia's file?

She was afraid she knew.

Lilia tried another approach. "Okay, I'll tell you what's in the file, and you'll tell me whether I'm right. That way, you're not giving away any confidential information."

"I don't have to even agree to that."

Lilia took a long shot. "But you want something. That's got to be why you're here."

"It could be that I wanted to see you again."

She was surprised enough to laugh. "That's not it. You want to make a deal, off the record, so you left your watchful stud at the office. Daylight's wasting; let's negotiate already."

He gave her a simmering look. "Not everything is negotiable, Lil."

"What do you want from me?"

If Lilia had thought she'd get the obvious answer, she was doomed to disappointment.

Montgomery glanced away, then back at Lilia. He spoke in a lowered voice. "I want to know why you think Fitzgerald's death wasn't an accident. I want to know what you're going to do about it." His smile flashed wickedly as she stared at him in astonishment. "And I want to know whether you have tattoos, as well."

LILIA BLINKED and Montgomery knew he had surprised her. He had no illusions that she didn't understand him. He also had no illusions that she'd readily confide in him.

He was proven right on both counts when she turned abruptly away to lie. "I don't know what you're talking about."

"Bull," he said, using her choice word. "You know something and you've accepted this chance to give the award in Fitzgerald's name as an excuse to get close to where he died." Her lips set and she kept walking, as if she hadn't heard him. "What did you find on his palm, Lil?"

She glanced toward him. "You must already know. Didn't anyone read it?"

"There was only one piece of data on it, the name and address of a firm called Breisach and Turner. That doesn't make sense. Even the identification sector had been erased."

"I know."

"How? What reader did you use?"

She smiled slightly, and Montgomery knew she would say something unexpected. She held up her left hand and the palm embedded in it. "I datashared, of course."

"Last night you said you wouldn't datashare with a corpse."

"Gid's corpse was no longer connected to his palm." She shrugged. "It was a nice clean palm in a box when I got it."

Of course.

"But there could have been viral software installed," Montgomery said, unable to hide his disapproval. "You could have been infected—"

"It was Gid's." She interrupted him with anger. "Do you really think he had anything that I hadn't already shared?"

Their gazes locked and held for a charged moment, and Montgomery wanted to ask about their marriage, their relationship, her feelings for Fitzgerald. Never mind what Fitzgerald had known, even if it had gotten him killed—he wanted to know how Lilia had felt about Fitzgerald.

But there was no possible justification for him to ask whether she'd been in love with her husband or not.

Rachel would have told him not to care. He had a hard time listening to her counsel about not becoming emotionally involved with humans. Something about their brave vulnerability, about their mortality, tugged at his heart.

Lilia tugged at that and a lot more.

She spun to walk away from him, her back straight. Montgomery claimed her elbow once more. She stiffened at his touch, a less-than-encouraging sign. "Answer one thing for me."

"I don't have to answer anything for you."

"Then answer a hypothetical question for me. Off the record."

She spared him a look. "Off the record? Is there such a thing in New Gotham?"

Montgomery touched his ear where the stud should have been. "It can be done."

"You could have other recorders on your person."

"I'm off duty." He held her gaze. "I swear it, Lil."

She considered him, indecision in her eyes. "You can ask whatever you want," she said finally. "I don't have to answer."

"Have you ever seen viral software that could erase a palm's identification sector?" He felt her hesitation, so carried on. "Because I haven't. The wiping of his palm's data surprised me. I didn't know it could be done."

She paused, then took a deep breath. "No. Never." When he waited, she said more. "I've never even *heard* that it's possible."

"Not even on the Frontier?"

Lilia shook her head with such finality that he believed her.

She was the kind of person who would know about all sorts of bootleg software. "Was there any other data buried or hidden on the palm?"

Lilia's eyes flashed at his implication.

Montgomery knew he was losing her. "Do you have interrogation software installed on your palm?"

"I'm not saying anything more without an attorney."

"Lil—" He pulled her to a halt. She didn't comply easily and several people looked askance at them. He pulled her closer, catching her shoulders in his hands as if they were lovers having an argument. Her lips parted, but there was still fire in her gaze. He dropped his voice to a whisper. "Do you or do you not have bootleg interrogation software installed on your palm?"

She started to pull from his grasp. "Let me go. I don't have to talk to you about this."

"Off the record."

She glared at him, her suspicion clear. "Even so."

Montgomery kept talking, hoping he could persuade her to confide something in him. "Because NGPD couldn't find anything beyond that address. Every sector was empty, according to the interrogation routine. Was there anything embedded in it, anything buried where official interrogation software might miss it?"

She studied him for a long minute. "Since when does anyone but me care about Gid's death?"

"I don't think his death was an accident."

Her gaze brightened. "Why?"

Montgomery shrugged, because he couldn't tell her all of the truth. "It never smelled like an accident to me."

"Isn't that persuasive," she muttered and made to turn away.

"There's something on your file," he said. "Tell me what you know and I'll tell you what I know."

She glanced back. "Maybe I don't know anything. Maybe you're lying."

"Maybe you'd like to know for sure."

Lilia shook her head. Then she held out her left hand, palm up. The display glinted through the window in her glove. "Go ahead: search me. We both know you don't need a warrant to conduct a random review of a citizen's palm."

"You're suggesting that we datashare in public?"

She smiled coyly. "Some people like it that way."

Her expression reminded Montgomery of Fitzgerald's tattoo and sent unwelcome heat through his blood. All the same, he admired her audacity. "We both know that I won't find anything if I do."

"Because I don't know, after all. Case closed."

"It's in your head, Lil, not in your palm." He was guessing, but her quick intake of breath told him that he was right. "It's too important a piece of information for you to store it where anyone could snatch it, with or without your consent."

He felt her shock, then she squared her shoulders. It wasn't common for people to use the equipment they'd been born with—most relied exclusively on the installed palm to remember everything—and he admired her resourcefulness and logic.

"I thought you already assessed my file and decided I was honest. There's no risk of me lying then, is there?"

"No. I assessed your file and decided that you weren't lying about the shade's murder. I also noted that you're inclined to be a little more opportunistic and self-motivated than most shade hunters. There's a strong pattern of behavior there." He paused, arched his brow, and pushed her. "Maybe it's about the comp. Is the price what we're really haggling about here?"

She was disgusted, just as he'd expected. "You're offering to pay me?"

"Not in creds."

"You're trying to blackmail me."

Montgomery held her gaze. "There's something on your file."

But she was unpersuaded. She shook a finger under his nose. "No. You're just trying to use my own fear against me. I know, because I've used this trick before and it's a pretty good one."

"Sure about that?"

She took a quick breath, and he saw her conclude that she had little to lose. She was far less of a rebel than she liked people to believe—he was already aware that what drove her was a deep sense of what was right, and a fearlessness in challenging the law or the Republic on moral grounds. It was both foolish and noble, and he found it intriguing.

And dangerous.

There were two possibilities: Lilia either knew the truth about Fitzgerald's death or knew enough of the truth that she would use all means, legal and illegal, at her disposal to learn the rest of it. Montgomery was pretty sure that she had a considerable inventory of those tools at her fingertips, so to speak.

One way or another, Lilia was going to dig out the truth about Fitzgerald's death and on the way, she might uncover the truth that was important to Rachel. Chances were good that Fitzgerald hadn't been a suicide. Chances were even better that Lilia would get herself into trouble in New Gotham.

Montgomery meant to do what he could to prevent that.

For the greater good of fulfilling his mission, of course.

AS MONTGOMERY watched, Lilia folded her arms across her chest and commenced a recounting of her vitals. "My file says that I am Lilia Desjardins, citizen, illegitimate daughter of Lillian Desjardins, father unknown; born 2064 in Minneapolis; widow of Gideon Fitzgerald. It says that I graduated from the Institute of Radiation Studies, summa cum laude, in 2090 and was admitted to the Society of Nuclear Darwinists in the same year. It probably says that I have achieved the Third Degree, that I worked for two years for the Society, and have since been employed by the circus on the Northern Frontier."

"So far, so good."

"My captures and kills are probably there too, as well as my address and other personal details." Lilia shook her head. "It probably even includes the last measured length of my hair."

"Forty-two inches," Montgomery agreed easily. "Although I thought it looked longer last night."

"I'm almost due for my annual."

"December 9. You should make an appointment soon."

Lilia glared at him and Montgomery stifled the urge to smile. He liked how she was unafraid to speak her mind.

Even though it must have proven costly to her in the past.

He sobered, knowing it could be more so in the future. The lie he had found on her file indicated that she had powerful enemies.

She caught her breath and averted her gaze, tapping her toe. "It probably also says that I was the consort of Maximilian Blackstone, then governor of the fifty-third state, currently a candidate for the office of president of the Republic."

"It does." Montgomery decided to ask. "Is it true?"

"Of course. You can see Max's election advertising everywhere."

"I meant about your being his consort."

"I was sixteen; he was almost forty. He had money and power, and I had a cute butt. It was kismet."

He had to ask. "Was it love?"

She sighed. "Love is for amateurs and innocents, Montgomery."

"Not you?"

She smiled tightly. "Mine is a learned response."

Montgomery wasn't fooled. People could only speak bitterly of idealistic love if, on some level, they remained idealistic.

"You and Maximilian. Anything for a price?"

Lilia laughed, although she sounded more angry than merry. "If I'd known then what I know now, the price would have been higher."

Montgomery felt his eyes narrow. "How much higher?"

"Are you negotiating for presidential candidates on the side?"

"Just curious."

"Well, save your curiosity, Montgomery. It's vulgar."

He didn't know what to say to that. He'd hit a nerve, but he didn't know what it was.

They walked in silence past an entrance to the nether-zones and the commuting conveyors that would be found on the upper level. An evangelist was expressing his conviction that Satan walked among them. Most of the commuters simply milled around the evangelist, ignoring him and his free download. A few, though, paused to make a furtive purchase of his download.

Montgomery cleared his throat. "No more guesses about your file?"

"You mean there's more?"

He nodded.

She snapped her fingers suddenly. "Maybe there's a hotlink to some of those news stories about the angel-shades I captured earlier this year. That was a big deal, for a day or so. And there would have to be a hotlink to the Society's denouncement of my find, not to mention the trouble I'm in with them."

Montgomery arched a brow, waiting.

She studied him for the barest moment. "You're not going to talk me into spilling my guts over a technicality. I don't believe that there's anything more on my record, unless it's something so trivial that even I've forgotten it."

"You're wrong." He spoke with surety. "It's too important to have forgotten, if it's true. Either way, I think you should know that it's there."

He saw the little frisson of fear in her gaze.

She knew what it was.

She knew it shouldn't be there.

Which meant that it *was* true.

Montgomery fought to hide his own shock. The child was dead, but it still cast a shadow.

Had Lilia's child been "harvested" right in the maternity ward? It was a horrifying notion, one that must have been devastating. He watched her with new respect. Not all women could have recovered from that emotional loss, much less have come up fighting.

On the other hand, how could she have become a Nuclear Darwinist? Didn't she have a problem being on the side of those who had declared her child a shade? But then, the fact that she worked for the circus and not for the Society implied that she didn't adhere to the Society's agenda.

Had Lilia fallen in love with Fitzgerald, and changed her mind as a result of that relationship? It made as much sense as anything, which wasn't quite enough.

She lifted her chin in challenge. "Then go ahead, Montgomery; tell me what my big secret is."

"We're either sharing information or we're not, Lil. Do we have a deal?"

She shook her head immediately and he wasn't really surprised that she turned him down.

Disappointed, but not surprised.

"No. I haven't had the opportunity to study your file and decide what the chances are that you're lying to me."

"You don't have that right."

"Actually, I don't need it. I've seen enough to know that there's no way that you'd violate your sworn duty to the Republic. Never in a million years. You're in for the pension plan if ever I saw anyone who was." She took a deep breath and glared at him. "You must have been ordered to forget your ear stud so some muckity-muck wouldn't be implicated further downstream. This is a lie or a setup or something equally unsavory that won't ultimately work to my advantage. So, we don't have a deal."

"Fair enough." Montgomery nodded crisply, then turned away. "You know where to find me when you change your mind."

He felt her watching him, and made an effort to remain visible for a long time. The farther away she thought he was, the better. Then she'd be less likely to be looking for him.

Montgomery had four hours before he had to report for duty and he intended to follow Lilia for every minute of it. He hoped Lilia found the inevitable trouble when he was around to help her.

He was already starting to think that was a long shot.

VII

IT WAS impossible.

Lilia's deepest darkest secret could not be on her file. She'd been promised. It had been years.

Montgomery was bluffing.

Lilia knew it had to be so, but she still had a cold lump of dread in her gut. She wouldn't give Montgomery the satisfaction of changing her plans, though. She wasn't that easily rattled.

It didn't help that Lilia was deeply suspicious of that last crumb of data that had been left on Gid's palm. She had to check it out, although she was well aware that someone could have predicted her response to a solitary data snippet. Her mother would have suggested that she had been set up. Lilia wasn't quite that paranoid.

Most of the time.

New Gotham was changing her perspective, but quick.

How exactly had it happened that there had only been one bit of data left on Gid's palm? Was Montgomery the one guiding Lilia's steps?

Or dragging red herrings across her path?

Lilia wished there was a way to know for sure. As near as she could figure it, solving the mystery of Gid's death was the best way to manage that. She licked her lips, tasted Montgomery's kiss, and shivered deep inside.

The man was distracting in either guise; she'd give him that.

BREISACH AND Turner's office proved to be in an old building that faced a paved parkette. The few trees around the park looked sad, their trunks surrounded by concrete, their branches valiantly stretching for the sky. Lilia recalled the trees pushing through the cracks in the pavement in old cities everywhere and had to admire the relentless optimism of nature.

The lobby of the building was bright, clean, and devoid of character. The suite numbers of the occupying businesses were posted beside the mailboxes, the list written in a careful hand.

Handwritten.

On *paper*.

Lilia gawked for a moment at ancient technology. She tried to touch the paper but it was covered by protective glass.

Paper. Huh.

Number 202 was the office for Breisach and Turner. There was a plastic sign by the elevator that said it was out of order. The sign was sufficiently old that the red letters had faded and it had a patina of dust. Lilia hadn't expected otherwise. With the price of juice, electrical conveniences were scarce and the building probably wasn't large enough to justify the expenditure for slave-shades to power the elevator.

She spent the climb reviewing her cover story. Given that she didn't know what had made Gid a murder victim—if indeed she was right that he had been one—Lilia wasn't in a hurry to confess that she was his widow. The people at the only address in his palm might know more than they'd like anyone to realize.

Lilia was counting on that.

She had to think that if they had been involved, they'd be expecting Lilia Desjardins. She hoped that she looked insufficiently like her official image that she wouldn't immediately be recognized.

It was a risk.

But a little fib might smooth the way. Lilia had created a file before leaving the Frontier, where she had better access to people with a cavalier attitude toward the forgery of official documentation, and it looked enough like the genuine article to survive a cursory glance.

A very cursory glance. A thousand creds didn't buy work of the same quality it once had.

She tapped it up onto her palm as she reached the second floor. The door to number 202 was open and a woman as neat, clean, and characterless as the lobby sat at a desk facing the door. She glanced up when Lilia made a show of checking the name lettered on the frosted glass of the outer office door against her palm.

She was Lydia Kushekov, a bureaucrat, she reminded herself. *A minion and a paid grunt, doing a job nobody else wanted to do.*

That part, at least, wasn't much of a stretch.

The woman behind the desk watched her. "May I help you?"

"Yes, I'm sure you can." Lilia replied pertly, wondering whose spirit she was channeling. "I've been sent to collect the effects of Gideon Fitzgerald, deceased." She displayed the edict on her palm, letting the receptionist read the "official" order demanding that she surrender all such goods to Lilia.

Lydia.

The receptionist repeated Gid's name, a little frown appearing between her brows. "That name doesn't sound familiar."

"But he worked here." Lilia oozed confidence as she launched into her fabricated story. "He died a few months back—August, um, second—and I've been sent by the lawyers to collect his things. All standard and customary stuff. He must have had something in his desk." She sighed and shrugged. "Even if it was an old comb, I'm supposed to bring it back. You know how lawyers are. I'll give you a receipt."

"But no one named Gideon Fitzgerald ever worked here."

Lilia frowned at her palm. "But that can't be right. Isn't this Breisach and Turner, Shippers and Expeditors?"

"It is."

"Is there another branch office?"

The receptionist's smile was less friendly as she rose to her feet. "No."

Lilia recognized that she'd worn out her welcome.

Already.

How interesting.

"Could I speak to the other employees?"

"I'm the only one, other than Mr. Breisach and Mr. Turner. Our drivers are independent contractors."

One of these three people had to be the reason Gid had had this address on his palm. One of them had to know something.

Maybe not this one.

Maybe the address had been intended to keep her from making a more obvious conclusion.

Then why was the receptionist so hostile?

While Lilia considered what to do next, she glanced around the office. There were two doors behind the receptionist's desk and, although they were closed, Lilia reasoned that they led to individual offices. One would be in the corner of the building, the other directly to its right. One for each partner. Lilia wondered who had scored the corner office.

Probably Breisach, as his name was first.

"But this is the address I was given." Lilia tapped busily at her palm and frowned, as if checking supporting documents. "I don't understand how it could be wrong."

"Well, it must be." The receptionist's tone turned glacial.

Maybe Gid had used another name. It hadn't been like him to be deceptive, but Lilia had to wonder whether he'd learned more from her than she'd imagined. Gid had been as honest as the day was long—Lilia had delighted in teasing him that that would get him into trouble one day.

There was no pleasure in thinking that she might have called it right.

Lilia pulled up an image of Gid and displayed it

abruptly to the receptionist, hoping to surprise her. "Do you recognize him?"

She shook her head. "I've never seen him before in my life."

Had she responded too quickly for her answer to be true?

When the receptionist came around her desk to encourage Lilia's departure, Lilia knew that she had lied.

Why else would she be anxious to be rid of Lilia?

"Maybe you just haven't worked here long enough to remember him," Lilia said lightly.

"I've been in this office for nine years. Is that long enough?"

"Could I speak to Mr. Breisach or Mr. Turner? Maybe they just hired him on a contract basis, like the drivers . . ."

"Neither of them are in." She took Lilia's elbow and her grip was firm.

"Then I'll come back later."

The receptionist was stronger than she looked. She practically hefted Lilia toward the door. "You needn't bother. They won't be available then either."

"They're both on business trips?"

"They're both unavailable for the foreseeable future." She definitely wanted to be rid of her guest, and Lilia was perverse enough to want to linger on that basis alone. "This address was clearly given to you in error, miss."

"But I've been working for these lawyers for years and they never—"

"Everyone makes mistakes," the receptionist said with heat.

"Can I get your name? Just to prove that I was here?"

"No." She escorted Lilia through the door with a firm hand. "Good luck finding information about your Mr. Fitzgerald, miss."

She'd remembered his name. Did she have a good memory, or had she heard it before?

Lilia glanced down at the receptionist's left hand, currently locked around Lilia's elbow, surprised by the strength of her grip.

That was when Lilia saw it: the end of a tattooed number, just peeking out from the cuff on her inner left wrist. It looked like the right side of a 3, or maybe an 8. The receptionist didn't realize that Lilia had seen it and Lilia didn't let on, but that sight certainly stole a lot of Lilia's resistance.

The receptionist was a shade.

She was a shade, working in an office, like a norm.

She was a known shade, a shade who had been captured and tattooed by the Republic.

Lilia couldn't make sense of it. Shades didn't have real jobs, not even crummy ones. Shades were supposed to labor unseen; the law code of the Republic made that clear. It was possible that a shade could evade detection and work as a norm, but the tattoo revealed that the receptionist was known to the Republic.

She had to be a fugitive. Who did Messrs. Breisach and Turner know that they could so blatantly break the law?

Lilia had no doubt that this shade knew more than she had admitted, and even less doubt that she would share any of it. Had it been the image of Gid that had turned her against Lilia, or had it been Lilia's own sparkling charm? Had the receptionist recognized her? If Lilia's reputation had preceded her, she had to think that it would have been counted in her favor by a shade.

Lilia was out in the corridor by the time she reasoned that far. The receptionist gave Lilia a firm shove to send her on her way and wished her a good day—with, it must be said, a certain insincerity. Before Lilia could reply, the receptionist shut the door firmly behind her.

Lilia grabbed the knob just as she heard the lock turn. She raised a hand, but the receptionist pulled down a blind over the window.

She knocked three times, but the receptionist was obviously ignoring her. Lilia walked down the stairs, wondering whether there even was a Mr. Breisach or a

Mr. Turner. Given that she didn't have access to the Republic database—as a certain cop did, a cop who had suggested they share information, a cop whom she didn't want to think about—there was only one way to find out.

She'd spy on them.

MONTGOMERY EXPECTED Rachel to make short work of her unexpected visitor. Lilia might be able to concoct a story and persuade many people to believe it, but Rachel wasn't easily seduced.

He stepped deeper into the shadows of a doorway, unable to suppress a twinge of satisfaction when Lilia emerged from the office building very soon after she entered it. He caught a glimpse of her frustrated expression before she pulled her veil over her face, and that made him smile.

Montgomery watched Lilia look up and down the street, and made a silent bet with himself that she wouldn't let the matter go that easily. She pivoted and set off in the direction from which she had come and he had to move quickly to keep track of her.

She might have looked as if she was walking back to the hotel, but three blocks later, she disappeared down a side street and Montgomery knew he had called it right.

Within five minutes, he was sure that she was circling back to the office building. It was reasonably easy to do, given that New Gotham's streets were laid out in a grid pattern. It might have been simple for Montgomery to pursue her, if Lilia hadn't seemed to have the sense that she was being followed.

Maybe she just worked with the assumption that the Republic was a hostile, backstabbing, double-crossing kind of place.

It wasn't a bad assumption, to Montgomery's thinking. Lilia had definitely picked up her pace. He caught a glimpse of her trim figure weaving between the rickshaws that seemed to fill this side street and broke into a trot himself.

The distance between them was growing too large.

He turned a corner, thought he'd lost her, then was sure he spied the broad brim of her hat turning the corner a block down.

He bolted after her, only to find the cross street empty. Montgomery moved slowly down its length, glancing into a shop to find her there at the counter.

Apparently she needed new gloves.

He fell back into a doorway and tried to be invisible just as she emerged. She looked up and down the street, as if she'd anticipated that he, or someone, might be there. Montgomery held his breath until she marched away from him, her skirts flicking with purpose.

Then he strolled behind her, ducking behind every obstacle he could but keeping her in sight.

Any man who had ever thought that making women dress in corsets and full skirts would make them less alluring had obviously never watched Lilia Desjardins move. The woman might have been dancing, and if she had been, it would have been in time with a provocative tune. Montgomery was fascinated by the neat indent of her waist, the sway of her hips, the fleeting glimpses beneath her hems of those snugly booted feet.

Yet her steps weren't mincing and feminine. She covered ground quickly and he had to stride to keep up with her.

And stay out of sight at the same time. She chose an utterly deserted street, probably just to thwart him, and a gap opened between them. When she turned down the cross street, Montgomery ran in pursuit. He found her moving even faster, already near the end of the block. He began to trot. He heard the bustle of a busy cross street just before Lilia dashed into it.

Montgomery sprinted into the thoroughfare, narrowly missing a collision with a cyclist, but he was too late. Lilia had disappeared into the jumble of rickshaws, shoppers, cyclists, and commuters. He spun in place, peering into the crowd. He was tall. She was tall. He should have been able to see her, moving decisively through the crowd.

But he couldn't.

He suddenly spied her broad-brimmed hat on the other side of the street and ran toward it. It didn't move, which brought him to a skidding halt with the fear that she'd see him.

But she'd dropped it on a tethering post. The hooded shades harnessed to a carriage and tethered there glanced up at him with dull eyes. The ribbons on her hat flicked in the breeze, as if to taunt him with his failure.

She knew he was following her.

Or at least that someone was.

Montgomery claimed her hat and considered his location. If Lilia had been circling back to Breisach and Turner, she was two thirds of the way there. Down two blocks and over one should bring him into the alley that ran behind the building.

Swinging the lady's hat, he strode in that direction.

MONTGOMERY KNEW he shouldn't have been as glad to see Lilia as he was.

He certainly shouldn't have been surprised to find her climbing a fire escape. He could hear her muttered curses as she pulled herself up on the bottom rung. He guessed that she'd tried a few times, although this time, she succeeded in pulling herself up.

The metal fire escape was attached to a building on the opposite side of the alley from the office, the stairs located around the corner and thus out of Rachel's view. It would give a good vantage of Breisach and Turner's office, although it was unconventional for a woman to climb a fire escape in her skirts.

But then, there wasn't much conventional about Lilia.

She'd knotted her veil over her hair after abandoning her hat, and the braid was slipping loose. Montgomery decided that he preferred when she looked a little disheveled.

How did she look when she slept?

When she woke up?

Montgomery stopped the direction of his thoughts. Unobserved by the busy lady in question, he leaned on the metal grating below, appreciating the view of her legs. A gentleman would have declared his presence, but Lilia fed his inclination to be ungentlemanly.

She climbed onward, oblivious to his presence.

She had exquisite thighs. He closed his eyes and knew he had to declare himself immediately.

"Missing something?" Montgomery asked in a conspiratorial whisper. Lilia's boot slipped from the next metal step in her surprise, and she caught the handrails more tightly.

"You!" She glared down at him.

"Me," he agreed.

"Why are you following me?"

He saluted her with her own hat. "If you're not worried about S&D taking you down again, maybe I am."

"Maybe you've called them," she said bitterly.

Montgomery shook a finger at her. "No. I told you the truth."

She studied him for a long moment, then tossed her braid over her shoulder. "Well, it doesn't matter now. Just leave my hat there and go away."

"I don't think so." Montgomery swung onto the lowest rung of the fire escape and pulled himself up easily. He climbed the stairs until he was immediately below her and offered her hat with a flourish.

"I thought I'd declined your offer to work together," she said.

"I thought you wouldn't be so good at getting yourself into trouble in my absence."

"I'm not in trouble . . ."

"Not yet. It's only the middle of the day, but you're already in public with your hair uncovered. I give you an hour." She touched her veil but he shook his head. "That doesn't meet code and you know it."

Lilia took her hat from him with poor temper. She removed the veil, her hair gleaming blue black in the sun, and pulled the hat onto her head. She leaned her hip against the stairs as she secured the hat with pins and knotted her veil under her chin. She looked as happy as a wet cat. "Better?"

"You've marked your dress with the rust." He fingered her skirts, purportedly to show her the damage, then lifted the hem slightly. "And did you tear your skirt climbing up here?"

"You're too perceptive by half," she said. She smiled impishly as she stuck out her booted foot, which had something soft and brown on the heel. "And you know what that is."

"Nice touch." Montgomery winced at the smell.

"Mine is a savoir faire that is seldom duplicated," she said with a cavalier sweep of her hand.

He heard laughter in her tone and glanced up to find her eyes sparkling in a most interesting way. He was only a step below her and their faces were level. She watched him as her smile faded, her eyes widening slightly as he leaned closer.

He could smell her skin, and a faint echo of an unfamiliar perfume. He could see the curve of her lips, the way they parted as she watched him. He remembered how her shoulders had felt under his hands, how she'd seemed both fragile and formidable. He was certain that he hadn't kissed her nearly well enough yet.

He should kiss her again.

Now.

Lilia caught her breath, her breasts rising and her eyes darkening. Their thoughts were clearly on the same track. Montgomery leaned closer and knew he didn't imagine that Lilia eased toward him. He lifted one hand to her veil, pulling it upward, and she only watched him.

The closest window opened abruptly alongside them, and a burly man leaned out. He glared at the pair of them, even when they straightened away from each other.

"It's illegal to use emergency exits when there is no emergency," he said, his tone belligerent.

"I apologize for troubling you, sir." Montgomery punched his badge up on his palm and flashed it. Quickly. "New Gotham Police. We're under cover, sir, a very delicate matter, and would appreciate your cooperation."

The man looked between them with suspicion. "Undercover?"

"Yes, sir."

"Narcotics?"

"Shades, sir," Lilia said in a deep voice. "Fugitives."

Her words made Montgomery's heart leap in fear. What had she noticed at Breisach and Turner? Or was that her favored excuse when caught in a transgression?

"Fugitives!" The man spat in disgust. "You should catch the bastards, put them to work."

"That's the idea, sir," Montgomery confirmed.

The man's gaze lingered on Lilia, his suspicion clear. "I didn't think there were any women police officers."

Lilia had obviously anticipated this objection, as she'd feigned a deep voice right away. He appreciated her quick thinking. "Undercover work, sir," Montgomery said.

Lilia fingered her chin. "You don't want to know how long it took me to shave this smooth."

The man chuckled, then nodded once.

Montgomery held up a finger. "If the Republic could rely upon your silence, sir, the world would be a better place for all of us." He wasn't sure that was true, but it sounded persuasive.

"Of course," the man said with a curt nod. "I hate shades, especially when they think they're as good as the rest of us." He had gotten taller in being called to do his civic duty.

"Thank you, sir."

"No problem, Officer. The Republic relies on all of us to do our part." The man shut the window and pulled the blinds on the inside, giving them a covert thumbs-up before he disappeared.

Montgomery glanced up to find Lilia watching him. "Careful, Montgomery," she said, her tone mischievous. "You keep doing stuff like that and I might start to like you."

Montgomery felt a dull flush rise on the back of his neck. He blurted out his foremost thought. "Why do you think Fitzgerald's death wasn't an accident?"

She inhaled and glanced away, her lips tightening. He didn't think she would answer him, but her words fell in a sudden torrent. "Gid was a statistician, a mathematician. He thought in terms of probabilities."

Montgomery remembered the first hundred digits of pi coiling around Fitzgerald's chest and understood another tattoo. "The probability of dying of radiation poisoning when you open your visor in a hot zone is pretty high."

Lilia nodded. "Gid used to joke that radiation was natural selection for Nuclear Darwinists."

"I'd think it was an occupational hazard."

"No. We prepare for it." She shook her head. "Gid said that only stupid Nuclear Darwinists die of radiation poisoning. We have the gear. We have the training. We witness the effects." She sighed. "And once you've seen someone die of radiation poisoning, you wouldn't wish it on your worst enemy."

"But he opened his visor."

"No." She shook her head vehemently. "No. Gid was the one who could calculate maximum exposure time in his head, given radiation levels, even to the point of taking protective gear and monthly exposure into account. The man was a human calculator. If he was conscious, he would never *ever* have opened his helm in a hot zone. And if he was unconscious, he couldn't have done it."

"Which means?"

Lilia's lips set. "Which means that someone did it for him."

Montgomery looked away from her. "There's another possibility, Lil," he said quietly. "He could have done it on purpose."

Suicide.

The unspoken word hung between them. The way she caught her breath told Montgomery that Lilia had thought of that before. He looked up and saw her dismay, saw the tears she blinked away.

"Never," she said fiercely. "Gid would never do that."

But it was exactly what she was afraid of.

"He denounced you," Montgomery reminded her. "You could have been the one who opened his visor."

"He didn't denounce me, not directly." She frowned. "Just my angel-shades. Besides I would have had to have been in New Gotham to do it, if I could have done it. I'm sure the databanks show that I haven't left the Frontier in years."

"If there's a way to fool the databanks, you'd know it."

She met his gaze. "I didn't kill Gid, Montgomery. I fought with him, but I didn't kill him. I didn't even know where he was."

He leaned against the railing beside her. "It seemed as if you didn't think it was him when his body was found."

"I didn't." She gestured helplessly. "We fought. I threw him out." She swallowed and glanced at him, her eyes a vivid blue. "I don't do well with distrust and unfair accusations."

Montgomery could believe that.

"My angel-shades aren't frauds. They're not surgical adaptations. I found them just as they are." Her lips tightened. "Gid should have believed me."

"I do."

Lilia eyed him for a long moment, then turned away. "Leave me alone, Montgomery."

He felt a pang of sympathy for her. She was afraid that she had driven Fitzgerald to suicide, and her need to know the truth was what had compelled her to finally leave the Frontier.

Montgomery hoped that she proved her fear wrong.

He wanted to help her do it.

He touched her chin, forcing her to look at him. He saw dread and defiance mingled in her gaze, as well as an unexpected vulnerability. His first assessment had been right: Lilia wasn't as cold as she wanted everyone to believe. "Even if Fitzgerald did kill himself, Lil, it's not your fault."

Lilia stared at him, then pointed across the alley. "Look!"

Rachel had pulled the blind aside to look out the office window.

"She's waiting for someone," Lilia said lightly, as if she hadn't looked so vulnerable just a moment before. Montgomery wasn't fooled. "Someone who's late."

The suicide subject was closed.

"How do you know?" Montgomery moved closer behind Lilia. He put a hand on her waist and felt her trembling.

She lifted her chin. "I don't, but if there isn't a story, I can make one up." Again, he caught a glimpse of Lilia's impish grin, the one that made his blood pressure rise.

Meanwhile, Rachel glanced over her shoulder.

"Then that person has arrived," Montgomery said, wondering who it might be. He moved his thumb across the small of Lilia's back, across the laces and boning of her corset.

He felt her straighten, heard her take a breath. He was glad to know that he wasn't the only one affected by proximity.

"And she knows that person," Lilia said. "I sure didn't get a smile of welcome like that."

Rachel closed the blind. A bit of light showed around its perimeter for a minute, then was extinguished.

They stood and watched for a moment, then Lilia swore with sudden force. Montgomery thought for a moment that he'd let his caress become too overt, but Lilia tried to push past him.

"Move!" she commanded.

"What's the matter?"

She planted one hand in the middle of his chest, trying to shove him out of the way. "They've left. She left with whoever came. That's why the lights are out."

"You don't know that . . ."

"No, but I can guess." Her eyes flashed with anger.
"And you distracted me. On purpose. Don't try to tell
me otherwise, Montgomery. You might be good, but
you're not that good." Before he could defend himself or
his amorous talents, Lilia squeezed past him. She nearly
crowded him over the railing with the volume of her
skirts.

"Look at the time, it's after four," she raged. "I've got
to get around to the front of the building to see where
they're going."

"After four?" Montgomery echoed.

His palm chimed right on cue. Lilia scrambled down the
fire escape, almost slipping in her haste. Montgomery
swore, then hurried after her. He would have lifted her
down, but she jumped before he got to the bottom. Evidently, she trusted him to follow her or didn't care whether
he did, because she began to run down the alley without
glancing back.

Montgomery stopped in the alley and took the incom-
ing call from his supervisor, doubting it could be anything good. He decided against opening a vid link.

"Monitoring says your earlobe feed is dead," Tupperman said and Montgomery knew he'd made the right
choice. "What's wrong?"

"I don't know. It seems fine from this end." Montgomery paused, as if fiddling with the ear stud. "How's
this?"

"No different." Tupperman exhaled in exasperation.
"They always say the new models are better and they're
always wrong. Book a review with Tech Support as soon
as you report today, Montgomery."

"Yes, sir. Reporting in twenty." Montgomery closed
the connection and looked around himself. There was no
sign of a tall shapely woman running in creamy skirts and
a broad-brimmed hat.

Lilia was gone.

And worse, he had no idea where.

* * *

THE MAN was too perceptive by half. Lilia ran as fast as she could, down the alley and around the corner. Was she running after the receptionist or running away from Montgomery's steady gaze? He seemed to be able to read her thoughts. In a way it was spooky; in another, it was a relief to put pretense aside.

Especially as he didn't seem to hold her choices against her.

Lilia had quickly become aware that Montgomery wasn't right behind her. Maybe one of his glow girls was calling him. Maybe he knew something she didn't. Maybe he was leaving her to her own resources. Maybe she was going to have to keep dropping items of clothing to keep him around.

It was a surprisingly appealing notion.

On the other hand, he'd made that move with his hand, keeping her from thinking straight right when thinking straight would have been the best option. Had he distracted her on purpose, to give whoever was at Breisach and Turner time to get away?

Lilia didn't know and she didn't like that one bit.

Montgomery messed with her game. It was better to be without him. After all, he'd casually voiced the fear that had haunted her since she'd had news of Gid's death. Had Gid committed suicide? Had it been her fault?

She'd owed Gid better than that. Lilia frowned, pushing the echoes of that last fight from her thoughts.

But if Gid had committed suicide, then who had killed Y654892?

Lilia peered around the edge of the building where Breisach and Turner kept their offices, but there was no sign of Miss Obstructionist. Lilia waited, trying to stifle a dawning sense that she'd been outsmarted. Maybe the receptionist had seen the pair of them when she'd looked out the window.

Maybe she'd exited the building through the netherzones. Lilia snarled at herself for missing the obvious: the receptionist was, after all, a shade, thus a member of that population for whom the underground network had originally been constructed.

Lilia ducked into the closest access, but the primary level was too crowded to find anyone. She supposed the commuter traffic had begun already as the conveyors were packed. There was no point in descending to the lower level; it was illegal for norms to go there, but more importantly, it was only expedient to use the lower zones when Lilia knew her destination. She had no idea where the receptionist might go.

Lilia reluctantly gave up the chase.

She walked slowly, letting the crowd push her where it would. *Nice lead, Gid,* she thought, trying not to become despondent over her failure so far to discover anything. *Where do I go from here?*

Gid, not surprisingly, had little to say for himself.

It wasn't the first time that her brilliant husband had left Lilia in his intellectual dust. Could he have killed himself over the fact that she'd tossed him out? Their relationship had always been unbalanced in terms of affection given and received.

She couldn't think about that. It made her feel too guilty. She had to prove her gut response right instead. Gid had been killed.

But by who?

Lilia did what she usually did when she needed to think. Later she would wonder whether Gid had been guiding her footsteps. Maybe somewhere in the cloudy nirvana—or in the gritty hellfire that Lilia always thought sounded like more fun—he'd been listening in.

Or maybe he had just known her well.

In that moment, though, filled with frustration from botching her only leads, a visit to the local parallel of where she spent most of her waking hours was the closest thing to psychological comfort food.

Lilia went to the circus.

Press Release
From *THE SOCIETY OF NUCLEAR DARWINISTS*
JULY 15, 2099

"Sunshine Heals" Heads to the Frontier

CHICAGO—Ernestine Sinclair, President of the Society of Nuclear Darwinists, announced today that the Society's successful and popular prevention program is expanding to new horizons. "There's a need that we can help to service," Ms. Sinclair said. "We're happy to work hand-in-glove with the Republic on this initiative, and to expand our program into new territory. Children throughout the Republic deserve protection from thyroid cancer and the Society is committed to ensuring a healthy future for all citizens." She noted also that expanding the program was a fitting way to celebrate the Society's seventy-fifth anniversary.

The link between radiation exposure and the development of thyroid cancer in children has been observed since the bombings of Hiroshima and Nagasaki. In the wake of Chernobyl, children were given doses of potassium iodide to prevent their thyroid glands from absorbing radioactive iodine from their environment.

It was Ernest Sinclair, founder of the Society of Nuclear Darwinists, who first tested the link between the ingestion of vitamin C as a preventative measure against cancers triggered by radiation exposure. The "Sunshine Heals" program was launched by Ernest Sinclair in 2040, whose own son suffered from thyroid cancer. In a tragic note, Ernie Sinclair, Jr., succumbed to his cancer shortly after the program was initially planned, and the inaugural "Sunshine Heals," which delivered oranges throughout the eastern seaboard, was dedicated to his memory. The cartoon mascot of Orville the Orange—affectionately known as Orv to children throughout the Republic—was based upon a drawing made by Ernie Junior when told of his father's plans.

"Sunshine Heals" has grown to a massive program,

consuming 54 percent of the Republic's orange produc-
tion and requiring fifty canola-fueled transport trucks. It is
entirely staffed by volunteers and funded fully by the Society for Nuclear Darwinists. <imagelinks>

Ernestine Sinclair has dedicated this year's program,
the fifty-fifth annual "Sunshine Heals," to the memory of
her father and to the older brother she never knew.

VIII

LILIA FOUND the local circus easily on the perimeter of town, on the old city side, of course, the muck of the Hudson alongside. She stepped beneath its welcoming arch—a concoction of scrounged wire and light bulbs that looked tawdry in the daylight, but would be magical at night—and took a deep breath.

Lilia preferred the circus before it opened to the public. The performers were awakening from their night revels and there was a sense of being privy to something that shouldn't be seen.

She liked being in on the secrets, big or small. In daylight, the circus didn't look the same—the lights were off, the faces were devoid of makeup, the sparkling costumes were folded away. What lurked behind the illusion was surprisingly mundane.

This circus was a bit smaller than Joachim's and Lilia thought of his characteristic comment that everything was bigger on the Frontier—an assertion invariably accompanied by a lewd wink. Lilia's boss was all of four feet tall, a lifetime circus performer who had lucked into ownership.

Or had worked himself senseless into it. Lilia still wasn't sure.

The New Gotham circus had three tents of good size, the biggest one striped red and white. The red was faded, so the tent—and presumably the circus itself—had been in business for a while. The same rows of banners hung between the tents as did at the Frontier circus, those brightly colored squares embellished with the watchful eyes of the Republic. Lilia could smell coffee and frying bacon and knew they were both the real thing.

Lilia wandered between the tents as if she belonged. People were chatting and working, mucking out the animals. It was like a family farm, one with elephants and llamas and tigers.

It was also a family farm in which almost all occupants were shades. A shade in faded sweats was teaching a younger shade to walk the high wire. Both had a sixth toe on each foot. The sixth toe—like a fifth finger or second thumb—was a pretty common mutation, so all circuses were well provided with trapeze and high-wire artists. The young shade kept glancing over her shoulder, even when the older one chastised her for not paying attention.

Lilia could name her tune: she was recently arrived.

It took time for any shade to learn that the hunt was over, and even more time to believe that the circus wasn't too good to be true. Most tended to suspect a trick; some clung to that fear longer than others.

At the circus, in contrast to the Republic's slave dens, shades were encouraged to choose names. The policy started for a practical reason: it was much easier to remember to call "Danny" than "Q871692." Also, giving names to shades made it less clear to authoritative eyes that they *were* shades, and not humans, either surgically altered or masquerading as shades.

The legal stuff wasn't Lilia's speciality. She simply knew that telling a shade that he or she would be able to choose a name was always the moment that the deal was made.

Sometimes shades already had names, if they weren't hiding out alone. Sometimes they knew what they wanted to be called; sometimes the other circus shades helped them make a choice; sometimes they took the name of a norm they've met. There were fourteen shades named Lilia at the circus on the Frontier and six named Joachim—one of which was a baby girl.

To have a name was a potent thing. Lilia often thought that shades would work at the circus for that right alone.

The humanity of shades was inescapable in the field,

before they had become dulled by poor nutrition, drudgery, drugs, and lack of sleep. It was easier to believe the rhetoric about protecting shades and offering relief to parents of shades, once the shades themselves were disheartened and sedated and looking pathetic.

Looking, in fact, like Sub Human Atomic Deviants. Lilia suspected that norms could only persist in believing that shades weren't really human because they'd never talked to one.

Maybe that was the plan.

The few other Nuclear Darwinists who did work in the field, the hotshots who "harvested" on behalf of the Society, were like Rhys ibn Ali, Lilia's personal choice of poster child for inhumanity, self-motivation, and unethical behavior.

What did Montgomery think of shades? The comments he'd made so far had been disappointing in that regard.

But then, she'd been disappointed when they'd been interrupted on the fire escape, as well. Lilia had been sure that Montgomery was going to really kiss her, to really go for a tongue tangler, and she'd been ready to participate. That would have been the rebel wild-boy Montgomery, in his high boots, faux leather, and velvet, the unpredictable twin Montgomery with the unruly glint in his eyes.

She wondered which version of him she'd see next.

His evil twin had her vote, no doubt about it.

"Can I help you?"

Lilia jumped. An older woman, twice as tall and half was wide as Joachim, watched her with the same suspicion Joachim would have shown to a stranger who arrived unannounced.

Lilia felt right at home.

The woman's voice was raspy, indicative of a habitual indulgence of one kind or another, and her face was lined with experience. Her eyeliner was too dark for her bottle-blond hair, and had been applied with less than a steady hand.

Same for the hair color.

"We're not open until six and we don't give tours." Her body language screamed "get out" and she was probably packing a weapon.

Although, so was Lilia.

Lilia wondered how fast this woman was.

A small shade hovered so close that she might have been the woman's shadow. The girl's eyelids were graced with the same turquoise as the older woman, also unevenly applied. She watched Lilia with open curiosity.

A girl shade, of perhaps nine years of age. Lilia's knees weakened right on cue. Shades of this age and this gender struck her as particularly vulnerable. This one had a third eye like Y654892, which might also have been responsible for the way Lilia's heart lunged for her throat.

Lilia offered her hand. "Lilia Desjardins, shade hunter. I work at a circus on the Frontier and hope you don't mind my visiting yours in off-hours. I felt the need for a little familiarity."

"Not *the* Lilia Desjardins?" The woman arched an artificially darkened brow. "The shade hunter who found those angels?"

"Angel-shades." Lilia smiled. "Right. That's me."

"Well! I'm Stevia Fergusson," the woman said, taking Lilia's hand and pumping it with enthusiasm. "I can't begin to say what a pleasure it is to meet you."

"Angels!" the little shade interjected. The cadence of her speech revealed that she was a little slow. "I see angels!"

"No, Micheline. You've seen no real angels. The ones on vid don't count." Stevia was patient with the girl, which Lilia liked a lot. "I've told you this before."

"Angels," Micheline whispered, her confidence unshaken.

Stevia looked Lilia up and down. "And here you are, just

wandering into *my* circus on a whim. Don't you have a staff now? A bunch of publicists trailing behind you, or aspiring shade hunters wanting to learn your tricks?" She snapped her fingers. "Hey, you must be a big guest speaker at the Society's convention in town."

Lilia laughed. She'd been within a whisper of being ejected from the Society for years and was looking forward to quitting in a blaze of infamy. "No, I'm not speaking."

Stevia seemed perplexed. "But you're the only one who managed to find an actual pair of angels . . ."

"Technically, they're shades with wings. It's a mutation."

Stevia ignored the correction. "They must be singing your praises at the Society, for being the one to finally find something profitable for the rest of us."

"Well, not everyone is that impressed."

"They just want a piece of it." Stevia leaned closer. "Because you're going to make Joachim a rich man."

Lilia smiled. Circus attendance had increased tenfold since she'd brought Armaros and Baraqiel onto the payroll. "I think you've got that right."

"Angels." Micheline hugged herself with delight.

Stevia lowered her voice. "So, tell me, just among friends in the business—who did the surgery and augmentation?"

"There was no surgery, none at all." Lilia said. "And it hadn't been done before either."

"Come on! Those wings?"

"The wings grow right out of their shoulders and are as tall as they are." Lilia shrugged and smiled. "It's the most remarkable mutation I've ever seen."

"Angels, then. Huh."

"Shades with wings," Lilia corrected, knowing it was futile.

Stevia looked around, then focused on Lilia again, her voice dropping to a whisper. "I've seen the images, and they're incredible. And their smiles are mesmerizing. Do they talk?"

"No."

"Remarkable."

There was something else remarkable about the pair, but it seemed rude to express it, especially in Micheline's company. Shades, very commonly, were retarded or at least mentally slow. They were like children, very sweet and simple. This had been used as justification for doing research on shades—of the "they'll never know the difference" variety of logic—but to Lilia, their innocence made their use as research subjects even more horrific.

It was a breach of trust.

The thing about these angel-shades was that their eyes shone with intelligence, more intelligence than was typical in a norm. They seemed to have no need to communicate verbally with each other. They watched everyone, their eyes bright, and Lilia swore they knew exactly what each person was thinking. Even Joachim, who was rarely spooked by anything, had confided in Lilia that he found it unsettling to be alone with them.

The public, though, couldn't see them often enough.

Lilia had assumed initially that their lightning intellect was a hint that they *had* been surgically altered. There was no one more cynical than Lilia Desjardins, after all.

But if they had been altered, the surgeon had been a hotshot, because they had no scars. The tests had even revealed that their skeletal structure was different, that their rib cages showed more commonalities with those of birds than those of humans.

It was a bit creepy to be in the presence of such a remarkable mutation, especially when the shades in question seemed bemused by such concern. Plus Lilia had never been able to shake the persistent sense that Armaros and Baraqiel had stalked her, that they had just let her believe that she'd captured them when in fact they'd chosen to surrender to her.

She wasn't, however, so troubled by this that she'd declined Joachim's bonus pay or the credit for the capture.

"It's a miracle," Stevia insisted. "I'd bill it as God sending his angels to us, to warn us."

Lilia had heard this logic before. "Of what?"

"Oh, I don't know." Stevia waved off the question. "I'd think of something that played well. The end of the world. God's wrath unleashed. Something that would look good in lights."

"And sell tickets."

Stevia smiled. "Of course!"

"I could show you my angels," Micheline confided shyly.

Stevia stroked Micheline's hair. "Ms. Desjardins is very busy." She turned to Lilia. "They seem large in the images."

"Taller than me."

"My angels too," Micheline added. "They're big, really big!"

"Micheline, that's enough!"

The young shade stepped away, her shoulders drooping with disappointment. "But I see them . . ."

Stevia bent to the girl, her manner gentle. "It's not the same, sweetheart, as seeing me and Lilia, though, is it?"

Micheline bit her lip and shook her head.

Stevia smiled. "See? Now, maybe you could go and put the kettle on for me, please."

Micheline nodded agreement, then scampered off.

"Micheline has quite the imagination," Stevia said, her gaze trailing the small shade. "She's always had the most vivid dreams. Sometimes I swear she even has them when she's awake."

Lilia watched the little girl run. She didn't tell Stevia that visions were rumored to be part and parcel of third-eye mutations. After all, there was no scientific proof, just a lot of mumbo jumbo and speculation.

She wasn't going to be the one to sign Micheline up for some extensive assessment of her abilities. Some research results weren't worth the price of learning them.

She also didn't want to take the risk of introducing a notion to Stevia, not without knowing her motives better. The Society might pay for a good research subject, after all, to smooth the transition from circus to slave-den.

It wasn't legal, but Lilia wouldn't have put it past them.

"Since she made friends with the tarot card reader's daughter, it's gotten somewhat out of hand." Stevia shook her head as they walked together. "I suppose, though, that it's harmless."

"She's very cute."

"Which makes her too easy to indulge." She cleared her throat and spoke more loudly, apparently for other ears to hear. "I don't suppose you might be returning to that hunting ground anytime soon?" she asked. "I could make it worth your while."

"I'm under contract to Joachim."

Stevia sidled closer. "But what if you found another pair and he didn't want them? Or even one. Who would you call?" The gleam in her eyes made it clear what answer she wanted Lilia to give. "A right of first refusal would suit me fine."

Lilia held up her hands in surrender, knowing that any circus owner would be more footsure around the legalities of contracts. "Joachim handles all the business aspects. Maybe you should just contact him directly."

"I will, and I'll tell him you suggested it."

"Sounds good."

Stevia gestured toward the plain tent pitched behind the biggest and brightest one. "Let me get you a cup of tea."

Lilia salivated at the prospect. It would be real tea. Little leaves plucked from shrubs, dried and oxidized, then immersed in boiling water.

"There's no need for that," Lilia said politely, not wanting to be beholden to Stevia for such an expensive contraband treat.

"Oh, but there is." Stevia smiled. "You see, I've been expecting you, Lilia Desjardins." Lilia's eyes must have widened, because Stevia chuckled. "The tea is on me, and yes, it's real."

Lilia should have known that a circus owner could be trusted to bait her hook twice.

MONTGOMERY HAD a bad feeling when the call came in.

It was early evening, the skies just turning dusky, the time that was usually a lull between daytime routine and the more dangerous night calls. He was restless, disliking that he had no idea what kind of trouble Lilia might have gotten herself into, disliking even more that there was nothing he could do to find out without leaving a datatrail. His new ear stud was tight and pinched his lobe, and the fact that he'd yet to figure out a way to disable it didn't improve his mood.

"I've got an anonymous tip from a public message unit in the netherzones," the dispatcher announced, his voice emanating from every desktop in the detectives' warren of cubes. "The caller reported sounds of violence behind a locked office door."

"I.D. on the voice?" Tupperman asked.

"He used a voice scrambler, sir."

"So, he knows more than he's letting on," Tupperman muttered.

"Maybe he's even the perp," Dimitri murmured. The other detective irked Montgomery with his jaded attitude and expectations that his seniority should be the only asset he needed.

"When and where?" Tupperman asked in a louder voice.

"A place called Breisach and Turner, downtown."

"I'm on it," Montgomery said, snatching up his helm before the dispatcher had finished giving the address.

Had Lilia returned to confront Rachel? Montgomery could believe that interview would proceed badly.

"Can't hurt, although uniform will check it out first," agreed Tupperman. "Dimitri, you're with Montgomery.

If it's only a B&E or a fight, you'll both get some exercise."

Dimitri groaned as he got up from his desk but Montgomery didn't wait for him.

They were walking to the bike garage, checking their equipment, when the call from the uniform division came in. "We need ident at Breisach and Turner," said a young officer and Montgomery broke into a trot.

"There's no fire, Montgomery," Dimitri said. "Didn't they teach you in Topeka that corpses wait?"

"And evidence gets destroyed if the site isn't secured," Montgomery snapped. "Get on the scene ASAP, that's what I learned. Even if it's bad, you've got a better chance of finding witnesses." He spared a glance to Dimitri, knowing that his fictional history in Topeka was a source of amusement in the department. "I figured you hotshots in New Gotham would be teaching me basic operating procedure."

Dimitri made a face but didn't answer that.

"I'll track down the message unit," he said as the pair started their motorbikes. Dimitri pinged the dispatcher for the reader's address and location. "Maybe we'll get lucky."

Montgomery knew it was too late. "He's gone."

"We'll get his prints."

"There won't be any." Montgomery was sure of it. "He thought to use a voice scrambler and a public reader, after all. He had a plan."

"If it was a he," Dimitri said grimly. "Some of those new scramblers provide gender switching too. Didn't they teach you in Topeka not to make assumptions, Montgomery?"

They peeled into the street, sirens blaring as they rode toward the office of Breisach and Turner. Montgomery couldn't go fast enough.

How far would Lilia go to get what she wanted? He could imagine that her determination and passion could easily lead her to make a mistake.

How far would Rachel go to defend herself and her

secrets? Montgomery didn't want to guess who might lose such an encounter.

He was through the door of Breisach and Turner well ahead of Dimitri, pushing the uniform cop aside, and almost had to turn back to heave in the corridor.

The dead woman on the floor was Rachel.

And she had been eviscerated.

STEVIA'S TABLE was set in an approximation of a Victorian tea table. There were mismatched china teacups and saucers, and a battered silver tea tin. Micheline stood by the table with pride.

"Did you collect all of these?" Lilia asked, letting the girl see her admiration. Micheline only managed to nod and blush.

Stevia cleared her throat slightly. "I don't ask."

Lilia understood that Stevia believed the collection had been pilfered in the old city. That was the philosophy of the circus: make use of what you find and don't ask too many questions. Lilia would have bet that Micheline had spent less time in the old city finding what she wanted—courtesy of that third eye—than anyone else might have been compelled to do, but then, Lilia was an easy mark for esoteric mumbo jumbo.

"You should get Micheline a radiation badge," she suggested. "Maybe a pseudoskin."

Stevia glanced up. "Why?"

"Well, if she's going into the old city to borrow supplies"—Lilia used circus lingo for illicit appropriation of goods—"then it would be a good plan to keep track of her exposure. That way you can ensure she doesn't get radiation poisoning."

"I thought you could only get that after a blast."

"No, it can creep up on you over time. It's cumulative."

Stevia grimaced, made a comment about people who detonate nuclear devices that was inappropriate for polite company, then indicated a chair. "Please, help yourself. What's ours is yours."

Stevia lifted the chipped teapot to pour and Lilia leaned across the table to catch a whiff of the good stuff before she could stop herself.

"Ceylon Black," she breathed with pleasure.

"Loose leaves, even." There was pride in Stevia's tone.

"My mother has always said that you couldn't get a decent cup of tea south of the Mason-Dixon Line."

Stevia snorted. "Well, she's never come to my table, has she?"

Lilia sipped with satisfaction, then met Stevia's gaze. "But why were you expecting me? How can that be? I came on impulse."

"Well, I didn't believe it either, if that makes you feel any better. But *he* told me that there was an overwhelming probability in favor of your coming here, and that odds were decidedly in favor of you appearing this weekend." She shook her head. "He had a strange way of expressing himself, so it stuck in my mind."

Probability. That was the only word Lilia had to hear to know who Stevia's visitor had been.

"Gid was here," she whispered.

"I don't know his name." She pursed her lips. "Early August it would have been. Maybe late July."

Lilia was too shocked to speak.

Gid had known he was in danger. He had guessed not only that she would come south, but that she would come to the circus at some point. Even that she would attend the conference.

It was disconcerting to realize that she was that predictable.

"He left you something special."

Lilia must have looked alarmed, because the older woman smiled reassurance. "Don't worry. It's nice."

Who else knew about this besides Stevia? Was she the kind of woman to keep her mouth shut? Or did everything simply have a price? Lilia couldn't guess the answer and didn't like it one bit.

MONTGOMERY COMPOSED himself, secured the scene, and looked again. Rachel had been left by the killer in the same posture as the shade Lilia had found dead in the old city.

It was such a distinctive way of leaving a body. Either this was the work of the same killer, or someone had done a copycat.

He couldn't avoid the realization that only he and Lilia had seen the images of the shade in Gotham.

Except that he had loaded her images into his desktop. Someone could have accessed them from there and the databank spiders might have automatically generated hotlinks.

Where *was* Lilia?

"Easy, dude," the younger cop said. "Don't puke on the evidence."

Montgomery swallowed and made a point of taking notes.

Rachel was dead.

It never occurred to his fellow officers that Montgomery knew the victim. There was no reason for any association to be made, and Montgomery wasn't the only one to have trouble with the scene.

He was glad that Rachel had been so careful about disguising their connection. Montgomery doubted there was a hint of it anywhere in the Republic databanks. He knew he would never have been able to manage that himself, much less have survived his first month in human society without her assistance.

And now she was dead.

And all her secrets with her. How would he complete his mission?

By the time Dimitri emerged from the netherzones, Montgomery had measured and examined the corridor and brushed the door for prints. They entered the scene together with the coroner's team and image grabber. The sight of Rachel's violated body made Montgomery think again about the consequences of volunteering.

Without Rachel and her information, he knew nothing. He wasn't the kind of person who could easily rely upon divine intervention to set things straight.

What was he going to do?

How was he going to return home?

Rachel was dead. Montgomery felt abandoned and isolated. He knew there must be other angels on earthbound missions, but he didn't know who they were. Rachel wouldn't have left any links to them either.

It was procedure, to limit the damage if one of them was captured and compelled to talk. Rachel, Montgomery was sure, would never have talked.

What happened to volunteers who died? It was all so mortal, so final. It was a denial of what she had initially been. Had she returned heavenward? Earthbound assignments were temporary and after a successful mission, volunteers regained their wings. The successful ones returned to their previous celestial existence.

But Rachel's life force was gone. Her body was merely a shell, a damaged one. Had her soul returned to the creator? Montgomery didn't know, he had no one to ask, and he feared the import of what he saw.

Even more importantly, with Rachel gone, there was no one to finish her mission.

Whatever it had been.

Except Montgomery. It stood to reason that her mission was more important than his. He had to know what Rachel knew while he could still find out. He had to finish her mission as well as his own.

There was only one resource available.

Montgomery stepped past Dimitri, pulled out his probe, and datashared with Rachel's corpse before anyone could stop him.

IX

To say that Lilia was surprised by what Gid had purportedly left her would be the understatement of the century.

"Well, here it is." Stevia laid a necklace in Lilia's hand.
"He left this with strict instructions that I should only
give it to Lilia Desjardins. Made sure I knew what you
looked like too."

Lilia stared at the cheap locket and chain pooled in her
palm. The "gold" was already chipping and the chain tinkled in her hand as if it had been made of aluminum foil.
There was a lavish *L* on the front of the locket.

It was the ugliest piece of jewelry she had ever seen.
Lilia tried to see some link between this clumsy locket
and the sleek piece of platinum on her left hand, both
chosen by the same man, and failed.

Had Gid left her a comment on the state of their relationship, or was this a kind of suicide note?

The tea seemed to curdle in Lilia's gut.

"Pretty, isn't it?" Stevia reached out a finger and caressed the locket's surface. "If it'd had my initial on it, I
might have forgotten it was yours," she said and it was
only half a joke.

Lilia was tempted to give the locket to Stevia, right
then and there, but Gid must left it for her for a reason.

Maybe it should have come with a cheat sheet.

"Well, aren't I lucky, then," she managed to say.

"I'll say!" Stevia poured another cup of tea for each of
them.

Against all expectation and belief, Gid, a man with discerning taste in all matters ornamental, had left this piece
of junk for Lilia. She felt like she'd been slapped, like she

was having that last awful argument with him one more
time.

But Gid had never been cruel.

Maybe it wasn't really from Gid.

Lilia pulled up a couple of images from her palm, including the one of Gid that she'd shown to Miss Conge-
niality at Breisach and Turner. She set it to scroll through
the images and asked Stevia to identify the man who had
left this.

Stevia picked Gid's image without hesitation. "More
than one admirer?" she teased.

"I just wasn't expecting anything like this."

"Who would? Why don't you put it on?"

Lilia lifted the chain around her neck with some hesitation. It nestled into the pin-tucked cotton covering her
cleavage, looking no less tacky than it had before.

"Perfect!" A romantic fantasy put a gleam in Stevia's
eye. "Maybe it's a proposal?"

"From my husband?"

"You're married to him? Ooo, then, maybe it's an invitation to a tryst. Or an anniversary present." Stevia winked,
then sipped her tea with a knowing smirk. "You should
open it and find out."

Lilia doubted that Gid had left any kind of message inside this locket, and doubted even more that it would be
romantic or unsuitable for other eyes. In fact, she would
have been surprised if Stevia hadn't already peeked inside herself.

Gid, being Gid, would have surely calculated the
probability of that to be quite high. People—like circus
owners—who survived on the margin of the law tended
to be curious. It kept them alive. Gid had learned a lot
about such people, courtesy of Lilia.

She smiled. "Maybe he just didn't use up his New
Gotham transit chip and wanted me to make use of it
while I was here."

Stevia laughed, but her curiosity was undisguised as

Lilia pried open the locket. The catch was a bit sticky but it gave suddenly, and whatever was inside splashed into Lilia's tea.

"Oh no!" Stevia cried and ran for a clean spoon.

It was a candy. Lilia could see it through the lens of the tea. It was one of those little sweet-and-sour candies shaped like hearts, the ones in pastel colors with red writing on one side.

LUV U 4EVER those letters spelled out, at least until they started to dissolve.

She knew then, and without a shadow of doubt, that Gid *had* left this for her. Nine years before, he'd proposed with the duplicate of this candy, a goofy fact no one knew except Gid and Lilia.

No one would have anticipated that he could be such a quirky romantic. Unexpected, that had been Gid.

Sincere.

Honorable.

Loyal.

So it was true that opposites attracted. Lilia blinked back tears, realizing too late what she'd lost and wishing things had been different. She wanted to erase that last argument, to travel back in time and chart her steps all over again.

Except that then she wouldn't have met Montgomery. She thought of the way Montgomery kissed and the way he made her yearn, tricks that Gid had never been able to master, and her tears came again.

It wasn't fair.

"Oh, it's melting away," Stevia said with disappointment. She put the spoon down on the table. "You should drink it. That has to be good luck, or at least better luck than chucking it out."

It seemed vulgar to tell Stevia that Gid was dead.

Lilia shut up and drank the tea, which had a strange taste courtesy of the dissolved candy, and wondered what Gid's point had been. He'd gone to a lot of trouble to prove that he had been the one to leave her this worthless piece of junk. It didn't make sense.

That wasn't typical of the logic-driven Gid Lilia had known.

Which meant that Lilia was missing his point.

THE SILENCE almost sizzled. Montgomery was well aware that his fellow cops were watching him with horror. There was a sizable gap around him. He was on one knee beside Rachel.

"Whoa, Montgomery, that's sick." Dimitri muttered.

Montgomery programmed his palm to download everything she had. His fellow cops were disgusted, but he had no idea how long it would be until one of them intervened.

"Is that how they do it in Topeka?" asked one uniformed officer with scorn. "Or just in the pleasure fringe?"

Montgomery spared them both sharp looks. "We've got a crime scene with no real evidence. She might have identified the killer herself before her death, or pulled up a relevant record. In Topeka, we aren't afraid to explore all the angles."

"Remind me never to go to Kansas," Dimitri muttered.

"Hard to believe anyone would have to tell you that," the uniformed officer said under his breath.

"Jesus," said the image snatcher and left the office.

Montgomery was more interested in the fact that Rachel's palm had been wiped.

Even the I.D. sector was blank.

The back of Montgomery's neck prickled. Rachel had had the same viral software installed as Fitzgerald.

By choice? Or had the killer installed it to ensure that she couldn't pass information to anyone else?

There was no way to know for sure.

He disengaged his probe and stood, feeling the relief of his fellows. He was relieved himself. The software persuaded him that the same person had killed Rachel as Fitzgerald, and he was sure Lilia hadn't killed her husband.

"Well?" asked Dimitri.

"Nothing," Montgomery said.

"You'd better be hoping that you end up with nothing," Dimitri said with the malice Montgomery had come to associate with the other cop. "A little digital souvenir could really mess with your palm, Montgomery." He looked as if he'd enjoy seeing that happen.

Montgomery ignored Dimitri and considered the scene. There were no signs of forced entry into the office—the windows were locked and the door had been slightly ajar when the first officers arrived.

Had Rachel known her assailant?

Whom had she met earlier today?

Why hadn't she already gone to Chicago?

The coroner arrived with his usual efficient bustle and urged the officers aside as he got to work. "Well, isn't this a mess?" he said cheerfully. "Anything touched?"

"Montgomery datashared with her," Dimitri said.

The coroner spared Montgomery a considering glance. "And?"

"Her palm was wiped, even the I.D. sector."

The coroner frowned and got to work, calling the image snatcher back to capture the specific images he wanted.

Where were Breisach and Turner? The pings Dimitri had left for those gentlemen weren't getting any replies. Maybe Rachel hadn't considered whoever had come to the office door to be a threat, even though she hadn't known the person in question.

She wouldn't have been afraid of Lilia.

Montgomery couldn't evade that unwelcome thought.

"Hey, this one's a shade," the coroner pronounced. He had pulled up Rachel's sleeve and her tattoo was displayed on her left forearm.

"That makes life easier," Dimitri said with pleasure. "Pack it up, boys. We're out of here."

The image snatcher put his camera away. "Waste of bytes there. I had some good shots."

Montgomery was shocked by the rapid change in their attitude.

"Punch this one in for me," the coroner said to Montgomery. "We can wrap it up with an I.D." He read Rachel's number from her tattoo and Montgomery tapped it into his palm with a request for identification from the central database.

"She used the name Rachel Gottlieb," Montgomery read as if he didn't know. "Harvested as an adult by the shade hunter Rhys ibn Ali in New Concord in 2090. She abandoned her assigned labor six months later, was immediately declared missing, but never found again." He glanced up, then displayed his palm to the coroner. "In her file image, she had darker hair."

The coroner peered at the image. "Still her, though. Look at those cheekbones. You can't buy implants like that."

"I thought she was a receptionist," said Dimitri. "Her being a shade explains why the partners aren't rushing to answer me."

"They smell more questions, tough questions," Montgomery said and the others nodded agreement. Breisach and Turner could be charged with harboring stolen property—the property of the Republic—if it could be proven that they had known of Rachel's shade status.

"She might have been more than clerical staff," the coroner said matter-of-factly. "She was quite the looker."

Montgomery was shocked by the thought. But Rachel had been devoted to her quest and pragmatic. He didn't doubt that she would have been prepared to make bargains, even unconventional ones, to complete her mission.

But someone had stopped her.

What had she discovered?

Dimitri eyed Rachel's file image, still displayed on Montgomery's palm. "Quite the babe, with her guts where they belong."

"She was obviously clever enough to pass as a norm and her defect was easy to hide. I wonder what it was."

The coroner cut away what was left of Rachel's clothing, baring her body to view with indifference. Montgomery inhaled sharply when her undergarments were cut away and discarded, noting how the other police officers gathered around to gape.

If she'd been a norm woman, her body would have been hidden from view.

"Everything looks like it's in the right place to me," Dimitri joked. The others chuckled, until the coroner rolled Rachel over. The cops stopped laughing, shocked to silence by the two long diagonal scars on her back.

Montgomery's mouth went dry. He had a pair exactly the same.

"Holy shit," whispered one. "What kind of mutation is that?"

"She must have had tumors removed," the coroner mused. "Or it could have been an extra organ. It's hard to say without full medical records." He glanced at Montgomery. "Are they there?"

Montgomery checked the file, then shook his head. "She had the scars when she was harvested, and they were why she failed the S.H.A.D.E."

Rachel's scars had been enough to condemn her. Montgomery felt a new awareness of his own vulnerability.

"Happens all the time." The coroner spoke dismissively, snapping his fingers for the body bag team. "She must have been a smart one. Too bad she didn't do her duty in serving the Republic."

"Yeah, on her knees in front of some senator," Dimitri smirked, earning himself no points in Montgomery's view.

The coroner almost smiled. "This one's out of our hands."

"You got her number, Montgomery?" Dimitri asked and Montgomery nodded. "Good, then I'll just retire it when we get back to the precinct. Don't you wish they could all be so easy?"

There was a chuckle of agreement. Rachel's body was removed like so much trash and the office given a cursory cleaning.

Montgomery found himself lingering for one last look. Other than the stains on the carpet, the office was as neat as it had been the last time he had visited Breisach and Turner. It couldn't have been a break-in or a random act of violence, or Rachel interrupting a thief. He suspected that she had died for something she had learned.

Like the shade in the old city.

Maybe like Fitzgerald.

Whatever it had been, Lilia was determined to learn it too.

"FORTUNE TIME!" Micheline sang as soon as Lilia's empty cup touched the saucer. Stevia smiled indulgently, and being a bit indulgent herself, Lilia followed the girl's directions.

"First turn it upside down," Micheline instructed. Lilia did so, ensuring that the last bit of tea spilled into the saucer. "Turn it three times, as the sun goes," commanded the little girl, then shook a finger at Lilia. "And make a wish."

Lilia wished for a clue in whatever Gid was trying to tell her.

Micheline pushed her hands away. "Ready for the future?"

"I'll have to have a word with the tarot-card reader," Stevia said under her breath.

Micheline turned the cup over with a flourish, then both Stevia and Lilia gasped. No one needed any special skills to see the images that these tea leaves had formed. There was a wiggly line on one side of the cup, and on the other, a winged man.

"An angel!" Micheline crowed.

"A dark angel," Stevia said with authority. She pointed at the wiggly line. "And a snake? I think that Lilia is going to be tempted sometime soon." She shook a finger at Lilia. "That husband of yours has something up his sleeve, that's for sure."

Lilia let Stevia believe what she wanted to believe. The "dark angel" in the cup gave her an idea—she wasn't going to think for one second about temptation.

She turned to the little girl. "Maybe I *am* going to see more angels. Would you show me your angels, Micheline?"

"They're just her imagination," Stevia chided.

But Micheline reached up and touched Lilia's forehead with her fingertips. They were a bit sticky with jam but landed right where Lilia's own third eye would have been, if she'd had one.

Lilia had the barest glimpse of Micheline's eyes rolling back before her lids closed. Was it for show? The little girl took a deep breath, her face serene.

"Yes. The angels will allow you to see them," Micheline whispered slowly, majestically. The hair on the back of Lilia's neck stood up. Micheline's voice had become reminiscent of the resonant tones of Armaros and Baraqiel.

"Tomorrow. They will show themselves tomorrow."

Lilia spoke softly. "Do you know when, Micheline?"

"Early. When it's still dark."

"Where?"

"I will take you."

"Where will I find you?"

Micheline lifted her fingertips from Lilia's forehead, then opened her eyes and spoke with authority. "I will find you at the circus. The angels will tell me where to go."

Stevia and Lilia exchanged a glance and Lilia nodded slightly, letting the other woman know that she'd take care of the child.

Could there really be more angel-shades?
It looked like she was going to find out.

MONTGOMERY'S DESKTOP was pinging when he got
back to his cube. At his touch, it summoned an array of
hotlinks for his viewing pleasure.

Although they didn't particularly please him. They
showed Lilia's activities in New Gotham, sorted by time
and date.

- *image: Y654892*
  source: datachip of Lilia Desjardins
  time stamp: 10/27/99, 21:03
- *vid: Lilia Desjardins*
  source: NGPD precinct vid-cam
  time stamp: 10/27/99, 22:36
- *vid: Lilia Desjardins*
  source: security cam, Breisach and Turner
  timestamp: 10/28/99, 12:37
- *image: R374591*
  source: police image-snatcher
  timestamp: 10/28/99, 19:47

Lilia's visit to Breisach and Turner had been noted by
the security video. He took the hint and looked at Lilia's
record. It was a different level of the databank, a deeper
one than he had previously viewed. Presumably the system had authorized a closer look at Lilia's records.

Her academic history at the Institute for Radiation Studies was the main difference Montgomery saw in the new
display. Lilia hadn't shown much academic prowess in her
years at the Institute. Montgomery would have expected as
much, given her apparent distaste for the Society's agenda.
Once again, he wondered why she'd bothered to apply to
the school in the first place.

What surprised him was that Lilia had received four

consecutive proficiency awards in one core subject, for exceptional skill in Dissection and Vivisection.

Montgomery sat down heavily. Dissection and Vivisection couldn't be for the faint of heart. Was Lilia's squeamishness an act? He followed the links through to the program of duties and the syllabi for the Dissection and Vivisection courses. They were, if anything, worse than he could have expected.

The databank and the Institute's records couldn't be lies. Lilia, however, had shown a tendency to manipulate the truth.

Was Lilia a shade-killer? Montgomery couldn't believe it.

Was he willing to bet his life on it? If his scars were revealed, he could be classed as a shade. Would she turn him in? Send him to the circus?

Or would she only do either if the price was right?

Montgomery spun in his chair. He liked Lilia's sense of honor. He liked that she bent the rules she saw as unimportant. He liked her fierce loyalty and he liked her passion. He respected that she presented herself as tougher than she was, if only to protect her idealism. He wanted her as well, his desire more than he'd felt for any other human woman.

Did he dare to trust his instincts?

Rachel had warned him about becoming emotionally involved with humans. She had said that his desire for Lilia was clouding his thinking. Instead of pursuing Lilia, he should focus on finishing the job that Rachel had started.

What had been Rachel's mission?

He could only think of one way to find out. Montgomery didn't miss the irony that he had to break the rules himself, just as Lilia did, to set things right.

He had to ask angels for help.

But first, he had to talk to Lilia about her proficiency awards in Dissection and Vivisection.

EVENING HAD fallen by the time Lilia left the circus. She wasn't sure whether she'd lingered over the tea table because she liked Stevia or because she had so little enthusiasm for the company of her fellow Nuclear Darwinists.

The evening ahead lacked a certain promise.

Lilia stuck to her principles, avoided the conveyors, and walked all the way back to the hotel. The lobby bar was filled with Nuclear Darwinists, mixing and mingling, and the din was considerable.

The last thing Lilia needed or wanted was cocktails, canapés, and chitchat. Her feet were sore, her back ached, she was hot and sweaty, and that dog poop seemed determined to cling to her shoe until the end times. She took one look at her fellow convention attendees and gave serious thought to going home, right then and there. After all, she had no leads left and big fat zip as proof that her instincts about Gid had been right.

But then, that had never stopped her before.

She could duck past registration, snag her bags, and head for the station without anyone knowing the difference. It was a tempting proposition, but that was, of course, when she was spotted.

"Lilia! There you are!"

Lilia knew without turning that it was Blake Patterson, Gid's old roommate and quite possibly the only person at the conference who would have hailed her with a friendly voice. He was also the only attendee she couldn't ignore.

Blake was a sweetie, despite the fact that he had a talent for finding Lilia at her worst. She was convinced that it was compare and contrast, like brides insisting that their bridesmaids wore dowdy dresses. When a person needed to look good, as Blake Patterson always did, that person needed to know where to reliably find a contrasting accent.

Enter Lilia Desjardins.

"Lilia! Over here!" Blake shouted across the lobby, then waved a drink just so Lilia couldn't miss him.

Or maybe to make sure that no one else in the lobby missed Lilia. She felt the hostility as her fellows noticed her, felt the temperature get downright frosty in the lobby.

The disapproval being exuded in her direction was just what Lilia needed to put some bounce back into her step. Her mother had always said that Lilia did best with an obstacle to overcome. She squared her shoulders, smiled, and pushed through the crowd toward Blake as if she was queen of the prom.

It was hard to miss Blake: he was six foot six, blond, and tanned, Adonis in the flesh. The tanning alone must have cost him a fortune at the spa—given the endless cloud cover over the Republic since the nukes—and Lilia always wondered how deep he was in hock. He was turned out splendidly on this occasion, per usual, and Lilia's bedraggled state did make the perfect contrast.

Even so, his sartorial flair lifted Lilia's spirits. It was refreshing to find a man who dressed like a peacock in the midst of dozens of scientists and math geeks who seldom surrendered their lab coats. Blake was wearing a cherry red zipped jacket and black pants fitted to show his long legs to advantage. His blond hair came to his shoulders and had been styled to look as if he had just sauntered in from a beach. His smile was so bright that it could have fueled the hotel's elevators.

He wrinkled his nose at her embellished shoe when she reached his side, then shoved a glass of something bubbly into her hand. "You're a wreck," he declared. "But I love you anyway." He gave her a trio of air kisses, alternating cheeks, a welcome that Lilia enjoyed more than she might have expected.

"Brilliant of you to suggest renaming the award for Gid," he breathed into her ear. "I hear the Council of Three approved it outright."

"There is no Council of Three," Lilia teased, then took a sip of wine. It was cold and hit her empty belly like a jolt of lightning. "We used to argue about that in the dorms all the time."

"No, you used to speculate on who the members

were," Mike MacPherson corrected. Gid's other long-standing roommate, Mike was standing behind Blake.

In his shadow, so to speak.

In contrast to Blake, Mike had gone with the safe male option of a navy blazer with taupe pants. His dark hair was touched with a bit of silver at his temples. Mike looked like the persistent researcher he was, the one who put in long hours in the Institute's research labs, pursuing drug patents and making money for the team. Lilia had always known she could have liked him better if he had changed jobs.

At least he'd ditched the lab coat for the festivities. Mike had also gotten a buzz cut since the last time Lilia had seen him.

Which might have been at her wedding. After all, no Nuclear Darwinists had come to Gid's memorial service. Lilia had no doubt that her conflict with the Society was responsible for Gid not getting the send-off he deserved.

Both Mike and Blake had earned their sixth degree and had the commemorative tattoos on their foreheads to show for it. Blake had chosen the eye in the pyramid, the Masonic symbol that had once appeared on Republic currency. It was a popular choice, as was the lotus mandala chosen by Mike.

"Hi, Mike," Lilia said and Blake jumped in surprise.

"Mike! I didn't see you," Blake exclaimed, predictably. Mike and Lilia exchanged rueful glances, because they had both been there and done that before, then clinked glasses.

"He's such a diva," Mike muttered.

Lilia almost spewed her drink. "Good thing we love him as much as we do," she whispered.

Mike grinned. "Doesn't mean we'll vote for him, though."

"I heard that," Blake protested. They drank and conversation stalled. Lilia felt Gid's ghost sidle up beside them. If the others had the same sense, no one mentioned it.

They drank.

"You two always took bets on who was Council of Three," Mike said brightly after a long moment.

Lilia rolled her eyes, even as she recalled Doc Mina's comments. "No one ever admits that the Council exists."

"But Lilia always managed to persuade me she was right and took my money anyway," Blake said with a smile. "You lie well enough to be a politician, my love."

"Is that a compliment?" Lilia asked. "Or does that mean that since you declared your candidacy, we can't trust you anymore?"

Blake, to her surprise, didn't smile. "Tell me then, can I count on your vote?"

Lilia looked at him hard. "I heard you'd gone over to the dark side. I'd hoped it wasn't true."

He had the grace to flush. "Okay, the Society isn't perfect, but I believe change is better accomplished from the inside. Running for Society president is the best way I know how to do that."

"Wrong, Blake. It's an empty position, everyone knows that." So much for *prudent*. The sparkling wine was already loosening her tongue. "The Council of Three make all the decisions, whoever they are these days. If you want to get anything done, you should run for the Council."

"Lilia!" Blake chided as only he could do. He'd make someone a good mother one day. "There is no Council of Three. That's just propaganda perpetuated against the Society." There was no conviction in his tone, so Lilia pushed. Mike watched.

"Be serious, Blake. Remember who you're talking to here. Who's running the show, if not the Council?"

"The nominated Board of Governors . . ."

". . . are a bunch of yes-people. Don't pretend you don't know the truth, not with me. We both know that you need to get on the Council of Three if you want to have a real say in things." Lilia took a gulp of wine. "Even better, you need to be the One."

Mike muttered a curse and excused himself. Blake looked a bit twitchy as he checked to see who might be listening. Then he shook his head, lowering his voice again. Lilia had the bizarre thought that they were leaning together like lovers and wanted to laugh. "That's not how it works, Lilia. A position on the Council of Three is an appointment, granted to those who have served the Society. Running for president is a start."

"You know a lot about this process."

He shrugged. "You were the one who used to speculate . . ."

"No. That was based on zero information or, at best, gossip. You sound as if you have hard data now. Where do you find out this stuff? Who's on the Council now, anyhow?"

"Lilia, we shouldn't be talking about this. There are things that shouldn't be said, not if you want to get ahead . . ."

"Or elected for Society president."

"Or that." He gave her a stern look. "Don't mess with the Council."

"What do you know?"

"Nothing. Just leave it, Lilia." Blake threw back the rest of his drink. "For your own good."

Interesting. Mike arrived then with refills—both Lilia and Blake fell on them as if they were parched.

She snapped her fingers, trying to recover the conversation's earlier playful tone. "Which reminds me, Blake." He looked at her warily. "You never did pony up that last fifty creds you owed me."

"For what?" Mike asked.

"I challenged him to prove that Doc Mina wasn't the master planner in charge of the Council of Three, and he never did it."

This time, Mike snorted his wine.

"I don't think we should talk about this," Blake hissed.

Mike continued as if he hadn't heard. "Did you hear, Lilia, that Rhys is lobbying for your ejection from the Society over those angel-shades? He says you were hunting illegally."

"There's a case of the pot calling the kettle black," Lilia retorted and snagged herself another glass of bubbles.

Hers had emptied with remarkable speed. She winked at Blake. "Rhys never did anything legal in his life. Hey, maybe he's Council of Three. What do you think, Blake?"

"Just leave it," he said through his teeth.

Lilia exchanged a glance with Mike. "Preelection jitters," Mike whispered and they nodded conspiratorially.

"Tell me, Lilia, why is it that I'm expecting a show when you present that award?" Blake asked.

"From me?" Lilia tried to look innocent and was sure she failed. She was better at demure than innocent.

The two friends exchanged knowing glances.

"Hurry, hurry. Get your tickets early," Mike said, sounding like a circus hawker, and Blake laughed. Lilia was relieved to see his easy charm make a reappearance.

"Speaking of a show." Blake nudged Mike. "Show Lilia your tattoo."

Mike's neck reddened and he averted his gaze. "I don't know . . ."

"Lilia, you'd better insist," Blake said.

Mike just got more red.

"Tattoos are forever," she replied. "There's always time."

"But you won't be able to see it once the hair grows back."

Lilia wondered whether she really wanted to see the tattoo.

She also wondered where it was.

She didn't even want to think about how Blake knew about it.

"Is this going to be in violation of S&D?" she asked.

"You won't believe what this fool did when he got his seventh degree," Blake said with a shake of his head.

The tattoo was on the crown of his head, on the seventh chakra to commemorate the seventh degree. Lilia exhaled in relief and Blake gave her an odd look.

"Where did you think it was?" he demanded. When Lilia blushed, Blake laughed. "Mind in the gutter."

"Hazard of early widowhood," Lilia replied, then

wished she hadn't. Gid's ghost seemed to get more tangible.

"Bend over and let me see," Lilia said to Mike.

He ran his hand over his head. "The hair's growing in, anyway."

"Quit stalling." Blake put his hand on the back of Mike's neck and pushed his head forward.

On the crown of Mike's head, visible through the short hair of his buzz cut, was an ever-smiling cartoon character.

Lilia was so surprised that she laughed out loud. "Not Orv the Orange? You put Orv on your head?"

"Isn't it insane?" Blake demanded. "The man passes his seventh degree, earns a reputation for exceptional lab work, and gets a cartoon character on his head to commemorate his achievement."

"Hey, it's not just any cartoon character," Mike protested. "This is Orv the Orange, official mascot of the Society of Nuclear Darwinists' *Sunshine Heals* program, beloved by children throughout the Republic . . ."

"See?" Blake interrupted. "Now he even talks like a publicist. Maybe the tattoo is messing with his head."

"Maybe the ink is dripping into his brain," Lilia suggested.

"Maybe it's the spirit of Orv himself," Blake said.

"It is Orv," Mike insisted as he put his hand over his heart. "He casts sunshine into my life with his very presence."

Lilia and Blake groaned.

"You're going to need a better story on a date," Blake said.

"Only if she shaves my head," Mike replied.

Lilia held up her hands. "I do not want to hear the rest of this conversation." She looked at Mike and giggled as she had a thought. "You'd better hope you don't ever go bald."

Mike shook his head. "Come on. Don't be so tough. Even Gid had Orv tattooed on his first chakra . . ."

Blake slapped Mike's back abruptly and the other man fell silent, his neck turning ruddy.

"Sorry," Mike muttered and they drank in silence.

They stared around themselves, desperately seeking a topic of conversation other than Gid or the Council of Three. Lilia thought it couldn't be more awkward, then Blake gave a low whistle.

"Praise be to the pseudoskin," he breathed as he looked at the hotel entrance. Lilia knew immediately who had arrived.

Funny how things seemed to look up whenever Montgomery appeared.

X

LILIA WATCHED Montgomery seek her in the crowd, felt his gaze lock on his target, then watched him stride directly toward her. He looked as grim as a reaper. She was surprised to feel her body respond to his presence, even though his evil twin was missing in action.

It had to be the pseudoskin. She tossed back the rest of her wine and met him halfway.

The pseudoskin was a marvel of modern technology, one that turned anyone remotely buff into a superhero. Half an inch thick, the pseudoskin was a slightly stretchy polymer embedded with lead mesh. The best pseudoskins required a body scan for the fitting, and were cast for the individual wearer. The matrices of the layers of lead mesh were computer-designed to overlap and create a radiation barrier. In the best suits—like Gid's first-string suit and undoubtedly the one Montgomery wore—the protection was equivalent to being encased in four feet of lead.

But so much more flexible. A pseudoskin fit like one's own skin—albeit a thicker and heavier version of the body's natural protective layer—hence the name.

Codpieces of reevlar, a dense inflexible synthetic resin that was virtually impermeable, and thorax guards of the same material completed the ensemble for both genders. The plan was to protect the reproductive jewels, so to speak, as well as the thyroid, those being the parts of the body most enthusiastic about sucking up radiation. In practical terms, people didn't wear the thorax guards much outside of very hot zones because the reevlar weighed so much.

Lilia found it funny how few men took chances with their codpieces: they wore them all the time. Any suggestion that this practice was overkill was greeted with hostility. She routinely abandoned hers, because, well, there wasn't much left to protect in that particular vicinity.

Montgomery didn't waste any time on formalities. "Where were you this afternoon, Ms. Desjardins?"

Lilia glanced to his ear stud, firmly in place, and wondered at his game. "Sightseeing. Why?"

"I'll ask the questions, Ms. Desjardins." His tone was firm but it was the coldness in his eyes that concerned Lilia.

"What's happened?"

He flicked her a quelling glance, one that didn't quell her one bit.

"If you're asking questions of a citizen, you have an obligation to tell that citizen why," Lilia continued, hating that she always seemed to be reciting law code in this cop's presence.

He eyed her for a second, then abruptly displayed his palm to her. The full-color image was of the receptionist at Breisach and Turner, eviscerated exactly the same way as Y654892.

Lilia had to turn away to keep her drink from ending up on Montgomery's boots.

"Two very similar killings reminded me of who had reported the first one."

Lilia had her hand over her mouth. She felt Montgomery watching her, measuring the duration of her gag reflex. It hadn't been long since she'd talked to the receptionist. "When did this happen?"

Montgomery didn't answer. "Where were you today? Do you have witnesses?"

She met his gaze, recognizing that she wasn't supposed to admit that she had seen him that morning and that he could be her witness. Where did his allegiance lie? She wanted very much to know.

"Isn't that the shade receptionist from Breisach and Turner?"

FALLEN   151

He wasn't surprised by the question or its nuances.
"How did you know her?"

"I didn't."

Montgomery gave Lilia a look.

She sighed. "I went to Breisach and Turner this morning. Their address was the last bit of information on Gid's
palm when I got it. So I went there, thinking they might
remember him."

"Ms. Desjardins, I remind you that the death of Gideon
Fitzgerald was deemed an accident and that you are not
doing yourself any favors by pursuing what is a closed
case."

She really hated his officious tone. Why couldn't he
have turned up in debonair mode?

"Why did you call her a shade?" he asked softly.

"Because she was one. I saw the end of her tattoo today."

He was taking notes on his palm and was impossible to
read. Again. "What time was that?"

As if he didn't know. "It must have been around noon
because I was hungry."

"And where did you go to eat?"

"I didn't." Lilia shrugged. "I was too upset to eat."

"Upset?"

"She was lying to me. She said she didn't know Gid
but I'm sure she recognized his image."

"That's hardly conclusive," Montgomery said, using
that quiet voice again. If he'd said anything remotely intimate, that voice would have given Lilia shivers.

As it was, she straightened and held his gaze. "In my
line of work, few things are ever conclusive. I run on gut,
Montgomery. I knew she lied to me and I had to think
about what the truth might be. I went to the circus."

He arched a brow. "Why?"

"Because there are fewer rules there, and that works
for me." She held his gaze with defiance and he simply
watched her, then turned back to his note taking.

"What time did you get back here?"

"About an hour ago. Blake and Mike saw me come in."
At his inquiring glance, Lilia gestured to the two men.
Blake was watching Montgomery with considerable in-
terest while Mike was more intrigued with his drink.
"Gid's old roommates. They were kind of grandfathered
into my affections."

Montgomery glanced at Blake, held his gaze in challenge for a moment, then looked back at Lilia. "Doesn't
look very grandfatherly to me," he murmured and Lilia
couldn't help but smile.

"He's watching you, Montgomery, not me."

Montgomery's eyes narrowed at that morsel of news.

Lilia laughed. "He's single. I could make introductions
if you're interested."

"Leave it," Montgomery said with such low heat that
Lilia met his gaze once again. The green of his eyes was
simmering as he watched her and she felt an answering
tingle start low in her gut.

She really needed to get to the pleasure fringe for some
orgasmic release.

Would Montgomery offer to be her tour guide?

Then he blinked and was officious all over again. "Let
me be blunt, Ms. Desjardins. You have spoken to or contacted two shades since your arrival in New Gotham, both
of which have been killed in the same way almost con-
current with your contact with them. You have no alibi
and your record shows a certain . . . disregard for authority and Republican law."

"I would never kill a shade," Lilia said.

Montgomery's voice was hard. "You're a fellow of the
Society of Nuclear Darwinists. You took top marks in the
compulsory Dissection and Vivisection classes. For four
years, you were the quickest and the best, and unfortunately for you, we're looking for a killer who knows his
or her way around a surgical knife."

"Dissection and Vivisection class was a long time
ago." Lilia spoke around the lump in her throat.

"I understand that surgery is not that different from being a good shot with a laze. It's an innate talent, from what our coroner says, and one that isn't forgotten."

Lilia swallowed. There was nothing she could say in her own defense.

Not even the truth.

"Do you own a surgical knife, Ms. Desjardins?"

"No. I never have."

"How uncommon."

"That's been said of me before."

His gaze searched hers, seeking weak points in her defensive walls. Lilia was sure there were none, but his stare was still disconcerting. "This is not a homicide investigation," he said quietly. "Yet. However, the deliberate abuse of shades has been noted in the history of most violent killers."

Lilia felt sick at the implication.

"Be sure that you have an alibi for duration of your visit, Ms. Desjardins. I'd advise that you stay away from shades." He turned to leave and Lilia cleared her throat.

"Montgomery." She waited until he glanced back. "Maybe you should watch *your* ass."

A glint lit his eyes, evidence that he recognized his own words from the night before. "And why would that be?"

"Everyone I talk to in this town ends up dead." Lilia shrugged. "Who knows? Maybe you've made the list."

He took a step back toward her, his voice dropping dangerously. "Are you threatening me, Ms. Desjardins?"

"Just making an observation. Lucky for you, you're not a shade."

Something flicked in his eyes, something that made Lilia wonder what she'd said.

"Enjoy your evening, Lil," he said quietly, then pivoted on his heel and marched out of the hotel.

She watched him go and knew that Gid would have calculated the probability of any subsequent enjoyment of this evening on her part to be very low.

Perhaps nonexistent.

She was innocent but couldn't prove it, which wasn't the most uplifting realization possible. And really, if Montgomery was looking for people who knew their way around a surgical knife, the hotel was booked with three hundred souls who had at least *passed* all four years of Dissection and Vivisection. Most of them had excelled at it, as those courses separated the proverbial wheat from the chaff at the Institute for Radiation Studies.

Every one of them was capable of having committed these two murders—they *were* murders to Lilia—but Lilia, who had shamelessly cheated in those courses with the assistance of a certain graduate student, was the suspect of choice.

She knew that she would eventually appreciate the irony of that.

The only person who knew the truth was that graduate student, who was rather inconveniently dead and thus unable to offer testimony on Lilia's behalf. There was no point in telling Montgomery the truth, as it would just sound like a handy lie that couldn't be corroborated.

On the other hand, it was obvious that someone who didn't know the truth was trying to set Lilia up. She looked across the lobby and knew she could limit the potential candidates to everyone in the Society except herself.

That wasn't very helpful.

Even less helpful was the fact that Lilia couldn't figure out why anyone would have it in for her. She knew she could be annoying on a small scale, but it was hard to think of herself of being worthy of the effort of being framed for murder.

Then again, maybe she was underestimating her ability to tick people off.

It had happened before.

LILIA WOULD have made her escape, but Rhys ibn Ali hailed her with a raised glass. "Lilia!"

"Lilia!" his cronies echoed, his chorus line.

"Our own rebel angel," Rhys said and they fell all over themselves laughing at his brilliant wit.

Lilia wasn't a big fan of Rhys. He was good-looking and confident, the kind of guy who believed that no rules applied to him. He was the Society's premier shade hunter, but only because they turned a blind eye to many of his less-ethical practices. They seemed to have a deal: they'd make him a star if he didn't talk too much about technique. It was a precarious balance because Rhys adored himself so much that he not only wanted to share intimate details of his brilliance with everyone, but failed to see that he had ever done anything wrong.

"I'm just heading up to my room, Rhys. It's been a long day and all that." It was the best she could do in terms of a polite brush-off. This was Rhys, after all. She tried to step past him, without success.

"You have to have one little drink first," he insisted. "I haven't had a chance to talk to you yet."

Lilia regarded him with suspicion. "Since when do you want to talk to me?"

"Since I had such a nice chat with Gid last summer." His smile didn't reach his eyes.

What did Rhys know? "Oh? I didn't realize you'd seen him."

Someone got Lilia a glass of wine—she didn't see who, and later that would drive her crazy—and she was so interested in Rhys' comment that she just threw half of it back.

Being drunk made it easier to be in his company.

"Oh, yeah." He glanced over his posse and they got the hint, each of them suddenly disinterested in the conversation. "It must have been just a couple of days before he died." He leaned closer, as snakelike as Lilia had ever seen him. "So, how long had Gid been *indulging*?"

Gid had been the cleanest piece of business ever born, but Lilia played along. "Hey, don't go talking it up, not right before the awards ceremony," she whispered. "The Society will be all over you."

Rhys eased closer and lowered his voice. "True enough. But what was he taking? He was really messed up. It's no wonder he died like he did. You fill your body with junk, it's only a matter of time before you forget to protect yourself."

"Did ever you see him take any drugs?"

"No. Gid wasn't stupid. If I'd seen, I could have gotten him kicked out of the Society. But his talk was enough to condemn him. When he said that I had to help him, I was sure he'd gone nuts."

"Really." Lilia refrained from observing that Gid would have to have gone insane to have asked Rhys for anything.

"Then I thought he was offering me an angel-shade." Rhys chuckled to himself. "That was why I listened as much as I did."

Lilia's glass was empty again. Clearly there was a problem with the humidity levels in the lobby bar, as all alcoholic beverages evaporated before they could be consumed.

A kid brought Lilia another, right on cue. He stared at her breasts, blushed, then fled.

Lilia drank.

Rhys meanwhile was in his element. If he thought Lilia would be devastated by his story, he could think again. Gid had never taken drugs in his life. Rhys was lying.

The trick was to figure out why.

And maybe to find the germ of truth in his story.

"He talked about angel-shades?" Lilia said, prompting him.

"An angel, just one. He insisted it wasn't a shade." Rhys laughed at the stupidity of this notion. "I mean, a *real* angel of the 'messenger from God' variety. Gid said that I had to help him avert disaster, as the angel had asked him to do. It was wacky stuff."

What had Gid found out?

Had he really talked to an angel?

And what had the angel told him?

"What kind of disaster?"

"I dunno. Come on, Lilia, it was nutty stuff." He drained his drink, nodding to himself. "Although it all makes a kind of sense since you'd turfed Gid out. Everybody knew he was crazy in love with you. He must have just lost it." He spared Lilia a glance. "Why'd you break up?"

Lilia decided that demure was a better social option than ripping out Rhys' throat in front of witnesses. "It's not your business."

"Ernestine's hot to kick you out of the Society. Why?"

"You know Ernestine better than me," Lilia said mildly. "I've never seen her naked, after all."

Rhys pointed finger at Lilia. "That's ancient history . . ."

"Is it? Maybe she's still hot for you. Maybe that's what's going on."

Rhys, predictably, found this logic appealing. "Hey. Maybe."

Lilia worked it. "Don't you think it's funny that Ernestine's playing hard with me over the angel-shades? Who would be your only real competition in the field? And what would be the capture of the century, and who made it?"

Rhys' dark eyes took on a hostile glint. "That should have been my capture and you know it."

"No, I don't."

"I saw them first."

"Then why didn't you capture them?"

He took a long slow sip of his drink. His manner was definitely resentful, which was interesting. Lilia remembered her sense that Armaros and Baruqiel had *let* her capture them and wondered if they had *not* let Rhys capture them.

"Don't be so cocky, Lilia. The Society's going to play hardball with you over this."

"Not that you've encouraged them or anything."

"Me? What could I do?"

"You say you saw the angels first. If that's true, you

could testify that they aren't surgically altered and save my butt."

Rhys' smile broadened. "Why would I do that, Lilia? What exactly would be in it for me?"

Lilia drained her drink and set the glass aside. "You know, Rhys, I can't figure out why people say such terrible things about you. You're just the heart and soul of compassion, a champion among men." She pinched his cheek, a little too hard, and he winced. "You truly are a soulless bastard," she whispered. "Maybe Ernestine *was* too good for you."

Lilia pivoted then, intending to make her exit, but found one of Gid's former classmates blocking the way to the stairs. He was tall and thin, a whisper of reddish hair drawn across the top of his head.

"Hi," he said, shoving his hand at Lilia in his nervousness. "You probably don't remember me. I'm Cecil O'Donnell and this is Rob McMurtry. We just wanted to say we were sorry to hear about Gid."

"Thanks." The pair looked so anxious to be acknowledged that Lilia couldn't have done anything else. "You sent donations, didn't you? I remember your names." They nodded and shuffled their feet a little, uncertain where to take the conversation from here. "You were in some of Gid's classes, weren't you?"

"Covert Tracking," Cecil confirmed. "Gid and I were lab partners."

"Basic Reports and Maintenance of Database Integrity," said Rob, then nudged Cecil. "That was one tough course."

Lilia nodded, having nothing to add to that.

A woman pushed between them to speak to Lilia as well. "Sorry about Gideon. He was a good guy." She gave a gruff nod, touching Lilia's shoulder briefly as if they were allies in some war that Lilia knew nothing about. "Tonya Erikson."

"Thanks, Tonya."

"Hey, here's someone you should meet. Here's our latest hotshot researcher," Cecil said, gesturing to a small dark-haired kid. "Nicholas di Giovanni."

It was the same kid who had brought Lilia her last drink. "Just call me Nick," he said, speaking directly to Lilia's breasts.

It seemed unlikely that they would call him anything anytime soon, but he appeared to be willing to wait it out and give them their chance.

Lilia wasn't. She made her excuses and went back to her unit.

LILIA WAS exhausted. She turned on the vid and it seemed that all six thousand channels were featuring someone, or something, having sex. Lilia was acutely aware of her own yearning to do the horizontal waltz and lack of a partner.

If Montgomery turned up again in renegade guise, she might surprise him.

Why was he living a double life anyway?

Which was the real Montgomery? Lilia was afraid it was the officious cop. She put the vid on autosurf to change channels every three seconds. She liked using one testosterone fantasy to set up another. It was better than sitting in silence, at least.

The channels swirled. She felt dizzy and disoriented and unfocused, which maybe was what she got for having a lot of sparkling wine on an empty stomach.

Lilia kicked off her boots and freed herself from her corset. She fell naked across the bed, not caring for once where the surveillance monitors were. She was sore and tired and a bit drunk. Her belly snarled and it had cause for complaint, given how little she'd eaten during the day.

Her body wanted to sleep, but her thoughts were spinning like the images on the vid. There was nothing in the room except the requisite Bible. For lack of a better option, Lilia pulled it out of the drawer.

The faux leather binding was embossed with the name of the charity that had donated the Bible—the Gideons.

There was something funny about that, given that Gid had been the most vehement atheist Lilia had ever known. Most Nuclear Darwinists were atheists and agnostics— Lilia had always thought it would be hard to make peace with the Institute's research plans if there was any chance of being judged for participating. She turned to the little information blurb about the Gideons, assuming they had been named after their founder.

But no. The name came from two chapters in the Bible, Judges 6 and 7, which told of the faith shown by one Gideon before God. Lilia booted up the Bible—which seemed to still be fully charged—and fumbled through the index, cursing the fact that the Bible's verses weren't in alphabetical order. Finally, she got chapter 6 displayed on the screen, but verse 22 nearly made her drop the Bible.

"And Gideon said, *'Help me, Lord God, for I have seen an angel of the Lord face to face.'*"

Lilia shut down the Bible abruptly. Rhys had said that Gid had seen an angel too. What if there were more angels? What if Gid had told other people? What if the Society hadn't been too tickled that he had decided to agree with Lilia?

What if the enigmatic Council of Three had decided to do something about Gid's potential insubordination?

Lilia was making stuff up and she knew it—it didn't help matters that her theory sounded good. Maybe that said more for the sparkling wine than anything else. She was really dragging now and knew she needed to get some sleep, spinning thoughts or not.

Maybe everything would make sense in the morning.

Maybe not.

She checked her palm for the time of sunrise and set her alarm so she wouldn't sleep past her rendezvous with Micheline. She crawled into bed, naked except for Gid's locket, and pulled the covers up to her chin. She fingered the locket as the changing light from the vid washed over the room and tried to find the key that would make everything make sense.

Like the philosopher's stone. Wasn't that supposed to have fallen from heaven, in Lucifer's brow?

Gid would have known what to do. Gid had always been practical and logical, while Lilia got sideswiped by passion.

Ever her mother's daughter.

Ever the one following her heart.

In lieu of Gid—because even the New Gotham hotel, with its many amenities, didn't have the afterlife on direct dial—Lilia called her mom.

LILIA'S MOM picked up immediately. "Lilia! Where have you been?"

There was nothing like being chided to make a person feel loved. "You know where I am." Lilia nestled deeper into the covers. The vid-screen painted the room in one color after another, one set of entangled limbs after another. Lilia ignored the periodic appearance of fur and turned off the sound. "Just thought I'd call and check in."

"And it's about time." Her mother glared at the feed just for effect. Lilia grinned back and her mother shook her head, almost loosing a torrent of thick red hair. She had tied it back with her usual haste and it was, as always, threatening to break free.

She was in the kitchen and undoubtedly cooking. No one much cooked anymore; it seemed so arcane and magical that it always fascinated Lilia. She felt a stab of homesickness.

"I thought you would call yesterday, after you got in."

"I was too busy with the conference," Lilia started to fabricate but didn't get much further.

"You're always too busy to call your mother. Of course, when I was your age, I never called my mother at all. I couldn't because she was dead, so I guess I should be grateful for small mercies." Lilia let that one go. "I just told Eva that you hadn't called—"

"Hello, Lilia!" Eva called.

"Hi, Auntie Eva. Save some leftovers for me." Eva was such a fixture in her mother's house that Lilia called her Auntie Eva, even though technically she wasn't related.

"Not much chance of that!" Eva chortled out of sight.

"As I was saying, I told Eva that you hadn't called yet and that I should go over and check on your unit . . ."

"It's fine, Mom. I'll only be gone for a week anyway."

"You were only gone for the day at Gideon's funeral when it was broken into before."

"But there was a notice in the daily upload about the funeral. Some opportunist was just enterprising enough to look up my address. The police said it happens all the time."

"Someone robbed your unit."

"No, Mom, someone broke into my unit. Nothing was stolen. I didn't—and don't—have anything worth stealing."

"It can't hurt to check on things."

"But you don't need to bother." Lilia yawned.

"I *should* need to bother, Lilia." Her mother punctuated this with a savage gesture to some innocent foodstuff out of sight. "You should have houseplants or a cat or even a parakeet, something *alive* in that unit to keep you company, something that I need to take care of while you're away."

"You know I'm not good at nurturing."

"On the contrary, I think you'd be wonderful at it, if you'd just let yourself try."

Lilia didn't argue. There was never any fire in her mother's commentary. It was all just suggestion, and suggestion made because she cared.

What kind of a mother would Lilia have been?

She'd never had the chance to find out.

"You look glum," her mother said.

This is why she hated calling her mother—the woman missed so little. "No, I'm fine. Really."

"I hardly think so, but I don't know what you expected, going to that conference with *those* people. Lilia, I still can't imagine what made you want to be a Nuclear Darwinist . . ."

"We've been over this, Mom." Lilia yawned again, knowing it was rude but unable to help herself.

"And you've never once given me a decent answer. It never made any sense. For years, you know, I was certain you had done it just to piss me off."

Lilia jumped a little, but her mother was too busy to notice.

"But then you brought home Gideon and I thought that maybe there had been some kind of divine plan." She sighed.

Lilia forced a smile. "And here I thought you'd cheer me up."

Her mother fired Lilia a glance that could have singed a lesser mortal, despite the flour on the end of her nose. "You aren't doing anything foolish, are you, Lilia?" She held up a hand when Lilia might have protested innocence. "I know how much Gideon's loss hurt. But that doesn't mean that there's more to his death than you've been told, or even if there is, that it's wise for you to pry into matters better left unexplored."

Lilia fumbled for an excuse, but her mother had had thirty-five years with which to observe her idiosyncracies. "I'm giving out the award they renamed for Gid. You know that. They invited me."

"And I know that a year ago if they'd invited you to do any such thing, you would have told them to go to hell and not come back. You might have even given them a map."

Lilia didn't know why it always surprised her when her mother revealed just where she got that gift for plain talk.

"Well, it seemed rude," Lilia hedged. "After all, Gid was serious about his membership."

"Another mystery," her mother muttered. "How anyone so apparently sane as Gideon Fitzgerald could find anything of merit in an organization of self-serving—"

"Mom, the line might be monitored."

Her mother shook a finger and what looked like fresh pasta on the end of that finger waggled. "Don't poke your nose into business that isn't yours to investigate, Lilia. I want you to promise me."

Since Lilia had already done what her mother had advised her not to do, she changed the subject. "You know, the food is terrible here. What are you making for dinner?"

Her mother turned and looked down at the counter with some pride. "Tortellini. Rodrigo brought some organically raised chicken today, and it was so plump and pink that I couldn't resist. I cooked it and diced it, then mixed it with cream and a little Asiago cheese."

"I'm salivating already."

Her mother spared a smile for the feed. "The basil in the window greenhouse was just about to bloom, so I made a pesto sauce, even though you weren't here to peel the garlic."

This was Lilia's only job in my mother's kitchen: she was allowed to peel and chop garlic.

And to eat.

It was a good deal.

"And Eva brought some of her cherry tomatoes for a small salad. I think we're just about ready, actually . . ." The doorbell rang in the background and Lilia heard Eva's high voice at a distance.

Some points belatedly got together to make a line. "Wait a minute. Is this the full moon?"

Her mother smiled. "Of course, Lilia."

"I forgot." Lilia hid yet another monster yawn behind her hand and fought the sense that she was being enveloped by cotton wool.

Or devoured by it.

Her mother shook her head. "To think I imagined that I had raised you right. I only make time on the full moon to make tortellini. They're so much trouble, and need just the right twist of the wrist to look right."

Lilia knew this story. "To look like the navel of Aphrodite."

Her mother's smile was quick. "A salute to the beauty of the Goddess." She glanced down and her smile broadened. "Who evidently doesn't have an innie."

Lilia laughed.

Someone called Lillian's name in greeting and Lilia's mom cast that smile over her shoulder. She leaned closer to the feed and let her voice drop. "Don't imagine that you've fooled me, Lilia. You didn't make that promise, which means you've already broken it. If you can't be good, at least be careful." She gave Lilia no chance to interrupt. "And go to church. Please."

With that uncharacteristic reminder—as sure a sign of her concern as anything could be—she touched the monitor with a decisive fingertip and killed the feed.

She was gone.

The hotel unit felt cold and empty. Lilia imagined being at her mother's home on garlic duty, joining her mother's friends at their feast. She could see the beeswax candles burning in her mother's kitchen, the warm golden light they cast, the laughter on those women's faces.

If home is where the heart is, Lilia's was in her mother's kitchen.

She sighed, just as the vid display faded. It was midnight. The image faded, as always, to the graphic of those two watchful eyes. It was an unwelcome little reminder that the Republic's fingers were shoved into the pies of all citizens' lives.

The image lingered for a long moment, just long enough to burn itself onto the retina, then the display faded to black. The room fell into shadow, but Lilia saw the eyes still. They were yellow against the darkness, a trick of physiology, seemingly watching her from whichever direction she looked.

It made her shudder.

She thumped her pillow, turned out the lights, and was dreaming of tortellini more quickly than anyone might have expected.

LILIA AWAKENED sometime later, although she couldn't have said how much time had passed. It was late, because the hotel was quiet. But some threat had awakened Lilia. Her heart was leaping and her mouth was dry, her senses on full alert. She thought she had had a nightmare, but couldn't remember one.

Then she realized she could barely move.

She was *in* the nightmare.

There was a slight sound, a whisper of a footfall on carpeting. Lilia turned her head, moving in slow motion, and saw the silhouette of a man framed in the open door of her room.

She knew the door was closed.

She knew the door was locked.

But he stood there, framed by the light of the corridor, all the same.

Then he slipped into the room, closing the door behind himself. The darkness swallowed his shape as he turned the lock. Lilia heard it click home and knew they were trapped in the room together. She tried to force herself to wake up, but she felt as if she was already awake.

If powerless. She tried to scream and made only a slight moan.

Her pulse went wild. She could hear him breathing, could feel him drawing closer. She could smell him.

This was no dream.

She was being robbed.

Or worse.

She wanted to blow him away. She wanted to surprise him, jump him and hurt him badly.

But she was paralyzed, trapped in her own skin as if she was encased in lead. Only her thoughts were free to race. A man was in her room and there was nothing she could do about it.

Except panic.

He moved to the closet, flicked on the light, began to rifle through her things. He went into the bathroom and Lilia saw the light come on, heard the tinkle of toiletries as he rummaged. He made no attempt to be stealthy, which meant he knew that Lilia couldn't do anything to stop him.

How did he know that?

The bathroom lights went off and Lilia knew things would get worse. He returned to the bedroom and walked toward her, purpose in his step. Lilia fought against her uncooperative body. She managed to lift her hand two inches from the mattress before it fell limply back down again.

He chuckled, just a little, not enough that she could recognize his voice. She did know, though, that he wasn't surprised by her state. She couldn't see his face, although she tried.

Just to make sure, he grabbed the bed linens at the foot of the bed and threw them over her head. She was bare from the waist down, restrained by a thin cotton sheet cast across her face.

It made her want to roar, but she couldn't even do that.

She was terrified. Her heart nearly jumped through the ceiling when he took her hand in his. He was wearing gloves, Lilia could feel the faux leather. She realized that he didn't intend to leave any fingerprints. There'd be no evidence of his presence except what he did to Lilia.

But what would be his crime of choice? Lilia feared one particular outcome, but he surprised her.

It was her left hand he held, a detail that should have warned her. Lilia moaned when she felt the metal probe slide into her palm. It snicked home and a tear rose to her eye when she realized his intention.

He was downloading everything she had.

Her breath came in anxious spurts and she fought to scream or save herself. It was pointless and he knew it. He took his time, so much time that he must have copied every single file. Lilia could see the faint glow from her palm through the sheet but nothing else.

He abruptly pulled out the probe when he was done.

Lilia felt violated and dirty and helpless. There were angry tears on her face, even as a wedge of light became visible through the sheet.

The door to the corridor closed behind the intruder with a decisive click, leaving Lilia in silence and darkness.

XI

Friday October 30, 2099

MONTGOMERY CHANGED into street clothing at the end of his shift, choosing purple lace with his customary black trousers and jacket and cloak. He'd blend into shadows better without the flash of white cuffs and collar.

"Big date?" Thompson teased but Montgomery just winked as he pulled up his hood.

His gesture wasn't accidental: it plunged his ear stud into darkness, so any interruption in the signal wouldn't be immediately noticed. He returned briefly to his cube, purportedly for his gloves, and bumped his desktop with his hip. He heard the slight snap of the connection to the wall port being broken. He couldn't remove the new ear stud and he couldn't damage the buried receiver, but he could still disrupt the signal.

For now. He left the precinct quickly.

None of his coworkers would have been surprised that Montgomery's steps turned toward the pleasure fringe. His standard excuse when he was late or unavailable was that he had been in the pleasure fringe. The other cops assumed he went there for the usual reasons, but the simple truth was that Montgomery preferred to be unobserved, no matter what he was doing.

The watchfulness of the Republic bothered him, on principle.

He and Lilia had that in common, at least.

Montgomery strode through the silent streets. It was two in the morning and the respectable avenues of the Republic were empty. He moved through the darkness confident that if he was observed, no one would be able to identify him. That silvery fog was creeping along the street again.

There were a thousand ways to disappear, even in the watchful streets and alleys of New Gotham. Montgomery was aware that Rachel had showed him all of the ones he knew. In fact, how to disappear had been the first lesson she had taught him.

He slipped from the street to first level of the netherzones, making random choices with practiced ease but steadily heading toward his destination. He felt Rachel's presence keenly, as if she was sitting on his shoulder, guiding his impulse. He followed every whim that he might otherwise have thought was his own.

Upon his arrival on earth, Montgomery had accepted the illusion that all was just as he'd seen it, quite literally, on the surface. He'd never thought about what made the commuter conveyors work or what made elevators go up and down or what kind of fuel powered the many labor-saving devices of the Republic.

Rachel had enjoyed opening his eyes to this slice of reality. The netherzones had been a shock to Montgomery and he'd never fully recovered from his first journey into the Republic's underworld. Rachel had revealed a hidden network of avenues and passages to him. Every street on the surface was echoed belowground and most buildings had basements that opened into the netherzones.

The hidden labyrinth was where the dirty work got done.

Rachel had told him of a rumor that a person could walk the length and breadth of the Republic without ever seeing the light of the sun. How else could the Republic move military equipment and troops without any evidence appearing on satellites? Montgomery had learned that there were passageways for police use only that did not appear on any maps, passageways with hidden and locked accesses known only to a few senior personnel.

In urban centers, there were characteristically two layers to the netherzones. The first layer, closer to the surface—often jokingly said to be between heaven and hell—was where the commuter conveyors were installed. Parking garages might have been on this level in former oil-rich incarnations of the Republic, but those vehicles had been supplanted by bicycles and rickshaws.

Petty crime was a persistent problem on this level, given the poor lighting conditions. Norms and shades whose defects were sufficiently minimal for them to work as domestics could be found on the upper level.

The second and deeper level was the exclusive domain of the shades. The doors were locked and posted with No Admission signs so citizens couldn't wander in and take a peek.

Rachel had taken him there, as part of her orientation tour.

There were usually fluorescent lights hung at intervals, because they were comparatively cheap to operate, but the intervals were long. There were no skylights: light coming down meant views available to those above. For shades, this dark realm of concrete and steel might be the only world they knew.

Montgomery could still hear Rachel explaining that the development of the netherzones had been a rational result of economic crisis. As the Republic collectively ran out of crude oil ("scraping the bottom of the $25,000 barrel of oil by 2030," in Rachel's words) there was an impetus to find other sources of energy.

It was still possible to buy gasoline, but it was expensive, even on the black market. There were still those who could afford automobiles and air transit, but a contrail high overhead would bring a crowd of norms to open-mouthed silence.

"Humans could have lowered their standards, but that's not the Republican way," Rachel had said with scorn. "They wanted everything to be easy, so they took the obvious answer. They reinstated slavery."

Who better to enslave than those believed to be inferior? By 2030, as if by divine plan, the human gene pool was filling with simpletons. That those children were the result of radioactive fallout was not an issue. Norms—notably like Ernest Sinclair—took what "nature" had given and put it to work. Those children with diminished IQ and mild deformities were perfectly good at generating electricity.

One of the most popular rationales was that they never knew the difference. Montgomery didn't believe it. He'd been shocked on that first trip to the netherzones, appalled to see shades harnessed to equipment, drugged and exhausted and compelled to work to the death.

Maybe that was why no one was allowed into the deep netherzones. Montgomery's overwhelming sense was that of the injustices that humans served upon members of their own species.

The shades were like the norms. They were human.

But norms made shades what they had become.

In the netherzones, the truth of human nature was inescapable. His first doubts about the merit of his quest had come to him in the netherzones and those doubts still haunted him. Should mankind be saved from itself? Was there enough good to merit the sacrifice made by him and others?

Montgomery wanted to believe that it was so.

He walked through the netherzones quickly, avoiding glimpses of what he didn't want to see, and felt an overwhelming kinship with Lilia. Her fierce rejection of this world and its implications was one of the first sensible objections he'd heard since his arrival.

Maybe all humans weren't the same.

Maybe that was justification enough.

Lilia awakened, feeling like something one of her mother's cats might have left on the kitchen floor.

At least she could move, although her body's response was still more lethargic than she might have hoped. She wondered whether her neurons were patching through a third world satellite feed instead of using her internal highways and byways to get the job done.

At least, she had awakened on time.

One glance into her closet and bathroom revealed that the intrusion hadn't been just a bad dream. Lilia checked her palm and confirmed that it had blithely surrendered everything it knew to person unknown at 01:16:47. It noted the time with perky precision, the faithless piece of junk, as well as the fact that every one of Lilia's passwords had been overridden.

Lilia was shocked. She had layers of passwords on her palm. They could only have been broken with some hotshot illegal software.

Or by the Republic itself.

Lilia thought of Montgomery's warnings and shivered. It hadn't been Montgomery in her room: the intruder had been too slender. And Lilia was sure that some very specific female bits of her would have responded with enthusiasm to Montgomery's presence, no matter how sedated she might be. That narrowed the options to someone less buff than Montgomery.

Who could have been sent by Montgomery to do his dirty work.

On the other hand, Montgomery had been the one to guess that Lilia didn't keep the good stuff on her palm. She couldn't believe that he'd bother with a palm rape.

Some individual unnamed had spiked something she'd consumed with a little pharmaceutical present, then left it to do its magic before breaking into her room. One of the glasses of wine she'd had in the lobby bar must have been doctored for her displeasure.

Too bad she didn't remember who had brought all of her drinks. There had been the first one from Blake. Mike had fetched her another. She'd gotten two for herself. Rhys—the creep—had bought a round, then sent his little weasel around to deliver another. What had the kid's name been? Nicholas. He'd talked mostly to Lilia's breasts, she remembered that.

It was oh-so-tempting to ask Montgomery for help. There had to be a hotel security vid, which he could access officially.

Lilia could offer sexual pleasure in exchange.

His evil twin might go for that deal, but she had a feeling she'd be seeing his officious cop side from here on in.

It was too bad, really.

MONTGOMERY HEARD the pleasure fringe as he drew closer. This zone of New Gotham was far from subdued and certainly not asleep. Cathouses were lit brightly and laughter carried through open doorways. Jazz music drifted from the windows of buildings filled with secrets and velvet shadows. Montgomery bought a handful of tokens and jingled them in his pocket as he progressed.

He always enjoyed the transition, the delicious sense that he was heading directly into temptation, if not damnation. There was joy to be found in the sensation of being human and alive, a luxury that he found alluring and seductive. He liked the vitality in the pleasure fringe, a savoring of life in defiance of how the Republic wished to constrain such pleasures, which he found refreshing and invigorating.

He didn't doubt that Lilia felt the same way about pleasure fringes. She was more alive than anyone he'd known—and tempting as a result. Distracting and seductive. He could sense the promise of humanity in her rebellious attitude and defiance, her determination and optimism. He could see the merit of saving mankind, if they had all possessed the noble recklessness of Lilia.

He wondered whether anyone other than Fitzgerald knew the location and design of Lilia's tattoos.

On the cusp of the pleasure fringe, the establishments seemed just a whisper from being legit. Any given bar could have been a restaurant, with a slightly different menu and clientele. The whores could have been women who worked in other occupations. The shade collecting money at the door of the peep house could have passed for norm beyond the neon lights, where he wouldn't have been dressed to display his hermaphroditism so well.

In the main traffic areas of the pleasure fringe, the stimulants were predictable and reasonably tame: there was caffeine and alcohol and cocaine. Clothing was scant but not tattered; flesh was unscarred, at least beneath the light of artifice. A citizen could buy sex toys or jewelry or cigarettes with tokens, and the purchase could never be traced. Clusters of citizens, mostly teenage boys, wandered in packs, discovering forbidden pleasures. The streets were fairly busy and there was a festive atmosphere.

As Montgomery moved farther into the pleasure fringe, though, the streets became rougher. The whores looked meaner. The shades were more radically mutated and more of them sold their bodies, or the sight of their bodies, right in the street. The bars began to look like destinations of no return, and Montgomery knew better than to buy himself a drink. The drugs for sale were plainer and their effects less easy to predict. There were dangers in the shadows. The rules were almost nonexistent.

This was where the controlling fingers of the Republic seldom reached and, given how little of merit was there, Montgomery believed that to have been a deliberate choice. The worst a citizen could do to himself in the deep fringe was self-destruct.

And maybe that was, in a sad way, performing a civic duty.

Was he being followed? Montgomery was never certain, so he acted as if he was. He impulsively ducked through a darkened doorway, passed through a grubby restaurant and into the dirty kitchen behind it. He ignored the protest of the cook and the scuttle of rats as he leapt down the access to the netherzones.

The accesses were usually in service zones, given that shades were the ones who used them. In the pleasure fringe, the accesses were seldom secured: this world was dangerous enough that it was unimaginable that anything worse could emanate from below.

Montgomery pulled his laze as he descended to the only level that existed in this part of town. He glanced back as the cook shouted again.

He *was* being followed.

Montgomery broke into a trot, dodging from shadow to shadow. Few people in the pleasure zone could afford slaves for power generation, so these netherzones were mostly deserted. The hidden passageways also tended to be simplistic in layout, lacking barriers and dead ends. Montgomery chose one stairway that smelled of perfume, guessing what he'd find at the summit.

He was right. He emerged in a boudoir with peeling gold paint on the walls, mirrors on the ceiling, and a pair of female shades entangled on the bed. This whorehouse had a Victorian motif: the draperies and gilt were as excessive as they were worn.

The redheaded whore had a third breast. The other had skin the color of coffee and luscious dark lashes. He couldn't see her defect and didn't want to know. The women were half naked and kissing, rolling across their mattress with such pleasure that Montgomery felt badly for interrupting them.

"Break time's over," he murmured and they jumped.

The brunette swore like a sailor and threw a pillow at him.

"Who are you?" demanded the other.

"It doesn't matter." Montgomery tossed them each a pair of tokens. "There might be a customer coming, one who likes a fight."

"Yum," said the redheaded one as she straightened her custom bustier and checked her lip stain in the gilt-edged mirror.

"My favorite," said the brunette.

"We could take you both," the redhead suggested with a hard stare.

"No time, unfortunately."

The brunette rolled from the bed and pulled on a poet shirt. The redhead lit a pair of candles in crystal-hung candelabra. "Lock the door from the outside, would you?"

"My pleasure," Montgomery said.

"You'd have to stay for that," the redhead said, sliding her tongue across her upper lip in invitation.

"Impossible, since I was never here." Montgomery left another pair of tokens on the dresser and the brunette smiled.

"There's the kind of man dreams are made of," she murmured. "He wants only silence and is prepared to pay for it."

"And leaves promptly." The redhead glanced at the door.

When Montgomery looked back from the threshold, the tokens had already been secreted away. He locked the door from the other side, then moved silently down the hall and into another room.

The blond whore being taken against the wall looked over her customer's shoulder in alarm, but Montgomery shook his head and held a finger to his lips. She had a keloid on her cheek, and the scar tissue had been augmented with a red tattoo to look even more like a crab than was typical. She'd even put sparkles on it and otherwise was quite pretty.

She glanced at her heaving customer and hesitated in promising her silence, until Montgomery placed two tokens on her dresser. Her eyes narrowed until he added another, then she nodded.

She gasped all the while as if lost in pleasure. Montgomery pointed downward, to the netherzones, then indicated the room, silently asking for the access point.

She arched a brow and looked at the tokens.

Montgomery added a token, but she only gave a minute shake of her head. When the fifth was added to the pile, she indicated a tapestry hanging on one wall. Montgomery understood that the access was behind it. She caught the back of her client's head in her hand and kissed him with false ardor, distracting him from Montgomery's progress across the room.

Montgomery headed down into the darkness again, without the climaxing client ever knowing he had been there.

He repeated his trick three times, passing through the kitchen of an oyster shack, jumping from the roof of a second whorehouse to that of a rowdy bar. He pushed through the crowd at the bar, disappeared into the band, ducked through the basement and into a service tunnel. There were old electrical conduits on the walls and grates in the floor that emitted the scent of sewage. Montgomery ran along it for as long as he could stand the smell, then emerged through a grate into a deserted alley.

It was darker and he heard the faint tinkle of calliope music from the circus. He moved down an adjacent alley, heading for his destination. It was after three and he had no time left to play games.

Fortunately, it wasn't far from this point to the first corner of this earthly paradise that Montgomery had seen. The moon was full and the clouds thinner than usual, the silvery light creating mysterious shadows in the night.

Montgomery walked quickly. Rachel had taught him to move with stealthy silence. He walked the last section of road with a heavy heart, feeling the lack of her presence, hearing her admonition to never let himself become emotionally involved with humans.

He must have broken that edict long before he'd met Lilia, because he missed Rachel and her blunt pragmatism.

He'd fallen further than he'd realized.

Could he ever go back?

Even assuming that he completed his mission and Rachel's, did he want to? It was a shocking thought. Everything he'd done had been geared toward regaining his wings and returning to what he knew.

But he recalled Lilia's kiss, the pleasure of her pressed

against him, and wasn't convinced that he wanted a life without sensation.

Was it better to feel pleasure and even pain than to never feel anything at all?

Once, Montgomery would have been positive of his answer but on this night, he yearned for Rachel's company and Lilia's touch and wasn't nearly so sure.

He emerged from the last group of trees and shuddered at the first sight of the warehouse, just as he always did.

Then he walked onward with purpose.

He'd returned a dozen times, despite Rachel's warnings to the contrary, but if he hadn't had such a strong memory of the place, he would never have guessed its secret use. It was made of red brick and had been a factory in the nineteenth century. Once there had been a multitude of high windows of small dense glass panes; now there were boards nailed over many of the windows. Inside was darkness and the crunch of glass underfoot.

The fields beyond the building had reverted to scrub. Queen Anne's lace had been blooming there when Montgomery had become earthbound, the frothy white flower heads one of the only things he could find attractive about his new home. The moon too had been full on that night, which seemed to have been a thousand years before.

He had changed in so many ways. He had been seduced by pleasure and sensation, more thoroughly than he had ever expected. He cared about humans, collectively and individually, something he'd never thought possible.

Was the change irrevocable?

In this night's cool darkness, Montgomery could see golden plumes of ragweed moving in the breeze. They were past their prime, their scent still pungent enough to tickle his nose.

The warehouse was utterly silent.

It seemed almost to absorb sound.

Montgomery hesitated before entering it. There was a lump in his throat and a tightness in his gut. It showed no signs of diminishing, especially when he returned here.

But he had too many questions to turn back now. He didn't even know for sure whether the angels had a fixed schedule or whether they simply did what needed to be done when it needed to be done. When he realized that he could have made this journey for nothing, he felt a very human pang of despair.

Was he becoming one of them? Or would the angels know when he needed their counsel?

There was only one way to find out.

Montgomery paused inside the building for a moment to let his eyes adjust to its darkness. The floor was rotted away in some places and it paid to be careful. He was climbing the stairs to the room that the angels favored as a pearly light began to emanate from ahead of him.

The light ran like quicksilver, filling the cracks of the floor and flowing along them, a gleaming luster that was reminiscent of opals and pearls. It steadily grew in brilliance and couldn't have been mistaken for anything other than what it was.

Angelfire.

They were coming.

Montgomery stepped into the room, shielding his eyes from their brilliance. He felt awe as their light touched him.

He had been like them, and he had chosen to throw it away.

He'd never understood that it could be a permanent choice.

Montgomery fell to his knees in the room, the light of the angels searing even though he had his eyes tightly closed. A bit late, he realized that he could no longer communicate with his fellows by thought alone, and that they didn't make any sounds. Could they hear him if he spoke?

He had to try. He prayed for guidance, he prayed for answers, he prayed for a way to complete Rachel's mission.

Most of all, he prayed that his former fellows would understand.

MICHELINE MET Lilia at the entrance to the circus, indicating that Lilia should take a bicycle from the communal rack. Micheline had already chosen a smaller bike with pink streamers on the handles and rode away without looking back. She made good speed, heading onto the darkened road on the far side of the circus.

It was shadowed and deserted. Lilia shuddered, refused to think about darkness, and chose a bike.

They rode for a good twenty minutes, moving farther from New Gotham, and Lilia wondered how far they had to go. Finally, the little girl pointed ahead and to the right. "There," she said.

Lilia could only see a copse of trees, their crowns silhouetted against the night sky and fathomless shadows beneath them. The cluster of trees troubled Lilia, as it seemed darker and more isolated. It looked lonely, to her view, too far from city lights. She might not trust people individually, but she felt better with more of them around her.

It was too isolated here.

Micheline rode on, untroubled. If anything, the child seemed excited. Lilia could hear a chirping sound that must have been crickets and could see a multitude of stars overhead.

She thought about her visitor of the night before, of being trapped alone and powerless to his whim, and shuddered again.

Micheline rode directly into the heart of the darkness beneath the trees, holding her feet out to either side and whooping with joy as she raced down the slight hill.

Lilia couldn't quite echo her mood. She biked after Micheline and was surprised to find a town beyond the cluster of trees.

An abandoned town. There wasn't a whisper of breath on its streets, not a sign of life, but not because of the hour. A glimmer of light caught Lilia's eye and she glanced down, noting that her radiation patch was emitting a slight glow. She looked past the trees and line of low buildings to see the silhouette of Gotham far to the right.

It wasn't a high radiation reading so it must have been a trick of seasonal winds to send the fallout plume back in this direction. The Republic, known for its caution in such matters, had probably ordered the town to be evacuated.

And the people had never come back. Lilia slowed her pedaling. It had been a small town, with an old main street lined with shops and apartments on the second floor overhead. There was an intimacy about this town, though, something about the scale of it that made its desertion more heart wrenching.

She could easily believe that she'd crossed through a portal to somewhere both within and beyond the Republic. She could have traveled back in time, back to a place where her skirts would have been the fashion for the first time.

But there was nothing whimsical about towns emptied because of the toxic plumes from old cities. Gotham, after all, had been abandoned for the same reason.

The difference was that in this town, Lilia had no sense that she was being watched. She felt like she was the last person alive, which was a much more creepy prospect.

She obviously needed more sleep.

At least, she knew where Micheline had borrowed supplies. Lilia was relieved that the little girl would take on less radiation over time than if she'd really been going into the old city.

Micheline, meanwhile, had leapt from her bike. She started to run toward an old brick warehouse. "Hurry!" she cried. "They're coming."

Lilia didn't express her skepticism. She left her bike beside the child's, then followed Micheline into the deserted building.

It was pitch dark inside and that was enough to make

Lilia hesitate. Micheline scampered across the wooden
floors with a confidence that Lilia felt obliged to echo.

She followed Micheline up the stairs with trepidation,
hearing the building creak all around her. Thousands of
small glass windows admitted the night's light, moonlight
slicing through some, others boarded to darkness. Glass
crunched under her boots when they were close to the ex-
terior walls, but Micheline headed to the center of the
building.

There was abandoned equipment that Lilia couldn't
name, shapes of wood and steel and rusted iron that
loomed out of the shadows on either side. There were holes
in the floor that had to be circumnavigated, holes that gave
glimpses of endless darkness below. Lilia smelled damp
wood, cold stone, and the wetness of the earth from those
openings.

She heard rats.

Or maybe bigger creatures of the night.

That made her hurry after the child.

Micheline had paused on the threshold of a room with
double doors. A filthy skylight far overhead glowed silver
with the light of the moon, although Lilia's eyes hadn't
adjusted enough to let her see the room's contents.

There were no angels, though. She knew that because
she couldn't see their light, that curious opalescent light
she'd seen once before.

"Angels," Micheline breathed with awe.

Lilia looked again. "No," she said. "No angels."

"Angels." Micheline spoke with confidence.

Was the little girl playing a game with her?

There was no chance to answer that. Micheline pivoted to face Lilia, holding her finger to her lips. When
Lilia nodded agreement and reached for the child's hand,
Micheline evaded her touch and scampered into the
room. Lilia moved quickly and quietly after her, suddenly afraid that something would happen to the child.
She didn't want to answer to Stevia for that.

Micheline fell to her knees and threw out her arms, her

pose one of rapture. She tipped back her head, her eyes squeezed tightly shut and began to whisper fervently.

That wasn't what stopped Lilia in her tracks. She'd seen people and shades do lots of strange things in her time, after all.

It wasn't the pearly light that began to glow in the middle of the room that brought her to a halt either. She'd seen that light once before.

It was Montgomery's delicious twin, his black faux leather cloak spread around him in a swirl, on his knees, his head bowed.

Lilia stared. The angel light touched the back of his head as lovingly as a caress, and she saw that his eyes were closed. His gloved hands were folded before his face, his posture submissive.

That must have been why her mouth went dry.

THE LIGHT grew ever brighter around Montgomery and he felt the room heat by increments. There was a vibration in his ears, a high sound that masked all other noise. He could have been surrounded by ten thousand humming bees, each emanating that pearly light.

"*Welcome.*"

He heard the greeting in his mind, more of his own thought than an utterance. He opened himself to the angel's voice, knowing that this communication was difficult for both of them.

Something brushed his head, ethereal fingertips sweeping his brow. It was a tender caress, one that made him think of a woman's hand. He had an urge to look upon the angel, but there was a pressure on the back of his neck, as if the angel sensed his desire but was reminding him to not look.

Flesh gave pain and pleasure, strength and weakness.

Montgomery understood the attitude of prayer as he never had before. He surrendered to the visiting angel, trusting her implicitly, and heard her more clearly.

"You must take Raziel's burden."

"Yes," Montgomery thought. *"But I need to know what it was."*

Silence stretched long and he feared that their communication was broken. He felt the angel straining, felt his thoughts burn with her presence.

Then the words came clearly again.

"You must identify the Council of Three, and eliminate them."

The imperative grew. There was music in this thoughts, half-forgotten potent music that lightened his heart and filled him with optimism.

Optimism he had forgotten.

"There is a divine plan and it is good."

Trust welled in Montgomery's heart. Faith in the future, in divine omniscience, in goodness triumphing over evil.

And he was aware of his role in the transaction.

He had to identify the Council of Three, whatever that meant.

Then he could return to the splendor he had known. He could return home. At the sound of the angel's voice, he yearned for his old invincibility and power. He wanted to shake free of the doubts that had plagued him since his arrival here. He wanted to be purposeful and confident and resilient again.

He wanted his wings back.

He would do whatever was necessary to earn them.

"It is not in you to be compromised, Munkar. Yours is the ability to see into the secret hearts of men, and that power will guide you to truth."

At the sound of his old name, Montgomery's tears spilled. The name resonated within him in its rightness and he knew, no matter that his form had changed, he was yet what once he had been.

"What of Raziel?"

There was sadness emanating from the angel even before she spoke. *"She cannot return to us now."*

"Then she is lost?"

"Her soul has returned to God, a divine spark rejoining with its source. She is no longer Raziel; Raziel is gone but her spirit continues."

It was both less and more than Montgomery had hoped.

It certainly was not a fate he wished to share.

He felt the brush of the angel's fingertips on the back of his neck. It was a sisterly caress, a mark of affection even though it burned slightly on his skin. It reminded him of the simplicity of the angelic state, of how clearly he had been able to think without the distraction of his body's hopes and demands.

Beneath her caress, his thoughts cleared and he was aware only of his need to complete his assigned task. And if distraction presented itself, he had to clear away its obstacle, so that he could fulfil his quest. Purpose filled him and he pushed to his feet, turning away from the angel's glory.

When he had taken a dozen steps, he opened his eyes and found himself surrounded by radiant angelfire. It shone through his hands, illuminating the bones and vessels, making him translucent. He meant to turn back, but he saw Lilia then. She stood in the shadows twenty feet ahead of him, her eyes round with surprise, gloved and booted and veiled and corseted.

Tempting.

Alluring.

Distracting.

Montgomery knew then what he had to do. His quest was all important, the risks higher than he had understood. He could not let desire for Lilia cloud his judgment.

Which meant he had to sate that desire.

Immediately.

XII

MONTGOMERY WAS surrounded by the angel's light as he strode toward Lilia. Her heart stopped cold. He was every bit as impressive without his pseudoskin, broad and tall and irresistible.

Determined.

It was time, Lilia decided, to get over her marathon run of chastity.

Montgomery looked inclined to help with that.

His gaze didn't waver as he closed the distance between them. He didn't hesitate or make small talk or pretend his destination was anywhere other than it was. There was only Montgomery in Lilia's world, his desire for her and the desire he fed in her.

For once in her life, lust was simple.

Montgomery reached to touch her cheek, his hand slipping smoothly past her ear, into her hair. Lilia felt the faux leather slide across her skin and parted her lips in silent invitation.

Montgomery bent his head, as if only claiming what was his rightful due, and kissed her deeply

It was faster and hotter than the last kiss, more impatient and less restrained. This kiss made demands that Lilia wanted to fulfill. She liked that he was less controlled.

She liked that he could be impulsive, even reckless.

She loved being the woman who had shaken his composure.

Montgomery cupped her face in his hands, holding her captive, tipping her toward him as he deepened his kiss. Lilia welcomed him. His tongue eased between her lips and Lilia let her own kiss turn demanding. Her enthusiasm didn't seem to surprise him.

In fact, he responded in kind. The careful and composed version of Montgomery was nowhere in sight. This Montgomery was imperious and impatient, demanding and delicious. Lilia wanted all of him.

Immediately.

He shoved his hands through her hair, discarding her hat and veil with impatience. He scattered the pins from her hair, kissing her as if he couldn't get enough of her. He spread her hair over her shoulders, then ran his hands over her curves with proprietary ease. He caught her closer, his hands bracketing her waist, and lifted her against his muscled chest. Lilia's hands were full of faux fur and faux leather, of animal and man and Montgomery. She held tight. His eyes gleamed as he smiled and Lilia's heart skipped a beat.

"Kiss me as if you mean it," he said, his words almost a growl. There was a gleam of challenge in his eyes and Lilia was only too glad to accept his terms.

"Only if you do the same," she dared and saw the flash of his smile before his mouth closed over hers.

Their next kiss was all tongue and teeth, all power and heat. They could have devoured each other. Lilia was on her toes, rubbing herself against him like a cat in heat. She pushed open the collar of his shirt, shoving aside the extravagant purple lace to kiss the warm flesh of his throat. She felt his pulse beneath her lips and ran her hands beneath his coat, wanting to feel all of him, taste all of him.

Montgomery kissed like a man driven to possess her, a man pushed past his boundaries. His mouth roved over her jaw, her ear, into her hair, nipping and tasting, as if he would own her with his touch. Lilia loved the honesty of his demands and when he caught her up in his arms, she knew what she wanted.

"I need you inside me," she whispered. She saw satisfaction flash in his eyes before he claimed her lips again.

She surrendered to sensation. He carried her to an adjacent room and laid her on a pile of canvas sacks in one corner. It might have been a feather bed for all Lilia cared. She could hear Micheline singing nonsense to herself in the other room, absorbed in whatever fascinated small shades. Lilia had a strange sense that the child was safe and didn't question it.

Not now.

Not with Montgomery on top of her.

Not with Montgomery touching her as if he'd never get enough.

Lilia loved the weight of his hips over hers. His reevlar codpiece drove into her own pelvis, a precursor to the real thing. She rolled her hips and he murmured a promise against her throat. Her fingers were snared in the velvet of his jacket, discovering his muscled strength beneath the glorious texture of the fabric.

"I need to see you," he said, his words hot and low. Lilia needed no more encouragement to get naked. He rolled her shoulders to one side, his hands making quick work of the back fastening of her dress. He spread it down over her shoulders with a smooth stroke and more of her temporary tattoo peeled away. Montgomery glanced at it, then at her, and shook his head minutely. He seemed amused.

Lilia didn't care what he thought of the tattoo or the Republic's motto. Her elbows were briefly trapped against her waist, snared in the partially unfastened dress, and for once in her life, Lilia didn't mind being captive. He pushed her shift aside, baring the curves of her breasts and bent his head to taste her. He eased her nipple free of her corset with his tongue and Lilia gasped with pleasure. She pulled her arms free, winding them around his neck and pulling him closer.

More. She wanted more.

When he finally lifted his head again, he held her shoulders in his hands, bracing his weight on his elbows.

"Nothing to say?" he teased and Lilia smiled.

"I told you what I wanted."

His smile was so wicked that it made her shiver. "A gentleman would give you a chance to change your mind," he mused, his gloved fingertips grazing her nipples.

Lilia arched her back. "I want you, gentleman or not. I want you now."

His finger unhooked the top clasp of her corset between her breasts. His eyes were as green as emeralds and glittered with intent. He cupped her breasts in his hands, sliding his thumbs across the nipples so that they stood at attention. He trailed a line of burning kisses down her throat.

Lilia knew where he was going with that. She leaned back, closed her eyes, and moaned when his mouth closed over her breast. She clutched the back of his head when his tongue flicked across her nipple. He rolled her other nipple between finger and thumb, driving her to distraction.

His caress felt so good.

Lilia had never felt so feminine or so savored in her life. She liked that he didn't seem to be in a rush, but was discovering her one increment at a time.

She was mussed and rumpled and aroused beyond belief when Montgomery finally slid down and ducked beneath her skirts. He cast the fullness of her petticoats aside, leaving her thighs surrounded by frills and lace. He braced his shoulders between her thighs and gripped her ankles in his hands. Lilia was open to his marauding tongue, captive to the pleasure he was determined to grant, and there was nowhere she would have rather been.

What power did this man have over her, that he could make her forget everything she'd ever known? Why was it that he could give her so much pleasure so readily? She felt both lucky and cheated, because she'd found him now but had been so long without him. Desire drove everything else from her thoughts.

That should have worried her, Lilia knew. That she trusted a virtual stranger was shocking, but not as shocking as the sensations Montgomery launched with his tongue. He held her down so that she couldn't squirm away. She writhed and bucked as he took her to the brink of orgasm.

He moved suddenly, cheating her of the thunder of release in the last moment. Lilia had no chance to complain before he returned to his task, bringing her even more quickly to the cusp of pleasure.

When he halted at the key moment again, she groaned in protest. Montgomery lifted his head, holding her down easily as she fought him with dissatisfaction.

"You tease!" she charged, furious with him for denying her. "I won't beg."

"You don't have to." He laughed, a marvelous sound that made Lilia's heart leap, then lowered his head again. "It's better if you have to work for it," he murmured, his eyes gleaming with intent over her skirts. "Everything is, Lil."

Lilia might have argued in favor of immediate gratification, but instead she gasped as his mouth closed over her once more. He was more demanding this time, rougher and faster.

Lilia loved it. For once, she wasn't the demanding partner, the one who wanted to explore the full range of sensation possible, the one who was a little bit too interested in physical pleasure. Montgomery wasn't daunted by her desire—he encouraged it and used it to redouble her satisfaction.

She respected that.

She could get used to that.

She wondered whether she'd finally met her amorous match.

She twisted beneath his caress, halfway thinking he'd cheat her again. She clutched his one hand in hers, spread her knees wide, and yearned for whatever he wanted to give her.

Again, she drew near the cusp of release, that simmering heat moving beneath her skin and driving her wild. She'd never been so aroused, never needed release so badly. Just when Lilia was sure she couldn't stand it anymore, Montgomery lifted his head. She moaned, but he moved swiftly to bury himself inside of her.

The surety of his move made Lilia gasp, the size of him made her sigh. "My turn," she said and he smiled in anticipation. She rolled over then, sitting astride him and holding him down. She moved slowly, loving how he caught his breath with pleasure. He gripped her buttocks and pulled her against him in silent demand, his eyes shining as he watched her. Lilia rolled her hips, liking the sight of his surprise, loving the feel of him inside her.

She might have teased him just as he had teased her, but Montgomery didn't give her the chance. When he was hardest and thickest, he caught her nape in one hand and pulled her toward him for a crushing kiss. His hand moved beneath her skirts and between them at the same time.

Lilia shivered as he touched her again. She clutched his shoulders and held on. There was plum lace against her skin and Montgomery's mouth locked on hers. When he moved inside her, she heard herself moan.

His gloved thumb moved against her in a deliberate and possessive caress; his other hand gripped her buttock and drove her against him in an insistent rhythm. Lilia felt her passion building to a crescendo all over again.

"Mine," he murmured into her ear, his assertion driving her over the edge. Heat surging through her veins, Lilia cried out with pleasure and tumbled on top of him.

Release left her trembling and edgy, limp yet unsated. He was still hard inside her. Montgomery studied her and once again he saw more than she expected anyone to see.

"Again," he said, his agile fingers allowing no surrender.

"I can't."

"You will," he insisted and Lilia felt her body recognize the truth. He rolled her to her back and claimed her anew, moving with sure strokes. She had the sense that he knew her better than she knew herself. He watched her so intently that she knew he would accept no compromise, that she could have no secrets from him.

At least in bed.

He demanded more and Lilia felt her body respond. It was wonderful. Their desire wasn't just equally matched: they each fed the other, the desire of one redoubling that of the other in a relentless crescendo.

Lilia arched beneath Montgomery, rubbing her bare breasts against his jacket. She felt wanton—she was half nude and he was almost fully dressed. She wanted to knot her legs around him and press her skin against his. She wanted to try every position she knew and learn some new ones. She wanted to spend days in bed with Montgomery's insatiable twin.

Once was not going to be enough. Not with this man.

Montgomery smiled a knowing smile as his fingers did their magic. Lilia felt her lips part in astonishment as the tide rose within her again. She rolled her hips, pulling him deeper inside.

"I want you naked," she whispered and he arched a brow.

"Too bad," he teased, then winked.

Lilia laughed. "Can't hold out that long?"

"I *won't* hold out that long." There was a very male gleam of pride in his gaze. "Neither will you."

He was so confident that Lilia would have liked to have proven him wrong, just on principle. She only managed to unfasten the collar of his shirt, to press her hands against his chest, before his touch distracted her again.

Montgomery knew his effect upon her, and he was doing it deliberately. It was as if he'd planned this seduction all along. Lilia found that idea surprisingly appealing, probably because she found Montgomery so appealing.

Especially when he smiled, as he did now. There was more to this man than met the eye and she found herself wanting to trade secrets with him. The leisurely curve of his lips as he watched her, the satisfaction in his eyes, the sense that he was holding back only to wait for her, all combined to push Lilia toward the edge again.

His arm tightened beneath her, holding her shoulders so that she was pinned against his chest. He kissed her with new force and she rose against him. She knotted her ankles around his waist, welcoming him deeper inside. Montgomery accepted her invitation, then flicked his fingers against her with surety.

And she was conquered again. Lilia shouted with pleasure and convulsed around him. This time, Montgomery roared as well, and they collapsed trembling in each other's arms. He murmured her name, then his eyes closed.

Lilia stared at the mucky skylight overhead as she caught her breath, her hand moving across the back of Montgomery's neck as he dozed. She was dazed and dazzled, content with sex for the first time since she could remember. She had no desire to move, no impatience to close the door on intimacy and don her armor again.

This man challenged her and understood her as no man ever had.

It was probably a bad thing that she didn't care.

It was definitely a bad thing that she heard that echo of male laughter again, the same laughter that she'd heard in the old city. Her mouth went dry when she saw that silvery fog slide across the warehouse floor.

STEVIA SIGHED when she heard Micheline come into her tent. Morning had come too soon.

Again.

Stevia stretched and sat up, hunching over her knees as her daily coughing binge began. "Put the kettle on, Micheline," she said when her coughing had slowed. "And bring me that gold bottle, please." Stevia shoved one hand through her hair, rubbed her eyes, and realized there had been no response. "Micheline, stop your daydreaming . . ."

Stevia glanced up in shock as someone much larger than Micheline loomed over the bed. One hand rose to clutch the front of her worn pajamas when she saw the man in a pseudoskin.

A stranger.

He smiled coldly and she knew nothing good would come of this.

Stevia scrambled for the laze beneath her pillow, but her fingers barely brushed it. He was on top of her in a heartbeat, his gloved hand over her mouth. She fought him but her hands slid off the pseudoskin, getting no grip on him. Stevia panicked and kicked, but he was younger and stronger.

He seized her laze, put the muzzle to her temple, then fired.

Stevia didn't even manage to scream.

The only mercy was that she never felt the knife.

As LILIA watched, the skylight brightened, casting a glimmer into the warehouse below. The light was warm, like that of a sunrise, but seemed more pearlescent. It was breathtakingly beautiful.

Even better, it seemed to dispel the silvery fog. Had she imagined it? And the laugh as well? Lilia had an uneasy feeling whenever she thought about the fog, so she decided not to.

Not right now. Instead, she studied Montgomery, the man of two identities, one of which was utterly fascinating. The other, the cop Montgomery, wasn't without his appeal either.

Even in slumber, Montgomery looked formidable and boxy. Even when he dozed, his proximity made her heart leap. He was a man of mystery whose many secrets she wanted to unfold. There was something about Montgomery that got to Lilia, that made her wonder if she'd been right about love being too much trouble or whether she'd dismissed its charms too soon.

He was fabulous in bed too, which didn't hurt. She stretched to kiss his ear, a curious warmth filling her hea

The brightening light shone on his black ear making its glassy surface gleam. Lilia froze and s

Montgomery's stud was back in place.

Which meant that the Republic was watching, and had been watching. No wonder he thought her temporary tattoo was amusing. She had a childish urge to wave to the monitor.

The eye of the Republic wasn't their only audience, though. The light from above took on a familiar opalescent glow.

"Angels!" Micheline exclaimed with delight from the adjacent room and Lilia swore. She'd forgotten her mandate to find more angels, she'd forgotten to guard Micheline, she'd forgotten every doubt she had about Adam Montgomery and his motivations.

In exchange for great sex.

And she didn't regret a thing. That was the most terrifying realization of all.

The man had made Lilia lose her edge.

Lilia was going to get over that, immediately if not sooner.

MONTGOMERY AWAKENED as Lilia shoved him aside. She scrambled to her feet, trying to adjust petticoats and closures with a haste that amused him. She was silhouetted in the light of the arriving angels, which made her look ethereal and bewitching. Her hair was loose, a dark tangle that contrasted with the smooth pallor of her back and the white ruffles of her undergarments. The light touched the muscles in her shoulders as she pivoted and he was captivated all over again by her blend of strength and femininity.

￼was something else he wanted to do all over

gomery rolled to his feet, adjusted his

ached to fasten the back of Lilia's dress

y from his touch, her eyes flashing with

locket she wore spun so hard that it al-

e chain. "Don't you touch me!"

Montgomery lifted his hands away. "A bit late for a change of heart, don't you think?"

Lilia shook a finger at him. "You deliberately distracted me."

He glanced around pointedly. "From what?"

She touched the temporary tattoo on her upper arm. "I forgot what I should never have forgotten." Then she reached and flicked that fingertip at his ear stud.

"It's out of service."

"And if I believe that, you've got some primo real estate in Gotham to sell me," Lilia snapped, her words halting when he lifted a finger.

The glimmer of angelfire crept across the hardwood.

The angels were back.

Lilia wriggled into her dress, fastening the back with no assistance whatsoever, then tapped her booted toe on the moving beam of light.

"There are angels here," she hissed. "They were here before, but this time, you won't distract me from what I need to do."

Her words struck terror into Montgomery.

She spun, her hair still loose, and reached into her skirts. He knew her laze had to be there.

She didn't manage more than two steps. Montgomery was behind her in one stride and clamped his hand over her mouth. He locked his other arm around her waist, trapping her arms against her sides. He held her tightly as he lifted her to her toes. Lilia fought and Montgomery felt her hidden laze against his thigh.

He hoped the safety was on. At such close range, the codpiece might not protect him, especially if the laze was on its highest power setting.

Unfortunately, he couldn't imagine Lilia using anything else.

She tried to kick him, even as the light became brighter, but he held her fast against him. He heard the resonant hum of the angels revealing themselves. Micheline held up her hands between Montgomery and the angelfire, almost basking in the angels' light. Lilia swore and struggled, but Montgomery held on.

"You will be silent," he murmured into her ear. She flashed him a mutinous glare and fought harder. "You will not distract them from their task."

Her eyes narrowed a little then and she stilled. He wasn't sure whether she was thinking about his advice or simply trying to trick him into relaxing, so he didn't release her. They flinched as one at the brightness of the angelfire, Lilia turning her face against his chest. They stood temple to temple, Lilia still trapped within Montgomery's embrace.

And once again, her curves and her perfume distracted him. Apparently, he hadn't sampled the lady's pleasures diligently enough. He was still hungry for whatever she had to offer.

"They'll dim their light in a moment, once they see there's no threat," he whispered and she nodded, her eyes still tightly closed.

Of course, she had seen angels before. He wondered, not for the first time, how Armaros and Baraqiel had surrendered themselves to her. He wondered whether Lilia truly believed that she had been the active player in that exchange.

He wondered if she would admit it, even if she had doubts.

The light dimmed then, and Montgomery opened his eyes to find the room bathed in opalescence. They could have been standing inside a gemstone. A lump rose in his throat at the familiarity of that gleam, one that he had once imagined was common to all of creation.

He'd gotten over that delusion.

On the other hand, it was hard to see the world clearly when surrounded by such bright light.

Three angels were revealed as they gradually eased the full splendor of their light. Their wings were whiter than white and stretched high over their heads. Montgomery felt a tingle as his human body responded to the electric-

FALLEN   199

ity of their presence. He was keenly aware that he was no longer one of them, no longer had much in common with their astounding beauty and grace.

What was Lilia's plan? She had stilled within his grasp, her eyes wide, and no longer battled him. Did she feel the same awe as he did? Or was she scheming a way to harvest all three angels for the circus?

That wouldn't happen as long as he had anything to say about the matter. Montgomery thought about Lilia's laze and tightened his grip on her as the tallest angel glanced his way.

Montgomery's heart stopped in recognition. It was the surgeon.

Which meant the other standing angel was the assistant, and the third, the third was making the sacrifice.

His mind stalled on the truth of what was about to happen, then his heart began to pound.

No. Not here. Not now. Not in front of his very eyes.

"Yes. Here and now."

The affirmation echoed in his thoughts, stunning him. Montgomery's knees went weak as the middle angel kneeled and bared his back. Montgomery's throat worked soundlessly but the surgeon merely nodded in his direction.

"He knows you," Lilia whispered behind his hand. "How does he know you?"

"You shouldn't watch this," Montgomery could only say. Lilia studied him with something that might have been concern. She frowned and looked back at the angels as the middle one put his forehead on the ground.

"What are they doing?" she murmured, her gaze dancing over the scene. "What's going on?"

Micheline sang quietly.

The surgeon raised his finger, kissed its tip, then bent toward the volunteer. Montgomery didn't want to watch but he couldn't help it. His gaze locked on the point where the volunteer's wings joined his back and he saw the spark of the first cut.

There was no blood, of course, only the brief and brilliant shimmer of light, as if an inner radiance was leaking through the wound. Lilia gasped.

The first wing fell a moment later. It looked lifeless on the floor of the warehouse, dulled and wrong and dead.

"Sweet mother of God," Lilia whispered in horror.

The surgeon glanced up sternly and Montgomery locked his hand over Lilia's mouth again.

He bent, placing his lips against her ear. "You mustn't distract them," he breathed and she nodded. It seemed as if she couldn't look away either, and she gripped his fingers with her own hands. He had the sense she was clinging to him, not trying to loosen his grip.

He didn't release her anyway.

The volunteer sobbed, his shoulders shaking with the trauma of his experience. The surgeon bent and slid his finger along the open wound. It seared closed with his touch, the volunteer straightening in shock at the pain.

Montgomery knew that pain. He knew that trauma and he knew that shock. His mouth was dry and, deep inside, he began to tremble. He was reliving his own sacrifice, more vividly than he would have preferred.

The removal of the second wing seemed almost anticlimactic, as it had to Montgomery not long before. The volunteer wept silently, the two diagonal lines on his back shining vivid red. He no longer gleamed with the opalescent light of the angels.

The assistant picked up the fallen wings and gathered the few loose feathers with efficiency. The surgeon implanted the volunteer's palm and the datachip in the back of his neck as the naked volunteer trembled.

Montgomery remembered.

He saw the tenderness in the surgeon's expression. He saw the compassion and even regret.

Then the surgeon framed the volunteer's face gently in his hands, bent, and kissed his cheeks each in turn. His manner was patient and loving, his compassion brought familiar tears to Montgomery's eyes. The volunteer wept openly and made incoherent noises that clearly startled him.

His first sounds.

His first tears.

His first experience of becoming earthbound.

The surgeon straightened and spared one piercing glance to Montgomery. It was a command.

Montgomery instantly understood that this volunteer would be his responsibility. He didn't know how to ensure that this volunteer merged into society, how to hide or protect him. He didn't know who the volunteer was or what his mission might be.

He only knew that he had a duty to pass along the kindness Rachel had done for him.

And he would do it. He would find a way.

Montgomery nodded once, noting that the surgeon didn't appear to be surprised by his agreement. It might have been arranged long in advance, a memory that Montgomery had lost along with his wings and his old name.

He had a new role now. On earth.

Until he fulfilled his quest.

The radiance of the angels increased steadily, so that Montgomery had to narrow his eyes against their brightness. The volunteer began to wail, evidently as he realized that he was being abandoned.

Just before Montgomery had to close his eyes completely, the surgeon turned to Micheline. He smiled sweetly, then reached back a hand to the child.

She didn't need a second invitation. She squealed with pleasure and ran to him, seizing his hand. Montgomery saw the angel lift her up just before the departing pair became too bright to watch.

"No!" Lilia screamed, tearing Montgomery's hand from her mouth. "I promised to take care of her!" She broke free of his grip and flung herself across the warehouse floor.

By the time she reached the spot where the angels had

been standing, they had vanished as surely as if they had never been.

And Micheline was gone with them.

Lilia turned in place, looking up at the skylight overhead. Her expression was desperate and anguished.

"Come back!" she cried. "Bring back the child!"

Montgomery heard in her voice that she knew her command was futile. He heard her despair and impotence. More than that, Montgomery heard the anguish of a younger Lilia losing her child to the Society of Nuclear Darwinists and the Republic, right in the maternity ward.

And he saw the truth of her heart.

Lilia would sacrifice anything, even herself, to protect someone weaker. She worked for the circus to save shades from the Republic's slave dens. And he realized that she had become a Nuclear Darwinist in the first place to find her child.

She was a shade hunter, but she had hunted one particular shade. Had the child died before or after Lilia had found her?

The volunteer moaned and reached for Lilia's skirts. He was still on his knees, still shaking from his ordeal. His hand closed over the fabric and tightened convulsively. Lilia turned and looked down at him. Montgomery halfway knew what to expect from her, given his realization, but she surprised him anyway.

Her features softened with a compassion that touched his heart.

She bent and touched the volunteer's face, gently easing away his tears, her touch as tender as that of the surgeon. This was her true nature, and one she rarely showed. On a daily basis, she spoke sharply and shielded herself because her heart was too vulnerable.

And that heart had been injured too many times.

"What have they done to you?" she whispered. "And why?"

The volunteer wailed wordlessly and Lilia gathered him into her arms, rocking him slightly in consolation.

She stood, holding him close against her left side, then pulled her laze.

She aimed it at Montgomery's unprotected chest. Her tone changed, becoming cold once more. She was the heartless shade hunter, the woman who would supposedly do anything for a price.

The problem was that Montgomery now knew which was Lilia's mask and which was her reality.

"If you think you're going to harvest him for the Republic, Montgomery, you'll have to take me down first." Lilia looked Montgomery up and down, then met his gaze once again. She removed the safety on the laze with her thumb. "Just between you and me, I don't think you're fast enough."

Montgomery folded his arms across his chest, knowing Lilia wouldn't shoot him, knowing she wanted him to believe otherwise.

He would have bet his last cred that Lilia would protect this volunteer with her very life. He was also sure that she had the bootleg software on her palm to merge him into society without anyone knowing the difference.

The solution he needed to fulfil his promise to the surgeon had found him.

He and Lil would make a perfect team.

XIII

LILIA HAD done a lot of unconventional things in her time, but holding a laze on a man while his semen seeped into her petticoats had to be a first.

Especially as she wasn't holding Montgomery hostage in demand for another round of pleasure.

He might have been in this situation a thousand times before, though, for all that it troubled him. He folded his arms across his chest, his gaze assessing and his expression impassive.

"What are you going to do with him?" he asked. "Harvest him for the bounty?"

"I'd never consign anyone to the Republic's slave dens."

"Is the circus so much better?"

"Ask the shades that sign up in droves."

"What about the angels?" He arched a brow. "Or should I say angel-shades?"

Lilia spared a glance to the spot where the angels had stood and down at the shuddering soul in her embrace. The red welts on his back were already fading. "I thought they were shades. I thought they *had* to be shades." She met Montgomery's gaze and found him more inscrutable than usual. "You said you believed in angels before this."

He didn't respond.

Lilia remembered her sense that the one angel had known Montgomery. "They knew you. Did you know they would come, the way Micheline knew?"

"Did she know? I wasn't sure." Montgomery glanced at the skylight overhead. The light coming through it had turned rosy and Lilia guessed that dawn was approaching. His move made his ear stud gleam.

"I guess now the Republic knows, as well," she said, not hiding her anger. "Or did they always know? Are you their spy?"

He smiled slowly. "I don't believe my ear stud is working."

Lilia told herself that her heart only went thump because she was a sucker for rebels and rule breakers. "You left it out yesterday."

"And it was embedded again, more tightly, when I reported for duty. You should know by now that you can't use the same trick over and over again, Lil."

She tried to not like how he said her name.

She lost.

Montgomery smiled, looking wicked and unpredictable again. Lilia's pulse leapt right on cue. "The transmitter in my cube that picks up the signal from my stud was smashed at the end of my shift. The cleaners, you know, can be so very careless."

"Are you sure?"

"I made sure," he said, his tone unequivocal.

"Whose side are you on, Montgomery?"

"My side," he answered without hesitation. "Just like you. And who knows, maybe we're both on the same side." He moved toward Lilia, looking long and lean and fearless, and her knees weakened. His words came softly. "Why don't we make a deal, Lil?"

Lilia immediately thought of physical debts to be rendered between them, but told herself to keep it clean. She held her laze a little higher and wondered whom she was trying to persuade. "I don't have to negotiate with you."

"Just how fast are you, Lil?"

Her gaze dropped to his holster and she considered that she probably didn't have it in her to shoot him.

And Montgomery probably knew it, perceptive beast that he was.

"What kind of deal?" Lilia lifted the laze as he eased closer, recognizing that he was trying to disarm her.

In more ways than one.

Montgomery halted, a mere step between them. The muzzle of the laze was almost against his chest, but Lilia was more worried about that than he looked. "Have you ever noticed, Lil, that your actions speak louder than your words?" He touched a fingertip to the laze. "And that they're a more reliable indicator of the truth?"

Lilia stepped back and lifted the laze again. "Don't try to persuade me that we should work together. I don't trust you."

"And I don't trust you, so that makes us even." He was giving her that bemused look again, the one that confused her.

He looked like Armaros and Baraqiel.

Who were real angels.

Lilia glanced down at the former angel who still clung to her side. The angelfire had died in his eyes when he'd lost his wings, but there was still intelligence gleaming there. He would be found a shade by the Republic if his scars were discovered, but he wasn't running slow like most shades.

She blinked. The receptionist at Breisach and Turner hadn't been dumb either.

Lilia glanced up at Montgomery. "That's why you cared about the receptionist at Breisach and Turner," she guessed. "You *knew* her. She was an angel, but she got caught. She was found a shade because of scars on her back, just like these ones."

It was Montgomery who took a step back this time, his expression turning wary. "You don't know what you're talking about."

"No, but I'm guessing and it's making a whole lot of sense." Lilia also liked what her guess told her about Montgomery's motivation. "Tell me: why did she earn the shade designation?"

Montgomery studied Lilia for a long moment, then punched something up on his palm. He flashed a pair of images at Lilia. The first was the one she'd seen before, the one of the eviscerated receptionist. Lilia was glad she didn't look away, though, because she might have missed the second image.

It showed the same woman, her back bare, and clearly displayed her pair of diagonal scars. They were exactly the same as the scars on the back of the man who leaned on her shoulder.

Lilia exhaled slowly as she wrapped her mind around the truth. There really were angels.

Angels who sacrificed their wings to pass as norms.

Angels whose sacrifice, if discovered, saw them classed as mutants and made them slaves of the Republic.

She immediately wondered how many of them there were.

"Why do they come?" she asked.

"To try to save humanity." Montgomery's tone was matter-of-fact, but Lilia wasn't fooled. His eyes were gleaming and she knew he cared deeply about the angels.

Just as she did.

"What happens to them?"

He met her gaze steadily. "They do their job, complete their assignments, and go back."

"They get their wings back?"

He nodded solemnly and she felt a little better about the injured angel she was holding. She was also more determined to help him.

"You know about the angels; you know about this place," she said, watching Montgomery. She knew he might not answer her questions. "The angels trust you. Do you help them?"

"What if I do?" He was cautious, just as she would have been.

Lilia gave a mock sign of resignation. "Then I'd have to revise my every prejudice against NGPD detectives. This is huge, Montgomery, a complete overhaul of my belief system. You'd owe me big time for a long time." She smiled.

"Would I?" Montgomery smiled back at her, his gaze warming. Lilia was sure that she wasn't the only one thinking about what they had just done.

Never mind what they might do next.

Montgomery reached for her, his fingertips brushing her cheek. Lilia strove to appear unaffected by his touch and lost that battle too. (She was thinking it might be too late to win the war.) He tucked a strand of hair behind her ear and stared down into her eyes. She knew he was going to kiss her again.

And that she was going to kiss him back.

"Answer one question for me," he murmured. Lilia stared into those green eyes and was ready to name her best orgasm of all time, or her favorite sexual position, or . . .

"Tell me what you said to Fitzgerald when he denounced you to the Society."

Lilia blinked.

Then she glared at Montgomery for changing the subject. "How do you know that I said anything?"

"I'm guessing. He told the Society that Armaros and Baraqiel couldn't be mutations, that it was too improbable to be true. That's essentially calling you a liar. I can't believe, Lil, that you would have let that pass."

Lilia looked away, unexpected tears clouding her vision.

"What did you say to him that left you thinking he might have committed suicide?"

Lilia swallowed. Maybe saying the truth aloud would let her dismiss the possibility that haunted her.

Maybe. Maybe not. Given what she'd figured out about Montgomery, Lilia was willing to take a chance on trust.

She wouldn't try to remember how long it had been.

"You're right. We fought, for the first time ever." She heaved a sigh. "He said a lot about my disregard for the rules and disrespect for the Society. He reminded me of my debt to them and to him. I was angry that he thought I was unappreciative after"—her words faltered—"after everything. I was furious that he wouldn't even come and look for himself. He called himself a scientist and I called him a stubborn idiot."

The silence hung between them, only the sound of the blond man's sniffles filling the air. Lilia stroked his hair and soothed him, knowing that she hadn't really answered the question. She glanced up to find Montgomery watching her, his gaze bright.

"I'm not proud that I lost my temper, but I can't lie that I did." Lilia took a breath and Montgomery waited. "I told Gid that I didn't love him. When he argued, I told him that I never had." Her voice was tight when she continued. "I told him that I had only married him because I owed him."

"Ouch," Montgomery said softly.

"I know." Lilia grimaced. "I thought he already knew, or at least suspected." She sighed and frowned at the floor. "It would have been kinder to have kept my mouth shut, but that's never been my best trick."

"Why did you owe him?"

"That's a second question, Montgomery. We agreed on one." Lilia was pretty sure that he wasn't going to let it go but his palm pinged, and it had a more imperious summons than Lilia's.

She noticed that he didn't activate the vid link.

"Montgomery," he said, reaching as he did to lay a finger against Lilia's lips. She felt what was left of her resistance to him melt, maybe because he had heard her truth and not condemned her.

"Montgomery!" The irritable voice of an older man carried from the palm. "Where in the hell are you?"

"Off-duty, sir."

"Homicide is never off-duty in New Gotham, Montgomery. It might be different in Topeka, but you're not in Kansas anymore."

Kansas? Lilia blinked. Montgomery was from *Kansas*? She'd never met a less likely farm boy in her life.

"Yes, sir."

"What the hell's the matter with your stud? I told you to check with Tech Support yesterday when you came on duty."

Lilia's eyes widened. Montgomery nodded, as if to say "I told you so," and Lilia found herself smiling in return.

"I did, sir," he said. "They installed a new stud and cross-checked it."

"Well, there's not a damn thing coming in on it now. Where are you?"

Montgomery's smile broadened as he surveyed Lilia. "Lost in the pleasure fringe, sir."

Lilia blushed.

"Consider yourself found, Montgomery. We've got a homicide and since you're in the pleasure fringe, I'll expect you to be first on the scene."

"Which is where, sir?"

"Address pending. Meet Dimitri there."

"On my way, sir." Montgomery watched for the displayed address, then terminated the connection. He didn't leave.

Instead, he laid a hand on the former angel's shoulder. Lilia watched something pass silently between them, then Montgomery took off his cloak. He slung it over the other man's bare shoulders and fastened the front clasp with a care that put a lump in Lilia's throat.

Montgomery pulled a handful of pleasure fringe tokens out of his pocket and gave them to Lilia. "Find him some clothes and talk to him until he's coherent. He'll learn fast."

"And then what?"

"And then he'll know what he needs to do."

"You know about this," Lilia guessed. "You were supposed to take him into the world. Why are you leaving him with me?"

"Because I don't have a choice. I have to report for duty."

Lilia started to smile, hearing what he wasn't saying. "Because you trust me. Go ahead, admit it, Montgomery."

He gave her a hard look. "I don't trust you as far as I could throw you," he said, but his smile softened his words. "But I think a potential shade can trust you to help him evade the Republic's many eyes."

"Thank you for that."

Montgomery leaned closer, his breath fanning her cheek, his eyes dark with intent. "And, Lil, if something happens to him, you get to answer to me."

"Promises, promises," she teased.

Montgomery kissed her ear, leaving her yearning for more as he pivoted and strode into the shadows of the warehouse.

MONTGOMERY WAS completely confident in leaving the angel in Lilia's care. Even if he hadn't been, the volunteer's wings were gone, so he'd not be of any value to the circus.

Which was, by strange coincidence, where Montgomery was going.

He had a strange sense that he had made a mistake in seducing Lilia, yet couldn't regret what they had done. The pleasure had been consuming, but fleeting. Too fleeting. It left him more hungry than he had been in the first place.

He'd missed something, but didn't yet know what it was.

Montgomery had a job to do before he could think more about Lilia. He reached the New Gotham circus, as instructed by his supervisor, first of the NGPD team. It was just after dawn and the circus had the morning hush that he knew from the pleasure fringe.

In fact, the circus had a great deal in common with the pleasure fringe. Not everything or everyone was as appearances might lead a visitor to believe. Not everything was legit and above the law. Deceptions and illusions proliferated beyond the reach of law enforcement. He felt a sudden affinity with Lilia, who was as much at home at the circus as he was in the pleasure fringe.

A burly shade met him at the entryway. The man had a third eye on his forehead, the same extra nodule as the shade Lilia had found dead in the old city.

"No admittance," the shade said, folding his arms across his chest. "We're closed."

Montgomery was startled. In the city, a shade would never confront a norm. A shade's eyes would never be clear of the cloud created by sedatives and his manner would never have been anything other than deferential.

In fact, it was hard to consider this man to be a shade, given his behavior. Montgomery understood why Lilia was so quick to defend shades as human.

"New Gotham Police," he said, flashing his badge on his palm. The shade's expression changed immediately. "We were called."

"Right over here." The shade led the way through the tents.

"I thought you'd know that already," Montgomery said.

The shade looked confused.

"Doesn't the third eye make you psychic?"

The shade laughed. "Only if it's real." He pulled at the skin nodule. "This one's an implant." His expression changed as he realized what he'd admitted. "I mean, it was there all along, of course, but my parents paid for me to have it augmented a bit."

"Right," Montgomery agreed easily.

"I always had the power to tell fortunes," the shade continued nervously, spreading his hands to show that the web between his fingers extended the length of an entire digit. "I was born with a caul. My mom said my fingers meant I was toast anyway, but Stevia said that my third eye needed to be more showy. She arranged everything." He gulped then and fell silent, sparing several anxious glances at Montgomery.

Montgomery had heard of norms in disadvantaged circumstances surgically adding a defect or two to get themselves work in the circus, but he'd never met anyone who had done it. It was illegal, and the doctors who performed such surgery did it on the sly.

It had to be a better fate than the Republic's slave dens. This shade's parents had paid for the illegal surgery to ensure that their child had a reasonably secure future. He could understand that impetus and the loyalty that such shades would feel to the circus owner who arranged the details.

He wondered again about Lilia's lost child. He could imagine that she would have fought to give her child a better life.

But she'd never had the chance.

The shade paused before a smaller tent, its stripes in shades of blue, and turned to confront Montgomery with some nervousness. "Are you going to report me, Officer?"

Montgomery met the shade's gaze steadily. "I'm a homicide detective. Unless you've killed a norm, your choices aren't my concern."

"Thank you." The shade was visibly relieved. "Stevia's in here. I didn't kill her, I swear it. I found her when I brought her coffee this morning." He pulled back the tent flap and the distinctive waft of fresh corpse caught at Montgomery's nostrils.

"Don't go far," he advised the shade. "And don't tell anyone what you saw. I'll need to talk to you before I leave and I'd like to be the first to hear your story."

The shade nodded. "Yes, sir."

Montgomery punched up the image snatcher in his palm and began to document the scene. He was particularly careful in his observations, given the context.

Because nothing at the circus was as it seemed.

Even the circus itself masqueraded as an itinerant operation, despite the fact that the New Gotham circus had stood on the same soil for decades. It was still set up in tents, as if poised to move at any moment, even though permanent buildings would have been possible and practical.

Nothing was as it seemed.

He glanced over his shoulder, thinking about the shade

who had guided him here. The shade owed Stevia his life
of comparative freedom and Montgomery guessed that
his loyalty would run far deeper than that of a mere em-
ployee. He guessed then that the killer wouldn't be found
within the circus' guy lines, that the circus operated more
as a family than as a business.

This was Lilia's world.

Lilia had a free and easy relationship with the truth, but
would fight to the bitter end for a noble cause. She was
incapable of doing violence to another person, in Montgomery's estimation, and Lilia considered shades to be
persons.

She'd said she'd owed Fitzgerald, and given that she'd
married him, her obligation must have been considerable.
He'd guess that no one could graduate as a Nuclear
Darwinist—and by extension have access to the Society's
databanks—without passing four years of the core course
of Dissection and Vivisection.

Montgomery had a pretty good idea what Lilia's debt
to Fitzgerald had been.

THE FORMER angel looked around himself with curiosity after Montgomery's departure. He stood straighter, as
if the pain was fading from his injuries. He was fair, his
hair a pale blond, and his eyes were blue. He was as buff
as Montgomery, if not quite as tall. He fingered the edges
of Montgomery's cloak, then smiled at Lilia, a sweet
trusting smile that nearly broke her heart.

He was in the wrong place to be trusting of strangers.

"I am Raphael," he said, his speech halting. "I must
take the train to New Seattle, please."

Lilia's heart skipped at the coincidence of hearing that
place named so soon after Montgomery had talked about
her file, then told herself not to make much of little.
Micheline had gotten her thinking about the past, that was
all.

And she was going to have to tell Stevia that Micheline

had gone with the angels. That wasn't going to be a fun conversation.

First things first.

Lilia offered her hand to the former angel. "Let me help you," she said and Raphael put his hand into hers.

He was so trusting.

So vulnerable.

Lilia had to fix that before she sent him on his way. He let her lead him from the warehouse, mimicking her gestures. He moved with increasing grace with every passing moment, as if he was learning at lightning speed.

It was just barely dawn. Lilia decided to push both bikes and abandon them in the pleasure fringe. She didn't want to leave any evidence of where they had been, of where Micheline had disappeared, of where Montgomery the protector met with angels.

She'd remember the place well enough.

She glanced over her shoulder to find Raphael staring up at the sky. She followed his gaze to see that a star was falling. It cut across the darker blue overhead, diving toward the horizon in a last blaze of glory. He was watching its course. Maybe he'd never seen one before.

When she called him, he didn't respond.

When she returned to his side and touched his elbow, he laid one hand over hers. His gaze remained locked on the falling star. "Mine," he whispered, but she didn't understand.

No one could own falling stars.

It was only when it had disappeared at the horizon that Raphael turned to face her, only then that Lilia saw the tears on his cheeks.

"New Seattle," he said, his voice thick with emotion.

"Yes," Lilia agreed. "But first I have to tell you some things about this place."

NEW GOTHAM had one thing in common with the world Lilia knew: the pleasure fringe was one place that

a well-dressed woman could lead a man, naked except for
a cloak, and no one even looked twice.

Raphael was even barefoot in dirty urban streets in October, but Lilia wasn't challenged once.

At least not by strangers. Raphael was another issue al-
together. He quickly revealed a fascination with shiny
items, and a talent for acquisition that would have made
him a terrific thief.

Somehow Lilia doubted that Montgomery would have
endorsed such a choice of career path. The more she
protested, the more crafty Raphael became, as if they
played a game.

There was no guile in him, yet, and his was the innocent
joy of winning a contest. By the time they'd gone three
blocks in the pleasure fringe, Lilia had returned the ring of
a hooker (who'd made the mistake of stroking Raphael's
shoulder), three watches and four cut-glass rings pilfered
from a street vendor's display, and the chain from an elab-
orate bell pull.

She had to wonder whether Montgomery had set her
up. She doubted that, although she imagined he'd enjoy
seeing what Raphael put her through. Montgomery might
even have expected it, given that he knew so much about
angels.

She finally found a haberdashery with stock that wasn't
too flash and pulled Raphael into the establishment. The
shop was down three steps from the street with a grill that
could be locked over the door. The dark carpet was of in-
determinate color and smelled faintly of spilled beer and
mildew. The walls were black and there were mirrors
mounted between the racks. Everything was a onesie, the
goods reclaimed or resold. An ad on one wall advised that
Joel's Clothes specialized in fitting the discerning gentleman and in repairing laze marks in better clothing.

A lean man with hollow cheeks, presumably Joel himself, stepped from between the racks of clothes. It was
quite the conjuring act for him to surprise a customer, as

he was dressed in a fuschia suit with black accents and mirrored cuff links.

Raphael went for the cuff links, like a dog for a bone.

Joel's gaze swept over Raphael and he smiled slightly in anticipation of a good sale. "And how may we be of service today?" He was unctuous and slippery. Lilia didn't doubt that he could be bought, so she gave him a story she wouldn't mind him selling.

"New sex toy." She sighed, as if she acquired new ones all the time, and found them somewhat troublesome. Raphael did his best to support the story as he tried on rings and bracelets, his fingers as fast as lightning. Lilia and Joel plucked them from his hands and returned them to the tray, Joel counting under his breath.

"Only came with the cloak on his back, hmmm?" Joel eased back the cloak, purportedly to guess Raphael's size. Lilia thought he was doing a more personal assessment, even as he fingered the faux-leather hem with appreciation. "Very nice," he said and Lilia wasn't sure whether he meant Raphael or the cloak. "I could give you a trade-in on this."

"I'm keeping both, thanks."

The salesman almost smiled.

"He needs one decent outfit, nothing too showy, nothing overly expensive." Lilia spied a sparkle disappearing beneath Montgomery's cloak and retrieved a silver bracelet from Raphael's fingers. She put it back in the tray with a smile, one that Joel didn't quite share. "Preferably nothing with pockets."

THE MURDER victim at the circus was one Stevia Fergusson, according to her palm, and she hadn't been dead long. She had been cut open exactly the same way as Rachel and the shade in Gotham, and it wasn't any easier to look at the third time.

More importantly, she was a norm. Montgomery had

no doubt that the same killer was responsible, but this death was a homicide.

The stakes had been raised.

The shade with the third eye said he'd found Stevia half an hour before Montgomery's arrival and pinged the police right away. He had no idea who could have disliked his employer so much, and hadn't seen anything. The pot of coffee he'd brought sat cooling on the table, his only interruption of the scene.

Dimitri gave Montgomery a look and whistled, before making a comment about being pulled away from hard labor. Dimitri looked as if he'd been dragged backward from bed for the call.

The coroner pronounced the body to be no more than an hour dead. Lilia couldn't have been responsible, but Montgomery wasn't going to volunteer to provide her with an alibi.

He'd figure out who was really responsible first.

And on the way, he'd discover why Lilia was being framed.

Montgomery got no further before his palm pinged an imperative. It helpfully accessed a circus security vid, showing that Lilia had entered this very tent the previous afternoon, with the victim and the girl-shade that Montgomery had seen taken by the angels. Lilia had not only been identified by the system, but her name was highlighted and blinking.

She really did have powerful enemies.

"One of your disappointed dates in the pleasure fringe?" Dimitri teased at the sound of Montgomery's ping. "Never leave a job half finished, that's what we say in New Gotham."

The other cops snickered at this.

Montgomery smiled. "No, it's just the central data-bank, doing investigative support."

Dimitri glanced up. "What are you talking about?"

The other cops and the coroner looked at Montgomery as well.

"It's seeking patterns in these deaths, searching the central databanks for connections." Montgomery could see from the expressions of his fellow officers that they didn't understand what he meant. "Aren't you getting its hotlinks?"

Dimitri glanced from side to side as he stood up, then he lowered his voice. "Are you running legit software, Montgomery?"

"Of course I am."

"But the system doesn't do that."

"Sure it does. I got the first message yesterday."

Dimitri shook his head. "No. There was a beta version of an upgrade that did that but they backed it out a year ago. The first perp it nailed was innocent and the New Houston Police lost a lawsuit after the execution. Didn't you hicks back out the upgrade in Topeka?"

"Well, sure," Montgomery lied. "I just assumed this was new. They upgraded and cross-checked my utilities when I came on board here. Everything I've got came from Tech Support."

Dimitri studied Montgomery for a moment, then swore under his breath and went back to his fingerprinting. He cast a dark glance at Montgomery. "So, that's how it's going to be, is it? A couple months off the farm and Montgomery's the new star."

"I don't know what you're talking about," Montgomery said.

Dimitri snorted. "Right. I wasn't born yesterday. They're giving you the better toys so you can be a star. I know how it works."

Montgomery and the coroner exchanged a glance.

"I don't know what you're talking about," he began but Dimitri interrupted him bitterly.

"I don't give a crap whether they've told you about the big plan or not, Montgomery. Here's the thing: you don't know squat about New Gotham, who to call and how things work, where things go down, and who the regulars are."

"But I . . ."

"You go ahead. You try to be a star, but I'll tell you now that they're going to regret not promoting me instead."

Dimitri went back to his work and the other cops turned their backs on Montgomery in a show of solidarity.

Obviously the data Montgomery was receiving wasn't being shared with everyone. He didn't believe he was targeted for promotion.

So what was going on? Were the messages coming from NGPD? The Republic? Or someone outside of the system who had hacked his way in? Was NGPD checking that he was who they thought he was?

One thing was for sure: somebody wanted Montgomery to decide that Lilia was a killer, against his own inclinations. His palm chimed again and Dimitri swore under his breath. Montgomery didn't want to look, not in front of everyone, but he did it anyway.

He wasn't surprised that Lilia had been detained at the train station for entering a restricted area.

He *was* surprised that she was alone.

XIV

LILIA ADVISED Raphael all the way to the train station and he listened avidly. He asked questions of greater subtlety and complexity as they walked. She only hoped she remembered everything of importance that he needed to know.

Some instinct for self-preservation kept her from telling him her name, and he never asked for it.

He was already moving with more confidence, and stepped to hold the door for a pretty woman descending from a rickshaw in front of the train station. The woman smiled at him and Raphael stared after her for a long moment, desire in his gaze.

Lilia decided to leave that alone.

Under her instruction, Raphael consulted the schedule and booked himself a place on the next train using his palm. Lilia watched and noted that someone had done some prep work in the Republic's databanks. It was brilliant and seamlessly done. Raphael had a personal history—albeit a spartan one—and some funds at his disposal. The info on his palm would pass a cursory exam and within days, his record would accrue more detail.

Was this what Montgomery did for the angels? Or were there others linked to the scheme? There was nothing Lilia loved more than a conspiracy, and she sensed that she'd found the tip of a big one. Raphael hadn't existed three hours before, yet his record showed that he was thirty-five and had been born in Paduca.

Someone inside the Republic was feeding garbage into the databanks. That made Lilia want to stand up and cheer.

Except that doing so would have blown the cover of the mystery hackers.

The train station was chaotic, filled with rickshaws, bicycles, stacks of luggage, porters with loaded carts, and running children. Vendors wove through the crowd, selling candy and downloads. Lilia overheard that Max had pulled into the lead in the presidential race, after coming off well in a vid debate.

But then, he'd always had the gift of gab. Lilia had told him once that he could sell tattoos to shades.

That hadn't proved to be so funny, in time.

She hugged Montgomery's cloak and led Raphael through the throngs of people in the station. It was dusty, the air filled with the smell of the steam engines. They found Raphael's train and the locomotive was already running.

Raphael kissed Lilia's fingertips. "Thank you for your help."

Lilia pulled her hand away, uncomfortable with his display of affection. Funny how he was just as buff and gorgeous as Montgomery but he did nothing to her equilibrium. "It was no trouble. You'd better get on board."

He caught her hand in his again and smiled. "Maybe you should come with me to New Seattle."

"No. Have a good trip, and, um, good luck at your destination."

Raphael leaned closer then and kissed Lilia's cheek. "I'll tell Delilah that you're well, then."

Lilia pulled back abruptly at the sound of her daughter's name. "Delilah? What are you talking about?"

Raphael smiled and trotted to the top of the stairs. The train gave a second whistle and began to pull out of the station. What did he know about Delilah? Lilia's hand rose to the locket from Gid, and her fingers closed on emptiness.

The locket was gone.

It was shiny.

She knew who had it.

"Raphael!" Lilia ran after the accelerating train when he ignored her. She leapt onto the bottom step and clung to the railing, swinging her weight onto the train. She lunged to the top of the steps and snatched at Raphael's sleeve. "Give the locket to me. Please."

"This?" The chain dangled from Raphael's fingertips, the locket swinging with the motion of the train. They stood at the top of the steps to the car, the ground blurring behind Lilia as the train gained speed.

"Yes, that." Lilia snatched and missed. "I knew you shouldn't have had pockets."

Raphael closed his hand it. "A memento for Delilah."

"I don't know who you're talking about," Lilia said with desperation. "It was a gift from my dead husband."

He watched her, that keen intelligence in his eyes. "It will mean all the more to Delilah then."

"No! I don't know anyone named Delilah. That locket is the only remembrance I have from my dead husband," Lilia said, reaching for Raphael's hand. "Give it to me, please."

The train switched tracks abruptly, throwing them both off balance. Raphael stumbled and Lilia thought he would fall down the stairs. She grabbed at him as he scrambled for the handrail.

She just had a glimpse of the intent in his gaze before he tossed the locket. If she hadn't seen that fleeting expression, she would have thought he'd dropped it

But instead, she knew he'd thrown it on purpose. The locket fell in the gravel in the train yard. Lilia leapt from the train in pursuit of the locket. She twisted her ankle when she hit the ground, but stumbled to her feet.

Raphael shouted, but Lilia ignored him. She sought the glitter of the cheap locket in the gravel between the tracks. Her heart was pounding and her hands were shaking. Delilah. How could he know about Delilah?

She had time to think how unlike Gid it was to give her a worthless piece of junk, how unlike her it was to risk her life for sentimentality, how unlikely it was that she'd find the locket again.

Then she saw it.

The locket was broken from its fall. Between the two thin walls that made the back of the locket was a hollow space.

Which held a black datachip.

The locket *was* a disposable piece of junk. What it concealed was its value. She should have known to smash it.

Once again, Gid had run intellectual circles around her.

Lilia glanced toward the station and found that a small disapproving crowd had gathered on the end of the platform. The stationmaster's thugs walked toward her, one swinging a crowbar.

It wasn't the most promising welcome she'd ever seen.

She knew then that she was in a restricted area without permission, the kind of deed that the Republic didn't favor among citizens.

Under the guise of straightening her skirts, Lilia jammed the datachip into her tightly laced boot. It pressed against her ankle, but she knew it was there. She straightened, holding up her gloved hands as she practiced her prettiest apology.

She would be demure. With luck, it would be enough to get her out of trouble.

Without luck, she'd be able to add resisting arrest to the charge against her.

Delilah.

LILIA LOOKED mutinous in the train station lockup, which didn't surprise Montgomery. Her eyes widened slightly when she saw him, then she settled into apparent indifference again.

Montgomery glanced over her quickly, noticing that she had a bruise rising on her cheek. Her skirt was muddy on one side, as if she'd fallen, and her sleeve was torn. Her cheap locket was gone and she had his cloak draped over her arm. After that one brief glance, she tapped her toe and considered the ceiling, as if she didn't know him at all.

That dawning bruise shorted Montgomery's circuits. He was furious with Lilia for entering a restricted area and for resisting arrest, but more furious with the stationmaster for allowing a woman to be injured. He took a deep breath and forced himself to be composed and indifferent.

"Can I help you?" the stationmaster asked, his tone indicating that he'd prefer to do anything else. He was a portly and older man, his eyes so narrowed with suspicion that Montgomery doubted he was capable of any other expression.

Montgomery made a show of consulting his palm as he spoke to the stationmaster. "I understand you have a Lilia Desjardins in your custody."

The stationmaster looked Montgomery up and down, obviously unimpressed by Montgomery's off-duty garb. "And what if I do?"

"NGPD." Montgomery flashed his palm and the man straightened. "That citizen is wanted for questioning in relation to a homicide here in New Gotham."

"That's her there," the stationmaster said, indicating Lilia with a jerk of his thumb. Lilia stared steadily back at him, unrepentant for whatever she had done. Not for the first time, Montgomery wanted to shake her. "If you're thinking of taking her into your custody, you should know that she was uncooperative. Me and the boys, we had to take her down hard once she got into the unauthorized zone."

"Or you could have simply asked me to accompany you," Lilia said tartly. "I was under the delusion that citizens had rights in the Republic."

"Not when they break the law," the stationmaster

snapped. "The train yard is restricted to ensure the safety of citizens."

"Then why don't I feel very safe?" Lilia retorted and hostility rose in the small space.

"Perhaps we might return to the business at hand," Montgomery interjected.

The stationmaster granted Lilia a cold glance. "You ought to take an impression of her teeth and charge her with assault," he told Montgomery, then pushed up his sleeve. "Look at this." There was a red bite mark just above his wrist.

"I think that then we'd have to discuss who assaulted whom first," Lilia said. "*That* was self-defense."

"Worked out real well for you, didn't it?" the stationmaster sneered. His two lackeys chuckled.

"It took three of you," Lilia said. "Against one little woman."

One of the lackeys took a step toward the cell but Lilia didn't even blink. Montgomery swallowed a curse and was glad that he had arrived as quickly as he had.

He wished she hadn't been so intent on making it worse.

Lilia glared at the lackey until he averted his gaze. Then she turned that look on the stationmaster. "I think if we tally the bruises, you'll be the one charged with assault. Or maybe with using unnecessary force. I was pushed from the train and the yard was where I fell. You could have treated me with courtesy."

"You were on a train without a ticket," snarled the stationmaster. "I'll add that to your list of charges."

"I was going to buy one on the train," Lilia replied.

"She's trouble," the stationmaster told Montgomery. "Never met a woman with such a mouth. You want to take her into NGPD's custody, you're welcome to her."

"That's exactly what I'm here to do," Montgomery said mildly. He completed the necessary files for the transfer.

Maybe, just maybe, he'd have the chance to give Lilia

a bit of advice. He flicked a glance her way, saw the set of her lips, and doubted the discussion would go well.

LILIA LEFT the station with her wrists handcuffed together and linked to a securoband that locked around her waist. Montgomery had found it difficult to cuff her, the scent of her skin and her proximity distracting him from the job. It was too easy to remember how she felt wrapped around him.

Never mind how much he wanted to do it again.

Apparently, getting Lilia Desjardins out of his system wasn't going to be simple. The fact that he didn't really want to be free of her spell might have been part of the problem.

He liked the idea that they were working together.

Montgomery's cloak was spread over the cuffs to hide them from casual view and he walked beside Lilia with one hand on the small of her back. It was all too easy to conclude that the woman needed a permanent escort, given her talent for getting herself into trouble. He was ready to volunteer.

"Don't say it," Lilia murmured when they were in the throngs of people in the station.

Montgomery said it anyway. "In some situations, you should just shut up," he muttered, hearing the anger underlying his own words. "You're going to have a whopper of a bruise on your face."

She flicked him a poisonous glance. "A small price to pay. I wasn't raped and I wasn't beaten up."

"It could have gone otherwise."

"A woman has to fight back, Montgomery. A woman has to show that she has some spirit, that she won't just roll to her back and let all comers have an easy go of it. They need to be a little bit cautious, a little bit surprised."

"Even if it makes them meaner?"

"They only get a shot in when I lose." Her lips set

defiantly. "And if I fight with my teeth and my heels, then they never guess what other assets I have."

Montgomery blinked. "They never took your laze?"

Lilia smiled up at him, confident again. "As chivalrous as it was of you to rescue me, I wasn't planning on staying long."

Montgomery didn't doubt that she would have taken care of herself. "What happened to our friend?" She glanced to his stud and he shook his head. "It's still out, at least until I get back to the precinct."

"He said he had to go to New Seattle. Just as you said, he had a plan. I blew your tokens on getting him dressed, showed him how to book a train ticket, and sent him on his way."

"How'd you end up in the lockup?"

Lilia frowned. "He wanted a memento of our time together that I didn't want to give. I also didn't want to go to New Seattle." She closed her mouth suddenly, as if there was something else she might have said but changed her mind.

They headed into the street, Lilia walking dutifully just before Montgomery. "Your story about the bulletin on me was a good one," she said as they dodged rickshaws and bicycles.

"It wasn't a lie, Lil." Montgomery saw her surprise. "The homicide was the circus owner—"

Lilia pivoted to face him so quickly that he nearly bumped into her. Her eyes were round with shock. "Not Stevia?"

"Stevia Fergusson," he agreed and she looked away with obvious distress. "A norm and one left in exactly the same way as the two shades. This one's a homicide."

Lilia swore. "The only upside is that I won't have to tell her about Micheline going with the angels." She looked up at him, her eyes bright. "Do you think they knew? Do you think they were protecting her from whoever attacked Stevia?"

"I don't know," Montgomery had to admit, then knew

he had to tell her more. "It gets worse, Lil. The system is fingering you as a suspect. It's hotlinking security vid files that put you on the scene just before the killings."

"I didn't know it did that."

"It doesn't. Remember how I said that you had powerful enemies?"

Lilia chewed her lip as she considered this. They turned as one and began to walk again. "Who hacks the angels' identities into the system?"

"I don't know."

"But we know at least that the system isn't impenetrable. There are ways to modify the Republic's information. There may be one group of hackers or a lot of independent ones."

"I'd put my creds on independents."

"Me too."

"Do you know anyone with connections?"

Lilia shrugged. "Depends on the price, doesn't it?"

Montgomery could see that she was thinking, even as every step took them closer to the precinct. He was ready to give her a bit more time to think about possible connections.

"Do you know anything about a group called the Council of Three?" he asked on impulse. He hadn't even tried a search yet.

Lilia looked at him in surprise. "They're supposed to be the secret team that runs the Society, but no one's sure they exist. Well, except Doc Mina."

"Doc Mina?"

"Don't ask. What do the Council of Three have to do with anything?"

"I don't know. I hoped you might know who they were."

Lilia laughed. "Hardly! Not for lack of speculating, though." She didn't seem to think they were a threat to take seriously. Montgomery would have to do some research on his own.

He lowered his voice. "We're going to go down Main

Street in a couple of blocks, Lil. It's always busy there."

Lilia slanted him a glance, her eyes dancing with the mischief that made his heart leap. "You should be worried that I might escape your custody in such a place."

Montgomery smiled. "I'm worried that you just might."

Her smile flashed. "You really know how to sweet-talk a lady, Montgomery." She leaned closer to him, her arm brushing against his, her lips tantalizingly close. "I'm going to tell you a secret, just for that. Gid left me something."

"Something like what?"

"A datachip. I need to read it, but not anywhere it can be tracked. I don't want to use my palm, because I was palm-raped and there might be a worm installed . . ."

"Palm-raped?" Montgomery stalled on that single word. "When? Where?"

"Last night." Lilia shrugged, no longer interested in the details. Montgomery didn't share her view. "Someone must have given me a Mickey Finn, probably in the lobby bar, then broke into my room. My palm said it was emptied at 01:16:47."

"Emptied?"

"He copied everything."

"Everything that was on your palm," he corrected and they exchanged a knowing smile before Montgomery sobered. "He? Who was it? Could you tell?"

Her gaze was assessing. "Not you. Beyond that, I'm not sure."

Montgomery wondered how she could be so certain.

"It's not like I'm overwhelmed with friends here in New Gotham," she added. "Can you access the security vid for the hotel?"

"Possibly." Montgomery wouldn't have been surprised to find that it had been someone from NGPD, since the system was so determined to frame Lilia.

"What's more important is that I read this datachip," Lilia said. "I need to know what's on it. I know where there are public readers that aren't monitored on the Frontier—"

Montgomery interrupted her, knowing what she wanted and realizing that they had very little time. "Go into the netherzones in the pleasure fringe then head uptown. In Forest Green, there's a beverage bar for sex-shades on the primary level."

"Their public readers aren't monitored?"

"They're all monitored here, Lil. But I can get around it."

She gave a shiver. "There's something about a man with the right tools," she murmured, then cast him a smile filled with promise.

"I'll meet you there at 15:00, just before I go on shift." He pursed his lips. "I'm going to have a lot of forms to fill out, what with you escaping from my custody."

"And your ear stud needing maintenance again," Lilia reminded him cheerfully.

"That too. It's already 10—I hope I'm not late."

"Main Street closing fast," Lilia said, jingling her cuffs with anticipation. "How am I going to get these babies off, Montgomery? Do you have a plan for that?"

"Just a key."

"Works for me."

Montgomery reached beneath the cloak and unlocked the cuffs with one hand. "You can cut the securoband once you're away," he advised. "Ditch it fast because it has a homing device."

"Does it? In that little thing?" Lilia shook her head. "It looks so innocuous, but the Republic thinks of everything."

There was nothing Montgomery could say to that.

They walked on to Main Street together, letting the crowd jostle them. It was busier than Montgomery had anticipated. Lilia held her hands as if they were still fastened together and walked beside him with careful steps. She might have been a respectable middle-class wife, her manner as unlike the Lilia he knew as was possible.

He slanted her a skeptical glance. "What's going on?"

She blinked. "Whatever do you mean, dear sir?"

Montgomery glanced behind them and to either side. "What happened to the real Lil?"

She laughed and her smile was wicked. "I'm trying to be demure. How am I doing?"

"A bit too well," he said. "But it can't last."

Before he managed to say more, Lilia proved his prediction true. She flung the cloak at his head and ducked behind a wheeled cart selling snacks.

Montgomery was plunged into darkness and he chuckled to himself before he pulled the cloak away. Lilia had lunged into the crowd and was covering ground fast. He shouted in mock dismay and gave chase without real heart.

If he'd been in uniform, the crowd might have stopped her, assuming that she was a felon of some kind. As it was, people watched her run, then glanced to him. Lilia chose to work with that, with her usual skill at improvising.

"He's a barbarian!" she cried, pointing back at Montgomery and holding her other hand over her heart. Montgomery noticed that she had managed to ditch the securoband already. "We've only just been introduced and he tried to touch my hand!"

She had pulled down her glove so that the skin on the back of her hand was bare. She looked down at the exposed skin and flushed crimson as if mortified. Another woman handed her a hankerchief to cover her flesh.

Men roared with anger at this breach of the rights of a member of the fair sex. Montgomery immediately found a wall of furious citizens confronting him, blocking him from pursuit of Lilia. He would have laughed if it hadn't been his role to look outraged and falsely charged.

Lilia, meanwhile, trotted away, surrounded by supportive women.

He blundered and blustered until she had completely disappeared from sight, then managed to talk his way out of the confrontation.

It was only when he reached the precinct that he realized he hadn't reminded Lilia to not return to the hotel.

Whoever was hunting her would look for her there first.

LILIA WAS starving. Hunger amplified her other reactions of the morning. She was overwhelmed with information, saddened by Stevia's death, skeptical of Montgomery's claim that the system was fingering her as the villain.

By his own admission, the system didn't do that.

She remembered his fleeting expression of cold fury when he'd come to the lockup in the train station and was sure that he was telling her a story, one intended to ensure that she behaved demurely for the rest of the day.

As if that would happen. She was going to eat, investigate, check out the datachip's contents, and jump Montgomery's bones again, either before or after she quit the Society for all time. It wasn't safe but nothing was safe. The stakes were high and Lilia believed that she could outsmart—or outmaneuver—anyone who was out to get her.

Even the Republic.

She wasn't going to worry about Delilah. Delilah was safe.

Gid had ensured it and Gid had been utterly trustworthy.

To Lilia's relief, when she got back to the hotel, the breakfast buffet was still set up, if picked over. Most people were in Doc Mina's special session, probably in dire need of artificial stimulants. Since she'd already paid for the meal with her conference fee, Lilia cruised the wreckage of the buffet. She'd be safe enough in a public area like this, especially if she kept her eyes open.

It had been a nice spread, for that kind of thing, with some sweet breads and "fruit," "coffee," and "tea," as well as the usual array of breakfast substitutes and energy pills. Lilia took a couple of Danish, which looked reasonably unextruded, and ate one right at the buffet.

She thought about chicken tortellini and salivated.

She glanced across the room, mildly curious as to who else had skipped Doc Mina's session. There were three dozen Nuclear Darwinists in the room, all pretending that Lilia was invisible. The last thing she expected was for anyone to acknowledge her, but Dr. Malachy was waving his cane, apparently at her.

Lilia glanced behind herself to be sure, but she was standing alone at the buffet. She waved back tentatively, and he flailed his cane with greater enthusiasm.

The mathematics professor from the Institute, Dr. Malachy had a full mane of silver hair and eyebrows so unruly that they seemed to possess lives of their own. He had walked with a cane for as long as Lilia had known him. Even though she had been abysmal at solving the convoluted mathematical formulas in his courses—she still had nightmares about derivatives—she'd always liked him.

She liked him enough to give him a chance to change his mind about inviting the conference pariah to his table. He could, after all, have been having a seizure or calling for more substitute dairy product for his "coffee."

All doubt was removed when he yelled at her. "Lilia Desjardins! Have you gone blind?" He rapped his cane on an adjacent chair. "Come here, my dear, and sit with me. I could use some scandalous company." He harumphed and settled back in his chair. "A man my age has to court rumor wherever he can find it."

Fair enough.

Lilia smiled, even as the others in the room began to whisper. Dr. Malachy returned to his breakfast, apparently considering his summons to be so irresistible that it was only a matter of time before Lilia claimed the seat beside him.

He pretty much had that right.

"Good morning, Dr. Malachy," Lilia said, being as polite a schoolgirl as she could manage to be.

"So, Gideon taught you some manners then, did he?"

Lilia sat down. "How nice to see you again."

He shook a spoon at her. "You mean that you're surprised that I'm not dead yet. Well, my dear, some days I'm surprised as well."

Lilia laughed and he winked at her.

Then he sobered. "Terrible business about Gideon," he said gruffly and gave her hand a pat. "Gave me a shock, that did."

"You and me both."

He shook his head. "It's a shame to lose a man with such promise. I've never encountered a mind so attuned to mathematics." He paused, then glanced around, as if waiting for a correction. When it didn't come, he made it himself. "Except my own, of course."

"Of course," Lilia agreed, realizing she'd missed her line. "Weren't you Gid's advisor at the Institute?"

Dr. Malachy nodded with satisfaction. "That I was. Do you know that I accused him of plagiarism when he turned in his first lab report to me?" He chuckled and shook his head. "I couldn't imagine that a second-year student could do such an intricate proof."

"Gid never cheated."

"No, he never did. Honest as they came, that boy." Dr. Malachy sighed and stirred his "coffee." Lilia didn't think it was the beverage that was troubling him. If he wanted to talk about Gid, the least she could do was give him a place to start.

"Dr. Malachy, do you know what Gid was working on?"

He snorted. "I wouldn't be much of an advisor if I didn't."

"I thought you had retired." Lilia got a sharp glance for that.

"You thought I was dead. We've been over that."

"No, but—"

"I always swore, Lilia, that I'd die in my lab, working until the end." He gave her another of those playful glances. "I didn't, however, think it would take so long."

"You'll probably outlive all of us."

"Terrifying prospect, that." He sipped from his cup, obviously less worried about that possibility than he claimed to be.

"But what was Gid working on?"

Dr. Malachy waved a hand. "Oh, more mathematical probabilities. I won't bore you with the details—I do remember that mathematics wasn't your strong suit, Lilia."

"No, it wasn't. Fortunately, I met Gid before I'd flunked out completely. He was a good tutor."

"Well, yes. He was motivated—" Dr. Malachy harumphed "—as only a young man prepared to court a lady's affections can be. You know, Lilia, if you hadn't been my student before you met Gideon, I might have thought that you pretended to be worse at mathematics than you were, simply because you were similarly motivated."

Lilia laughed. "I didn't have to pretend. I still have nightmares about calculating the area inside an ellipse."

"And this from a Nuclear Darwinist. Amazing. How do you calculate half-lives?"

"I ask Gid to do it for me."

"Well, that won't work any longer, will it?" He cleared his throat, then made a joke to ease over the moment. "Unless you have abilities beyond most of my students. Have you had a third eye removed?"

Lilia spoke lightly, her tone dismissive despite the leap of her pulse. "That would make me a shade, wouldn't it?"

They laughed politely together, then he shook his spoon at her again. "Odds were against you being as incompetent as you were, given that you'd been accepted into the Institute. I've no doubt that Gideon took encouragement from your difficulties."

Lilia had never considered that Gid might have thought she'd been exaggerating her incompetence. "Maybe he did."

They sat in silence for a moment, then Dr. Malachy cleared his throat. "I wondered, you know, whether the two of you would be happy. You have quite passionate opinions about the Society, Lilia, ones that I doubt Gideon shared."

"Married people don't have to agree on everything, Dr. Malachy. In fact, it's probably more interesting to disagree on some—"

He interrupted her with a wag of one heavy finger. "I always wondered why you even became a Nuclear Darwinist."

Lilia said nothing. Something about his steady stare made it impossible to summon a lie, even for the best liar on the Frontier.

"If memory serves," he said, "and you may be fairly warned that mine usually does, you arrived at the Institute with your bias against the Society fully formed. Rather a strange course of study for one so vehemently against the Society's practices, wouldn't you say?"

"Would you believe that I enrolled to annoy my mother?"

Dr. Malachy laughed. "Yes, of you, I would believe that. But time has clearly failed to mitigate your opinions. I would have thought that Gideon would change your thinking."

"Maybe I've seen too much."

"Maybe you haven't seen enough. Nothing is ever black and white, Lilia, and nothing is ever fully good or fully evil. Life would be much simpler if that were the case. We could all make the right choices if things were laid out so neatly for us, which truly would change the world. Instead we must choose the lesser evil."

He leaned closer and Lilia smelled the smoke of his pipe clinging to his jacket. It was a reassuring scent and one that made him seem all the more paternal. "You have to balance your view, Lilia," he said gently. "You have to acknowledge the good that is done by the Society, the care given to shades, the emotional and financial relief given to the parents of shades who can entrust them to other hands. A disabled child is a terrible burden upon a family."

Lilia gritted her teeth at the familiarity of this argument. "They should have the choice."

"And who could choose dispassionately?" he demanded. "Who could perceive the greater good through the haze of obligation?"

Lilia remained silent, knowing how precious it would have been to have had the chance to choose for her own child.

"What about the drugs developed by the Society?" Dr. Malachy argued. "Our drugs alleviate pain and suffering throughout the Republic at large. They could never be patented without our research."

Done on shades.

Like Delilah.

Lilia swallowed at a memory she didn't want to review.

"What about the research, like Gideon's, that more precisely quantifies the risk of radiation exposure? Did you tell him that his work was for a bad cause?"

"No, of course not."

"Did he think that you disapproved of his work? Did you extend your distaste of the Society to include your husband?"

Lilia was shocked by this suggestion, but Dr. Malachy had evidently given it some thought. "No!"

He watched her over the rim of his cup, his gaze shrewd. "How could his alliance with the Society and your determination to be against everything connected with the Society not have been an issue in your marriage?"

"That's a very personal question." Lilia made to leave the table but Dr. Malachy put a hand on her wrist.

"I was very fond of Gideon. He worked many hours since your discovery of those controversial shades, so many hours and so far away from the Frontier that it is difficult for me to imagine that you spent much time together before his death."

Lilia didn't answer. If Gid hadn't confided in Dr. Malachy about their split, then she wasn't going to tell tales.

"My concern, Lilia, is for Gideon and his frame of mind at the time of his death."

"What do you mean?"

"I would hate to think that such a fine man believed himself to be unworthy of his wife's affections." He gave Lilia such a hard look that she realized his implication.

But now, thanks to the ruthless slaughter of every person she contacted, Lilia knew it wasn't true. She spoke with confidence. "Gid didn't commit suicide."

Dr. Malachy raised a brow. "How probable do you think it would be for an expert in the calculation of radiation exposure to have erred so fatally in assessing his own circumstance?"

"I think it was pretty low."

"As do I." Dr. Malachy was stern, his gaze relentless. He'd discarded the official cause of death for the same reason as Lilia, but derived a different solution. "How probable do you think it would be for Gid to fail to turn in his research?"

Lilia blinked. "I thought you knew what Gid was working on."

"He didn't turn in his results. It was most unlike him, perhaps a sign of emotional devastation." Dr. Malachy leaned forward, his expression intent. "I remember that tattoo. He had the melusine already, of course, but she had no face until he met you."

Lilia felt the color drain from her face. She hadn't imagined that anyone else knew about Gid's tattoo. Dr. Malachy probably could figure out that Gid had been celebrating a sexual conquest, but not why Lilia had chosen to surrender.

Not unless Gid had told his trusted advisor the truth.

Delilah.

XV

DR. MALACHY pushed back in his chair. "I do not intend to make you uncomfortable, Lilia. I always felt a kinship with Gideon."

"I know that he was fond of you, Dr. Malachy."

The professor harumphed and frowned into his cup for a long moment. Lilia rose to excuse herself, then he spoke. "It seems plausible that Gideon and I could have shared a similar amorous disappointment. It's whimsical, of course, but I'm old enough to have license to be whimsical on occasion."

"You disagreed with your wife?"

"Never had the chance. The lady in question and I did discuss marriage. She shared your skepticism of the Society's merit and we argued about it. In fact, she broke our engagement as a result of that argument."

"I'm sorry." Lilia sat down again. "What happened to her?"

"I don't know, not for certain." His next words were so softly uttered that Lilia had to lean closer to hear them. "She went to Gotham, to visit her sister. It was thirty years ago."

Lilia straightened. "Not *then*?"

"*Then.*" His gaze drifted from his coffee cup to the almost-empty room. "I've often wondered whether we could have come to a compromise, if we'd talked one last time, if I hadn't been so proud." He sighed. "I would have liked Gideon's story to have had a different ending."

"I'm sorry, Dr. Malachy."

"So am I." He patted her hand. "Just as I will always be sorry to have lost Gideon. The truly bright lights don't come very often." He gathered his cane as if he'd excuse himself.

"Dr. Malachy, what was Gid working on?"

"It's not that interesting to the layman."

Lilia refused to be insulted. "It's interesting to me. Besides, how will I know whether I come across his research results, if I don't know what I'm looking for?"

Dr. Malachy's gaze brightened. "He was calculating the patterns of radiation effect in the population over time, and making extrapolations from those calculations. It's the kind of quiet work that few people heed, but it's sufficiently challenging that it can be its own reward. I would have liked to have seen his results."

"Do you know why he was in the old city?"

"Maybe he just wanted to see it. The destruction of Gotham is impressive and I wouldn't be surprised to find any Nuclear Darwinist sufficiently curious to plan a sightseeing expedition." His gaze fell on Lilia's glowing radiation badge.

"Busy month at the circus," she said quickly. "I had to double up to clear the time to come to the conference."

Dr. Malachy nodded, his expression mild, and Lilia realized that he'd probably heard a lot of excuses in his time. He stood and braced both hands on his cane. "I had the sense that Gideon was on the cusp of a big discovery, but that was just my feeling. He never said anything, although I wouldn't have expected otherwise. He liked absolutes in his reporting. That was why I had hoped he had sent you something."

Lilia shook her head. "Nothing."

"Ah, well, then, we'll never know."

"Too bad his palm was wiped clean," Lilia said.

Dr. Malachy wasn't surprised. "Researchers can be proud of their attributions and many program their palms to erase their contents upon the cessation of the pulse." He patted Lilia's shoulder. "Mind you don't get reckless in Gideon's absence. It's easy to forget the value of our own lives when we're bereaved."

"Was there ever a Mrs. Malachy?"

He averted his gaze. "No. So I won't be the one to tell you that it gets easier, Lilia, or that the ache of loss goes away." He looked at her steadily, his eyes bright, and his voice turned hoarse. "I've never lied to my students and I don't intend to start now. I can only hope that trust is repaid in kind."

With one last hard look, Dr. Malachy strode away, leaning more heavily on his cane. He looked older and smaller as he crossed the floor, and Lilia sighed that he had taken Gid's death so hard.

Did he know that she had lied to him? She felt the press of the datachip against her ankle and wondered whether she should have told Dr. Malachy about it.

But she didn't even know what was on the datachip. Better that she met Montgomery and knew what she had to offer before she handed it over to the Society. Gid had chosen not to do so himself, which made it highly probable that there was a good reason for his choice.

MONTGOMERY'S PALM had sent him two more alerts regarding Lilia being the likely killer of Stevia and the shades. It was as if someone somewhere was becoming impatient with him. He lingered in the precinct locker room to read them again. Was there a backup team to move into action if he didn't arrest Lilia?

He jumped when Tupperman spoke behind him.

"Montgomery, I've been looking for you." The older man looked haggard and must have been coming off duty.

"Yes, sir."

Tupperman stopped beside Montgomery, unzipping his pseudoskin as he stood in front of the lockers. He heaved a sigh and frowned. "Long night."

"Yes, sir."

"I never get used to the bad ones. I guess that's a good thing."

"I'd think so, sir. A sign that we're all human."

Tupperman spared Montgomery a sharp glance. He swallowed, then spoke quietly. "I want this killer."

"Everybody does, sir."

"No. I want this killer and I want him today. I don't, however, want you taking ridiculous chances to close the case."

"I don't understand what you mean, sir."

"I don't want to lose a man, Montgomery, especially you."

"Sir, can you tell me about these alerts I'm receiving?"

Tupperman seemed to be choosing his words. "No. Not specifically. The system sometimes works in mysterious ways." He impaled Montgomery with a glance. "The system works for the benefit of the collective, not that of the individual."

Montgomery understood that he was being warned. "Yes, sir."

Tupperman heaved a sigh. "What you might not know, Montgomery, is that we have something in common. I came from Topeka as well. It's been awhile but I have fond memories of my time there."

Did Tupperman mean the earthly Topeka, or was he implying that he shared Montgomery's celestial origins?

"And now the bad news," Tupperman said with a frown. "I know how bright the lights of the city can be to a young man fresh from Topeka, because I've been that man myself. All the same, I don't want to lose a man over an equipment malfunction."

"I don't intend to be lost, sir."

"No one ever does. The fact remains, Montgomery, that you enter high-risk areas during your personal time and that's dangerous. I've never seen such dysfunction in an ear monitor, for example. The cleaning staff never broke a transmitter connection, not until last night. And now this morning, your stud is fried, as well."

"My rotten luck, I guess, sir."

"Maybe." Tupperman unfastened his boots and straightened to look Montgomery in the eye. "Maybe not. Your visits to the pleasure fringe have been noticed. Tech Support thinks that the ear monitors might be more susceptible to radiation exposure than previously believed."

"I turn in my radiation patch monthly, sir."

"Of course you do, and it's within tolerance. Trust me, I made that argument." He sighed. "But the matter has gone above me."

"Sir?"

Tupperman held Montgomery's gaze and spoke quietly. "You're to report for a complete physical exam, tomorrow at 11:00."

Montgomery's heart stopped cold. They'd find his scars. "I had one in Topeka, just three months ago, sir. A physical is only required on an annual basis, per protocol 786B."

"My superiors don't give a shit about 786B. They want your monitor fixed and they want it fixed now. I know you're busy right now and I did my best to have it postponed." Tupperman shook his head. "Tomorrow is the longest they'd wait. Be there."

"Yes, sir."

Tupperman peeled back the left shoulder of his pseudoskin with a wince. He watched Montgomery so steadily that Montgomery wondered what the older man was trying to tell him.

Tupperman wore a T-shirt under his pseudoskin, exactly the way Montgomery did.

Did he do it for the same reason? Their gazes met.

"Goddamn pseudoskin," Tupperman muttered as he rolled his right shoulder. The tight pseudoskin didn't move. "Ever since I took that shot in the shoulder, it catches. Give me a hand?"

"Of course, sir." Montgomery wasn't fooled. Tupperman got in and out of his pseudoskin daily and Montgomery couldn't believe that he didn't do it alone. "Maybe you should take some therapy to loosen up the joint, sir."

"Maybe."

Montgomery eased the tight pseudoskin over Tupperman's right shoulder. He could just discern the ridge of an old scar on the older man's right shoulder blade. There was another scar on the left shoulder, the mirror image of the first.

"You took a hit, sir?"

"Right across the back from a shotgun, just before I transferred in. My back was so full of shot that they had to slice me open to pick it all out." He nodded once curtly. "I don't miss those ranchers in Kansas, that's for sure."

They were from the very same Topeka.

But Montgomery didn't have a cover story on his file.

"I want this killer, Montgomery," Tupperman said with quiet heat. He quickly peeled off his pseudoskin and hauled a shirt over his shoulders. "Don't let me down."

"No, sir," Montgomery said, his thoughts whirling. He had an ally at NGPD, one more than he had expected.

But then, since he was going to fail his physical exam the next day and lose his job, the alliance was immaterial.

Or was it? He had no chance to ask Tupperman more because Dimitri entered the locker room.

LILIA EYED the schedule and decided against the keynote luncheon. Never mind the inevitable faux-flesh entrée, just hearing the patent applications always gave Lilia a headache.

She showered and changed instead, choosing a frilly navy ensemble that she'd never put on her back before. She put Gid's chip in the left cup of her corset, liking the security of having it close to her heart. Then she slipped out of her room, with plenty of time to meet Montgomery, and descended to the netherzones by the back service stairs. They were metal stairs, unembellished in a concrete stairwell. Lilia tried to be silent, but the slight click of her heels echoed loudly.

A grate was locked across the entrance to the netherzones, barring access. Lilia pulled her laze and blew off the lock, taking pleasure in destroying something in New Gotham.

The primary level of the hotel netherzones was filled with laundry facilities and kitchen prep zones. The shades working there might as well have been robots for all the animation they showed. Lilia waited in the shadows until the supervisor turned away, then made a run for the second set of stairs.

The lower netherzones were darker. No one wasted juice on lighting these industrial wastelands. Pulleys groaned and cogs clattered as an army of shades used their physical abilities to generate power for the hotel. Lilia refused to look at them, knowing that she'd only feel compelled to do something if they were bound to the equipment.

She waited at the base of the stairs, willing her eyes to adjust to the shadows. There was a soft sound then, like a footfall on the metal steps overhead and behind her. Lilia jumped and turned, her hand on her hidden laze.

Nothing.

She must have imagined the sound. That kind of delusion could happen to anyone who was hungry, tired, hung over from a palm-rape drug, or otherwise operating at less than her full capacity.

One of these nights, she had to get some sleep. Lilia hurried to the sliding steel door that led to New Gotham's labyrinth. She put her hand on it, then her ear.

There was only a distant hum. Lilia tested the door, found it wasn't locked, and slid it open. The New Gotham netherzones snaked out in half a dozen poorly lit directions.

Lilia headed into the darkness of the labyrinth, in search of Forest Green's beverage bar.

It took her an hour to find it. There were a dozen comparatively attractive shades in the beverage bar, most nursing a cup of something dark. There was little conversation. The music was horrible, twentieth-century disco dance music, and loud enough to mask pretty much anything.

Montgomery was there in his twin guise, lounging against the counter and looking like a wolf on the hunt. He looked, if anything, even more dapper and sexy than usual.

Maybe Lilia was just glad to see him.

Her heart certainly was. It skipped and cavorted at the very sight of him. Montgomery smiled and beckoned as if he'd just spied exactly what, or whom, he wanted.

Lilia could relate to that.

There was at least one norm behind the counter, so Lilia shuffled toward Montgomery, trying to look dull. It was a challenge, given that she felt so alive in his proximity.

"You're late," he said when she reached his side. He pulled her close, as if not expecting an answer, and kissed her leisurely. Lilia hung onto his shoulders and surrendered to sensation.

It was all too easy to forget that they had other things to do.

When he lifted his head, he had the same look of intent as he had had that morning. "Are you ready for your lesson?" he asked, his words low and silky.

The proprietor chuckled. "Keep it clean, would you? I've got a license to protect."

"It's your mind that's in the gutter," Montgomery said, as if affronted. "I'm teaching her to read."

"Right." The proprietor rolled his eyes. "I don't want to know the details."

Lilia glanced between them, keeping her expression blank.

Montgomery opened his hand and there was a datachip on his palm. He spoke slowly, as if she might not comprehend his words. "This is the daily download. The news. Do you know what that is?"

Lilia nodded, playing her dumbest dumb bunny for the audience at hand. The shades were disinterested in whatever games she and Montgomery were playing, but she didn't trust the norm behind the counter. The eyes of the Republic were everywhere.

The proprietor watched, glowering, as he washed cups.

Montgomery held Lilia close against his side as he guided her to a public reader. She doubted it was a coincidence that it was the very end one, located in the darkest corner of the beverage bar and the farthest one from the proprietor.

Montgomery sat down at the reader and pulled her onto his lap, keeping one hand locked around her waist. She could feel the strength of his thighs beneath her, and his reevlar codpiece pressing into her buttocks. She wriggled and Montgomery caught his breath. "Easy," he muttered and she smiled at him.

The proprietor would see Montgomery's cloaked shoulders and a whole lot of frilly petticoats. Even the display would be blocked by the two of them. Montgomery furthered the illusion of his seduction by locking his hands around her waist. She arched her back, wanting more.

Montgomery chuckled against her neck. "Behave," he counseled.

"Behaving is no fun," she whispered.

"I thought you were being demure."

"I don't think I have a talent for it."

"You can say that again," he teased. "How about we try for innocent?"

She met his gaze, understanding that he was casting her own words back at her. His gaze was steady, his eyes that vivid green. "I'm not sure I want to be amateur again," she murmured.

He didn't blink. "I'm not sure we make the choice."

Lilia's heart pounded at his implication. She studied him, knowing it would be very easy to fall for Montgomery. Maybe too easy. Dangerous.

But it was a tempting proposition all the same.

He leaned closer, watching her carefully, then kissed her. It was a teasing kiss, one intended to persuade her. His tenderness, the hint of his own vulnerability, nearly undid her.

She dared to imagine a future with Montgomery.

She liked that fantasy a lot.

Montgomery broke their kiss and she watched him catch his breath. She wasn't the only one affected.

He smiled at her and arched a brow. "Time for the business at hand," he murmured and cupped her breast in his hand. He caressed her through her clothing, bolstering the illusion that she was no more than an instrument of pleasure.

She probably shouldn't have enjoyed it as much as she did. There was something exciting and forbidden about being fondled in a public place. When Montgomery reached under her skirts, she wondered how far he would take things.

To her disappointment, his hand went into his own boot.

He did caress the inside of her left knee en route, though.

"Tease," she whispered and his grin flashed. He retrieved a thin film from a receptacle hidden in his boot, then spread it on the daily download datachip. "What's that?"

"It's a scrambler, a film that degrades when exposed to air," Montgomery breathed the words in her ear, disguising what he did by kissing her. Lilia shivered. "It also messes with the central databanks." He pushed the download chip into the port, then nuzzled her neck provocatively. "Start reading."

Lilia scrolled through the news, pretending it was much harder for her to read than it was. Montgomery certainly complicated the matter, distracting her with his touch as he did. "Maximilian Blackstone's presidential campaign received a boost yesterday, although not from his own efforts," she read carefully and slowly. "The president announced a new treaty neg, neg—"

"Negotiated," Montgomery supplied, his hand easing beneath her skirts. The smooth faux leather of his glove eased over her bare thighs and Lilia had a hard time concentrating on the news. "You shouldn't," she murmured.

"We have to keep up appearances," he insisted, his

fingertip on the top of her thigh. Lilia caught her breath and kept reading.

"*Negotiated* with China on his official visit there, but the agreement fell far short of expectations in the Republic." She caught her breath as Montgomery's fingertip caressed her most tender spot. He smiled against her throat. Lilia swallowed and read on. "Blackstone's polled popularity rose 10 percent yesterday alone, even as the president began his return journey to New D.C."

Lilia noticed that the download had opened another window on the screen, one that usually wasn't there.

"Where's your datachip?" Montgomery asked in an undertone. "We don't have a lot of time."

"It's in my corset," Lilia confessed. "I'm thinking maybe you should get it." She spared him a challenging glance and saw his eyes brighten. "Left cup near the middle."

She should have known that he'd leave her gasping when he removed it. He unfastened the back of her dress in record time, his exploring hand sliding up the front between corset and bodice. Lilia read the news with increasing difficulty as Montgomery caressed her nipple, slipping his finger and thumb between the corset's cup and her flesh. He had the chip, passed it to his other hand, pushed it into the ancillary port, and continued to stroke her skin.

"You are frightening," she breathed and he chuckled.

"Experience," he teased. Montgomery fastened the back of her dress again, his fingers making quick work of the fastenings.

A spreadsheet abruptly displayed in the extra window, distracting them both.

"It must be Gid's research results."

"Keep reading," Montgomery advised and Lilia read aloud the details of the new treaty.

Meanwhile, she studied Gid's spreadsheet. It documented the population of shades in both raw numbers and as a percentage of the total population of the Republic, every year for the past seventy years. Gid had starred the data from the first decade as being incomplete.

"So what?" Montgomery murmured.

It did look innocuous. "We're missing something." Lilia had never been good at interpreting statistics without Gid telling her the answer.

Which presumably was what he was trying to do.

Montgomery scrolled up and down, and they both sought patterns or significance. The numbers of shades increased dramatically after each major emission of radiation. Gid had separated the most recent fifty years regionally and all the familiar hits were there. D.C., Houston, Mexico City, Seattle, Gotham.

"Big spike after Gotham," Montgomery said.

"No surprise," Lilia whispered. "Really dense population there at the time of the hit."

"Then the numbers drop after each big hit."

"It's a cycle: radiation has the greatest effect on babies who are in utero when the mother is exposed. Mutations peak about five months after the detonation. After that, defects diminish at a steady rate until they reach normal levels."

"Or until five months after the next hit."

"Pretty much."

"So this isn't news."

"But maybe the quantification is." Lilia knew she wasn't the only one who failed to see Gid's point.

"Someone palm-raped you to get this," Montgomery muttered, his frustration clear.

"And Gid anticipated that." Lilia glanced over her shoulder as someone entered the beverage bar.

It was the shade from the front desk of the hotel. They weren't anywhere near the hotel, which meant that Lilia *had* heard a footfall on the stairs.

The shade had followed her.

"What's the matter?" Montgomery asked.

"That's the shade from the hotel. She followed me."

Lilia pushed to her feet. "I need to find out who she's working for."

Lilia got up, but must have looked somewhat adversarial. The shade took one look at her and ran.

To MONTGOMERY'S dismay, Lilia bolted after the shade from the hotel. He retrieved both datachips in a hurry, shrugging at the proprietor's knowing smirk.

"They keep them on electronic leashes, just because of wolves like you," the proprietor shouted, but Montgomery wasn't listening.

He was running after Lilia.

Again.

That fog was sliding through the netherzones, making him shiver when it touched his boots. Montgomery ignored it and ran after Lilia.

The shade went down one walkway and turned abruptly down another. Lilia chased her, yelling, for all the good that did. They navigated alleys and broad thoroughfares. The fog got thicker and deeper, more silvery and sinister. Montgomery didn't like it one bit. The shade dumped trash cans behind herself, leapt over open grates by swinging from the pipes overhead, disappeared into the steam of local power generation.

Lilia followed suit, Montgomery right behind her. Lilia pulled her laze, but Montgomery shouted at her to put it away.

She grudgingly did what she was told.

He doubted that would last.

The shade knew the labyrinth, Montgomery realized quickly. She was fast, agile, and evasive. He suspected he would hear later that the shade had an unfair asset in her flat shoes.

But maybe Lilia was more motivated. She slowly gained on the shade. The two were maybe fifty paces ahead of him when Montgomery saw the shade's hair slip from her braid.

Lilia pounced. She grabbed the shade's hair and wrapped the length of it around her hand, hauling her to a stop. The shade screamed, then spun to fight, kicking at Lilia like a wild dog. The fog was waist deep in this corner, swirling about Lilia and the shade like a tornado.

As if it would pull them under.

But fog didn't do stuff like that.

Lilia had the shade against the wall in record time. "Why are you following me?" she demanded as Montgomery drew closer. "Who are you working for?"

The shade glanced around herself, panting, then whispered.

Lilia shook her head and leaned closer as the shade whispered again. "Maybe she has a voice box mutation." Lilia muttered and bent her head even closer.

Montgomery was still half a dozen steps away when the shade lunged for Lilia and bit her ear.

Lilia shouted, then loosed her grip for a precious second. That was all the shade needed to wriggle free, as lithe as a fish. Montgomery bolted after the shade, but she squirmed through a space too small for him to follow.

And disappeared from sight. The fog closed after her, disguising her figure as surely as if she'd planned it that way.

Lilia swore eloquently as she came to a halt behind him. She exhaled with frustration as the fog wound sinuously around them. "Zero for two, Montgomery. You're screwing with my legendary good luck."

"You shouldn't have just run after her. It's dangerous."

"I'm used to solving things alone."

"We're supposed to be working together, Lil." Montgomery was irritated and didn't care if she knew it. "Maybe I was wrong when I thought we'd make a great team."

"Maybe you weren't." Lilia smiled at him and things didn't seem so bad after all. "Sorry. I've never worked with a partner I could trust."

"Well, maybe that should change."

"Maybe it is." Her smile broadened and her eyes lit

and he could have spent the day staring at her. The fog cosseted them, closing them off from the world in their own little cocoon. It was chilly though, its touch slithery.

Montgomery shivered. "This fog is so strange."

"I feel as if it's following me," Lilia agreed. She flicked a hand at it, but it didn't disperse. "Do you get it a lot here?"

"I've never seen it before. It's unnatural."

Lilia shuddered and looked at the fog with revulsion. "It touches like a date with fast hands. I don't like it."

He stared at her for a moment, surprised at the accuracy of her summary. "Let me see that ear," he said then, and wiped the blood from her lobe. She leaned her forehead against his shoulder and he felt her shiver. His arms closed around her protectively. "You could take fewer chances, Lil."

"I have to solve the puzzle. Why is that data so important?" She frowned, then looked up at him. "We're in New Gotham. Gid died in Gotham. Maybe that's where we can find the key."

"You're not going back into Gotham without a better plan than that."

"No. Not yet anyway." His palm chimed and she glanced up at him. "You're late for work." The bruise on her cheek was becoming more purple with every moment.

"Is it too much to ask you to try to stay out of trouble?"

That impish grin wreaked havoc with his pulse. "Probably. I'll try, just for you."

Montgomery didn't believe it. "I'll try to get the security vid from the hotel, and find out who came to your room." Gratitude lit her eyes and sent heat through his veins. "Don't go back to the hotel. That's where they'll be looking for you."

"Whoever 'they' are." Lilia shrugged. "I'm not going to run and hide, Montgomery, not until I figure out who killed Gid."

As much as he admired her determination, it terrified him. "It's risky . . ."

"Life is risky. If I'm not going to take any chances, I might as well be dead." She reached up and touched her lips to his before he or could argue, sending a blaze of desire to his toes. He closed his arms around her, ignoring the pervasive fog, remembering the heat of her locked around him.

And a man laughed in close proximity.

MONTGOMERY BROKE their kiss and pulled his laze. Lilia had pulled hers as well and they stood back to back, staring into the fog. "Who's there?" Montgomery called and the laugh came again.

Louder.

Darker.

"Just like in the old city," Lilia muttered. At Montgomery's inquiring glance, she continued. "I heard this laugh in my helm when I found the dead shade."

"In your helm?"

She nodded.

"No wonder you were spooked," he said. "There are no stray frequencies in the old city."

"That's what I thought."

Montgomery surveyed the area around them as the fog withdrew slightly. There was no evading the sense that it was sentient, and evil. "Lil, you need to be careful," he began, knowing that he was wasting his breath.

Lilia smiled at him and her eyes were dancing with that vitality he found so intriguing. "You know, Montgomery, my mother would like you just fine." She put one hand on his chest and leaned closer to whisper. "Funny thing is that I kind of like you myself."

She'd never change, and he was glad of it. Montgomery abandoned the argument and kissed Lilia as thoroughly as she deserved.

But not nearly as thoroughly as he wanted to.

His palm, after all, was chiming an imperative.

Officials without Leads in Horrendous Attacks on Gotham

NEW GOTHAM—This morning, in the daily press update, the head of Republican Security admitted that they are no closer to naming the culprits responsible for the attacks on Gotham just five days ago.

Lucas O'Shaunessy, appointed Chief of Republic Security just three months ago, acknowledged the possibility that the mastermind behind the coordinated attack might never be known. "It's not unlikely that he or she participated in these suicide attacks. If nothing else, the majority of people who do know who planned this assault are dead, which makes investigation difficult."

It has been determined that no less than fifty synchronized assaults were launched more or less simultaneously upon Gotham on the morning of July 11.

At this time, it is known that the assault began at approximately 9:05 a.m. when suicide bombers exploded nearly thirty dirty atomic bombs in central Gotham's public transit system, spreading radiation and chaos throughout the city at the peak of morning rush hour. Dirty bombs are conventional explosive devices surrounded by radioactive material, and are small enough to be carried in backpacks or briefcases. Officials now speculate that these bombs, even given their number and the damage they caused, were only a diversion. It is unclear how many citizens were killed by this phase of the assault.

Almost simultaneous to the detonation of the dirty bombs, it appears that atomic bombs were detonated on Gotham's streets. Although mushroom clouds were observed, as well as fireballs and a subsequent surge in radiation emanating from the city, it is unclear precisely how many devices were detonated or what method of delivery was used. They were not dropped from aircraft, as Gotham remains a no-fly zone and no aircraft were observed overhead. According to a representative from the Society of Nuclear Darwinists, the radiation levels recorded indicates that the cumulative blast was in the vicinity of forty kilotons, or roughly equivalent to three times that released upon Hiroshima in 1945. The Society representative also said that there were differences in the pattern of the blast, which indicates that the devices were detonated on the ground. He refused to speculate upon survival rates within the city.

Additionally, sixteen small aircraft targeted nuclear reactors in New Jersey and Pennsylvania between 9:00 a.m. and 9:15 a.m. Although two planes were shot down within the restricted air space over each reactor, the others succeeded in crashing into their targets by 9:30 a.m. The damaged reactors include four at the Susquehanna nuclear facility, one at Hope Creek, two at Oyster Creek, and three at Limerick, Pennsylvania. Radioactive material has been confirmed to be leaking into the atmosphere, although the Republic has yet to release an accounting of the extent of the damage sustained or the current status of the reactor cores. Journalists have not been allowed into the controlled access space surrounding any of the reactors, but all residents are being evacuated from a potential fallout plume stretching from Philadelphia to Hartford.

Emergency services are still overwhelmed in the region, while hospitals and shelters in surrounding regions are struggling to deal with the influx of those who had been Gotham residents and those evacuated from the potential fallout plume. Fires continue to rage in Gotham and the Republic has forbidden emergency services personnel to intervene. The damage to bridges and the blockage of several tunnels where they emerge into the city has both hampered the evacuation and prompted speculation that ground zero of the bombs was at these locations.

Ernest Sinclair, president of the Society of Nuclear Darwinists and in attendance at the President's press conference in New D.C. this morning called the incident a "horrific example of man's inhumanity to man." According to Dr. Sinclair, the Society of Nuclear Darwinists is actively advising the Republic upon the appropriate emergency response in changing conditions. A spokesperson from the Society noted that the prevailing winds from the southwest during the summer months will "virtually guarantee" that Gotham is within the fallout plume from the nuclear reactors. The unofficial spokesperson, who preferred to remain unnamed, reminded reporters that the fallout and long-term effect of the Chernobyl disasters in 1985 and 2009 were far less than anticipated. (It should be noted that there are those, however, who dispute the official research results from Chernobyl.)

Given the evacuation of Gotham and the unwillingness of the government to expose law enforcement officials to unnecessary levels of radiation, is it unclear how any investigation can be pursued. Seven different international terrorist groups known to be hostile to the Republic have claimed responsibility for the devastating attack, although Republic officials insist that they are giving no credence to any one claim over the others.

Critics are becoming increasingly vocal, demanding explanations as to why only two of the attacking aircraft were shot down in restricted air space, the ready availability of small aircraft licenses, the apparent lack of security on public transit, and the apparent lack of a cohesive evacuation plan for Gotham. There has also been criticism of the Republic's lack of preparedness for such a disaster and the lethargic speed of response. Mr. O'Shaunessy admitted his agency's apparent ineffectiveness in facing this recent challenge, calling the lack of preparation for such a concerted attack "a failure of imagination." He is expected to announce his resignation within days.

XVI

THERE WAS nothing so wonderful as a bed with her name on it. Lilia went back to the hotel, locked the door of her unit, and slid a piece of furniture against it for insurance. She cleaned up her ear and climbed into bed.

She was asleep within moments.

Lilia awakened to the soft chime of her palm. The light coming through the window of her hotel room had changed, evidence that it was early evening. She rubbed her eyes, yawned, and looked at her palm.

It had received a message while she napped, marked "urgent." Her palm, at least, had known better than to wake her up for that. She yawned again. Joachim was probably missing her expert advice.

But no: it was from the Society.

Maybe they'd amended the conference schedule. Lilia yawned wide enough to swallow the vid screen on the wall, sat up, and tapped her palm.

The Society was revoking her fellowship, effective immediately.

Within an hour of her planning to quit in a glorious show of defiance.

Unfair!

Lilia was on her feet, spitting sparks, and wide awake. How dare they do this to her?

When had the Society ever expelled a fellow who had paid up his or her dues? When had they ever turfed a fellow right before that fellow honored one of their nearest and dearest? No doubt about it, they were afraid of what Lilia might say when she got up in front of everyone.

And so they should be.

It must have been their diabolical plan all along to lure

her south under false pretenses. She wouldn't put such scheming past Ernestine. Lilia wanted her conference fee creds back. Her impulse was to throw on some clothes and go rip someone apart—preferably Ernestine herself—but Montgomery's point was well taken.

Leading with her passion was, after all, what they'd expect from her. Leaping in where angels feared to tread was pretty much Lilia's trademark.

And Ernestine would be looking forward to the confrontation.

There was something satisfying about the prospect of making Ernestine wait for it. Vengeance was a dish best served on elegant china, with all the frills.

Lilia's mom had taught her that.

While Lilia dressed for success, she formulated a plan.

She didn't understand the spreadsheet from the chip in the locket, but the way that Gid had passed it to her indicated its importance. It stood to reason that the only item left on his palm had a connection to the list, which meant she'd missed something at Breisach and Turner. The receptionist who had stood guard at that portal had been dispatched from fulfilling her angelic mission, which made Lilia suspect that she'd known the truth too.

Clearly, Lilia needed to break into those offices and look for . . . well, that was where the plan showed its weakness. She'd go there under cover of darkness and look for something that seemed to have a connection with what she knew.

Sometimes a person had to hope for the best.

Because there was a chance of her having an active evening, Lilia was glad she'd brought her one tailored evening suit. It was a jazzy little number with trousers, a tuxedo cut for a woman, one that nudged the boundary of the decency code but didn't cross it.

Plus, she felt hot when she wore it.

That couldn't hurt.

There was something, Lilia was convinced, about crisp black lycrester that made a woman feel like an irresistible siren. A fabric that could have been made in heaven, lycrester was smooth to the touch, soft and supple, held a crease but didn't wrinkle. It seemed too good to be true, which was why it cost a bomb, which was why Lilia planned to still have this suit when she died.

And it would fit.

Sadly, given the trim cut of the suit, her laze was less unobtrusive than would have been ideal. She wore it anyway, rationalizing that people might be more respectful of her opinion that way.

That plan worked for about three seconds.

LILIA EMERGED from the stairwell to find that the shade on the front desk was different. Had Bite Queen gone AWOL? Lilia asked the new shade on the front desk about her predecessor. Even with a thorough description, Lilia got only a blank stare in reply.

Maybe the shade had had her memory wiped. One heard about such marvels, but only in whispers behind closed doors at the Institute.

It wasn't legal, but that didn't mean that it wasn't done.

Just to make her evening complete, a hotel security representative appeared at Lilia's side. "Excuse me, madame, but would you please surrender your weapon here at the desk?" His smile was tight, as if it was painful to him. "For your safety, of course."

As this seemed likely to have the opposite effect, Lilia protested. "I'm registered and authorized to carry my laze."

His disapproving look proved that he was a man who failed to appreciate the charms of black lycrester. "The hotel's corporate policy expressly forbids the possession of firearms on any of its properties."

Lilia considered his own weapon. "Funny then that you have a laze."

He smiled again and Lilia wished he would stop. "There is an exception for security personnel hired to ensure the safety of hotel guests and employees." He put out his hand.

"Ms. Desjardins, isn't it? While you are our guest, you are required to surrender your weapon to security."

Lilia was tempted to leave right there. The problem was that she wanted to have her say to Ernestine, right now in the main ballroom where the Society fellows were congregating. The security dude wouldn't let her head deeper into the hotel with her laze, no matter how well she argued.

"What are you going to do with it?"

"Your weapon will be held in a secure location and returned to you upon your departure from the hotel." He checked the desktop in front of the shade. "You're scheduled to leave Sunday, aren't you?"

"That's right." Lilia folded her arms across her chest. "What if I want it sooner, to possess on property not held by the hotel? A girl can't be too careful, you know."

"You can always check out, Ms. Desjardins." He looked as if he'd like nothing better, which—predictably—made Lilia perversely think about extending her sojourn in nirvana. "When you do, your weapon will be returned to you."

"But not before?"

He offered that smile again. Lilia was annoyed enough to offer him a perfect mimicry of it, which seemed to disconcert him. Her mother had taught her to never let people like this guy to take control of the situation.

Lilia surrendered her laze, with obvious reluctance. "Well, I have a few questions for the hotel, so if you're their appointed representative, maybe you could answer them." She showed him her wounded earlobe. "A shade in the employ of this establishment bit me this afternoon. I must insist upon seeing the health and inoculation records for the shade in question."

His eyes narrowed. "Do you know the shade's number?"

"No, but she was working on the front desk when I checked in, so you should be able to retrieve her number from the shift records."

He began to tap at his palm. "You'll have to file an injury report . . ."

FALLEN 263

"No, you'll have to file the injury report on my behalf. I'm late for an appointment. The shade bit me and ran."

"And where did this occur?"

"In the netherzones. At a beverage bar in Forest Green. There can be only one."

He looked up. "What were you doing in the netherzones? That's off-limits for citizens."

"I'm not just a citizen. I'm a shade hunter."

"You were hunting shades?"

Lilia decided to recast herself as hero, because she was in a tight spot and didn't much like his attitude. It was only a small revision to the truth. "The shade was acting suspiciously. She went into the netherzones and I followed her. I cornered and caught her, she bit me and escaped."

"Did you see where she went?"

"No. You have this fog in your netherzones that makes it hard to pursue anyone."

He blinked. "Fog? I've never seen fog down there."

"Well, there's a ton of it this weekend. It even came up into the street last night. I'm surprised you put up with it, but then there's no accounting for regional differences, is there?" Lilia forced the tight smile and he blinked at her.

The fog wasn't normal.

Other people couldn't see it.

Except her and Montgomery.

Interesting.

Lilia walked away before he could stop her, seething still about the sacrifice of her laze. She was starting to remember why she'd always found an excuse to miss this conference.

And now, contrary to every probability Gid could have calculated, she was deliberately looking for Ernestine Sinclair.

MONTGOMERY WAS on patrol when he first heard the whisper.

At first he thought he was imagining it. The streets were filled with that silvery fog again. He marched through it, keeping to the patrol path he had logged earlier, and tried to decide what to do.

If he showed up for the physical exam, his scars would be found.

If he didn't show up for the physical exam, he'd be terminated.

Neither option was particularly appealing. He'd offered to take patrol, so he could think.

Too bad he had more questions than answers. Who was framing Lilia and why? What did Fitzgerald's statistics mean? What had Rachel known that had gotten her killed? If Rachel had discovered the identities of any of the Council of Three members, what would she have done with the information?

She would have remembered it, Montgomery was sure, instead of recording it on her palm.

But she would have filed the proof. He thought of Breisach and Turner's offices, the filing cabinets along the walls there, and wondered whether he had missed the obvious.

"Munkar . . . "

Montgomery froze. The whisper knew his name.

The fog rolled across the street in front of Montgomery, all quicksilver and mystery. It had direction, like the current in a river. It flowed into the access to the commuter level of the netherzones, as if it had purpose.

Montgomery watched it for a long moment, weighing his options, then decided to accept the invitation.

The stairwell to the commuter conveyors was filled with the dark opalescent light of the swirling fog. It was cold and made him shiver when he stepped into its tide. It also seemed to pull him into it.

"Munkar . . . "

The summons rose from the netherzones precisely as the fog descended there. Montgomery went after it. The fire door shut behind him with a decisive click, even though he was sure it had been latched back when he passed through it. The darkness closed around him, the only illumination coming from the fog.

That male laughter echoed in his ears again.

It had to be a figment of his imagination.

But Lilia had heard it too.

Twice.

BLAKE WAS at the door to the ballroom, a second glass of sparkling wine in his hand just for Lilia. It was the last thing she needed, so of course, she accepted it with a gracious smile. He whistled loud enough that several people turned, then bowed low. "Divine! Lilia, you look scrumptious!"

"Blake, I'm not dessert."

"Maybe you should be."

"For you? I thought your taste was for other delicacies."

He grinned. "I can still appreciate a masterpiece without committing to it." He offered his elbow. "What better tonic for all of us than a party?"

There was something to be said for that, though Lilia thought it would be graceless to say that she'd have preferred the party to have a different guest list.

She scored a point for *prudent*.

The room was elegant. The men were all in black tie, the women in gowns, many of them glittery enough to make the lycrester look mundane. To Lilia's surprise, Mike had hit on a trend before it was over—there were lots of Orv tattoos in the crowd. Blake was in his element, shaking hands and looking for votes. He sparkled more than the chandeliers, jewelry and bubbles combined.

Nuclear Darwinists had gathered from near and far, but Chicago was the hometown of the vast majority of attendees. That made sense, Chicago being the location of the Institute of Radiation Studies. Unlike others, Lilia made no jokes about the Midwest being dull: if being dull ensured that home was the only major Republican city left unbombed, then "dull" worked for Lilia. Her beloved Mont Royal hadn't been nearly so lucky.

Otherwise, there were few Nuclear Darwinists from cities spared nuclear destruction. That was the turf of abstract theorists. And old cities? Only shade hunters like Lilia ever went there, and even she wasn't reckless enough to live in such a place.

Waiters slipped through the crowd with trays of tall glasses and there was a happy burble of conversation, one that was destined to get louder the longer the free booze flowed. She liked that Gid would be honored with an award at a presentation like this: it commemorated his passing with a certain style.

The best part, though, was that people didn't know what to do about her. As the widow of one of the Society's favorite sons, and a guest invited to present the award renamed in his honor, they should have been making a fuss over her. As a fellow who had refused to cede to the Society's demands to surrender the angel-shades—well, angels—for research, Lilia should have been chucked right out the door. She enjoyed watching the war of emotions on so many faces.

Being the center of controversy—and having some sparkling wine in her veins—put a little bounce in Lilia's step.

Lilia threw back some wine and considered the other occupants of the room. She had to guess that the members of the Council of Three would be in attendance. A Council meeting would explain the quick and timely decision to revoke her fellowship.

So, who were the Council members?

Ever the gracious gentleman, Blake tried to divert her with small talk. Lilia had to wonder why he allied himself so visibly with her, given that he was running for Society president. Old times' sake maybe? It could only hurt his campaign, but she appreciated the gesture.

Until he tried to warn her.

"Who's your best guess for Council of Three?" she asked as she openly assessed the crowd.

"Lilia, just do yourself a favor and leave things alone."

"I will when someone tells me what Gid was working on."

Blake leaned closer, dropping his voice another increment. "Listen to me. This isn't a game. You could get hurt."

"For asking questions?"

"Yes. Gid was on Society business . . ."

"Well, duh. He worked for the Society—"

"Not *that* kind of Society business," Blake interrupted her for probably the first time ever and Lilia met the warning in his eyes.

"Council of Three," she guessed in a whisper.

He held her gaze steadily, neither affirming nor denying.

That was good enough for Lilia.

Her scalp crawled. *Gideon, what have you done?* "Who's the Council of Three right now?"

Blake straightened. "I don't know."

"You're lying."

He looked around and dropped his voice. "You don't understand what you're getting into."

"And you think I can't handle it. Thanks very much."

Blake evidently saw that his strategy had misfired, because he gritted his teeth. "Look, I'll find out what I can for you. Does that make a difference?"

"Not one bit." Lilia snagged another glass of wine. "If you find out anything juicy, you probably won't tell me."

He set his lips, proof positive of that.

Lilia was annoyed, not just by Blake's assessment of her, but by his alliance with the administration of the Society. She couldn't trust him anymore. He could be warning her off just to protect the Society, which was not one of her agenda items.

All the same, this wasn't the place to fight it out. People

were starting to notice. Lilia summoned her best fake smile. "Okay, Blake, let's call a truce. If the presidency is what you want, then I hope you win."

He smiled, hiding his thoughts with an ease that made Lilia miss the Blake she had known. "Never one to mince words, are you?"

"Well, I wouldn't wish the job on anyone, but then there's no accounting for taste, is there? I'd even vote for you, and put my little nail in your coffin if they hadn't revoked my fellowship today."

He blinked. "They what?"

"You must have known." He paled though and Lilia knew he hadn't known. Her judgment of him softened slightly. "Go ahead, ditch me," she advised. "Being seen with me is a liability to your campaign."

"Oh, no, that's not true," he said without conviction.

He wanted to run so badly that Lilia patted his arm with sympathy. "Go now. It's only going to get worse."

His eyes narrowed. "What are you going to do?"

Lilia smiled and indicated a woman on the other side of the room.

"Don't provoke her . . ." Blake said, but it was too late.

Lilia Desjardins had nothing left to lose. She charted a course toward Ernestine Sinclair, current Society president.

Lilia's favorite piece of toxic waste.

THE LOWER netherzones were filled to the rafters with fog. Montgomery strode into the fog to find its source.

He immediately felt dirty.

It was a slithery fog, touching Montgomery in a strangely intimate way, like an unwelcome lover with fast hands. He remembered Lilia's words all too well. He descended into the fog as one slips into a pool of water. The fog engulfed him. He felt violated every place it touched his pseudoskin and had the unreasonable urge to scrub himself down.

When it had closed over him completely, his response

changed. Every hair on his body rose and he tingled from head to toe. It wasn't fear and it wasn't dread: it was lust that the fog awakened. He was raging with sexual desire as he never had been before.

Montgomery wasn't easily spooked, but this fog was different. He froze, listening. He could hear the rhythmic squeal of a dozen treadmills close at hand. He could smell the perspiration of the shades who walked those treadmills, could hear their labored breathing. Gears ground and belts whined, evidence that even the labor of shades had to be maximized.

"*Munkar* . . ." The voice beckoned him onward, deeper and louder than it had been.

Who knew his old name? Montgomery had to find out. He could see his feet and an increment of the poured concrete floor. He held his laze high as he began to walk deeper into the labyrinth.

He didn't know how far he walked before the lights brightened and then winked out.

He was surrounded by silvery fog.

Montgomery only hoped he saw whatever was stalking him in time to blow it away.

IT WAS almost too easy to hate Ernestine Sinclair. In her absence, Lilia wondered whether she'd missed some redeeming feature of Ernestine's character. In her presence, Lilia was too busy loathing Ernestine to care.

First, she was the daughter of the founder of the Institute, Ernest Sinclair himself, one of Lilia's least favorite action heroes. Secondly, she was president of the Society, just finishing her term, a job that Lilia was convinced that no sane individual could want.

Including Blake.

Finally, she was a plain old-fashioned bitch. Inescapable, yet no one seemed to see this truth but Lilia.

Ernestine pivoted and locked Lilia in her sights. As she strode closer—a stalker in evening attire—she smiled.

Lilia smiled back, putting a bit more malice in her smile. Hungry barracudas had nothing on those smiles.

Ernestine, Lilia noticed, had chosen a swastika for her third-eye tattoo, which meant that she was both Sixth Degree and insensitive. Lilia knew that it was an ancient symbol for the sun and protection from the evil eye, but everyone was aware that it had passed into the vernacular of symbolism with a nastier association.

"Lilia," Ernestine said, showing her father's ability to command the attention of everyone within hearing distance. "How nice of you to make a final appearance at a Society event."

"Final? Should I be careful what I eat here?"

Ernestine's smile thinned. "I can only assume that you've received the official revocation of your fellowship and that this will be our last chance to see each other."

"I came to present the award renamed in Gid's honor, and I'll happily retire my fellowship after I've done so."

Ernestine laughed her throaty chuckle, the one that had every man within twenty paces looking her way. She'd laughed like that at the Institute, when the two women had lived in the same dorm, and Lilia was surprised that she hadn't upgraded any of her charms in the intervening years. "That's not how it's going to be, Lilia."

"Why not? I came all this way, specifically to present the award. You knew that was why I was coming."

"Lilia, don't pretend you don't understand. My father would have been appalled by your presence at our conference. It's a sad commentary upon our culture at large that so many individuals"—Lilia got a look to punctuate precisely which individuals Ernestine referred to, as if anyone had any doubt—"see only the potential for personal profit in their associations with the Society."

"I don't know," Lilia said, helping herself to another glass of wine. "It could be argued that the Society itself was founded for the purpose of profiting from shades and mutants. How about those government research contracts?"

This was a somewhat unpopular remark.

"Securing the future of those unfortunates who have birth defects attributable to radiation exposure is a social responsibility," Ernestine scolded. "But surgical manipulation of subjects, many of whom are incapable of protesting their fate, well, Lilia, that's beyond the pale."

"I don't think that minor surgical alteration of children who are already not passing as norms—even if they are— is any more morally suspect than enslaving those born with defects." Lilia took a restorative sip of wine. "Especially since those defects are the result of our species bombing the crap out of each other. Collectively, we're not innocent either way."

"But surgical alterations are done despite the will of the child."

"Tell me, how does a child in utero protest his mother being exposed to radiation?"

"Lilia, it's not the same thing." Ernestine was impatient. "The importance of ensuring the defense of the Republic is beyond question, and ours is not to question the decisions of those with far more information."

"Oh, I think as citizens, that's precisely our obligation."

"We can hardly argue politics here."

Lilia felt her temper begin to boil. Unlike her smug fellows, Lilia saw these altered kids all the time. They appeared with hopeful parents, who had effectively mortgaged their souls for the surgery. Every single one of those parents was desperate for a chance to see their child's future secured. Joachim hired the kids to do general labor, to take care of animals or cook, whenever he could.

Which wasn't all the time.

Lilia tried not to think about what happened to the ones he had to turn away. She didn't always succeed.

Ernestine smiled her nasty smile. "Perhaps we should have invited you as a special guest for another reason this year, Lilia, given your recent infamy."

Lilia had a very bad feeling. It might simply have been due to the venom in Ernestine's tone.

"I don't know what you're talking about."

Ernestine smiled and lifted a single fingertip.

Her gesture prompted the sudden appearance of the official photograph of Armaros and Baraqiel, Lilia's angel-shades. *Angels*. They filled the wall display with their brilliant glory; their beaming smiles alone had to be a good ten feet wide.

The room fell silent. Lilia had to think it was awe.

"You look as if you're proud of this lie," Ernestine hissed.

"I'm glad that we aren't going to pretend that this little exchange is about the circus or surgically altered children."

"You're the one who's falsifying—"

"Allow me to present the angels," Lilia said, casting her words over the room. "Two individuals whom I persuaded to join the circus earlier this year."

A murmur passed through the crowd and Rhys ibn Ali looked daggers at Lilia.

"Please refer to them by their assigned shade numbers." Ernestine snapped.

"They don't have any." Lilia decided to push her. "They have *names*. They are Armaros and Baraqiel."

Disapproval rolled through the room like a dark tide.

"Names!" Ernestine spat, raising her voice to carry to the corners of the ballroom. "It is forbidden for shades to possess names, according to the law code, just as it is forbidden for a Nuclear Darwinist to capture a new mutation and not deliver that specimen to the labs of the Institute—"

"Angels aren't a new mutation. We've been talking about them for millennia."

"They are not angels!"

Lilia turned to the image. "They look like angels to me."

Ernestine seethed. "*Anyone* could tell you that the statistical probability of such a complex mutation occurring, even as a result of radiation exposure, is infinitesimally small . . ."

"Thirty-three and a half million to one. Against."

Silence filled the ballroom.

Lilia had their attention.

She could work with that.

Lilia strode toward the display, knowing the amplifiers would be embedded in the ceiling there. "That a winged fetus would be born alive and survive to adulthood roughly doubles the odds against. That there would be two such mutations in close proximity to each other, both of whom would mature to adulthood and simultaneously avoid capture by the Society for those years of development is beyond the capacity for statistical computation."

Lilia paused for effect. "I know this, not because I excel at the calculation of statistical probabilities—in fact, I stink at it."

They laughed at that admission.

"I know this because my late husband, Gideon Fitzgerald, could calculate the probabilities of anything, to nine decimal places, in his head. When I found Armaros and Baraqiel, Gid and I had our first argument ever. He was skeptical, perhaps even more skeptical than you are, and he told me the mathematical justification for his response. He calculated the odds to be less than one in seventy-six million."

"Which only proves that they are surgically modified," Ernestine insisted. "We all know the accuracy of calculations by Gideon Fitzgerald."

"No, it proves nothing," Lilia retorted. "The probability is overwhelmingly against anyone finding a pair of shades mutated to fit our mythical description of angels, but it's still not impossible. Improbable, but not impossible. In fact, that's exactly what happened: the lab reports prove that it *is* possible."

"Lab reports can be adjusted to prove anything," Ernestine insisted. "How gullible do you think we are?"

Lilia surveyed the group coldly. "Perhaps I missed

something in my training, but I always believed that a
Nuclear Darwinist of repute observed all of the data before making a decision. I was taught that an open mind
was the greatest asset of an intelligent scientist. Let me
show you the test results."

Ernestine laughed. "We have no need to see the lab reports you bought to endorse this claim! We wouldn't even
give them credence by asking to examine them." There
were murmurs of assent from the crowd. "We have a reputation to protect—"

"Where does it say that we know everything?" Lilia demanded. "The radiation levels in the atmosphere of this
planet increase almost daily—we all know that—which
means that humans are exposed to a constant and an increasing barrage of radioactivity. I don't think any of us
can say where, or if, our species' mutational process will
end." She paused for a breath. "We're all guinea pigs, boys
and girls, in the greatest biological experiment of all time."

Oh, that was a popular statement. There appeared to be
a good chance of Lilia being stoned for heresy.

Or would she be burned for that?

"And now," she said, turning to the display. "Now, the
angels have come. Maybe Reverend Billie Jo Estevez is
right and they've brought a message to our kind. Don't
you think we should ask what it is, instead of slicing them
up into little pieces to see what they're really made of?"

The room erupted in anger and remonstration then.

She raised her voice in challenge. "Look into their
eyes and tell me that they wouldn't know the difference if
you subjected them to vivisection."

The mood in the ballroom turned ugly.

Ernestine looked daggers at Lilia. "Proud of yourself?"
she hissed.

"Pretty much, yes," Lilia said and accepted another
glass of wine from a waiter who obviously appreciated
her black lycrester.

"Your own husband, Gideon, denounced you formally
to the Society review committee, Lilia. The person who

knew you better than anyone else believed that you were lying about this. That's why it was decided that you weren't the appropriate person to present the award renamed in his honor."

"Fair enough," Lilia said. "I want my conference and travel fees reimbursed, because you invited me here under false pretenses. I want my hotel bill paid. I want my fellowship fees for this year refunded and I want my laze back."

Ernestine's eyes narrowed. "Is that all?"

Lilia pretended to think about it. "I think so."

"Then stop at the registration desk and have your I.D. bead updated. Your professional designation has to be removed from your file."

"And my creds returned to my file."

Ernestine sneered. "I should have known it would be about the creds for you."

Lilia smiled. "I should have known you were evil, right to the core. The really sad thing is that I could spend all of eternity in your company in hell." She drained her glass and put it on a passing waiter's tray. "I'm thinking I should reform my ways, before it's too late."

With that, Lilia walked out of the hotel ballroom, feeling lighter on her feet than she had in years. The Society of Nuclear Darwinists, after all, wasn't a club to which she had ever really wanted to belong.

XVII

"WELCOME, MUNKAR." It was the same voice that had called Montgomery onward, at once everywhere and nowhere. "Somehow I knew you would answer my summons." The voice was deep and dark, an old voice worn as smooth as a serpent.

It was masculine and beguiling. Ageless and ancient. Montgomery understood that he'd been summoned by the darkest angel of all.

Lucifer.

"Yes," the voice agreed easily. "Who could have anticipated that you and I would meet? Our teams don't mingle much anymore." The voice chuckled. "But then, there is that delightful Lilia, who doesn't seem to be allied with any team."

At the mention of Lilia's name, Montgomery remembered the feel of her against him. He imagined her skin beneath his hands, her mouth beneath his own, her breath against his throat. He felt his erection straining against the reevlar of his codpiece.

His companion laughed. "Perfect! That's precisely what I needed. How accommodating of you, Munkar, to see to my desires."

Montgomery could discern a shadow then, a silhouette of a man against the fog. He seemed to be only a dozen paces in front of Montgomery, although it was difficult to be certain. The shadow was only a tone darker than the silver of the fog and became less distinct if he looked straight at it.

"Who are you?" Montgomery asked, although he thought he knew.

"That's not an easy question to answer. Maybe you should try another one."

"What do you want?"

"Focus, Munkar. All inquiries benefit from a certain focus. We all want so many things, don't we?"

Montgomery thought of Lilia again. It was as if the fog stirred his passion and manipulated his thoughts. He was tempted to shoot and ask questions later, but wasn't sure precisely where his companion was. If he was going to fire, he wanted the shot to be fatal. "What do you want from me?"

"Well done! There's a veritable list, of course, but you've made an admirable beginning."

"To what?"

"Desire."

Montgomery almost felt the exhaled word roll across his flesh. It could have been a caress, one that stirred him even further.

Montgomery took a step back.

"Preferably illicit desire. Maybe we should call it lust."

"I don't know what you mean." But Montgomery did, all too well.

"What's the point of falling, Munkar, if you don't enjoy the earthly benefits?" that voice whispered. "Why sacrifice so much and get so little in return? I don't have to be the one to tell you that the pleasures of the flesh are vastly underrated by the celestial crowd."

"What are you talking about?"

"When you lust, Munkar, you feed my manifestation. All of the seven deadly sins are good for me, of course, but lust is my favorite. How about you?"

"I couldn't say."

"You mean you *won't* say. I can teach you about pleasure, Munkar, teach you things you've never dreamed of knowing."

He sauntered closer, looking more substantial with every step.

"Why would you do that?"

"For the fun of it, of course."

"To serve your own ends, I'd guess. Lust feeds your manifestation because you haven't got a form of your own," Montgomery guessed, half remembering a story he had been told long ago. "Being cast into darkness meant that you can't take flesh, not really, and that you gain in power only when you can feed on wickedness. Human wickedness."

His companion hissed briefly before continuing his persuasive argument. "Are you in human company now, Munkar? I'm thinking so." His voice dropped to a whisper. "Why don't you secret yourself away with Lilia for a week or two, and satisfy your every desire? Forget the rest of the world and its woes."

Montgomery's body responded with predictable enthusiasm to this notion, although he knew that this dark angel's goal was to distract him. "I have things to do."

The voice dropped. "I know you sampled her once. How many more times will it take to sate you? Is it even possible? Think of those lips, those breasts . . ."

Montgomery found it far too easy to do so.

"Perfect!" His companion laughed, a rich rolling laugh, and stepped out of the protective cloak of the fog. He was naked and black, so black that his skin might have been carved of ebony. He was muscled and possessed of a certain radiance, a dark opalescent glow that reminded Montgomery of the fog. He had presence and Montgomery could feel the weight of his gaze. He moved with complete confidence, untroubled by his nudity, and had an impressively large erection.

Lucifer himself, emperor of all dark temptation. "Yes," the dark angel said. "My moment has finally come."

That was when Montgomery understood what was wrong with his relationship with Lilia—as long as he saw her as an object of desire, as long as he lusted after her, he would never be satisfied with their lovemaking. With lust, he served only this prince, the Prince of Darkness. He sacrificed the luster and glory of his being for empty earthly pleasure.

But if he loved Lilia, then all of that changed. Love was the expression of the divine, love was what made everything worthwhile, what made every act holy.

And it would be so easy to love Lilia.

"You must have been majestic once," Montgomery said, seeing him as a shadow of his former self.

At his disparaging tone, Lucifer unfurled his wings. They were massive and leathery, like the wings of a bat, and stretched up to brush the roof of the netherzones. "Miss yours?" he asked playfully, then leaned closer. "You could join me, Munkar. I could give you back everything you've lost and then some. We could rule together . . ."

It was out of the question. "You will never rule anything."

"I will rule the earth and the Republic, very soon now," Lucifer retorted. "The time has come, or did they forget to tell you that part when you volunteered? You're too late, Munkar, the course is set. I have the perfect plan and the candidate who will make all things possible." He leaned closer and hissed. "Why not join the team that will be triumphant?"

"It's never too late," Montgomery insisted.

Lucifer laughed at this defiant hope. "The Revelation of Saint John, chapter 9. Know it?"

Montgomery shook his head. Rachel had given him a Bible to study but its mix of speculation, misinformation, and truth had been too time consuming for him to study in depth as yet.

His dark companion cleared his throat and posed to re-cite. " *'I saw a star that had fallen from heaven to earth, and he was given the key to the shaft of the bottomless pit.'*" He smiled and gestured to the netherzones. "Here we are, Munkar. What have you done with the key?"

"There is no single key to the netherzones."

"I'm speaking metaphorically, of course. And there *is* a single key. I even know her name." He leaned closer, his breath as dark as brimstone. "Her name is Delilah. Where is Lilia's child?"

Montgomery fired his laze, right into the heart of the specter before him. He squeezed off three shots in rapid succession, but they sliced right through the dark angel before him.

One shot burst a pipe behind Lucifer, and it erupted with a sizzle and began to spew steam into the nether-zones. Montgomery smelled a fire starting, then a boiler blew. His three shots had trashed infrastructure but left the dark angel unscathed.

He hadn't taken substance.

Yet.

Lucifer, meanwhile, laughed. "Listen and learn, Munkar. My triumph is imminent and you can be a part of it. Send me the child and you'll be seated upon my right hand. We'll rule together." He leaned close again. "It's an offer you'd be a fool to refuse."

"Liar!" Montgomery shouted, but he was alone in the netherzones.

The lights came back on, all at once, and an alarm rang. He jammed his laze back into his holster and ran in the opposite direction from Emergency Response.

The Devil wanted him to change teams.

Which had to mean that he was close to thwarting something. Montgomery navigated a course to Breisach and Turner, hoping he could discover what Rachel knew.

Before it was too late.

A MINION caught up with Lilia in the lobby and insisted on removing the professional credential from her I.D. bead. She bent her head for the foul deed, seething all the while.

At least she looked fabulous.

It was a surprising relief to let the lie go, because really it had been Gid who had graduated twice summa cum laude, not Lilia.

And they couldn't erase her tattoos.

Lilia's satisfaction faded when she got to the front desk, because the security dude wouldn't return her laze. She wasn't checking out and those were the rules he lived by.

So she went to Breisach and Turner unarmed.

She felt as if she was going naked.

Which might have made the journey more interesting.

Lilia must have looked dangerous all the same—and she *was* in a pretty foul mood—because no one messed with her and it was past curfew. Maybe the good citizens of New Gotham weren't that brave. Maybe the few people who were on the streets sensed trouble emanating from Lilia's person and they scattered from her path.

The area around Breisach and Turner's offices was quiet. Lilia could see lights in the windows of upper floors of buildings, apartments over store fronts, and the occasional shadow of someone moving behind blinds.

The front door of the building was unlocked and the lights were off. Moonlight streamed through the sidelights at the entry and slipped over the transom to paint a patch of silver on the foyer floor.

Lilia slipped over the building's threshold, acting as if she had every right to be there. Once inside, she listened. The building was silent. Lilia was glad of the moon, a welcome old ally. She could see the stairs dimly and stared up them, feeling a bit of trepidation.

She reached the second floor and paused, but heard only sounds from outside. A cat yowled, someone shouted at it and something shattered. Lilia took a deep breath, told herself she was perfectly safe, and acknowledged that this was a lie. All the same, she went down the corridor to Breisach and Turner.

The door was locked.

But there were no witnesses. Lilia put her wedding ring on her index finger and broke the glass in the door with one swift stroke. Shards tinkled to the floor inside. Lilia picked up her pace, just in case there was a silent alarm. She put her ring back where it belonged, wrapped the end of her scarf around her hand, reached through the glass, and unlocked the dead bolt.

She went straight through the reception area to the office where the shade receptionist had peeked out the window. The moonlight shone brightly enough through the blinds to let her see dim shapes.

Lilia had hoped for a desktop with a blotter display like Montgomery's but no luck. There was a table in the room that looked as if it was made of wood. *Wood*. It must have cost a fortune. It had no drawers, no display, no electrical feed.

The building was starting to feel like a museum to Lilia.

One wall was completely filled with metal cabinets, each of which had four doors, one over the other. They were graceless and bulky and quite deep. Lilia had no idea what they might be or why anyone would bother to manufacture anything so hideous.

Let alone collect a whole row of them.

There was a little white box on the top drawer of the leftmost cabinet. When Lilia squinted at it, she realized it was a label of some kind. She could make out the hand-written script *"A–Armistice"*.

The one immediately below said *"Armstrong–Berkshire"*.

And so it went, one to the next, reminding Lilia of that old set of encyclopedia volumes that someone had tried to sell to her mother. Lilia and her mother had had a huge fight about them: Lilia had been fascinated by the faux-leather binding and the thin pages of paper, but her mother had called them a waste of money.

Actually she had called them "a bourgeois souvenir of Victorian social aspirations and the cultivation of appearances." When Lilia had complained, she'd been invited to look up anything she wanted to know in the public-access areas of the Republic's databanks, preferably at the public library, where the connection was fast and free and comparatively anonymous.

There was a metal tab beside the handle on each drawer. It wasn't rocket science to figure out that this was a clasp of some kind. Lilia depressed it, pulled on the handle and a massive drawer rolled out toward her.

She yelped and ducked as it clattered right over her head. It finally lurched to a stop, the depth of the drawer being—surprise—the depth of the cabinet. It was obviously on casters and heavy enough to have a momentum of its own.

The drawer was stuffed full of files, files made of *paper*.

That stopped Lilia cold. She fingered them in awe, looking over the array of drawers and trying to imagine how much paper was collected here. It too would be worth a fortune. The only time she had ever seen paper, actual sheets made of compressed wood fiber, had been when she had looked at that encyclopedia.

Never mind shipping and expediting—maybe the partners of Breisach and Turner had retired. They could sell this paper and buy themselves a tropical island. Maybe two—his and his luxury retreats.

But the paper was still here, thus unsold.

Maybe what was written on it was important. Lilia pulled out a file and flipped it open, unable to keep herself from fingering the corner with reverence.

She carried the file over to the window—the writing was small—and read a bit. It was a customer file for Armstrong Manufacturing and was filled with shipping documents, invoices, and receipts. The very fact that the documents were on paper told Lilia that they were old, and in fact, they were all dated from the 2040s. That the paper had been kept meant that the data likely hadn't been processed electronically.

Lilia paused. And *that* meant that whatever information was here was not in the Republic databanks.

Her pulse skipped.

Pulp triumphed over bytes. This was lost information, or information that the Republic didn't even know existed.

She knew then that somewhere in this array of files was the bit of info Gid had wanted her to find, the bit that the receptionist had been defending, the bit that had condemned them both.

But there were thousands of documents, hundreds of files, and time was a-wasting.

A quick peek revealed that every drawer was full, arranged in an orderly fashion. Lilia zipped through the other office, just to make sure the problem wasn't bigger. That room contained only a chair and a table similar to the one in the first office.

Back with the files, Lilia looked up *Breisach and Turner,* but found no file. *New Gotham Circus* didn't have a file either, nor did its proprietor *Stevia Fergusson,* although that had been a long shot. *Gideon Fitzgerald* didn't have a file and neither did *Lilia Desjardins. Y654892* had no file. Lilia's mother had no file. Neither did *NGPD. Adam Montgomery* didn't have a file. Lilia even checked *Armaros* and *Baraqiel.* No luck.

Gid had died in the old city. She tried *Gotham, Rockefeller Plaza,* even *Prometheus. Angel. Satan. Lucifer. God.*

Nada.

These files were starting to tick Lilia off. She wanted a good search engine but they didn't have one.

She leaned against the wall and looked up at the moon. It was high overhead, its shape fuzzy through the filter of the blinds.

Someone had shipped something somewhere, years ago, and the record was here. What had anyone been shipping that could have been important enough to get Gid killed?

The moon rolled across the sky overhead and Lilia glared at it, wishing her old friend could tell her the answer. The moon would have been here. It must have stood witness. Wasn't there supposed to be a man in the moon?

The moon was round.

And kind of yellowish.

Lilia snapped her fingers and dove for the filing cabinets, seeking the drawer for *S,* as in *Society of Nuclear Darwinists.*

The moon was almost like an orange. Orville the Orange and the Society's *Sunshine Heals* program had been launched in 2040, which was less relevant than the fact that somebody had to move those oranges around every year.

To ship and expedite them, as it were.

The Society of Nuclear Darwinists did indeed have a file at Breisach and Turner. Lilia snagged it out of the drawer, barely able to get her fingers around it because it was so fat. Decades of oranges, she guessed, none of which might have anything to do with anything.

She shut the drawer, bracing herself for an exciting night of reading. Lilia couldn't snag the data as it hadn't been digitized. She'd have to discover whether there was anything worth reading here the old-fashioned and time-consuming way.

Here?

She couldn't just steal the file—could she? She hadn't really been joking to Ernestine about changing her own game—stealing certainly would be against the law.

But then, who would know? The receptionist was dead. Did Messrs. Breisach and Turner check their paper files? She was debating the merits of reading in the office—in an uncharacteristic attack of conscience—when she heard the front door to the office open.

Lilia froze, the file clasped to her chest.

Maybe she hadn't really heard anything. She held her breath, ever optimistic.

But no. A beam of light moved across the outer office floor, then was extinguished.

Lilia might still be in the dark, but she clearly wasn't alone anymore.

LILIA DUCKED into the shadow that would be behind the office door when the visitor opened it more widely. Maybe she could leap past the new arrival and run before he or she was aware of her presence. Lilia pressed her back against the wall, clutched the file, and waited.

He shut the door to the outer corridor quietly, but he hadn't left. Lilia heard his boot on the broken glass. She heard him breathing quietly out there, waiting and listening as if he also suspected that he wasn't alone.

She had to strain her ears to hear his cautious footfalls in the outer office. That meant she was dealing with a seasoned professional, a thief who was both armed and dangerous.

One who should have been able to hear Lilia's heartbeat.

She felt his presence coming closer, smelled him more than she heard him. She sensed that he looked into the other office, then stiffened as he approached the one she occupied. Lilia saw the shadow of him through the crack between the door and the frame, a little sliver of darkness that entered the office.

He didn't advance far into the room, which didn't give Lilia any chance to make a run for it. She waited, trying to not have heart failure in the interim.

His light flicked on and she peeked around the door in time to see it play over the filing cabinets.

"Paper," he muttered. "Brilliant."

Lilia just about fainted when she recognized his voice.

Tit for tat, though. She'd get even with him scaring her like that. "You'd have more charm, Montgomery, if you didn't try to freak me out all the time."

Montgomery nearly went through the roof. He swung the flashlight around and Lilia held up a hand to block the light in front of her face. He swore so eloquently that she couldn't help but smile. He was in evil-twin guise, which made her heart soar.

"Gotcha," she said.

Montgomery went one better, though. He swooped in, caught her against his chest, and kissed her like he was never going to stop.

It worked for Lilia.

It worked just fine.

"WHAT THE hell are you doing here?" Montgomery demanded long moments later. "I thought you were staying out of trouble."

Lilia was in a trim black evening suit with her hair coiled up. Even without making any infractions of the S&D code, she was the sexiest woman he'd ever seen.

And she kissed as if she wanted to eat him alive.

"I had a relapse," she said, giving him that impish smile. "I could ask you the same thing, you know."

"I'm part of an official inquiry."

"I don't think so. You told me that there was no investigation about the secretary's death, because she was a shade."

"Maybe that changed."

She looked up at him, all sparkle and mischief, and relief made his heart skip a beat. The system was still feeding him reasons to arrest her, someone in the Society was out to get her, and she was just fine. He shouldn't have been surprised that Lilia protected herself—she'd been doing it for a while.

And maybe it was better that way. After his physical the next day, he wouldn't be able to help her at all. Montgomery tried not to worry about that.

"And that would be why you've forgotten your eye of the Republic stud?" she teased.

"They had to remove it at the beginning of my shift to

assess why it isn't working. I think the angelfire shorted it out." He didn't tell her that he'd probably worked his last shift.

"They're going to think you were staring at a nuke." Lilia regarded him with a twinkle in her eye. He noticed that she was clutching a fat paper file. "So, Mr. Straight and Narrow, have you got a warrant for this official inquiry?"

"It doesn't matter."

She let her eyes round. "Are cops allowed to break into private offices in New Gotham whenever they feel like it?"

"I was going to knock, but the door was already open. I'm investigating."

"And what did you find?"

He smiled. "A citizen with a talent for finding trouble."

She smiled back, untroubled by his assessment. "It's a gift."

Montgomery sobered. She was in a serious predicament that was getting worse. He needed to be sure she knew how bad it was. "I need to ask you a question."

"That sounds ominous."

"What happened to your child, Lil?"

She took a step back and he saw the wariness in her eyes. "I don't know what you're talking about," she said, but he could hear the lie in her tone.

"You had a shade child. It's on your file. I told you as much the other day."

"What's past is past . . ."

He wanted to shake her. "No, Lil. Someone powerful has pulled that detail up to an accessible level of your file, probably to discredit you, certainly to affect your future."

Fear flashed in her eyes. "I don't believe you. I was promised—"

"Then someone lied, or changed their mind." He leaned closer. "What I need to know, Lil, is where is the child?"

She paled. He could see as much even in the darkness. "Dead," she whispered.

"That can't be true."

She started to argue but Montgomery shook his head. "No, Lil. The truth."

She swallowed and looked away, stepping away from him in her consternation. She was as upset as he had ever seen her, although she fought to pretend otherwise. "Hidden," she said so quietly that he barely heard the word.

Montgomery's heart clenched. There was a child and the Devil himself was seeking her. He didn't doubt that there would be others. "No one is ever really hidden in the Republic, Lil," he said gently. "You know better than that."

"Gid took care of it!" she said, then clapped a hand over her mouth. He saw dismay in her eyes.

"That's what you owed him," he guessed and she turned her back on him.

"I married Gid because he said he loved me," she said, her words tight. "And he proved it."

Montgomery knew he didn't imagine that she was shaking. She took a deep breath, pivoted, and met his gaze with the old fire back in her eyes. "I don't know where she is," she said with such bravado that it had to be a lie. "And I won't begin to speculate, for anybody. I don't care what price I pay. She's safe, Gid ensured that, and I won't be the one to put her in jeopardy."

What did it take to earn Lilia's loyalty? She would protect that secret until her death; he could see it in every line of her body. Montgomery was impressed by Lilia's fierce devotion to those she loved.

He was shocked by how much he wanted to be in their company.

He wasn't going to get there by pushing for the surrender of her secrets.

Instead, he tried to coax her smile. He folded his arms across his chest and regarded her, letting his own lips curve in a smile. "I'm going to add a notation to your file, Lil."

She responded to his attempt to make peace immediately by giving him a smile of her own. "Do I get to know what it is?"

"I'm thinking that you should never be considered for police work."

"Now there's a way to break my heart."

"You left the door ajar and unlocked," he chided gently. "Anyone coming along the hall would have seen that and known that someone was in these offices." He tapped a finger on the tip of her nose. "You put yourself in danger too easily."

She eyed him, looking strong, sexy, and skeptical. "Who cares?" she demanded softly.

"I do."

He saw a glimmer in her eyes, which might have been a tear, but she brushed it away. "And there are so many people strolling along the hall outside the offices of Breisach and Turner in the middle of the night." She shook her head as their palms chimed midnight in quiet unison. "Montgomery, I'm thinking this isn't much of a risk."

They both straightened at the sound of footsteps in the outer corridor.

"You're right," Montgomery muttered. "Your luck *has* bailed."

XVIII

Saturday, October 31, 2099

"GET BACK," Montgomery said through his teeth, then flattened Lilia into the wall when she didn't move fast enough. They were behind the door, chest to chest. The only things separating them were clothing and that file.

Even the fat file was an insignificant obstacle. Montgomery could feel Lilia's curves and smell her perfume.

One taste of Lilia Desjardins hadn't been nearly enough. He thought of Lucifer, of his own revelation, and knew what he wanted.

All he had to do was convince Lilia.

When he couldn't make her any promises about the future. He had to finish this quest to protect her and her child, but success would mean his own return to the heavens.

And Lilia again would be alone.

So would he. It wasn't an enticing prospect.

The outer door to the offices opened, creaking slightly on its hinges, then closed again. Broken glass crunched under a boot.

Montgomery slid his hand down Lilia's side, searching for her laze. He would have preferred to not fire his own weapon again, especially on a secured investigation site where he shouldn't have been. The smooth fabric of her evening suit invited more exploration than would have been smart.

The woman had a talent for distracting him. Montgomery resolved to make love to her more slowly the next time.

More thoroughly.

He couldn't find her laze and she shook her head minutely, as if guessing what he sought. He couldn't imagine that she'd left it behind voluntarily but the story would have to wait.

Because Montgomery smelled gasoline.

Gasoline? The scent was only vaguely familiar and he was momentarily uncertain of his conclusion.

The intruder stepped into the office where they were hidden. The file drawers clicked in succession and Montgomery feared that the visitor would notice that one file was missing.

But the drawers were being opened too quickly, and the smell of fuel was getting stronger. Montgomery peered around the door. A man in a pseudoskin was dumping the contents of a large gas can across the tops of the filing cabinets. The drawers had each been left open and a bit of liquid splashed inside. A veritable fortune was being poured into the files, which were worth a fortune in their own right.

Then he understood. Paper, which had the advantage of holding data outside of the Republic databanks, had the disadvantage of being flammable.

What if Lilia hadn't claimed the right file?

He couldn't take the chance.

Montgomery stepped out of the shadows, his laze aimed at the intruder's heart. "Freeze!"

Lilia snagged Montgomery's flashlight and shone it on the intruder. He was wearing a pseudoskin and a closed helm, and was just another anonymous man in black.

The intruder froze. Could he have been surprised by their presence? He must have seen the broken glass in the outer door, but then maybe he hadn't been able to see that well with the tinted visor of his helm down.

He lifted one hand and moved to put the gas can down before raising the other. There was something in his upheld hand, though, something small that he held between finger and thumb.

Montgomery couldn't see it clearly, but didn't trust

him one bit. He took a step forward, keeping his laze trained on the man's chest. "Put the can down slowly."

The intruder lowered the can toward the floor.

Suddenly his upraised hand moved, and he struck something against his belt. He had been holding a match and with the strike, it flared to life. In the same instant, he flung the gas can at Montgomery.

Montgomery ducked and the can clattered against the wall behind him. Too late. The intruder threw the lit match into the closest filing drawer and turned to run. The flames leapt up with surprising speed, hungrily devouring the gasoline. They jumped to the next drawer almost immediately.

Montgomery aimed his laze at the fleeing arsonist.

"You'll spread the fire!" Lilia shouted, in the same moment that Montgomery realized the same thing.

He swore and gave chase. The intruder was already in the outside office, running for freedom. He kicked a trash can behind himself in the corridor. Montgomery was close behind him, shouting for him to freeze and halt, which had no discernible effect.

Too bad he wanted this guy alive.

The intruder jumped over the bannister in the stairwell. Montgomery raised his laze, thinking he might be able to injure him, but there was no clear shot before his silhouette disappeared into darkness.

The door to the street slammed in the foyer down below.

"Someone will see him," Montgomery said, putting his laze away with dissatisfaction and not really believing as much.

Lilia came to a skidding halt behind him, armed with his flashlight and that fat file. "No, someone will hear him and by the time they look out the window, they'll see us."

She was right.

It would be stupid to exit the building on the street level.

It would be equally stupid to remain in the building.

There was a lot of smoke spreading into the hallway and absolutely no chance of returning to the offices of Breisach and Turner. The fire alarm began to ring and it would only be moments before the emergency crews arrived.

Lilia wasn't any happier than Montgomery. "You could have just fried him, you know, and saved us a whole bunch of trouble."

Montgomery slanted a look at her, then started down the steps. "Remind me to make that note on your file. You *would* make a lousy cop."

"Well, forgive me for having doubts about your policing capabilities right now," she said, trotting right behind him. "I thought it wasn't about what you were packing, but about how fast you were. What were you waiting for, Montgomery? An invitation with a bitmapped target display?"

"I couldn't get a clear shot." He was talking through his teeth, and if Lilia had been smart, she'd have let it go.

He knew better than to expect that.

"I hate to be the bearer of bad news, but the building is on fire and that gasoline is a good guarantee that the whole thing will go. I wouldn't have let a little potential damage to the common areas stop me."

"Then maybe it's a good thing you didn't have your laze. Where is it anyway?"

"The hotel security staff confiscated it." Now she was growling. "*Theoretically,* they'll return it when I check out."

Montgomery didn't ask what would happen if they didn't. He could imagine. "It wasn't potential damage to the building that stopped me," he said instead. "He's more useful alive than dead."

"What? So he can hunt us down and kill us?"

"Leave it, Lil." He marched down the stairs.

She darted after him, waving his flashlight. "Tell me, who would know if you broke the law? You said that your monitor was fried. I can be bought, if you're worried about me testifying against you."

He paused to confront her. "Do you really think they

don't take a burn print from every police laze as soon as it's issued?"

That set Lilia aback. "I'm not used to considering the Republic to have a lot of foresight."

"You should get over that. The stupidest thing you can do is underestimate your opponent."

"So now I'm up against the Republic?"

"Weren't you always?" He sighed, not really expecting, or needing, an answer to that. "Haven't you heard that dead men tell no tales, Lil? This guy knows something and seeing how everyone else has ended up dead, I thought a live informant would be a nice change."

"Are you being sarcastic, Montgomery?"

"You figure it out."

She trotted after him and he could practically hear her thinking. "They'd never get a laze print from a burned building."

"Don't be so quick to assume that the whole building will go. There are always bits and pieces left."

"And that would be the piece they found? Come on, Montgomery, you've got to be luckier than that."

Montgomery wasn't ready to count on it.

Sirens blared in the distance, drawing closer with every heartbeat, and Montgomery spared her a look. "Would getting caught at the scene of an arson be a sign of good luck?" She opened her mouth to argue with him and Montgomery had had enough. "Move it, Lil. We're not going to be here to welcome the fire department."

"Not even as the official voice of law enforcement in the community and witnesses of an offense made against property?"

Instead of replying, Montgomery seized her hand and dragged her down the stairs into the netherzones. Montgomery didn't doubt that she'd interrogate him as soon as they were away from the scene. He had a few questions of his own but needed to find a more private place to talk.

He was so irritated with Lilia and himself that Montgomery made a classic mistake.

He let his guard down too soon.

They entered the deep netherzones beneath the office building when Montgomery realized his error.

He heard a sound behind him.

A footstep. Montgomery spun and saw the silhouette of a man taking aim at Lilia. He understood immediately that the arsonist had only slammed the door to the street, and had kept running down the stairs. Then he saw the laze fire.

Montgomery leapt toward Lilia, flinging her behind him and putting himself in the line of fire. He pinched off a shot himself, but it was too late.

Searing heat dinged his right shoulder, making his shot go wide of the mark. The hit made him spin, even as he heard Lilia shout his name. He heard the arsonist running, out of the light and into the protective darkness, and swore under his breath.

"Get down!" he roared at Lilia, hoping that for once she did what she was told. He fired after his attacker, shooting blind into the netherzones.

The second shot seemed to come out of nowhere. It grazed across the back of his shoulders, leaving a burning trail. Montgomery fell heavily to one knee, like a drunk fighting to remain on his feet. The third shot grazed his temple and he fell to the ground, dazed.

He felt the slick heat of his own blood. The concrete floor of the netherzone was cold under his cheek, a welcome respite from the damage done by the laze. He felt his grip slacken on his own weapon and felt the darkness close around him.

Lil snatched his laze from his fingers. He heard her swear and saw the flutter of paperwork falling all around him. She fired four shots into the distance and he wondered idly whether she'd hit anything.

It was hard to care.

The drifting documents reminded him of feathers. The pain reminded him of his choice to volunteer.

He was back in that warehouse again, his world ending

all over again. He was going to die while he was earth-bound, losing everything over a stupid mistake.

He'd find out what had really happened to Rachel because he would share her fate.

"THE BASTARD got away," Lilia said with frustration.

Again. She expected Montgomery to add the correction but he didn't.

She lowered Montgomery's laze. "I could have nailed him if I'd had my own weapon," she complained to the prone cop. "How do you deal with this antique? The repeat is terrible."

Montgomery still didn't answer. He looked like a felled giant, stretched large and dark across the concrete floor.

Lilia bent down beside him, fear filling her heart. "The confiscation of private property by zealous hotel personnel has to be against some law somewhere. Doesn't it?"

She considered the scattered papers from the file that she had stolen from Breisach and Turner's offices and didn't think she should argue about stolen property anymore.

Montgomery wasn't just silent, but far too still.

Lilia had a bad feeling. His cloak had been shot right from his back and had swung over one shoulder to splay across the floor. His jacket and shirt were sheared from his skin. There was blood coming from his right shoulder and his back, as well as a nasty welt on his left temple. The sight of a dark puddle spreading steadily across the concrete made her bile rise.

Montgomery couldn't be dead, not when she was starting to count on him.

Not when she was starting to unravel his inconsistencies.

Not when she hadn't had nearly enough of him.

Worse, he had taken a hit that had been meant for her. It couldn't kill him: that wouldn't be right. She owed him and she wouldn't have a chance to even the score if he died.

But Lilia knew the world didn't always play by her rules.

Montgomery was bleeding copiously and he had lost consciousness. He was still breathing. She could feel his pulse when she put her fingertips to his throat but it wasn't as strong as she would have preferred.

Lilia wished she had paid more attention in Emergency First Aid. This was one thing she couldn't solve by herself.

Fortunately, there were paramedics close at hand. She heard them arrive overhead and wished she could know for sure whether the arsonist had really fled this time.

Or whether he was lurking in the shadows, waiting for a chance to finish Montgomery off. The netherzones were dark but not quiet, and once again Lilia had the sense that she was being watched. She shivered as that silvery fog began to roll toward her again. She certainly wouldn't have wanted to be abandoned in this place.

She couldn't just leave Montgomery unguarded while she got help. Leaving him vulnerable would be a lousy reward for his taking a hit for her.

Bad karma too.

Could she drag him up those metal stairs?

There was only one way to find out. Lilia bent and grabbed Montgomery's elbows. If she could get him into the light, she could still keep an eye on him as she ran upstairs for help.

The man was like a dead weight, even without a pseudoskin. Lilia managed to pull him a short distance with a large effort, then paused to catch her breath.

She realized she might not be helping him by revealing his presence to the paramedics. He was off-duty and had entered a crime scene, without a warrant. He was already in trouble about his ear stud. She wondered whether he could lose his job over this.

But his life was more important than his job. She'd fix

him up with Joachim, if necessary, get him a job as a security guy at the circus.

Lilia liked the sound of that. She bent and hauled Montgomery toward the bottom of the stairs. She gave him one last tug into the pool of light, then shoved her hand through her hair.

The light played over his head and shoulders, painting his fallen figure in shades of yellow. She could see the damage from the laze on his back more clearly and the raw flesh made her wince in sympathy.

She could also see his scars.

Lilia blinked and looked again.

They were precisely the same as those of the shade receptionist. Lilia stood and gaped, knowing that she was wasting precious time and unable to move just the same.

It was all making sense.

The angels knew Montgomery because he had once been one of them. He knew about the warehouse and the ritual there because he had participated in it. He knew how Raphael would adapt because he had done it himself.

She wondered when.

She wondered why.

She understood how he knew the receptionist, and why he cared so much about her death, even though she had been a shade.

She'd been classed as a shade because of her scars.

If Lilia summoned official help, Montgomery would be classified as a shade too. The very idea made her feel sick, sicker even than the sight and smell of his blood.

It was out of the question.

But if he completed his mission, whatever it was, he'd leave her and the Republic forever. The prospect made Lilia dizzy.

She still had to do right by him. She retrieved his cloak and tucked the faux fur and velvet over his shoulders, hiding his scars from view. She pushed him back from the pool of light, hoping she wasn't making his injury worse by moving him so much.

"Montgomery, you've got to help," she whispered urgently, giving him a shake. "We have to go to the pleasure fringe and I can't drag you all that way."

He didn't move. His eyelids didn't even flicker.

The sirens echoed loudly from above and the smell of fire carried down the stairwell. Lilia heard the firefighters pounding up the stairs toward Breisach and Turner. It would be just a matter of moments before they came into the building's basement, if only to find an auxiliary water source.

The silvery fog slid across the floor of the netherzones, looking to Lilia's fanciful eyes as if it was making a beeline for Montgomery. There was a decided lack of intervening angels.

Time for Plan B.

Lilia darted farther into the netherzones, her heart pounding that Montgomery was alone for even a moment. She didn't know what she was looking for, but she recognized it when she saw it.

There was a rickshaw parked in a lot nearby and it was neither locked nor secured. It might as well have had an invitation nailed to the front of it.

Addressed to her.

Her luck was back, in spades. Lilia stole the rickshaw without a moment's hesitation. Moving Montgomery into it was easier than she expected.

Maybe terror gave her extra strength.

Or maybe it was another power of black lycrester.

MONTGOMERY AWAKENED, groggy and in pain, in the darkened back of a jostling vehicle. There was a jumbled stack of paperwork tossed onto the seat beside him. His back hurt more than his temple or his shoulder. He checked and discovered that his clothing was shredded: whoever had put him in this rickshaw must have seen his scars.

Fearing the worst, he pulled himself forward and peered out the front of the moving vehicle.

Lilia, in her black evening suit, was pedaling the bike of the rickshaw. He would have recognized her figure anywhere, never mind her determination. She looked particularly stylish and overdressed for a rickshaw laborer, even though her hair had come out of its coil. They were rolling through the netherzones at a good clip, nearing the periphery of the pleasure fringe.

She wasn't harvesting him for the Republic, or even the circus.

He grinned, knowing he'd guessed her motivation accurately. Her actions never lied.

"So, what's your plan, Lil?" he asked lightly, noting how she jumped in surprise. "Are we running away together?"

"*You're* running away," she said, firing a hot glance over her shoulder. He didn't miss the flash of relief in her eyes or the way her gaze ran over him. "I'm just the cheap help."

"Since when? I thought I couldn't afford you."

She cast him a wicked glance, one that made his pulse leap. "Maybe I'll take the comp in trade."

Montgomery couldn't argue with that plan. He didn't have the chance anyway: they went over a seam in the concrete and he nearly fainted at the pain. The rickshaw had lousy shock absorbers.

"Sorry," she said with a grimace.

"You didn't cast the floor, Lil," he said, hearing how tight his voice was with the pain. "It's just one of those things."

"You need a tissue regenerator," she said with purpose. "Any likely candidates in the pleasure fringe? At home, I'd ask the guy with the tattoo parlor. He drinks and sometimes messes up, so he calls the generator his insurance plan."

Montgomery smiled at her pragmatism but knew he had to ask. "The EMS team must have been right there. They would have had a tissue regenerator. You could have just whistled them up, Lil."

"I didn't think you were in the market for a tattoo, Montgomery."

He'd guessed right: she *had* seen his back.

"So, we're going to the circus instead?"

Her glance was contemptuous. "You're a cop, Montgomery. Nobody pays admission to the circus to see cops."

He couldn't stop his grin. It wasn't about the comp, after all.

"Two passages up, take a right, Lil," he said. "I know the bartender in that jazz bar. He'll get rid of the rickshaw and help us get to the cathouse."

"Oh, so I'm killing myself to get you one last hurrah?"

He chuckled, hearing the bite of jealousy in her tone. "Something like that," he conceded and his smile broadened at her disapproval. "You haven't shown me your tattoos yet, Lil, and it was your idea that I repay you in trade."

She biked in silence and he wondered what she was thinking. She followed his directions and dismounted, then walked back to him. To his surprise, she looked shaken and uncertain. She framed his face in her hands and her eyes were wide. "I thought you were dead."

He pulled her close. "I guess I'm tougher than I look."

"There's certainly more to you than meets the eye."

He arched a brow. "I'm not alone in that."

She studied him for a moment. "So, when do you leave?" she whispered, her heart in her eyes.

He couldn't lie to her. "When my quest is fulfilled."

She nodded and averted her gaze, her throat working. "So much for my legendary luck," she quipped, then reached up and kissed him sweetly.

He tasted her fear and wanted only to reassure her. He pulled her closer, deepened his kiss, speared his fingers into her hair. She was softer and more vulnerable, more open to him than she had been yet. Her trust sent a welcome heat through him, made his pulse race, made everything within him quicken.

He was alive.
He was mortal.
He was in love.

MONTGOMERY LOVED to mess with her mind. Lilia knew it, but she was too glad that he was conscious again to complain about it.

She also liked the glint of mischief in his green eyes and the curve of his smile as he watched her. Something had changed between them and she didn't want to examine it too closely in case it vaporized.

Every moment she had with him, after all, felt like a gift. Or a theft. An unexpected treasure to be savored. She'd never forget him, she knew it, and she wanted to collect as many memories as possible in the time they had together.

The cathouse he'd chosen had a Victorian theme and a pair of whores who regarded him with affection. Lilia refused to speculate on any reasons for that. They were suspiciously quick to cede their room and promise their silence. Lilia refused to consider what Montgomery done to earn such loyalty.

The women also fetched the cathouse doctor, who had a bootleg tissue regenerator. It was a small unit, probably so it could be easily hidden away, but the doctor assured them that it worked quickly. As much as Lilia respected pirated technology and its timely appearance, she intervened before the unit could be installed on Montgomery.

"Is he going to get extra thumbs?" she demanded.

The good doctor smiled. "Those aren't the default extra appendages it grows."

The whore with three breasts laughed, but Lilia didn't appreciate the joke.

"Well, override the default. Muscle tissue, veins and arteries, and skin only. No appendages of any kind."

"Demanding," the doctor said to Montgomery.

"It gets worse," Montgomery agreed easily. Lilia

didn't like how he grimaced as he settled himself on the four-poster bed.

"I like him just the way he is." Lilia shrugged.

The whore with the golden skin smiled. "Who says your opinion is the only one that counts?" she purred, running her fingertip down Montgomery's boot.

"I do," Montgomery said quietly and offered Lilia his hand. He gave her a hot look to go with it, one that both surprised and pleased her. She went to stand beside him, liking how his hand engulfed hers. His grip was strong and she knew she could get used to having him around.

Permanently.

Although that looked like it was too much to ask.

In the interim, she'd give him anything she had.

"Can they be trusted?" she asked after the whores and doctor were gone.

"It's all in the tokens," he muttered. "You could say that I have a credit here."

"I don't want to know the details."

He squeezed her fingers and pulled her to sit on the edge of the bed. He looked pale, in need of blood as well as tissue, but that would come. He leaned back against the headboard and closed his eyes as the regenerator hummed busily. Lilia thought he might sleep, but he surprised her. "What file did you take?"

"The file for the Society. I hope it was the right one."

"Let's find out."

"You should rest."

"I can do that while you read to me." He gave her a bright look and Lilia got the file. It was a mess, seeing as she had snatched up all of the invoices and jammed them back into the folder in her haste to get Montgomery to safety. Her fingers shook at the close call they had had, but she refused to dwell on it.

Instead, she sat beside him on the bed. Montgomery watched and waited. It took Lilia awhile, but she sorted the file's contents into chronological order again.

"Why did you pick the Society's file?" Montgomery asked.

"Someone has to ship all those oranges," Lilia said. "See? Breisach and Turner has been shipping the Society's oranges for the *Sunshine Heals* program on their hybrid canola-electric fleet."

"That's not suspicious." Montgomery frowned and took the sheet from her. "Even though it's an old contract."

"But this is suspicious." Lilia handed him another piece of paper. It was a bill for additional charges, given excess weight of the payload picked up in 2069.

"More oranges, or heavier ones?" Montgomery asked.

"Maybe." Lilia found the invoice from the previous year, for a shipment of roughly the same number of crates of oranges, and played compare-and-contrast.

"The weight on the 2069 invoice was eight or nine times higher, for roughly the same quantity of oranges." She glanced at Montgomery. "That was some kind of iodine they'd injected that year."

He shook his head. "There must have been something else in the shipment."

"There's no way of knowing. This initial contract says that the shipments are to be packed and sealed in the Society's warehouses."

"What else could they have shipped, under Orv's banner?"

Lilia flipped through the file and stopped cold.

Montgomery leaned forward. "What have you got?"

She lifted it out of the file with uncertainty. "An insurance claim for four trucks lost in the 2069 attack on Gotham."

"Bad timing?" Montgomery mused. "They must have been four trucks loaded with *Sunshine Heals* oranges to be in this file."

Lilia recalled one snippet of information from her years at the Institute and sat back in astonishment.

"What is it?" Montgomery asked, seeing her shock.

"It's my suspicious mind at work again."

"Tell me."

Lilia swallowed. "A ten-kiloton nuclear device fits on the back of a flatbed truck."

Montgomery checked the insurance claim. "Which was what these four vehicles were."

Lilia tapped up a bit of history on her palm, her heart racing with the implications. Montgomery sat straighter, sensing her dismay. "I was right," she said, wishing she'd been wrong. "Experts speculated not only that the bombs had been detonated near the ground, but that the total force of the blast had been forty kilotons."

The two of them eyed the stolen file.

"How much extra weight was there?" Montgomery asked.

Lilia tapped up a Gid-worthy calculation on her palm. She did it three times to make sure, then met Montgomery's gaze. "Enough for those boxes to have contained enriched uranium, not oranges."

Montgomery looked away, frowning. "What did the Society do?"

Lilia was pretty sure they both knew.

"What else is in the file?" he asked after a moment.

Lilia flipped through it to the end. "The last item is a letter of intent from 2070, confirming that Breisach and Turner will continue delivering the Society's oranges."

"Breisach and Turner figured it out."

"And the Society made a deal with them to keep them silent," Lilia concluded. "Did your friend ever actually meet the partners?"

Montgomery sobered, then tapped his fingers on the desk. "Breisach died in a skiing accident last winter."

"Turner?"

"She never said much, but she was upset last August. Turner had had a rickshaw accident but died in the hospital."

"Of what? A broken leg?"

"Supposedly of a mistake with his medication, an inadvertent overdose."

"In August," Lilia mused. "At the same time Gid died."

Their gazes met and held for a potent moment.

Lilia knew there had to be more. The hit on Gotham was old news, thirty-year-old news. Gid couldn't have been killed for figuring out that the Society was responsible. "Do you still have that datachip?"

"And one last scrambler," Montgomery said, reaching for his boot. "There's got to be a public reader in this place."

XIX

THERE WAS a public reader, although it was hidden. Montgomery hadn't expected otherwise. The reader was in a small room off the reception area, hidden behind a framed oil painting. The painting turned out to be on a hinge. Montgomery managed to make it down the stairs under his own steam, the tissue regenerator having done a quick job on his shoulder. Lilia guessed that the owner had paid for a speed upgrade, so that any injured whores could get back to work more quickly.

They'd decided not to worry about the quality of his manufactured tissue, at least for the moment. He liked his increasing sense that they were a team and a pretty good one.

The owner advised them to be quick about their usage before he left them alone. "The juice cost kills me," he said.

Montgomery grimaced once he was gone. "You always said that everything has its price, Lil."

"In the pleasure fringe, it can be a lot more than you expect."

He put the scrambler on Gid's chip and pushed it into the port. The spreadsheet came up immediately but didn't look any more significant to Montgomery than it had the last time.

Lilia's gaze brightened and he wondered what she saw. "Look. Here's where the shade populations bottom out, then spike again. The dates are familiar ones: numbers diminish through the 2030s, then spike in 2035 and 2036."

"Just after the first hit in the Second Global War," Montgomery said, remembering his dates.

"The spike probably began its upturn four to five months after the nukes," Lilia told him. "The greatest damage occurs in utero, when the mothers are exposed."

"Nice."

"It's a weapon, Montgomery, not a welcome wagon." She tapped the display with excitement. "The same pattern repeats: over time the shade population diminishes, until our next spike . . ."

"The years 2051 and 2052. The Pacific Rim Conflict."

Lilia nodded. "Then the same cycle occurs. The shade population numbers drop through the 2060s. Notice that they reach lower lows than previously, both in raw numbers and per capita."

"And then Gotham was hit," Montgomery said, with some impatience. He could hear sounds of activity in the foyer of the cathouse and didn't like the possibility that they might be observed. "Lil, this isn't news."

She straightened and he knew she was going to say something outrageous. "Quick question: who has the most to lose if there are no more shades?"

"Everybody."

"No." Lilia shook her head. "Not everybody would suffer equally. Individuals would be inconvenienced or be compelled to do more physical labor themselves, but one organization would cease to have a rationale for existing. A rich organization, with connections at all levels of government, connections based upon its exploitation of shades."

Montgomery knew which one she meant. "You've got no proof."

"Do you have the images from the palm of the shade who wanted to meet me?"

Montgomery tapped into the NGPD database and pulled it up.

"I've got to love organized men," Lilia murmured, then leaned over to expand the first image. The image was a shot of traffic, time-dated in the lower right corner: 08:38, July 11, 2069.

Montgomery tapped up the news file on the Gotham strike to confirm the time. "Just before the detonation," he said softly.

The image was grainy, but the logo of Orv the Orange was clearly visible on the crates loaded on one truck. The truck was bigger than the other traffic entering the tunnel, looming large over the bicycles and rickshaws. Above the entrance to the tunnel were signs and beyond that was a distant cityscape.

"Do you know where this is?" Lilia asked.

"It says it's the bridge into Gotham."

"There's a crater on the other end where one of the bombs was detonated. I went around it the other night."

"And this image was purportedly taken just before the attack."

Lilia was insulted, as he'd known she'd be. "Purportedly?"

"It could be a montage, Lil, put together after the fact. You can't even detect the good ones these days."

"No, it is what it looks like it is."

Montgomery swivelled in the chair, feeling compelled to be the devil's advocate. So to speak. "Prove it."

"Why would anyone have taken pictures of these trucks before the attack was known? Obviously because someone had a whiff of what was going to go down."

"Then why haven't the people who had this image come forward in thirty years?"

"I can think of a whole bunch of reasons for that, most of which involve the suppression of information by a central authority," Lilia said, her tone tart. "Although I probably shouldn't say as much in the company of an official being compensated by the central authority to administer its information-suppressing policies in this particular geographic area."

Montgomery smiled.

"Don't go cop on me again, Montgomery."

"You need more than speculation, Lil."

She eyed him, then lowered her voice. "Tell me again: how does the angel thing work?"

Montgomery was surprised by the question. He glanced away, then back at her, knowing she'd want to watch his expression closely. "You volunteer and you get an assignment." He swallowed. "You make the transfer, and you do your job."

"And then?"

He held her gaze. "And then you go back."

He saw her lips tighten just before she turned back to the display. He wasn't surprised that she changed the subject. "I'm going to bet that there are images from each of the points where the nuclear bombs were detonated in Gotham in 2069."

"So, the Society's oranges got caught in the crossfire when Gotham was bombed. So what?"

"So, I wonder whether those oranges ticked. I wonder whether that's what Y654892 wanted to tell me."

Montgomery leaned forward. "Lil, you know that the Society of Nuclear Darwinists is a prestigious organization with well-established influence and credibility. Where's your proof?"

Lilia's lips set and Montgomery knew she wasn't going to give it up. "We can get proof."

"I don't think so. There can't be any left after thirty years."

"Not so. Uranium 238 has a half-life of 4.46 billion years, Plutonium 241 a mere 24,110 years. Time is on our side, Montgomery—thirty years here or there barely factors in."

"You are not going into the old city—"

She interrupted him. "If I'm right, the debris from the trucks themselves will be the hottest wreckage—"

"Inconclusive data. It'll never hold."

"You could be more helpful, you know. For the good of humanity and all that."

"It's irrelevant. The players are probably all dead."

"No, no, it's not old news. It's tomorrow's news."

He regarded her with suspicion. "What do you mean?"

"Look at that shade population curve, Montgomery. We're running low, lower even than before." She spoke with quiet certainty. "They're going to do it again."

MONTGOMERY WAS horrified, but it made perfect sense. "Where? When?"

"Where are they sending the oranges?"

"Didn't they take the program to the Frontier this year?"

"Thousands of miles of turf," Lilia said with a grimace. "We have to do better than that."

Montgomery searched, aware that his scrambler couldn't last much longer. It began to fizzle as the results displayed and both of them leaned close to the display, anxious to read as much as possible.

"They're warehousing them in Estevan," Lilia read.

"What's there?"

Lilia clicked the hotlink. They had time to read that Estevan was a former military base, current population ninety-seven. The scrambler fizzled and Montgomery automatically popped the datachip from the port.

"Obviously not their target of choice," Lilia said with frustration. "We're missing something."

"Let's go back to the beginning," Montgomery suggested. "Who's they?"

"Council of Three, probably," she said and Montgomery's pulse leapt. "They're supposed to be running the show and ensuring the Society's existence would have to be high on their agenda."

"But who are they?"

"That's the tricky part." She leaned against the wall, obviously thinking.

"Fitzgerald?" Montgomery asked.

Lilia didn't dismiss the idea out of hand. "Maybe. But then, why would they kill him?" Montgomery could think of several reasons, but Lilia shook her head. "If Gid was involved at all, then his advisor, Dr. Malachy, would have been the one to bring him into it. He knew Ernest Sinclair and has been a member of the Society virtually from its inception."

"Sounds like a reasonable choice."

Lilia smiled. "But I like him."

"Your gut instincts aren't untrustworthy," Montgomery said.

"And then there's Rhys ibn Ali. He'd be my choice pick for an evildoer. The Society looks the other way when he breaks the rules."

"So, he has influence."

Lilia cast him that mischievous grin. "As much as I hate to admit it, it's easier to believe that Rhys is sleeping with somebody who has influence than that he's part of anything clandestine. The man has zero discretion."

"It could be an act."

She was unconvinced. "Which brings us to Ernestine."

"Society president?"

"Heiress apparent and president. She's been doing Rhys for years. Blake said the presidency was a stepping stone to the Council and she's almost done her term."

"What about older fellows?"

"Doc Mina is being given the nudge out of the Institute, so she can't be on the Council. In fact, she's pretty bitter about their decision to ditch her."

Montgomery thought that could be an act as well, but he didn't want to interrupt Lilia's thoughts. She knew these people, after all, and he was interested in her impressions.

She snapped her fingers. "The guy who'd been booked for the keynote, Paul Cosmopoulos, is a possibility. He's involved in the drug patent program, a big part of the Society's income base."

"Is he here?"

"I don't know." Lilia grimaced. "At the Institute, I skipped all the drug-testing-protocol courses that I could. I don't even know what Dr. Cosmopoulos looks like." She took a deep breath, glancing toward the door. "He could be anybody."

"That's not the most reassuring comment you could have made," Montgomery teased because she looked so concerned. She fell silent and he sighed. "We need to know where to begin."

"Oh, that's easy. We need to retrieve Y654892's palm."

"He was killed in Gotham."

"I'll guess that the wolves didn't eat his hardware."

Montgomery looked away while he thought. He'd be breaking the law by going into the old city, and treating himself to some radiation exposure. It was a long shot, but the only clue that they had.

On the other hand, Lilia's theory, even without proof, neatly explained the angel's insistence that he eliminate the Council of Three. Meeting Lilia could be the reason he'd been assigned to NGPD.

That assignment had run its duration, though. He'd already fired his laze without authorization or explanation a good half dozen times, and his physical exam would terminate his employment at NGPD. Tupperman had as much as said he couldn't help him.

Montgomery had nothing left to lose.

But he had a whole lot to gain. He plucked the tissue regenerator off his shoulder and turned it off, flexing his arm to check its progress. His back was much better and he felt stronger.

"What are you going to do?" she asked quietly and he grinned at her. He saw her eyes widen, saw her catch her breath, and he loved that she was as aware of him as he was of her.

"I'm thinking, Lil, that it's time you showed me your tattoos."

Lilia began to smile. "Do you have enough tokens left to get us a room with no peepholes, Montgomery? I'm a bit shy."

The very idea of Lilia being shy made Montgomery laugh but he wasn't going to argue with her.

He had better things to do.

MONTGOMERY WOULD leave when his mission was done. Lilia didn't want to know the specifics of his assignment, didn't want to know the precise parameters of his time on earth. It wasn't like her to duck the truth, but Montgomery was already someone she'd come to rely on.

She wished he'd stay.

She knew it wasn't for her to ask.

They returned to the whores' bedroom and the massive gilt-edged four-poster bed. Montgomery was more lithe on the stairs, the tissue regenerator having done its business well enough. He was preoccupied already, thinking about their course of action, and Lilia sensed that he'd be gone soon.

She wanted his undivided attention one last time.

Even if she had to show him her tattoos.

He closed the door behind them and she pulled the heavy drapes. She lit the candles on the sideboard, feeling Montgomery's gaze follow her. The room was filled with mysterious shadows, the decor decadent and luxurious. It was perfect. Lilia turned down the bed, smoothed the sheets, and plumped the pillows.

She turned to find Montgomery leaning against the door, his arms folded across his chest. That little smile played with his lips, the one that made Lilia's blood pressure rise. His chest was bare, his shirt and jacket having been dispatched for the tissue regenerator, and he wore only his cloak. Without his reevlar codpiece, Lilia had no doubt what was on his mind. He looked like a pirate king, an unpredictable rogue with pleasure on his mind.

She stood in the middle of the room and unfastened her hair. The braid had already come loose but she shook out the heavy weight of her hair, letting all forty-two

inches of its dark curtain surround her. Montgomery's
eyes gleamed as she unfastened the jacket of the black lycrester suit. Her corset was as black as the suit and she
knew it contrasted with her pale skin. She removed her
boots and set them aside, then wriggled out of her
trousers. She folded the lycrester carefully, giving Montgomery a good view of her assets as she did so.

She crossed the floor barefoot, pausing before him. He
seemed prepared to let her set the pace. She unfastened
his cloak and set it aside, then ran her fingertips across
the breadth of his chest. She understood why he hadn't let
her see him nude before, but now she wanted a good look.

It might be the only chance she got.

She reached up and kissed his earlobe where his
monitor had been, letting her fingertips dance over the
flesh wound on his temple. It was already closed, as was
the shot to his shoulder. She urged him to turn with a caress of her hand and he did so, displaying his back to
her.

Lilia ran her hands across his repairing flesh lightly,
then traced the length of his scars with a fingertip. It was
hard to believe that he had had wings, though not that hard
to believe that he had been an angel. His body was
beautiful, perfect other than the scars, as well crafted as
a piece of fine sculpture. She couldn't imagine how it
had felt to lose his wings, but she had seen Raphael's
pain.

She bent and touched her lips to the scar tissue. Montgomery caught his breath. He turned and reached for her,
his fingers sliding into her hair as he kissed her with
sweet urgency. Lilia found herself on her toes, arching
against his strength. Her nipples slipped over the top of
her corset and she rubbed them against the hair on his
chest. His kiss deepened, became more demanding, and
she felt his desire press against her belly.

They parted, their breathing heavy, and Lilia smiled at
Montgomery as she reached for the fastening of his

trousers. He pulled off his boots and cast them aside, his trousers following suit.

He was nude before her. Nude and magnificent, so splendid that Lilia caught her breath. He took her hand in his and kissed her fingertips, his eyes gleaming with promise. Then he spun her around, eased her hair aside, and pulled her laces free.

The corset fell to the carpet and Montgomery bracketed Lilia's waist with his hands. He bent and kissed the tattoo at the base of her spine, then slid his thumbs across it.

"What do they mean?"

"Each degree is commemorated by a tattoo on the appropriate chakra," she said.

"Chakra?"

"Chakras are power points in the body, according to old mysticism. They govern facets of our life and mark developmental milestones. We tattoo them in order." She glanced over her shoulder at him. "That's the first chakra, at the base of the spine. It symbolizes an awareness of self and our physical bodies, as well as self-preservation."

"Your tattoo is an apple." His expression turned quizzical.

Lilia smiled. "I've been called a temptress many times."

"I wonder why." Montgomery grinned, then lifted Lilia in his arms. He kissed her as he carried her to the bed, then laid her across the linens. He spread her hair over the sheets and studied her as if she was a marvel.

"Consider me tempted," he whispered, then bent to tease her nipple with his tongue. His hand wandered to her pubis and Lilia knew the moment that he saw the second tattoo.

"The second chakra is in the genitals. It represents earthly desire and physical temptation."

"A snake," Montgomery said and looked at her. "Temptation that can't be trusted, maybe?"

Lilia smiled. "Exactly. Desire, sexual pleasure, maybe at the price of other things. That snake's name is Maximilian."

He met her gaze and she knew he recognized the name. "Delilah's father," he said and Lilia couldn't stop her lips from tightening.

"He called them to harvest her at the hospital. Right away. It's a lesson I don't intend to forget."

He slid his hand across her smooth skin, as if he was trying to ease away her pain. "But not all desire and temptation is bad, is it?"

Lilia slid her arms around his neck and pulled him closer. "Definitely not," she whispered, daring to hope for her one desire. "It's only bad when it exists alone." She saw the fleeting glimmer of his smile and her heart clenched with the conviction that he agreed with her.

Then he kissed her once again. They savored each other, exploring, sampling and tasting and enjoying. Montgomery caressed Lilia as he had before, his gaze bright as she writhed beneath his touch.

She let him see the fullness of the pleasure he gave her. She felt unveiled in his presence, naked, without secrets. It was liberating and new. Montgomery didn't judge her or find her lacking. He didn't disapprove of her or condemn her.

Was this his gift to her before he left forever?

It wasn't nearly enough.

"There's one more," he said finally, moving his fingertips to her belly. Lilia made a sound of protest and he laughed. He traced the spiral of text there and it tickled Lilia.

"The third chakra is at the navel," she told him, knowing he wouldn't leave it be. "It governs identity and autonomy."

"The mission of your life, maybe?" he said and it wasn't really a question.

After all, he'd read the tattoo.

And he wasn't holding her past against her.

Lilia was fresh out of secrets. She reached for Montgomery and pulled him closer, wanting all of him and wanting it now.

He seemed only too glad to comply.

HOURS LATER, they were still entangled on the bed. Lilia knew that the sun was rising, because the draperies were becoming lighter around the edges, but she was in no rush to leave their slice of heaven.

Montgomery ran a fingertip around her navel, tracing the spiraled course of her daughter's name. "Delilah Louise Desjardins," he whispered, then bent and kissed her flesh. His eyes were very green when he looked up at her. "Your daughter."

Lilia nodded, her throat tight.

Montgomery ran his fingertips across her skin, making her shiver. "I'm glad Fitzgerald found her for you."

Lilia took a shaking breath, needing to tell him the whole story. "He found out why I'd really come to the Society. I told him one night when I got too drunk. But Gid looked for her. He didn't tell me until he'd found her. She was working in a mill. They use children to do repairs in the small spaces under the equipment, even though some of them get killed."

"Why was she made a shade?"

"She had a third eye, just like Micheline. At the mill, they noticed that she knew things would happen before they did. Gid had tracked her number and located her, then found out she was being transferred to the Institute for a new study." She took an unsteady breath. "He accessed the protocol . . ." she began and couldn't continue.

Montgomery caught her closer, sensing her dismay. "Let me guess: she wouldn't have survived the test."

Lilia shook her head. "She was only nine. Just a little girl. I begged Gid to help her. I promised him anything, everything." Her tears were running freely. "He stole her from the Society and faked her death. He hid her in New

Seattle in a traveling commune." She heaved a sigh. "It was against everything he believed."

Montgomery spoke quietly. "But he did it for you."

"I didn't even believe him, for the longest time, but I knew Gid couldn't lie to save his life." Lilia swallowed. "He lied, though, to save Delilah's."

"Did you see her again?"

Lilia shook her head and her tears fell, scattering across her cheeks. "Not since they took her. Gid said it would be too dangerous and I knew he was right. But still." She caught her breath. "I held her for just a minute when she was born and then she was gone. Forever. My mother didn't even get to see her."

Lilia wept then, wept as she never had since Delilah had been harvested. Montgomery caught her close and rocked her. The heat of his skin, the tenderness of his embrace, was comforting to her. Lilia let loose and cried from the depths of her soul.

"What about Maximilian?"

Lilia laughed shortly. "He was the one who pinged the Nuclear Darwinist on duty in the hospital." She knew her words were bitter but she didn't care. "Max took one look and that was all he needed to deny his own child. I didn't expect much sympathy from him myself. He'd made it clear that he didn't need a pregnant consort or a dependant." She caught her breath and buried her face in Montgomery's chest. "I was the one who called him to the hospital. I'd thought that seeing the baby would change his mind."

"You couldn't have known."

"I should have known. There is no compassion in Max. I was young and stupid and trusting."

"Innocent?" Montgomery asked and Lilia glanced up at him.

"Innocent," she agreed. "But I got over it."

He laced his fingers with hers and his voice dropped low. "Is that a permanent change, Lil?"

Her breath caught. "I'd thought so, for the longest

time." She tightened the grip of her fingers on his and her words became thick. "But lately, Montgomery, I've been feeling like a bit of an amateur."

He smiled and kissed her temple. "Me too," he whispered and her heart skipped. He closed his arms around her and held her tightly and Lilia was content—for the moment—to hear his heart beat under her cheek.

"You should have had another child," he said eventually and she heard the anger in his voice. "You would have been a good mother."

Lilia would have laughed if it hadn't been so sad. "Don't you know, Montgomery?"

He pulled back to look at her. "Know what?"

"The graduation present that the Institute gives to all of its fellows is a sterilization." Lilia saw his shock and dismay. "The idea is that we might not manage to make impartial assessments of our own offspring. I guess I'm proof positive of that."

He frowned. "So the price of saving Delilah was sacrificing your chance to ever have another child. Did you know?"

Lilia nodded. "I couldn't just let them have her. I couldn't let it be."

He held her tightly again but she sensed a difference dawn in his mood. He seemed preoccupied.

"What's the matter?"

"You haven't heard anything since?"

"No. The commune moved three or four times in rapid succession and then disappeared." Lilia corrected herself. "Well, that's not true. Raphael said he'd give Delilah my greetings. He promised to protect her."

Montgomery was surprised. "He did?" At her nod, he smiled. "Good. *Good.*"

Lilia held Montgomery's gaze and the words didn't fall easily from her lips. "Can angels be trusted, Montgomery?"

She wasn't just asking about Raphael.

Montgomery smiled slowly, warmth filling his gaze.

He bent and brushed his lips across hers lightly, then slid a fingertip across her cheek.

"Absolutely, Lil," he said with a quiet force that filled her with new confidence. "You have my word on it."

MONTGOMERY'S PALM pinged. He checked the message and his mood became grim. They might have been taking a break, but the killer showed no such inclination.

"What's going on?" Lilia asked.

"You're not going to like it."

"Show me." She straightened and looked determined.

"Another shade. Do you know this one?" Montgomery flashed an image of another eviscerated shade.

Lilia grimaced and looked away to compose herself. "You need to stop doing that to me," she complained. "Can I just see the shade's face?"

Montgomery tapped, editing the image, then displayed it again.

Lilia leaned against him as she examined it. "That's the shade who followed us, the one who bit me. She worked at the hotel, on the front desk. Now she's been killed too?"

Montgomery nodded.

"It's really bad luck to follow me, that's for sure." Lilia fingered her earlobe.

Montgomery figured there was no point in evading the truth. "She was left in your hotel room, shot in the head with your laze."

Lilia was outraged. "But I don't even have my laze! That security guy confiscated it at the hotel."

Montgomery tapped his palm. "He swore an affidavit to Dimitri that he returned the laze to you when you departed from the hotel last night."

"Liar!" Lilia was livid. "I never got it back. He's lying."

"There's a full alert out for your arrest, given that you're a violent person who is a threat to society at large."

Lilia paled. "Me? I didn't do it, Montgomery. I would never cut a living person like that. I couldn't."

"That's not what the system thinks."

She bit her lip and looked away.

"Lil," he said softly. "I know you didn't do it. I know you didn't have your laze last night, because you would never have used mine otherwise. And there's nowhere you could have hidden it without me finding it."

She looked at him, a glimmer of hope in her eyes. "It would have been nice if you'd just trusted me."

Montgomery smiled. He did and she already knew it. "Maybe this would be a good time to tell me how you cheated in Dissection and Vivisection."

All the fight went out of Lilia's shoulders. "You've guessed."

He spared her a knowing glance. "You can't even look at the image of a corpse. How could you possibly be responsible for these savage killings? There's no way you could have even shown up for those classes."

Lilia smiled that he had seen through her so well. "I couldn't tell you before. It was just my word against the databanks."

"Fitzgerald." There was no doubt in his tone.

Lilia nodded.

"He helped you pass the core courses because he was crazy for you. He knew that you wanted to find your child, and you needed to graduate to have access to the files."

Lilia nodded again. "But I don't understand. How did they find a corpse in my unit?"

Montgomery grimaced. "Someone complained anonymously about the smell." He stood and got dressed. "So, there's only one thing to do, the way I see it."

She glanced up, a question in her eyes.

"You're under arrest, Lil."

Lilia leapt to her feet and backed away, her expression outraged. "I don't think so!"

Montgomery was untroubled. "It's for your own safety."

"That's what they all say."

"We need evidence. It's in the old city. We're not going

into the old city without pseudoskins. Mine is in the precinct and yours, I'll assume, is in your hotel unit. So, the plan is that I arrest you, we go to the precinct, and then return to your hotel room to confirm your story."

"I'll go alone . . ."

"No." He shook his head. "There's a guard posted at the hotel, looking just for you, and every cop in the city has received this all-points bulletin. You're considered armed and dangerous, by the way, and the bulletin is marked shoot to kill." He looked at her, wide-eyed, naked, and vulnerable. "You'll never get into the old city without me, Lil. So, are we a team or not?"

She smiled that mischievous grin. "You're irresistible sometimes, Montgomery."

He sighed with forbearance. "Only sometimes? I'll have to work on that."

Lilia leapt at him and gave him a triumphant kiss. "I can help."

XX

THE ONLY good thing was that Lilia had been busted in black lycrester. She looked like a million creds at the precinct, even securobanded to Montgomery's desk.

She lounged, as if she had all day, and wished Montgomery would get it in gear.

She could hear the other cops chatting in their cubes and eavesdropped shamelessly. Unfortunately, the cops were talking politics, always a yawn-fest for Lilia.

"I'm telling you," one said to the other. "You shouldn't waste your vote on Matheson. That Maximilian Blackstone is the man we want in New D.C."

Lilia's ears pricked up.

"No. No. I don't like his style."

"I don't like that we'll end up in another global conflict if President Matheson is reelected."

"He just negotiated a new treaty with China!"

"The last official trip before the election? The timing is too good and the deal was made too fast. He wanted to get out of there and they wanted to be rid of him so they agreed to agree for the moment. Nothing will come of it."

"You're too skeptical."

"You believe too much of what you're told, Thompson. There'll be another war. You'll see. Matheson shouldn't have even gone to China, but no, he had to chase all that positive vid." The first cop snorted. "Never mind what it cost us to fly him and his entourage and all the vid boys from the press halfway around the world. Wasteful, that's what Matheson's administration has been. They deserve to be thrown out on their . . ."

Fly. Lilia thought of Hiroshima and an airplane delivering a payload.

They wouldn't.

Would they?

The other cop laughed. "And you think Blackstone will be better? You're the optimist."

"At least Blackstone hasn't learned how to milk the system yet. We've got a chance to get a few good years out of him."

Although Lilia tended to agree with the first cop's skepticism of politicians, he was totally wrong about Max and his ability to work the system. Max could coax blood from a stone, if it meant more comfort and wealth for Max himself. Lilia was tempted to contribute that tidbit to the conversation.

Truth be told, it was part of what she'd liked about Max. He was so self-motivated that he was completely predictable.

"Hey, you gonna watch the president's return tonight?"

Thompson snorted. "I thought you disapproved of waste, Dimitri."

"It's my kid, he's fascinated with planes." The cop chuckled. "He's got the course of Republic One all traced out and we'll watch it all on the vid."

"How can he trace the course? The trajectory is classified."

"Ah, he guesses. Who knows if he's right, but every time the president goes anywhere, he's figuring out the range and the likely refueling stops. Can't be bad for him to be doing extra math. He's gonna go places, that kid. You'll see."

"Only if he's right." Thompson laughed.

Dimitri didn't laugh. "You watch. He says they'll refuel in Estevan tonight."

"Twenty creds on it, Dimitri."

"You're on."

Estevan.

Lilia's heart pounded.

Was it just a coincidence?

The most efficient way of delivering a nuke, after all,

was from an aircraft. The Republic had been hampered in recent wars by the expense of fossil fuels and the shortage of aircraft big enough to carry a heavy payload like a big bomb.

But the president's plane was the biggest one in the air.

Lilia reminded herself that Republic One wouldn't be a bomber, fitted to deliver a payload like a nuke. There were a lot of reasons why it was a crazy idea.

But it made a compelling kind of sense.

Montgomery, however, would demand proof.

They needed to know just how heavy this year's shipment of oranges were. Breisach and Turner's paper file had ended in 2070. She was sure that any electronic record had been destroyed or disguised.

Unless it had been pirated.

Maybe by Y654892.

They had to get his palm immediately, if not sooner. Lilia stood and pulled at the securoband just as Montgomery came back into his cube. He looked harassed as he freed her from the desk. She left the precinct in his custody, knowing from his expression that she shouldn't say anything.

Montgomery spoke when they were in the midst of a crowd. "I've persuaded Tupperman to deport you to the Frontier, but his decision can be overridden." He spared her a dark look. "Given your recent run of luck with the system, that could happen at any time. I can get you into your unit; get changed ASAP. We have to hurry."

"We do," she agreed firmly.

"What's up?"

"I think I know the plan," she whispered. "If I'm right, the president's life is in danger."

Montgomery started. Lilia told him about her suspicions and he was as skeptical as she'd expected.

"We haven't got a shred of proof."

"Y654892's palm. That has to be what he wanted to share. It explains everything."

"Not necessarily. Someone else has to know the inside

story, Lil," Montgomery muttered. "Someone has to be willing to talk."

"Dr. Liam Malachy," she said, knowing a brilliant idea when she had one. Montgomery glanced her way. "Not only was he Gid's research advisor, he might have pointed Gid in the direction of these findings. Plus he lost the love of his life in the attack on Gotham."

"If the Society executed that hit and he found out about it, that could put him against the Society," Montgomery mused.

"I thought he had had some regrets. I thought he wanted to say something else." She gave Montgomery a smile. "Maybe, after thirty years of silence, he's ready to confide in somebody."

"It's worth a try," Montgomery agreed. "But be careful."

"Prudent," she said with easy confidence. "That's me."

It said something about the man's perceptiveness that he didn't appear to be convinced of that.

ROTTEN LUCK: Dimitri was guarding the crime scene.

Montgomery remained with him outside Lilia's hotel unit. There was no concern with her disturbing evidence as there'd be no homicide investigation.

"So, that's our shade killer," Dimitri sneered. "Maybe we shouldn't be stopping her."

"She's being deported to the Frontier," Montgomery said in his impassive tone.

Dimitri snorted. "Is that the way you handle crime in Topeka? You let someone else solve it for you?"

"It was Tupperman's decision." Montgomery wasn't surprised when she reappeared, either by her choice of clothing or by her expression. She carried a bag and he assumed her helm was in it.

She had to be wearing her pseudoskin under her street clothes, which perfectly adhered to the S&D regulations. He caught a glimpse of her heavier boots and smothered a smile, knowing that little with this woman followed expectation.

He left Dimitri standing sentry at the door and escorted Lilia to the front desk.

Once checked out, Lilia proceeded from the front desk to the security counter. The way she smiled with all of her charm told him that the security guy was in for a surprise.

Montgomery eased close enough to overhear but not intervene.

"Excuse me?" Lilia asked sweetly. "I was wondering if you could give me your name, please."

"Marvin," the security guy replied. He had the wits to be wary, at least.

"Just Marvin?" Lilia's smile broadened. "You must have a surname, otherwise you wouldn't adhere to the Naming Convention."

"Marvin Gregorivich."

Lilia typed something into her palm and Marvin looked uneasy. Montgomery was sure that Lilia was enjoying herself a great deal.

"Thanks!" She started to turn away, sparing Montgomery a quick conspiratorial wink.

"Hey, wait a minute," Marvin called. "Why do you ask?"

Lilia hesitated and Montgomery knew she had planned this in advance. "Oh, it's a long story. You wouldn't be interested."

"Of course I am," Marvin said with annoyance. "I want to know why you typed my name into your palm."

"It's a free country." Lilia grimaced. "Well, depending upon how you define your terms. But I can type what I like into my palm."

"I don't think so." Marvin was right beside her, looking antagonistic. "Why did you want my name?"

"Well, I could tell you, if you insist."

"I do."

Lilia took a deep breath. "You see, technically I'm agnostic, but since making that religious choice, I've seen a lot of things and met a lot of people, and it just seems to me that there's something missing from the agnostic equation."

"Like what? God?" Marvin snickered, proud of his joke.

Lilia watched him. "No. Accountability." Marvin's grin disappeared and he looked wary again. "There are a lot of people who do immoral things yet profit from them, people who lie and deceive and get away with it. So I decided that I'd start keeping a list, not just in my palm but in my head too." Lilia leaned closer to the security representative.

"You and I both know that you lied, Marvin. It looks like you're getting away with it, but I've got your name on my list, so fair's fair."

Lilia pivoted to walk toward Montgomery, Marvin fast on her heels. He spared an anxious glance at Montgomery, then touched Lilia's sleeve. "What are you going to do with that list?"

"Nothing," she said lightly. "For now. But one day I'm going to die, Marvin. And when I get to wherever I end up, I'll turn over my list. *'Here'* I'll say *'Here's a few souls who should burn in hell for all eternity, just in case you missed them.'*"

Marvin gaped at her.

"You know how bureaucracies are," Lilia continued. "I'm sure a few souls and their dirty deeds just slip through the cracks in some kind of clerical error. It never hurts to have an independent audit report." She smiled, obviously enjoying his uncertainty of what to do. "I figure I'm just doing my part for the betterment of the species. It's in the job description, after all."

Marvin started to sputter. "Officer! Did you hear that? She threatened me."

"With the possibility of eternal damnation?" Montgomery arched a brow. "If that were a Republican offense, sir, we'd have to close all the churches."

Lilia gave Marvin a cheerful wave. "Bye now! Have a *great* day, Marvin!"

"He won't recant his sworn affidavit," Montgomery whispered to her. "It might affect his reputation."

"I know that. But maybe he won't be so quick to lie in the future."

"That's good enough for you?"

"It's all about the greater good, Montgomery. You should know that." She cast him a sparkling glance, one that made his heart skip. "By the way, I'm not joking about my 'Reserved Seating for Hell' list. Behave yourself."

"Message received, Lil."

"There's Dr. Malachy," she said, staring at an older gentleman with a cane who was entering the main ballroom. "I need a last word with him, um, to deliver Gid's last message."

"There was no last message."

She leaned closer. "You know that and I know that, but your partner has no idea."

Montgomery nodded. "The beverage bar in thirty."

"I'll be there."

IT HAD to be synchronicity to see Dr. Malachy right when she needed to find him. Lilia caught up to him quickly.

"Dr. Malachy!" She put her hand through his arm as they walked together into the big ballroom. Another buffet was being spread for the conference attendees. "Just who I've been looking for."

The professor looked briefly alarmed, then summoned a smile. "And why is that, Lilia? I have no ability to appeal your ejection from the Society."

"Oh, never mind that. I wanted to talk to you about something important."

He arched a scraggly gray brow. "More important than your Society membership?"

"Yes." Lilia looked him in the eye. "I want to talk about Gid."

"There are counseling services, my child . . ."

332 CLAIRE DELACROIX

"I want to talk about his last research project. The one you sent him on."

"That was between Gideon and myself."

"It was once. I know what he found."

Dr. Malachy frowned and glanced around the pair of them. Thanks to Lilia's status, there was an even larger gap around them than the previous day. He lowered his voice when he spoke. "Just what do you know about Gideon's research?"

"Everything," Lilia asserted. "Gid left me his data."

Dr. Malachy's nostrils flared and Lilia knew that he knew not only what Gid had been doing but its import. She'd found an ally. "And who else has seen it?" he demanded in a whisper.

"No one." Lilia shrugged and smiled, ever the competent liar. "I couldn't make sense of it. It must be his final results."

Dr. Malachy inhaled sharply. "Is it in your palm?"

"No. On a separate datachip."

"You must give it to me," he insisted with heat.

Lilia shook her head. "I can't just pass it to you here, where anyone could see."

A big factor in her inability to surrender the datachip was the fact that Montgomery had it, but Dr. Malachy didn't need to know that just yet.

"Besides, I'd like some information in exchange," Lilia said. "Maybe we could make a deal."

He smiled ever so slightly. "And what would that deal be?"

"An answer to a question, one honest answer."

He straightened, clearly excited. He probably assumed she would play her ace for something lame, like a request for protocol for appealing her ejection.

She gave his arm a minute tug. "I was thinking the netherzones would be ideal for this exchange."

"Perfect."

Lilia pulled him to a stop when he might have gone

back to the lobby. She didn't want the other cop to see what she was doing. "No, let's go through the kitchens."

Dr. Malachy readily turned his steps in that direction. He moved with such purpose that Lilia knew she'd made the right choice.

DR. MALACHY was more nimble than Lilia'd expected, but then, he'd probably thought that precious data had been lost forever with Gid. The pair made their way through the kitchens and into a service stairwell. They got down the stairs to the first level of the netherzones with reasonably good speed.

He halted and turned, panting a bit, his expression avid. "This will do." He gestured to Lilia's palm. "Now, turn it off."

"What?"

"There will be no monitoring of this conversation. You've already said too much that could be observed."

"You can't turn off a palm."

"Of course, you can." He tersely dictated a string of commands. Lilia punched them into her palm, as he did the same with his own, and the displays in both palms faded simultaneously.

Lilia stared at her palm in shock. She'd never felt the tiny electrical impulse that the palm stole from the body, but she noticed when it was gone. Her left hand felt a bit numb. Dead. She felt kind of lost without her electronic leech, spy, and memory aid. "I never knew that was possible."

"For obvious reasons, the Republic would prefer that no one knew," Dr. Malachy said, dismissive of such details. "Now, what's your question?"

"Wait a minute. How do I turn it back on?"

He gave her the commands and Lilia punched them in, relieved when it flashed and tingled once again. He glared at her and she turned it off, as obedient as she'd never been.

"Now, your question."

Lilia took a deep breath. "Who was the head of the Council of Three in 2069, who ordered and planned the attack on Gotham?"

His eyes flashed with surprise. "What are you talking about?" His words lacked conviction and Lilia knew she had to persuade him that she wasn't just guessing before he'd answer.

"You know what I'm talking about. The attack on Gotham was organized by the Society, in order to replenish the population of shades and ensure the Society's longevity."

"Gideon did not tell you this."

"No. Gid charted the shade population over time. It reached a dangerous low immediately before the attack on Gotham, one that would have threatened the stability of society at large if nothing had been done. Gid's data show that if that downward trajectory had continued, the entire justification for the Society would have disappeared, probably within a decade."

Lilia took a step closer to the professor, who was looking a bit bewildered, and softened her voice. "Someone decided to do something about that, to be proactive in ensuring job security for Nuclear Darwinists everywhere. I think you know who it was. I think you've known for thirty years." She put her hand on his arm. "Who killed your fiancée, Dr. Malachy? It might have been done indirectly, but it was a murder all the same."

He considered her for a moment and Lilia knew he was weighing his options. "You've made a good bit of conjecture here, Lilia. Have you any proof of this?"

"Gid's datachip."

"You had best give it to me. As I was his advisor, those results were doubtless intended for me. I may understand the data better than you do, my child, and this is a matter of considerable delicacy."

He knew! Lilia would have given the chip to him, right then and there, but Montgomery still had it.

She smiled at the professor. "You haven't answered my question yet. We had a deal."

"Fair enough. But where is the datachip, Lilia? Is it safe?"

"It's hidden, where no one will find it but me. You don't need to worry about it falling into the wrong hands."

"Good." Lilia saw his smile, the barest warning that she'd miscalculated, then Dr. Malachy took a swing at her with his cane.

THE NEXT thing she knew, Lilia was down on the floor on all fours, her brains scrambled. She could feel something warm running down her cheek.

She'd made a big mistake.

Lilia looked up as Dr. Malachy stepped over her again, his features twisted with anger. "Stupid cow!" She rolled out of the way in the last moment and his cane struck the railing, its metal head making the balusters ring.

Dr. Malachy swore.

Lilia climbed to her feet and tried to run up the stairs. He deftly hooked the cane around one of her ankles and brought her to the floor again with a quick gesture. Lilia fell hard on her rump and wondered whether she'd chipped her tail bone.

Bruises were the least of her worries. Dr. Malachy was more agile than she'd realized and a lot stronger.

Plus he was intent upon killing her.

The solitude of the netherzones no longer seemed like such a good thing. Lilia got to her feet in a hurry as Dr. Malachy snarled, swung, and missed.

"I let you live," he snarled. "I argued for your life to be spared and this is your thanks."

"You only wanted Gid's datachip," she guessed.

"I dislike loose ends."

This was Lilia's last chance to find out more, so she goaded him. "Maybe you don't even know who was on

Council thirty years ago," she said, her tone condescending. "Your research was never that significant, was it?"

"Stupid woman," he muttered and took another swipe. He was learning from her evasive tactics: when Lilia dodged the blow at the last minute, he twisted his wrist and redirected the cane. It caught her painfully across the left arm.

Lilia *wanted* her laze, which was rather inconveniently sealed in a plastic bag at NGPD. Marvin had just gone to the top of her Destined for Hell list.

"You killed Gid," she speculated.

"Gideon signed his own death warrant. I told him to tally the statistics and leave the matter be, but he defied me." Malachy and Lilia circled each other. "He learned a fatal curiosity from you." He raised his cane. Lilia dove for his feet. His weight teetered, and he rained blows down upon her back.

Something cracked and Lilia hoped it wasn't one of her vertebrae. Her preference would have been his cane.

"Just like Johanna," he muttered, his breath coming faster. "Impossibly stupid, stubborn cow."

Lilia figured he was talking about his fiancée, though she was surprised at his terms of endearment. He couldn't have loved her, not if he called her names like that. So he hadn't been sharing his own sad history over breakfast; he'd been trying to find out how much she knew.

Tit for tat. Lilia went after what he knew. "Johanna guessed what was going to happen to Gotham," she guessed. "That was why you really fought. She wasn't stupid at all."

Dr. Malachy growled in recollection. "She went to try and stop it, stupid, stupid girl. She couldn't stop it, no one can stop something like that once it's started."

"Why not?"

He swung and missed. "It's planned that way, obviously. If you weren't female, you'd see that. Women never understand anything of importance."

"Then explain it to me." Lilia's dumb bunny tone won her more than a respite.

He straightened, his expression filled with malice even as he couldn't resist the chance to show his mental superiority. "Any decent plan ensures that very few individuals know the entire scheme, and that stopping one individual doesn't stop the incident. It's only logical."

"Incident? Is that what the Society called the termination of several million lives? Just an *incident*?"

Dr. Malachy lunged toward her. Lilia tried to evade the cane, slipped, and he kicked her in the gut. She fell down a trio of steps, somersaulted backward, and came up on her feet.

"It was for the greater good!" he roared.

"Of who?" Lilia shouted back.

He came down the stairs toward her, breathing heavily, his eyes ablaze. "It was the divine plan. The Society was anointed with the task of safeguarding shade children and making their lives useful. Ernest Sinclair created the Society and devised the plan to ensure its longevity . . ."

"Ernest Sinclair ordered the attack."

He didn't agree or disagree. "But Johanna, a mere Nuclear Darwinist Second Degree, thought she could undo the good work of the Society. She left the Institute and went to Gotham because she was too much of a fool to see the truth."

"And so she died."

He bared his teeth and raised his cane. "It was natural selection. Only the fittest should survive."

Lilia gasped outrage, which gave him the opportunity he needed. His cane flashed, the hook caught her under the arm, and he heaved her toward the railing. Lilia caught at the cold metal with her hands, but he twisted one hand behind her back and lifted her from behind.

Lilia was looking down the center of the stairwell, down to the floor of the lowest netherzone. She watched a drop of blood from her temple fall and splatter, and figured she'd be right behind it. She eyed the distance to the concrete floor and, even without Gid's aid, calculated the probabilities of her survival from such a fall to be quite poor.

She would have liked to have thought that it was her own sense of impending doom, of a personal nature, that gave her new strength, but it was what Dr. Malachy said.

"I wonder how long it will take the shades to notice that something is different about their stairwell," he mused. "Poor creatures. They're lucky we find a reason to let them live."

Lilia's blood boiled at his attitude.

Where was Montgomery?

She had to stall for time. "Don't you want Gid's datachip? Push me and you'll never find it again."

Dr. Malachy laughed. "It would suit me if no one ever found it, if indeed you ever had it. Either way, your death will be convenient. You are somewhat of a nuisance, Lilia." He pushed her a bit farther over the rail and Lilia felt her weight dangle in space.

"Actually, I lied about hiding the datachip," she said. "I gave it to the cops."

"I don't think so. I think you're lying now."

"Give me the satisfaction of knowing who ordered the attack, at least," Lilia said. "Seeing as I'm going to die anyway. What can it hurt?"

"There is always one on the Council who leads," he hissed in her ear. "It was ever thus. From the Society's inception until his death, it was Ernest Sinclair who dictated all policy, for the good of all of us. We exist for the benefit of mankind, Lilia. That was the basic lesson you were supposed to learn at the Institute, the one that you were too stupid to grasp."

"That enslaving part of the population can be justified?"

"That the greater good of the species justifies all." With that, Dr. Malachy gave her a final push.

The loose end was no longer the datachip: it was Lilia.

MONTGOMERY BURST into the stairwell in time to see Lilia hanging from the railing. He didn't want to fire his laze and draw attention, so he crept silently and quickly down the stairs.

The old man gave Lilia a shove.

Lilia snatched at the balusters and clung there for a heart-stopping moment. She fought for a grip on the metal. Her assailant raised his cane to batter Lilia's fingers, but Montgomery tapped him on the shoulder.

"Is there a problem?" he asked.

The older man spun, swinging his cane at Montgomery. Montgomery ducked, then decked him after the follow-through. Malachy faltered, looking old and feeble, and Montgomery almost regretted what he had done.

Lilia managed to get a grip on the railing and hung on panting. "Don't trust him," she said, but Montgomery had already seen the glint of malice in the old man's eyes.

Malachy coughed weakly and fell to one knee. Montgomery eased closer, knowing it was expected of him, and the old man came up fighting.

Montgomery decked him again.

The old man was so surprised that he lost his balance and toppled backward. His feet went out from under him and he cried out. His head hit the lip of a lower step with a fearsome crack. He lay there motionless, sprawled over the stairs with his head higher than his feet.

Blood began to run down the metal stairs.

Montgomery gave Lilia a hand and pulled her over the railing. "Okay?"

"Pretty much." She tapped at her palm. She nursed the bruised knuckles on her other hand, warily keeping her distance from Dr. Malachy.

"What happened?"

"He tried to kill me." She spared Montgomery a glance. "I guess that means my theory was right."

"But we still have no evidence of it."

"My ribs hurt like hell, and I'm going to have some major black and blue. Doesn't that count?"

Montgomery shook his head. They looked as one at the fallen Malachy.

"You know, a better person would call a paramedic," Lilia breathed. There was hostility in her tone. "But if he isn't already dead, I'll give him time to get there."

"What happened?"

"They nuked Gotham, for the good of the species." She heaved a sigh. "He knew about Gotham all these years and kept quiet. He knew that the Society would strike again—in fact, he dispatched Gid to correlate the statistics."

"He sent Fitzgerald on a mission he wouldn't be allowed to survive," Montgomery said quietly.

Lilia nodded.

Montgomery felt the need to say it. "So the Society was responsible for Fitzgerald's death, not you."

He wasn't sure what she would have said, because something flicked on Malachy's palm in that moment. Lilia approached the old man cautiously, her gaze flicking between his face and his palm.

He was still.

"Careful," Montgomery advised.

Lilia touched his throat, her own heart leaping. "Even he can't pretend to have no pulse."

There was a familiar spinning golden graphic on his palm, the logo of the Society of Nuclear Darwinists. They leaned closer and at the bottom of the display were three tiny glowing words:

Erasure 35% Complete.

The percentage number was ticking higher at lightning speed. "It's a worm," Montgomery said. "It's erasing his palm on his death."

"He's got to be Council of Three," Lilia whispered.

"One down," Montgomery said. "I wonder who the others are."

"There's only one way to find out." Lilia slammed her dataprobe into his palm.

Montgomery's heart stopped cold at her audacity.

The percentage froze at 52 percent complete. Neither of them breathed for an instant.

Lilia took a shaking breath. "All we have to do is breach his firewalls and hope that the important data wasn't among the 52 percent that's already gone."

Montgomery almost smiled. "That's all."

Lilia gritted her teeth and bent over their linked palms. Montgomery would have bet his last cred on her beating the system, but she didn't have a chance.

Malachy's palm sent a message. Montgomery saw the icon and was horrified. "To who?" he demanded.

"Persons unknown. Two of them."

Montgomery swore. Malachy's palm had sent a message of its own volition, presumably to the surviving Council members.

"It's erasing again," Lilia said with dismay. "Faster now."

"Pull out."

She pulled out her probe and stood beside Montgomery. The Society graphic on Malachy's palm stopped spinning. It flashed once, then twin hemispheres closed over the logo from behind, seeming to devour it. When the logo had turned into a featureless golden globe, his palm extinguished.

"The other two know he's dead," Montgomery guessed.

"They probably know I'm with him." Lilia looked up, her expression frightened.

"And they know where we are," Montgomery concluded. He seized Lilia's hand and leapt down the stairs to the netherzones, hoping they hadn't lingered too long. "We need a bike and we need to get into Gotham. The only good thing is that we probably won't be followed."

Lilia snorted. "Get serious, Montgomery. Every guest in this hotel is packing a heavy-grade pseudoskin. I'd be surprised if we *weren't* followed."

"You do know how to put things into perspective."

"It's a gift."

Montgomery kicked open the steel door allowing access to the lower level of the netherzones.

Lilia peeled off her street clothes and chucked them

aside. She even gave the pile of petticoats an extra kick
for good measure. She hauled her helm from the bag she
carried and put it on, then put the bag on her back.

"Leave it behind," he counseled and she laughed.

Her eyes were dancing and she looked vibrantly alive.
"My black lycrester suit is in there. Until death us do part
and all that."

Montgomery hoped it wouldn't come to that.

XXI

LILIA LOST her heart completely when Montgomery commandeered a bike from a loyal citizen, failing to mention to that citizen that his motorbike would be hot if and when it ever returned to New Gotham to be claimed.

He also gave the citizen the name and service number of some cop named Dimitri.

He got a ping on his palm about Lilia's nefarious deed. "Let's get out of here," he said and she agreed.

Montgomery drove nearly as fast as she would have done.

He headed for the tunnel and it could have been instant replay. The geiger on the bike ticked up a storm when they emerged in the old city. Lilia heard the wolves, just as she had before, but they weren't as close.

Maybe it was too early to dine.

Lilia shivered when they turned into Rockefeller Plaza, still felt cornered. She saw the eyes of the wolves only once they were in the square, as the canines closed ranks behind the bike on their silent feet.

Lots of yellow eyes and shaggy silhouettes.

That made her nervous.

Montgomery pointed to the indent in the square where Lilia had found the murdered shade without turning on his speaker. Light shone in the recessed space in front of the fountain.

Someone was obviously waiting for them.

The little hairs on the back of Lilia's neck prickled.

Montgomery didn't hesitate, but then, whoever was waiting would have heard the bike already. There was little point in delaying the inevitable. Lilia saw that pairs of torches had been lit, one on each end of each step that descended into the pit. More had been lit around the perimeter.

A figure sat on the lip of the dry fountain, exactly where Y654892's body had been. Lilia knew it was the same spot because there was a bloodstain on the stone.

It was a woman and Lilia didn't know her.

It's true that Lilia couldn't have recognized a woman in pseudoskin and helm, except that her pseudoskin was salvaged and patched. Everyone Lilia knew with a pseudoskin—all Nuclear Darwinists—had a snazzy new model like Gid's.

None of those people would have risked their health and welfare, even to disguise themselves, by wearing a substandard suit.

She guessed that Montgomery's associates were the same.

Lilia could see now that there was an inscription carved into the stone behind the gilded statue of Prometheus.

"Prometheus, teacher in every art, brought the fire to earth that hath proven to mortals a means to mighty ends."

Funny it didn't say anything about pride coming before a fall. Prometheus hadn't had a great ending to his story, and mortals weren't doing too well on that score either.

Maybe fire from heaven was more trouble than humans could be trusted to handle.

The wolves howled behind them as the woman held up a small square item.

It was a palm.

Lilia's heart leapt. She knew whose palm it had been.

The woman touched the base of her helm, activating the speaker. "Is this what you're looking for, Lilia Desjardins?"

A shiver slipped up Lilia's spine that the woman knew her name. She glanced back nervously to find the wolves half as far away as they'd been a moment before.

Moving as silently as shadows.

Salivating.

Montgomery revved the bike and the wolves backed off a bit.

"They won't come down here," the woman in the pit assured them. "Not with the fire."

Lilia activated her own speaker. "You sound pretty sure of that."

She laughed. "They know that fire means we're serving wolf."

"They always said Gotham was a dog-eat-dog world," Montgomery said in an undertone.

"You'll have to leave the bike behind," the woman said. "And come alone. Like you did last time."

Lilia exchanged a glance with Montgomery, wishing she could see his eyes more clearly. The tinted visor disguised his expression, but he handed her off the bike as if she was a noblewoman descending from a carriage.

"Time for some prudence," was all he said.

"Don't stay up here alone," she murmured. Montgomery got off the bike, leaving it running, and descended a couple of steps behind her. He pivoted and drew his laze, guarding her back.

The wolves immediately swarmed around the motorcycle and past it. They didn't go down the steps. They surrounded the square and looked down hungrily, their toes on the lip of stone.

"You must come here often to know so much about them," Lilia said as she went down the rest of the stairs. She refused to think just yet about how they would get out of here.

One problem at a time.

The woman had the dark filter lowered so that Lilia couldn't see her features. "You could say that. I live here."

"You can't live in Gotham. It's too hot . . ."

"On the surface, it is. And there are the wolves, of course."

Lilia realized then that there were dark openings

around the perimeter of this recessed square. "Gotham doesn't have a netherzone."

"Not officially. Nothing's been built here since the bombs."

She watched Lilia, apparently at ease, apparently waiting.

"There was a netherzone here before?"

"Subways are literally paths beneath the surface of the earth."

Lilia had never thought about it, but the woman was right. "Didn't they flood?"

"Some of them did." Lilia heard laughter in her tone. "Knowledge is power."

Lilia glanced back at the wolves, who watched avidly, and was aware of the press of time. She'd been in the hot zone just a few nights before and needed to watch her exposure. "I came for the palm."

"I knew you would."

"How?"

The woman lifted the filter of her visor and Lilia could see her features. She was older, probably contemporary with Lilia's mother, and there was intelligence in her gaze. Lilia noticed that much, as well as the node on her forehead.

"Because the stories about the third eye are true?"

"In a way. You have to learn to see with it. You have to learn to trust it. I've had good teachers." She smiled. "Besides, it was only logical that you'd come back."

Lilia was feeling a bit skittish about this stranger being so calmly certain of what she would do. "Is the third eye how you know my name?"

"No." She lifted the bootleg palm. "Yvan knew it."

"Yvan? That was his name?" Lilia was relieved that he hadn't just been a number. Yvan was preferable to Y654892. When the woman nodded, Lilia tried again to push her to the point of surrendering the palm. "You survived here in Gotham, with Yvan."

She seemed amused by this. "Not just Yvan."

"But why stay here?"

"Where else would we go?"

It had never occurred to Lilia that people might remain in the old cities, much less that they would choose to do so. But then, those who were visibly shades had little to gain by declaring themselves alive.

When Lilia said nothing, the woman leaned closer. "Yvan was obsessed with finding the people who did this to us. He thought he could ensure that there was justice."

"He wanted to stop it from happening again," Lilia guessed.

She nodded. "Once he realized their plans."

"And he died instead."

She glanced up suddenly, as alert as a rabbit hearing pursuit. Lilia listened but couldn't hear anything. She glanced back at Montgomery, who shrugged.

"How did they put the homing device on you?" the woman demanded.

"What are you talking about?"

"It's probably in your palm," she said, almost to herself.

A homing device? It wasn't possible . . .

Lilia heard the engine then. It was coming closer.

Lilia looked down at her left hand in horror. Had the intruder installed a souvenir in her palm, as well as copying its contents? Or had Dr. Malachy had viral software on his palm?

Either way, whoever was following them had been led directly to them by Lilia's own palm. She turned it off, even though it was too late.

Montgomery swore and lifted his laze. The engine grew louder, the bike turning into the plaza. The wolves turned to watch the new arrival and Lilia realized the strategic disadvantage of being in a pit.

Her momentary distraction was all the advantage the other woman needed. The woman disappeared into the darkness to one side of the former pool.

"Hey!" Lilia shouted to no effect. "Hey!"

"Lil!" Montgomery bellowed, but Lilia ran after the shade.

The woman knew where she was going and Lilia didn't. She was more accustomed to running in her pseudoskin than Lilia was, and hers was probably lighter.

But Lilia wanted that palm.

Even if it meant running into dark tunnels with no idea of where they led.

IT WAS dark and wet in this old-city netherzone. Lilia was terrified by the darkness and really didn't manage to think any further than not letting the woman out of her sight.

She scrambled down stairs and along ramps, then into a tunnel of some kind, and Lilia was as close behind her as she could manage to be. A desperate fear that she might get lost alone in this maze kept Lilia running despite her exhaustion. The only light was cast by the woman's helm, which had apparently been retrofitted with a flashlight.

Lilia regretted never having done the same to her own.

She turned into a tunnel that was long and straight. There were rails on the ground, two shining rails, and Lilia remembered her comment about subways. More than paths under the ground, they had run trains underground in many cities, a fact that she'd always found hard to believe. The ground was covered with heavy gravel and there were puddles in between the tracks. Lilia shivered, feeling entombed beneath the abandoned city.

But the two women weren't alone. As Lilia's eyes adjusted to the darkness, she saw that there were thousands of tiny eyes gleaming in the shadows, watching with interest.

Rats?

Or feral cats?

Or very large cockroaches?

Lilia bolted after the shade, who was making good

time down the tunnel ahead of her. She was feeling all her Malachy-inflicted injuries but would worry about them later.

Assuming she survived.

The woman took a branch to the right, two more to the left, scurried across a tiled platform to the other side, and ran down another tunnel. Lilia was panting, but determined to not lose her.

Lilia turned a corner and was shocked to find no light ahead of her. The darkness would have swallowed her whole, and her heart constricted in terror.

Then someone grabbed Lilia's arm and pulled her hard to the right. Her back slammed against a brick wall.

"We don't have much time," the shade said tersely. She flicked on her helm light and offered Yvan's palm. "There are images here that provide all the proof about Gotham you'll need. You have to take this and reanimate it . . ."

"But why don't you? Why haven't you told anyone?"

"Who would have believed us?" She shook her head and frowned. "And in a way, it seemed irrelevant. What was done was done so there seemed little point in coming forward."

Lilia saw her meaning immediately. "There was only the risk of identifying yourselves as shades and being harvested."

She nodded.

"What changed?"

"Gideon Fitzgerald. He didn't know what he did with his research, not until it was too late. He must have shown his statistics to someone . . ."

"He was dispatched by his advisor, Dr. Malachy."

To Lilia's surprise, she caught her breath and glanced away. "Yes," she said quietly. "Telling Liam would be enough."

"Wait. You know Dr. Malachy?"

"I thought I knew him better than I did. Thank God I found out the truth before I married him."

Lilia stared at the woman in shock. "You're Johanna?"

She nodded.

"But I thought you were dead."

"It was easier to let people believe that, than to face them after I'd failed to stop them. At least I understood what was happening that day and what to do to save myself." She nodded firmly. "And I could see the pattern, when Yvan started to gather his shipping data again."

"But Gid—"

Johanna held up her palm. "This was the message Gid sent Yvan. I datashared it, in case Yvan's palm was lost and I needed to find you."

Lilia caught her breath as an image of Gid appeared on Johanna's palm. The display was pulling hard to one side and his face was distorted. She saw the date on the bottom of the display and her heart stopped cold.

August 2.

Lilia swallowed when Johanna started to replay the message, her chest clenching as Gid glanced over his shoulder in obvious fear. He expected to be overheard. His manner was furtive.

He knew the danger he faced.

Lilia could imagine that he had calculated that the risk was worth the potential price.

Oh, Gid.

"All right," he said quickly, "I'll come and see your evidence because there's no other logical way to end this." He looked hard into the vid. "But if anything goes wrong, if anything happens to me, then you have to contact my wife, Lilia Desjardins." He gave Lilia's palm address. His rueful laugh was painfully familiar. "Lilia's the only one who will believe this."

All too soon, Gid killed the feed.

"They must have followed him," Lilia said.

"Didn't you wonder why the wolves never ate his corpse?"

Lilia hadn't wondered, but then she hadn't known much about wolves and their dining habits just days ago.

Johanna shook her head. "They collected him fast, too fast for us to intervene."

"I thought he'd been in the city a week."

"No. He was picked up immediately and put back in the city later that week, just before the patrol came through. They wanted his palm."

"They wanted to know what he knew." It wasn't out of respect for one of their own—their speed had come from a desire to limit potential exposure.

Johanna smiled. "But Gideon didn't leave that info there to be found. Too bad he only got as far as Thirty-fourth and Third or we might have beat them to his body."

"Am I right? Are they going to do it again?"

"Of course. Everything's easier the second time. A precedent means no need for a justification."

"But where? When?"

Whatever Johanna was going to say was never uttered. Lilia felt the laze beam more than saw it, the distinctive sizzle of it on her left. The shot singed the shoulder of her pseudoskin and she ducked instinctively.

Which only gave the assailant a clear shot at Johanna.

By the time Lilia had straightened, Johanna was slipping to the ground, dead.

Lilia quickly reanimated her palm because she wasn't coming back into the old city soon. She needed Johanna's data and wasn't up to cutting her palm loose.

Datasharing with a corpse was the only answer.

Lilia knelt, swallowed her revulsion, and slid her probe into Johanna's palm. She tucked Yvan's palm into her belt. Johanna's passwords were predictable and her firewalls were feeble, sufficiently weak that Lilia's palm overrode them automatically. The datashare was fast and dirty.

Lilia straightened when the download was complete. She still had to get out of Gotham alive.

She pivoted and in the weak light cast by Johanna's helm could see two men wrestling. They were fighting over possession of a laze, presumably the laze that had just been used to kill Johanna.

Johanna had a laze of her own.

It was ancient but it would do. Lilia ripped it out of Johanna's holster, then didn't know whom to shoot.

Two men in black pseudoskins and helms, virtually indistinguishable from each other. In the dim light, it was impossible to guess which was friend and which was foe.

One was Montgomery.

THE MEN fought over the laze, first one claiming it then the other. Lilia pointed Johanna's laze at one, then at the other, but couldn't pull the trigger.

She wanted to be part of the solution, not part of the problem.

One man sucker-punched the other, who bent over in pain. He wasn't down, though, because he abruptly kicked the laze out of the hand of the first. The weapon flew high, then fell with a clatter in the shadows beyond the reach of Johanna's fading light.

Lilia went after it. She had a laze in each hand, and no clue whom to shoot.

The men parted, panting, the one who had had the laze straightening. He pushed up the filter on his helm and held up his hands. "Lilia, don't shoot."

"Mike!" Lilia couldn't make sense of it. Mike MacPherson?

"I followed you to be sure that you were okay."

Lilia remembered that Mike had been at the cocktail party when she'd gotten the spiked drink. He was a man in a pseudoskin and could have been the intruder to her room.

He was seventh degree. Attaining the top honor had to get a Nuclear Darwinist into the inner circle.

And he almost ran the research labs.

She wanted to know what he knew, so she let him talk.

The other man pushed up his filter and Lilia saw that it

was Montgomery. He said nothing, but pulled his own laze, which put Mike at a definite disadvantage.

Mike started to talk. "Lilia, he just killed that woman when he was aiming for you." He took a step closer to appeal. "Look at your shoulder. You've taken a hit. He almost got you. We've got to get you some medical care."

Mike had followed them and Lilia knew his gesture wasn't born of goodwill.

Mike didn't stop talking. "Lilia, you have to be careful here in New Gotham. Gid knew that the New Gotham cops are crooked, so they got rid of him."

"I thought it was the Society that Gid learned the truth about."

"That's what they want you to think. NGPD is on the take, from Maximilian Blackstone's campaign."

"What are you talking about?"

"Don't you watch the polls? Blackstone is going to get elected and he wants to get rid of the Society. He's had evidence planted against the Society so that he can 'reveal' in his inaugural speech that Ernest Sinclair and the Society were responsible for the attack on Gotham. He wants to take charge of the shade labs and claim the licensing revenue from the drugs we've developed. It's a lot of money, Lilia, and the only way the Republic can seize it is to discredit and eliminate the Society."

"What about Dr. Malachy?"

"He's been working with Blackstone's people, planting doubt in the Society, finding details that can be used against us. They need someone on the inside to make the story plausible. Can't you see what's at risk here?"

Lilia knew Max well enough to find this possible. This kind of bold, self-serving grab for revenue and positive PR (not to mention wealth and power) was totally characteristic of him. Its very sneakiness was quintessentially Max-like.

Plausibility didn't make it true.

Mike continued in a hurry, perhaps believing that Lilia was on the cusp of being convinced. "NGPD is a part of it. How else can you explain that sloppy autopsy report? Not a single question as to why Gid was in the old city, which is off-limits by senatorial decree."

"I wondered about that."

"I talked to Gid at the end. He was part of a clandestine effort on the part of the Society to stop this before it started. Gid learned that the Republican government actually executed the attack on Gotham and that Maximilian Blackstone's people were trying to pin it on the Society. Gid must have had proof, or gone to get it."

"And the cops were in on it?" Lilia didn't dare look at Montgomery. He had to know that she wasn't persuaded.

"Sure. Who better to plant evidence in Gotham and New Gotham without being monitored? Breisach and Turner was set up as a false company, with paper records—Lilia, who on earth still stores paper records? It was all a scam. There never was a Mr. Breisach or a Mr. Turner."

Montgomery was as impassive as only he could be.

"They must have thought they'd gotten away with it, then Gid showed up, asking questions. I guess he wasn't as circumspect as he should have been and they realized what he was doing. They got rid of him, but then you appeared. Nobody knew how much you knew. Didn't you think it was a coincidence that you got roughed up your first night here?"

Lilia removed the safety on Johanna's laze. "I didn't tell anybody about that."

"I saw. My room overlooks the street and I saw. I didn't realize it was you until later, Lilia, I'm sorry. I don't know if I could have gotten down there in time to help even if I had known it was you."

"It's the thought that counts, I guess."

"And what about the shade who was following you? She was registered to the Republic and assigned to NGPD."

"I didn't know that."

"I checked her records in our own databases. And now your cop escort is helping you run, to see where you'd go and who you'd contact, to see where else the information about Gid has leaked and to plug the holes. I tell you, Lilia, he almost got you. Let's take him down and get out of here before we take on too much radiation exposure. You've already seen too much this month. I owe it to Gid to take care of you."

Lilia lowered the weapon, letting Mike think she was persuaded. "At least no one dropped a chunk of building on me."

Mike reached for one laze. "Maybe they would have if you'd gone to Thirty-fourth and Third."

Lilia took a step back and feigned confusion, inviting him to fill the apparent gap in her knowledge.

"That's where Gid died," he said with easy confidence.

"How do you know where he died?"

"It's in the autopsy report."

"No, it's not," Montgomery said, then shrugged. "Sloppy."

Mike's eyes widened slightly as he realized his mistake. "Then it's in his file. That must have been where I saw it."

"No, it's not," Lilia said quietly. "I read it all."

Mike looked between the two of them. "I mean, I was just speculating as to where Gid might have gone . . ." he began, then lunged for the laze in Lilia's left hand.

She fired once, just enough to stun him.

"Lilia!" His shout echoed off the old subway tunnels, but there was nothing he could say to stop what she was going to do.

She'd found Gid's killer, in the most unlikely of places.

"This is for Gid," Lilia said and gave Mike time to take one step back before she blew him away.

MIKE DIDN'T blow far, just fell back against the wall as the laze burned into his chest. Lilia fired until his pseudoskin was disintegrated, until the flesh and muscle were burned away, until she could see the bright white of his sternum.

The smell of his burning skin made Lilia gag but she couldn't stop. She felt Montgomery step beside her, guessed he wouldn't approve, and still couldn't release the trigger.

It wasn't just for Gid.

It was for the receptionist.

It was for the hotel shade.

It was for Stevia.

For Montgomery.

For Delilah.

Bile rose in Lilia's throat just as Johanna's helm light flickered and died.

"I think his marrow is fried." Montgomery's hand fell over hers and he pushed Lilia's finger from the trigger.

She let him do it. When she lowered the laze, she was shaking. Montgomery claimed Mike's laze and tucked it into his belt.

The glow from the laze had already faded to nothing. It was dark, dark as pitch. Lilia thought about the weight of the city above them, thought of the convoluted course they had run. There was no way she could retrace her steps. There was no way she could get out of this labyrinth.

Lilia started to panic.

The weight of Montgomery's hand fell on her shoulder. "Remind me to never tick you off."

"Is that a joke?"

"Not a good one." She heard the smile in his voice. He must have felt her shaking, even through the pseudoskin. "Are you all right?"

"No. I don't do darkness."

Montgomery flicked on a light in his helm and gave her a crooked smile. "Better?"

"You could have done that sooner."

"I wanted you to appreciate it."

Lilia was thinking of some very earthy ways to show her appreciation when Mike's palm began to glow. The Society logo appeared on the small display, spinning just as it had on Dr. Malachy's palm.

Erasure was already 60 percent complete when it sent one message.

Montgomery swore as the palm faded to nothing.

"We've got to get out of here," he said.

"I don't know how . . ."

"Good thing you didn't blow me away then." He stood and hefted Mike across his shoulders, bending a little beneath the other man's weight. Lilia deliberately did not look at whatever was dripping from Mike's chest. Montgomery grunted as he started to walk. "Pick it up, Lil. I can't carry both of you and I'm not coming back."

The man knew how to issue a compelling invitation.

XXII

To Montgomery's relief, it didn't take long to reach the recessed space where they'd started. A wolf howled from the top of the stairs as soon as they appeared.

"No sneaking out of this party," said Lilia with enough verve that he was reassured. She'd frightened him three times in short order: when she'd run after the shade, when she'd finished off the other Nuclear Darwinist, and when she'd admitted to her fear of the dark. Having her back in fighting form meant there was a better chance of them getting out of Gotham.

"Certainly not," said the woman waiting by the statue of Prometheus. Montgomery stopped cold. She was wearing a deluxe and pristine pseudoskin, and the filter on her helm was dark.

They had found Council member number three.

She had a laze trained on them.

"Really, Lilia, I must congratulate you on your unexpected resourcefulness. Mike has proven to be so efficient in the past, indispensable really. It's a shame to lose him." She gestured to the statue. "And what a choice of setting for our final interaction. You've chosen a fitting place to die."

"Doc Mina!" Lilia said in obvious shock.

"And who else did you expect? Ernest Sinclair?" The woman laughed at her own joke. "Even the Society for Nuclear Darwinists can't rouse the dead. Not yet anyway."

She was sparkling, hubris personified, so filled with confidence that it had to mean bad things were in store for somebody.

Montgomery had a favorite choice. He lowered Mike to the ground, knowing he needed to be agile.

"First of all, I must insist that you surrender your weapons," the woman commanded.

Both Lilia and Montgomery hesitated.

The woman was no idiot, although she was reckless. She fired at their hands to encourage cooperation, singing the back of each of their gloves. Montgomery jumped backward and she laughed.

He thought it would be a bad idea to say that he preferred negotiating with the sane.

He and Lilia put the safety on each weapon, slowly, then tossed them into the space.

As he bent, he opened a link on his palm to Tupperman. He kept his hand turned toward his thigh so their captor couldn't see its activity. Tupperman wouldn't be able to intervene, but this Doc Mina might give enough evidence to incriminate the Society.

Once all three lazes were surrendered, the woman turned and fired at the canola tanks on all but one of the three bikes. The fuel splashed onto the stone and the wolves scattered, snarling.

Montgomery and Lilia moved closer together.

"I must say that I'm quite struck by how neatly this has all turned out. I can see the headline." Doc Mina raised the dark filter on her visor and Montgomery could see her features. She raised a hand as if running it across the headline. " 'A rogue Nuclear Darwinist and a crooked cop, executed by a valiant member of the Society's corps, who surrendered his own life for the sake of justice.' It's simply too perfect. We shall have to compose the scene, to maximize the impact."

Montgomery wasn't keen on arranging his death to suit the Society, but he doubted he had a choice.

Doc Mina considered them as a pert sparrow considers a choice bread crumb. "Of course, it might not make the headlines of the daily upload tomorrow, given other events."

Her import was obvious. "The Society is going to detonate a nuke," Lilia guessed.

"Tonight," Montgomery guessed.

"What better culmination of the annual conference for the Society of Nuclear Darwinists? It's simply too delicious. The pièce de résistance, as they would say on the Frontier."

"Chicago," Lilia guessed. "It's the only major Republican city that didn't sustain an attack in this century."

"And on the trajectory of the president's return flight from China," Doc Mina said. "How clever you both are. Refueling in Estevan will prove to have been a bad strategic choice."

"You're going to hijack it," Montgomery guessed, wanting her to confirm the plan.

"No, it will be grounded and replaced by our own bomber in Estevan. Republic One is the only plane cleared to pass over the Republic without interception, after all." Doc Mina sighed in mock sympathy. "I can't tell you how complicated it's been to arrange for the planes to be confused by air traffic control. Fortunately, the functions are automated and computers tend to believe what they're told."

"Someone will figure it out," Lilia said.

Doc Mina laughed. "But that's why the president will be our guest on board. No one will command that he be shot down, will they?"

"It's wicked," Lilia said.

"He's insurance," Doc Mina said coldly. "And there's not a thing you can do about it now."

"I thought you were being ousted from the Institute," Lilia said.

Doc Mina laughed. "What better cover for The One than to appear to be on the periphery of influence? I'll tell you now that they never will manage to be rid of Doc Mina and her cultural studies program—but that will be attributed to my tenaciousness, not my power. It's a perfect scheme, as you can see."

Montgomery hoped that Tupperman was paying attention, and that his trust wasn't misplaced.

A faint pearly glow began to emanate from the statue of Prometheus. Montgomery straightened slightly.

Tupperman wasn't the only one paying attention.

Maybe there *was* a divine plan.

Doc Mina didn't notice the light. "It's so thankless to have secured the future of the Society so brilliantly and to have no one left with which to share the triumph. I was thinking, Lilia, that once your friend is eliminated, you and I could watch the detonation together."

"Watch from where?"

"On my palm, of course. We commandeered an old weather monitor and reconfigured it for our viewing pleasure. Poor Liam was quite looking forward to it, although of course, the tower will be destroyed at some point in the detonation. Even so, it's so seldom that one has the opportunity to witness the cloud formation at leisure."

"Perhaps there's something of interest we can show you first," Montgomery said.

"I think not," Doc Mina scoffed. "There is nothing of interest that you might offer in this forsaken place . . ."

"How about an angel?" Lilia suggested as the light brightened still more. "I thought it was your one desire to see one."

Doc Mina's tone turned condescending. "Please, Lilia, how gullible do you imagine I am?"

"Look to your left and find out," Montgomery advised.

She looked, keeping the laze trained on them all the while. She couldn't have not looked and she couldn't have guessed that it would have been so dangerous to do so.

Because as soon as she turned, the angel revealed himself in his full glory.

LILIA SQUINTED at the brilliance of the light, then Montgomery threw himself on top of her.

"Don't look!" He locked his gloved hand over her visor to be sure she had no choice. He forced down the dark filters on both of their visors.

Lilia could still see the white light. She would have sworn that she could see the bones in Montgomery's hand, the matrix in his pseudoskin, as that brilliant light shone. It was like finding herself in the middle of the sun.

Or being at ground zero of a nuclear detonation.

Lilia was starting to understand why people in the Bible always fell on their faces when they saw angels.

Then she smelled something burning, something a lot like flesh. Lilia gagged and Montgomery tucked her more tightly beneath him. It was hot and getting hotter, the stone heating beneath them. She wondered whether their pseudoskins would melt.

Then she heard Doc Mina screaming.

The light reached a crescendo and faded to that luminescent glow that Lilia knew from Armaros and Baraqiel. After what seemed an eternity, Montgomery released her. They stood and turned, able to watch as the angel let his light fade to a faint glow.

"Angels can control their radiance?" Lilia asked.

Montgomery nodded. "They not only choose to whom they reveal themselves, but can choose how brightly they appear."

The angel folded his wings behind his back again. He smiled, benign, elegant, and ethereal, then raised his fingertips to his lips and blew a kiss.

To Lilia?

To Montgomery?

She couldn't be sure.

He faded from sight then, as surely as if he had never been, and there was only the sound of Doc Mina's moans.

MONTGOMERY KNELT beside Doc Mina and datashared, patching the feed back to the precinct.

"Tupperman's been listening to the whole thing," he told Lilia grimly and she knew she had something to learn from this man about foresight.

She chose not to look at the dying professor and tried not to inhale. Even through her filters, the smell of cooked flesh was bad.

Doc Mina breathed her last just a few minutes later and Montgomery nodded as he got to his feet. "Got it. The others can take it from there." He considered the wolves at the top of the stairs. "We've got more immediate problems."

The bikes parked at the top of the stairs might as well have been a thousand miles away. Wolves milled around them, eyes shining in expectation, and time was of the essence. An alarm in Montgomery's palm was ringing with quiet persistence, reminding them both of their excessive exposure. Montgomery reclaimed his laze and handed Johanna's to Lilia.

"Maybe you could call up one of your angel pals again."

"It doesn't work like that, Lil."

"How does it work, then? Why did the angel come?"

"I don't know. They answer to a higher authority."

Lilia was confused. He'd been one of them, hadn't he? "How can you *not* know, Montgomery?"

"Part of the plan is that volunteers forget." Montgomery cleared his throat and looked down at Mike. "Right now, I'm thinking that there can only be a homicide investigation if there's evidence of a murder."

"I've heard that before." Lilia was dismissive. "Let's get out of Gotham and talk about the law later."

"Like a body," Montgomery continued. "A body is evidence of a homicide, especially a body of an individual who has lost his life due to the intervention of another individual. And of course, once you have a body, you have other evidence to gather, like the weapon and the location of the victim's demise and . . ."

Lilia straightened, seeing the direction of his argument. "So you're going to charge me with murder for killing Mike?"

"You could probably get a lawyer to argue that it was

manslaughter, but you might still sample the Republic's hospitality for a while."

"Thanks for the reminder."

"There can only be a homicide investigation," Montgomery said, "if there's evidence of a homicide."

Lilia was shocked by his implication. "You're going to leave him for the wolves."

"Officially, no."

"But . . ."

"Maybe we got separated in the tunnels," he mused. "Maybe you and I found our way out, but couldn't find your friend. Maybe my alarm went and we had to leave, lest we become overexposed."

"Careful, Montgomery, I'm falling hard for you."

He laughed, a rich sound that made her want to laugh with him. "Besides, I don't think we'll make it if we carry him." He gave Lilia a nod. "We'll take Doc Mina's bike."

"Because it's the one that will still run?"

"And lucky for you, it's not stolen."

"Because you can't have a theft investigation without evidence of stolen goods?"

Montgomery only smiled.

Lilia sighed, knowing she was completely lost. "What about the angel?"

He gave her a quizzical glance. "What angel?"

"What angel? How can you say that . . ."

Montgomery winked and flashed that killer smile, then claimed one of the burning torches that Johanna had lit on the steps. "C'mon Lil. Let's get out of here."

He swung the flame at that first wolf. The beast snarled and took a step back. Montgomery fired the laze he carried in his other hand, keeping them at bay on both sides. Lilia made to follow his lead, but first she paused to open Mike's visor.

Even though she knew he was already dead, Lilia liked the idea of him suffering a bit more.

It wouldn't take long for the wolves to get him anyway.

Montgomery, bless his heart, pretended not to notice.

"Lil! Move it or lose it!" Two thirds of the way up the stairs, Montgomery tossed the burning torch into the pack of wolves and they barked in fear as they scrambled out of the way. Lilia was right behind him, flailing fire in every direction. It didn't take long for the wolves to decide that there were easier pickings.

Lilia looked back as the bike roared out of the plaza and saw their shadows slipping down the steps toward Mike and Doc Mina.

The sight made her shiver and hang on tight.

"Where to?" she asked, feeling full of promise for the future.

Montgomery paused for a beat, long enough to make her dread his answer. "The warehouse," he said slowly. "Of course."

Of course. Lilia's heart sank.

His mission was completed.

Montgomery was leaving.

THEY USED the chemical showers on the New Gotham side of the tunnel, then continued to the warehouse in silence. Lilia had nothing to say and Montgomery didn't seem inclined to talk.

She wasn't going to beg.

She didn't want to know if it would matter.

Instead, she focused on practicalities. They sat together in the angel room of the warehouse as Montgomery fed details to his supervisor.

Doc Mina's palm proved to hold a wealth of information. The entire scheme was there, documented in excruciating, self-indulgent detail.

The plan to use Gid to confirm the Council's suspicions about shade populations was there, as was an increment of alarm that he somehow figured out the reason for his research.

The good partners at Breisach and Turner had apparently balked at shipping a bomber in parts to Estevan. It seemed that they had figured out what had happened at Gotham and the deal with the Society for a perennial shipping contract of oranges had been a ploy to shut them up. They'd played along, until they'd seen the pattern developing again. Mike had engineered the skiing accident for Mr. Breisach and Dr. Malachy had been the helpful gentleman who had escorted Mr. Turner into his rickshaw, only to ensure that man's injury in a subsequent accident. Doc Mina had been the doctor to administer the false and fatal dose.

Lilia had been a wild card, because the Council had no idea how much she knew. Mike had followed her and executed everyone she talked to, cleaning up behind Lilia with the obvious intent of eliminating her once her investigating was done. She'd been denounced to make it less likely that anyone would believe whatever she claimed.

It was perfectly logical, but they hadn't counted on the intervention of angels.

Lilia had to like that.

She didn't have to like seeing the light of angelfire illuminating the skylight overhead. "They're coming for you," she said softly as Montgomery stood.

"Yes," was his only reply. His gaze was fixed skyward, his manner distracted.

"I love you, Montgomery," she said, her heart aching and her voice thick.

He turned and glanced back, a smile curving his lips. There was a sadness in his gaze, though, a sadness that made her fear what he would say. "I know, Lil," he said with quiet heat. "Your eyes told me first."

That he didn't reply in kind told Lilia all she needed to know.

There was a hard lump in her throat, and she wanted to cry as she had never cried for Gid. She was tempted to leave, to not watch him exit her life forever, but she couldn't deny herself one last glimpse.

She averted her eyes from Montgomery as the light brightened, marveling that this was only a fraction of the radiance they could release.

That was when she realized she wasn't the only mortal in the warehouse.

A trim older man in a pseudoskin, his hair cut very short, stood in the doorway. He was watching her. He lifted a finger to his lips when she saw him, then gestured back to Montgomery and the arriving angels.

Montgomery had told her once before to not distract them.

Lilia bit her tongue and watched, hoping she'd made the right choice.

MONTGOMERY KNEW what he had to do.

He'd never made promises he couldn't keep and he wasn't going to make Lilia a promise now, not when he wasn't sure he could deliver. White light filled his vision and his thoughts, burning away doubts and lies. Montgomery reveled in the clarity it brought to him, in its cleansing power, and knew that it could only be one thing.

Angelfire.

He bowed his head as the radiance grew brighter around him and prayed that his request would be fulfilled.

"You have done well, Munkar." The words resonated in his thoughts, honest and caring, devoid of guile.

"I was not alone in this."

Montgomery let the image of Lilia fill his thoughts. He thought of her stubborn pursuit of justice and her willingness to put herself at risk for a cause she'd embraced. There was something noble about her quest, something admirable about her knowing the odds were stacked against her and not changing her course as a result.

She was passionate.

She was idealistic and optimistic.

She was quintessentially human.

He didn't want to leave her.

"Your time as a volunteer is ended, Munkar. Your quest is done."

Montgomery knew that he felt more than desire for Lilia, more than admiration, more than the love that angels felt for all of God's creation.

It was the love that humans shared for each other.

That love was both alien and marvelous, uplifting and devastating. He thought of the burden and reward of flesh and knew there was only one choice. Risk was the price of admission but the potential reward made any sacrifice worthwhile.

He wasn't ready to abandon mortality.

Much less Lilia.

"Arrangements have been made for the return of your wings . . ."

The angel spoke with the calm detachment that had once been familiar to Montgomery and now was utterly foreign.

He interrupted the angel.

"I want to stay." He felt the angel's shock at his request and hastened to explain himself. *"I request another assignment. There is much to do. Lucifer is manifest . . ."*

The angel spoke calmly. *"We know of this, Munkar."*

"But he has targeted Lilia's child . . ."

"You cannot aid her, Munkar. Not without revealing her location to those who watch."

"But she is in danger . . ."

"Raphael is worthy of his assignment." The angel showed an indifference—or confidence—that Montgomery couldn't share. He had spoken with Lucifer and felt his malice.

"I need to stay."

The angel seemed startled by Montgomery's intent. He fell silent, then spoke with caution. *"It was not the plan for you to do so."*

Montgomery sensed the angelic resistance to what he asked. *"I can't just leave, not now, not when so much hangs in the balance."*

There was a pause that seemed to last half an eternity. *"You argue with the urgency of a human, Munkar."* The angel's tone was cautious but Montgomery wasn't fooled: his request was possible. *"Be advised, Munkar, that we may not be able to intervene in future on your behalf. If you die in human form, there is no return to our abode. The soul returns to the divine, a spark reuniting with the flame, but your wings and your celestial existence will be lost to you forever. We have already lost Raziel and have no desire to lose another volunteer."*

A sense of purpose filled Montgomery. *"I understand."* Even he heard the defiant hope of humanity in his own words.

"You choose with your heart." There was amusement in the angel's tone. *"Perhaps you know best where you belong, Munkar."*

He felt the heat of the angel drawing near, felt the singe of a kiss planted just below his ear, and his tears rose at the greatness of the gift he was being given. *"Be well, Munkar. Know that you are blessed and that you will be missed."*

"Thank you," he whispered audibly, but the angel wasn't done with him.

"I have a charge to entrust to you. See that she has good care."

The angel's light began to fade as Montgomery opened his eyes. He saw a young girl release the angel's hand, her eyes wide with wonder. She smiled and turned to him, and he realized that she was the small shade from the New Gotham circus.

"Micheline!" he heard Lilia breathe behind him.

"Angel," the little girl said to Montgomery and he offered his hand to her. She put her fingers in his and stepped away from the fading angelfire, her trust and confidence making him smile. "They said you would take care of me," she said.

"Yes," Montgomery said and turned to Lilia. "We will."

Joy made Montgomery's heart pound and he turned to

find Lilia watching him with trepidation, her hands at her mouth. Micheline ran to her and Lilia pulled the child close, her tears spilling as she stared at Montgomery. Her heart was in her eyes.

He had something to tell her but Tupperman stepped out of the shadows in that moment, an ignition card in his hand.

"I HAD a feeling you'd stay," the older man said to Montgomery as Lilia hugged Micheline. The little girl sat on her hip, showing a confidence in the proceedings that Lilia couldn't echo.

Montgomery was staying?

He offered the ignition card to Montgomery. "We'll trade vehicles. It will take longer for your disappearance to be tracked that way."

"Did we intervene in time?" Montgomery asked.

The older man nodded and Lilia felt relief. "Pick up a daily download tomorrow, wherever you are. It's going to be fine." He spared a glance to Lilia. "Drive carefully. I'll be in touch."

He winked, smiled at Lilia, then departed quickly with the ignition card from the hot bike.

Silence filled the warehouse. Lilia wanted desperately to know what was happening but wasn't sure what to ask. Montgomery surveyed her, his eyes gleaming. He looked proud and satisfied, although she wasn't sure why. Her own heart was pounding. "He's another one?"

Montgomery nodded, his gaze unswerving. "I didn't know until yesterday."

"How many are there of you?"

He shrugged and smiled. "I don't know. Maybe I'll find out."

"You are staying, then?"

Montgomery nodded and took a step closer. "I asked for another assignment. I guess I'll be reporting to Tupperman this time."

Lilia swallowed, not feeling nearly so tranquil. "Here in New Gotham?"

"Not necessarily."

Montgomery took the last step between them and lifted Micheline from Lilia's embrace. "Could you go see what kind of vehicle he's left us?" he asked the child, who scampered away to do his bidding.

Then Montgomery lifted Lilia's hand in his and laced their fingers together. He watched her as steadily as Armaros and Baraqiel could, and seemed to be waiting for something.

It was now or never.

"You could come home to the Frontier with me," Lilia said, her words falling in a rush. "My mother cooks a mean chicken tortellini, you know, and—"

Montgomery's fingertip fell across her lips, silencing her. She met his gaze, surprised to find his eyes sparkling with laughter. "You've been working at the circus too long, Lil," he said quietly.

"How so?"

"You're baiting your hook twice." Montgomery smiled. "I love you, Lil. Wherever you are is where I want to be."

Lilia had no chance to respond in kind. Montgomery bent and kissed her so thoroughly then that she didn't have a shred of doubt left in her heart.

They stepped into the twilight to discover that Tupperman had left them a touring bike with a sidecar and a full tank of fuel. Micheline was already exploring the stash of provisions. Lilia tucked her into the sidecar and closed it securely. Micheline looked as if she was going to go to sleep.

"You should try my mom's tortellini before you make such a big decision," she teased when he started the bike.

Montgomery laughed, a rare and welcome sound. "Your mother already made the only force that could change my life, Lil."

She got on the bike behind Montgomery, knowing that they'd be home on the Frontier the next day.

Home.

With Montgomery.

Fighting together for justice in the Republic.

It couldn't get any better than that.

Terrorists Charged in Chicago Attack

NEW D.C.—In a daring last-minute intervention, an attempted assassination attack upon the president has been thwarted.

Late last night, on the president's return from his treaty mission to China, Republic One landed at the Estevan airport on the Frontier. The terrorists planned to kill all aboard, but were foiled when their plans were prematurely revealed. Republic One landed as scheduled, but the terrorists were overwhelmed and killed by Republic forces.

A large quantity of enriched uranium was discovered at the airport, leading to speculation that the terrorists had even more fearsome plans for the Republic.

"Diligent police work led to the timely infiltration of a key terrorist cell in New Gotham," said a spokesperson for the Continent Security Commission. "It is our honor to be of service in protecting our leader and commander. The investigation is ongoing, however, and the threat of terrorism omnipresent."

Initial reports indicate that the assassination attempt might have been made by rebel forces working on behalf of the Chinese.

The president of the Republic issued a brief formal statement from the White House today, expressing his gratitude to and admiration of the Republic's police forces, calling them "tireless and vigilant." Presidential candidate Maximilian Blackstone has challenged the official version of events, insisting that the Republic is disguising the near-failure of security forces in defending the president. He cites the president's own budget cuts, made to what Blackstone labels "critical defense." Blackstone has vowed to double the military and defense budgets of the Republic if elected.

GUARDIAN

THE EYES OF THE REPUBLIC ARE EVERYWHERE....

A victim of what she believes is a malicious kidnapping, seer Lilia Desjardins quickly realizes that her abductor is on a divine mission. Rafe, a fallen angel, is trying to ensure that Lilia reaches her true calling as an oracle for the Republic, and if that results in a closer relationship between the two of them in the meantime, well, he doesn't mind that at all.

Filled with visions of her destruction should she succumb to Rafe's charm, Lilia knows she has to leave him behind. Unfortunately, by fleeing his guardianship, Lilia sets the wheels of fate in motion, as assassins become drawn to her. As Rafe races against time to save Lilia, he knows he isn't just saving her for the good of the Republic—he's saving her for himself.

> "Wonderful characters and mythology... beautifully written"
>
> —Bookloons.com on *Fallen*

In paperback October 2009 from

CLAIRE DELACROIX

978-0-7653-5950-6 • 0-7653-5950-2

www.tor-forge.com